Charlotte E Hart
THE END

****

THE END

An erotic novel
The second part of The Stained Duet
Copyright ©2017 by Charlotte E Hart
Cover Design by MAD
Formatting by MAD

All rights reserved

Without limiting the rights under copyright reserved alone, no part of this publication may be reproduced, stored in or introduced into a retrieval system, or transmitted, in any form, or by any means (electronic, mechanical, photocopying, recording, or otherwise) without the prior written permission of both the copyright owner and the above publisher of this book.
This is a work of fiction. Names, characters, places, brands, media and incidents are either the product of the author's imagination or are used fictitiously. The author acknowledges the trademarked status and trademark owners of various products, bands, and/or restaurants referenced in this work of fiction, which have been used without permission. The publication/use of those trademarks is not authorized, associated with, or sponsored by the trademark owners.

Charlotte E Hart
THE END

License Notes

This book is licensed for your personal use and enjoyment only. This book may not be resold or given away to other people, or used for any other reason than originally intended. If you would like to share this book with another person, please purchase an additional copy for each recipient. If you're reading this book and did not purchase it, or it was not purchased for your use only, then please return to your favourite book retailer, or copyright owner, and purchase your own copy. Copyright infringement of this work, or any other works by Charlotte E Hart will exact legal proceedings. Thank you for respecting the hard work of this author.
ISBN: 9781981742349

Charlotte E Hart
THE END

Table of Contents

Chapter 1
Chapter 2
Chapter 3
Chapter 4
Chapter 5
Chapter 6
Chapter 7
Chapter 8
Chapter 9
Chapter 10
Chapter 11
Chapter 12
Chapter 13
Chapter 14
Chapter 15
Chapter 16
Chapter 17
Chapter 18
Chapter 19
Chapter 20
Chapter 21
Chapter 22
Chapter 23
Chapter 24

Acknowledgements

THE END

By

Charlotte E Hart

"ASK AND YOU SHALL RECEIVE ..."

Chapter 1

ALANA

You'd think after some declaration of commitment we'd be basking in contentment. Me easing this pain away from my skin somehow. Him admiring the decadence of a night fucking his way through his new plaything, thankful for my acceptance of his heavy handed liberation. We should be lying with each other, reminiscing of the night's activities and enjoying each other's touch. Accepting this new found love I've tumbled into. That's what should be happening. It's what happens in all the tales I write, but it's not happening here. I can't even comprehend when it occurred, or why I let it occur in the first place. Maybe it was something to do with the post fucking haze my body languished in, my limbs too weak to offer protest. Or maybe it was my lacking ability to say no when he started wrapping the rope around my wrists. I don't know. I don't care either. I'm still too exhausted to move or offer resistance to whatever he's planning next. I'm just tied to the bed frame, my wrists attached to the post by the floor and my head continually shoved onto the floor should I attempt levering it upright.

Charlotte E Hart
THE END

I've cried so much, apprehension mingling with tension, created by fear inching in with every passing minute, and yet for some reason I feel safe here. This post my fingers grip onto feels like a solid structure within my grasp. It literally keeps me grounded as he roams my skin; tasting, delving, and biting into whatever he feels like. It allows me something to cling on to, hold tight too. And the only time it feels any less is when I let my mind wander back to my old life, reminiscing in some way about its disconnect to this space I'm in now. But the moment I let myself drift back there, or find an avenue to manage the continued pain he's inducing, he shoves my head to the floor and growls at me, seemingly noticing my meander away from his preferred treatment of me.

He sounds as feral as the air around me feels. He's been that way for hours now, hardly giving me a reprieve since he first carried me into this room. We haven't slept, nor moved from this space. He's barely said a word, choosing to talk with his lips on my skin instead. The sheets above me are still covered in my blood. I'm near drained dry of orgasms, regardless of the one that's building again. I can't think past the feeling of my thighs trembling, and I'm struggling to even hold myself up on all fours anymore as he's requested. I'm just a mess of prostrate flesh and broken skin, still ready to let him carry on in his adventure around my body regardless. His story, I suppose.

My legs finally give way as something tightens around my ankle and drags me backwards, stretching me against the floor until I'm flat on this carpet, too tired to care about the surface's cleanliness.

I'm done here. Finished. Literally fucked.

THE END

"Weak," he mutters behind me, his weight leaving my body and allowing me a moments respite from him. Weak? It's probably true. My life is spent behind a laptop, sitting on my backside, little thought to exercise involved. I rub my cheek into the carpet and let myself rest in the relaxed nature of it for a few minutes, not caring for the stench that permeates my nostrils. I just need a break from him. I can't do this anymore. Much as I might adore every fucking sensation he's delivered, every touch. I'm just too exhausted to move now, let alone deal with more from him. "You don't deserve dates from me." The sound of those words makes tears spring to my eyes again, some morbid fascination in my lacking abilities fuelling them. "You've shown me nothing but your pretence."

I don't know what that means. I've given him everything through the night. Let him pull me, push me, turn me and defile me. There isn't a hole he hasn't been inside, a word I haven't accepted as alright, or a humiliation I haven't endured. I've been slapped, bitten, spanked and gripped tighter than I've ever felt. I've given him everything I've got to give, breathed through it and remembered I love him on the way, but now there's nothing left but my shattered limbs and more tears, ones I didn't think I had left. "If you want your dates, you'll fucking earn them from me."

He leaves after that. I hear the door click closed as I stare through the glistening in my eyes and try to focus on my bedpost again, hoping for more grounding in the middle of this oddity. It offers nothing now, though. It's just wood. As solid as it was before but no longer something to hang onto or cling to for support. That sensation left me the moment I heard him leave me alone.

Charlotte E Hart
THE END

My fingers gently flop from the gnarled frame, the tension in them evaporating the moment they fully engage with the floor. So fucking tired. So fucking drained. It's enough for me to choose closing my eyes rather than acknowledging the tears or their effect on me. I haven't got enough mind power left to deal with that either. I just need to sleep, and to find my comfort in that. I'm not mad nor upset by his words. I haven't got the energy to be either. I'm as empty of thought as I ever have been. No stories. No words. No deadlines. I'm just vacant inside, short of a slight tremor still skating through me. Hollow.

The door opens again as I'm dozing off. It hardly wakes me, rather stirs me into acknowledgement of some kind. I don't care. I can't move anymore or think, and I've no interest in opening my eyes again. He could do whatever now and I'd just take it, little effort to sentiment involved. Not that there has been any sentiment from him as far as I can tell, other than regressive intent. It's all felt like a dive into untamed waters, calm, considered even, but nothing about this has been a Blaine I've indulged in before. He just got lost in me.

His fingers scratch around my wrists, undoing the rope that holds me here. They loosen slowly, each thread seeming to speed my descent into sleep. I'm not lulled there or held, more forced by the exhaustion holding me still. It's time to sleep it off. Wake tomorrow. Talk about it then. My body's half lifted from the ground and part dragged somewhere. It makes me open my eyes slightly, wondering where I'm going, but it's just a blurred dark room to me until I see a large cage coming at me, its door open. Panic swells somewhere deep down, inducing a spurt of energy to rise up. It makes me brace my body in his arms, my legs trying to gain leverage on the floor and propel me away from it.

"Blaine?" coughs out of me, barely able to speak after all the screaming and tears that have come from my throat. He wants me in there, doesn't he? He wants to cage me like an animal. "Please. No." He doesn't stop dragging me at my plea. He chuckles a little, his fingers gripping tighter as he tries to manoeuvre me. "No," I snap out again, twisting in his hold and wrangling my head round to face him. "Fuck you. Let me up." The cage door creaks as I bash my arm into it, slamming it shut before he gets a chance to move me inside. "I'm not going in there." He wraps a hand around my arm, turning me onto all fours again and widening the door. I'm not going in there. I'm not. I struggle with everything I've got left, my legs scuffing the carpet, hips and stomach muscles engaging to curl me away repeatedly. Still he holds firm, the wire surface repeatedly hitting my shoulder as he pushes me forward. Oh god, I'm nearly in. It makes me snap my teeth at him and manage to bite into his arm, some of my own feral intent suddenly bursting through my previous exhaustion. "Get the hell off me," spits out, as I glare up at him. "I'm asking you, Blaine. Let me up."

He smiles. It's the first one I've seen for hours. It lights up the dark blur I was in, making my frantic attack stop without thought. Fucking man. I snarl slightly, energy pulsing through my veins as he slowly lets go of my skin and lowers me to the floor again.

"See? You've got so much left yet, Alana." My snarl continues as he walks away, his jeans' covered arse as appealing as ever. Why has he got those on? He should take them off so I can bite him again, suck his cock even. He hasn't let me do that. "You're done when I say you're done. Not before. That's the way this works for me." Arsehole. My snarl turns to more of an irritated smirk as he crouches four feet away and smiles again, his eyes level with mine as I stay on all fours. "You behave like an exhausted fucking dog again and I'll treat you like one."

"Screw you." I'm not going in that cage. Never will I be put in a cage.

"There's my brat," he says, his smile still in place as he stretches his arm to something behind him. I don't remove my eyes from his. I couldn't care less what he's got behind his back. I'm energised again, either through what he's done or the thought of sucking cock. I'm not sure, but my shoulders click around regardless, losing themselves in the thought of more fucking. "Hungry?" My head tilts at him. What an odd thing to say. "How much begging do you have left?" I narrow my eyes, wondering what that means as he stands up and points to the floor in front of him. "Let's find out how far you're prepared to go for me."

"What?"

He brings his hand around in front of him, then opens it to reveal a cooked sausage. I near laugh at the thing in such context, his hand lying far too close to his cock for it to be comfortable. Although, the vision does make my stomach rumble. Seems I am hungry. I flick my eyes between it and the other thing I want, his jeans still obscuring my view of it as I gaze on.

"Come beg for it," he says, his tongue slowly licking over his lips. He just dangles it there, his thumb and forefinger resting on its end, tempting me with all kinds of imagery that has nothing to do with a sausage. "Beg well enough and you can suck that treat you're after when you're done." My own tongue licks my lips, mirroring his movement. It's a tense moment, one that fills me with dread at what I'm becoming. I'm going to beg for a sausage, aren't I? Not that I care for the meat on offer, not really, it's the other thing I want. My treat. I'm enthused by the thought of having some control of it, of him. I want nothing more than to hear him moan and groan as I pull my lips around it, slipping it into my throat, hearing him pleased by me. It makes me feel dirtier than I already am, like I want to crawl this drab carpet, arse in the air to get to him and show him my need. And I don't stop the first slight movement of my hand as I lift it and let my leg follow. I just crawl, my body proudly displaying my want for him as I keep focused on the thing I need. His face flattens as I get closer, the smile turning nefarious with every inch closer. It shakes my nerves a little, making me wonder what he's going to do when I get there, but rather than do something to scare me further he just waits and holds the meat out to me.

"Tease me with it," he says. "Suck it like you will do me."

Liquid pools between my thighs at his words. I feel it dribbling down their insides, tormenting a new ache that's beginning. It's not like the ache he creates in me, not like the one I've endured all night. This one burns through me of my own making. It teases me as I lower my head to the meat, wetting my lips as I go. I nibble at first, the end of it slipping inside so I can taste it. It's divine, causing my stomach to rumble again. Hungry. He was right. I'm starving for it. Ravenous, actually. So much so that I barely control the need to chomp down on it and devour it. My jaw twitches with the thought, almost giving in as I slip more of it inside my mouth. He shakes his head at me slowly. A warning, I suppose. I smile into the movement again and let my lips travel back along the length of it, sucking its meaty taste inside as I go and then moving back up again. It makes me squirm with my own thoughts, my thighs separating as if inviting the unknown in. For someone who's had nothing but filling all night, I feel empty, desperate for something to sink inside me and fill me up again.

I carry on. Long licks first, and then short ones follow, making me imagine the dog he called me, and then sucking, my lips drawing back and forth, pulling the meat in further with every draw on it. It tugs in his grasp, the meat flexing and bending, waiting for me to snap my teeth into it.

"Careful," he says, his frame shifting around in front of me, his knees sinking down to the floor. I watch as he begins undoing his fly, his cock in his hand before I let the meat slip from me again. He leans in, offering his cock to me at the same time. "Wider," he mutters, his hand coming to rest behind my head. "Take both of them." I should smirk, but nothing about this here feels silly. It feels grubby, dirty, as if he's priming me for something other than what's happening at this precise moment. The thought makes me gasp slightly as I inch forward again, my mouth reaching wider to fit them both in. It doesn't stop my thighs widening too. My knees shuffle outwards, announcing something I'm trying not to think about as I suck in the taste of him. It makes me groan as I run the flat of my tongue along his ridges, tasting him for the first time in ages. I'm greedy for more of that taste, so much so that I stretch further still, making my jaw ache to accommodate the two entities. He's not watching me anymore. He's leaning back, his thighs spread and eyes closed as I gobble down on what he offers me. And I'm still fucking squirming like a slut, my arse writhing about in the air hoping to tempt him into fucking me again. "Bite," he murmurs, his breath laboured as I carry on. "Eat." My top teeth cut into the meat, snapping a small piece off. "Swallow it down, take me with it." Fuck, the thought half halts me as I position the meat and look to him, my lips hovering around the end of him. "Swallow or I'll help you fucking swallow." He says it as he tugs the back of my head, proving his point. I slowly draw forward again, trying to tell my throat what to do, but it won't. It feels conflicted, indecisive about the two things. He grabs tighter and pulls himself upright, his other hand reaching over my body until he finds the one thing I'm aching for. "Take a breath," he snarls. One finger sinks in first, the movement yanking me forward onto his cock again, the feel of it making my mouth widen in a gasp. The instant I do, I swallow, unable to stop the contraction around the one thing I was nervous of. I stop breathing and just let the moment halt itself in the middle of whatever this is. I just let him lodge himself in there and finger around me, more fingers pushing in to join his first. Oh god, I'm so full. And then he moves his hand, his thumb climbing and sinking into my arse too. I try to heave in another breath, but gag on the sensation. He hisses in response to the movement, then groans as his hips buck into me.

"Again," he growls, a temper coming from the tone as he pulls back a little with his hand and then drives it in again. It's push and pull, his hand forging me on to get his cock deeper as I hold any breath I've got left. On and on it goes, his balls slapping my chin as I get comfortable with the position. "Fuck," comes out of him at one point, followed by another groan as his hand twists and turns, flicking my clit and winding me into a frenzy. It's all I can do to stay still as my backside screams for more from him. It writhes and turns, egging him in deeper, all the time trying to keep my head still and accommodate him. A spank comes so hard I shunt onto him again, barely able to stop my eyes watering from the impact. And then it lands again, and again, until I'm gagging constantly, unable to stop the want to vomit rising through me. "Keep going," he spits at me, his hips beginning to fuck into me like he's about to come. And the fucking groan that comes with it, the feral intensity of its sound in the room as I squirm and offer my arse at him again, that alone makes me want to come. I want to shout harder at him, want to feel a sensation of coming by spanking alone. I know it's there, I felt it with that other Dom, and when the next one lands on my skin, driving me onto his cock again, I know why. It rises through me, sending chills across my spine as his fingers brush my clit repeatedly. I swallow without thought, edging him further in and not giving a damn if I die or not. I'll suffocate for this. I don't care. I want him deeper. Need to have him there.

He groans again, his hips stilling against me as he releases my backside and unloads his come in my gullet, the feel of its creamy texture making me nearly come. I squeeze my eyes shut, trying to stay alive with barely any air and relish the intimacy of the moment, but it's hazy now, unclear, like I'm going to pass out any minute. I snap my gaze up to him, my head shaking in his hold as he applies more pressure to hold me in place. I need air, desperately. I find him smirking at me, dead eyes fuelling the look as his fingers drag along my cheeks, holding me close. I tug again, noises coming from my throat as I try to yank from his grasp and jerk. It just makes him hold tighter, amusing himself with my fear as his hands pinch in. So I stop and hold myself still, my body trembling. The reaction makes him soften his hold, letting me inch my head away slowly, the length of him sliding out as I do.

Eventually I collapse to the floor, hands bracing me off it as I gulp in breaths of air and let saliva cough and splutter from me. I want to cry, vomit and bile rising again as I try to find comfort in what he achieves in me. It's vile in its own right, disturbing. I'm here, arse in the air as he chuckles above me and finds new ways to humiliate and defile me. It's enough of a thought to retch new bile again, another wave of nausea coming before I can swallow it down.

"You let that out and you'll be in that cage behind you." I clamp my mouth closed, stopping the small amount of sick from coming through my lips. He means it. I can hear it in his tone as I keep staring at the floor. I'm not even sure why I didn't end up in the cage beforehand. He's far stronger than me and could easily force me in there if he wanted. "This is about you earning your rewards and learning to trust. So far, you're earning well. Don't fuck it up." My eyes crawl up his jeans, stopping at the cock that's still in his hand. He swipes his fingers around it, pulling it back and forth, waking it up again. "Be a good girl and you'll get more rewards."

I swallow as I watch his hand, the thought of rewards making me suck back my own vomit rather than risk the thought of going anywhere near a cage. I'm not a dog. I will never be a dog. This might all be new and different, but I'm not a fucking animal to be locked up.

Although, it appears I did just do as I was told because of the thought of punishment.

I frown at the thought, pushing myself a little higher as I begin to understand the dynamics of this. It makes me scan my eyes back to the cage, looking at its still open door. Push and pull. Reward and punishment.

"It's simpler than you might think," he says, his finger suddenly on my chin and twisting me back towards him again. "Look at yourself. Look at the blood and bruises. Tell me if you feel them." He tugs my chin downwards and pushes me back onto my knees, forcing me to see the marks littering my thighs and arms. I gasp immediately, struggling to cope with the images on display as I scuttle backwards. More bile comes up my throat, racing for freedom as I scan limbs of colours and welts. I turn my arms, frantically searching for pain. Each and every bruise, the occasional bite mark interspersing, should be causing me horrendous pain, but there isn't any. I'm sore to touch, swelling ensuring the specific places of his intent, but there's no real pain, not to concern me, anyway.

"Why doesn't it hurt?" The question's mumbled rather than asked as I keep searching myself, turning and twisting to see what he's caused on me. I don't even want an answer from him. I want to find it myself, understand it. Nothing really hurts. No real sense of agony, the sort that should be making me run a mile, screaming for escape.

"Your mind and your body are two different pain centres," he says, softly. It makes me stop my frantic scrabble and look at him. I find a small glimmer of his former persona striking through the heated haze in here as he smiles a little. He rolls his shoulders around and enjoys the feel of his hand still stroking himself, all the time looking at me with a sense of relaxation taking hold of him. "You're learning to use them separately, Alana. You will need to with me."

"But it should ..." Hurt. I should be in agony now, ready to call the pshyc ward and have him, or me, put into a home for the mentally disturbed. I look back at myself, trying to fathom what the hell I've just been a part of. "This is insane, Blaine. This isn't normal."

"No, it's not," he says, a small chuckle coming from his lips as he lowers himself to the floor to sit in front of me. "It's far from normal. *We're* far from normal." He crosses his legs and smiles again, causing me to look over his perfectly poised frame, near panting for more of it on me. "Insane is an interesting word, though. Don't you think?" I don't know what I think. In fact, I'm not even sure if thinking has anything to do with this. "Sadism could be described as insane. It's certainly an unreasonable need given human evolution. It's why I'm a psychology professor. It teaches me about people and their desires, offering solutions in my own mind. I've spent hours analysing myself, finding a reason. Others too." He leans back on his hands, seemingly wanting conversation as he scans over my limbs and smirks occasionally, amused with the response of his own desires on my skin.

"You want to talk about this now?" I'm not sure what I should think about that. I'm here, exposed, bloodied and battered, near fucking exhausted if I'm honest, and he wants to talk?

"You asked for dates."

"This is a date?"

"This is a reward. A prelude to dates."

"What is rewarding about us having a conversation?"

"You're in my mind. Ask questions before I fuck you again." He sits up, his fingers tapping the floor in front of his crossed legs, a smirk still on his face. "You won't get the chance often, Alana. Use the time wisely to advance as much knowledge as you can before I close down again. Research."

My mouth opens. Nothing comes out. There are so many questions and for the life of me I can't think of one. Nothing comes to mind. I feel like I'm barely conscious and he wants to have in depth conversations about sadism and insanity? Jesus. I lean back away from him, trying to find a coherent thought in the midst of this carnage, occasionally looking over my skin for inspiration. "Or you could go in the cage. If you're not fucking quicker than this you might anyway."

"I'm exhausted," I snap out, irritated and tired. I can't think now. I've got nothing left in my mind other than exhaustion and the need for sleep.

"You're not half way done yet," he replies, lifting himself from the floor. "You want the rewards, you'll work fucking harder."

Six seconds is all I get between him coming at me and the instant grab of my hair, yanking me sideways as he starts towards the cage again. My legs scramble, my fingers reaching to push him off as I shout out a 'no' in protest, but nothing stops my drag across the floor. That cage is coming, whether I like it or not, and there's no stopping him or his pull on me.

Chapter 2

ALANA

It's morning again, or perhaps afternoon, I don't know. Seems I've become lost in a fog of clouded judgement and recklessness, neither caring for nor bothered by what I'm becoming. He's here next to me, his breath easing in and out as if he's having some peaceful dream while I lie against bloodstained sheets. He fucked me while I lay in them last night, the weight of his frame pushing me deeper into the blood as he did. I'd like to say it was lovemaking, but it wasn't, not in the traditional sense of the word, anyway. There was barely a sense of connection that I remember, or maybe there was and I was so out of it that I couldn't quite latch onto it. It was just a sea of fucking, aggressive in nature and barely recognisable as something other people do. It's certainly not something I've written about before now. There was no eye contact after the cage, no lips mingling even. He flipped me around as if I was just a vessel to be inspected, used.

I was left in that cage while he called me every name under the sun, then told me of the things he would do if I wasn't smarter with my thinking next time, until eventually he got me out and used me for anything else he felt like. It was as feral as the last time and as confusing as the day in my apartment, but still I wanted it, all of it. I didn't stop him or say no. In fact, I remember my nails digging into him, asking him to devour what was left of me and prove himself right in some way, perhaps show me that all of this isn't wrong. That it's normal somehow. That the conversation he was beginning, the one that was apparently my reward, a prelude to dates, was reason enough to endure his wrath on my skin.

Dates.

I muse the word to myself as I look around the barely lit room, wondering what kind of dates we'll go on. It just seems like a hotel room, barren of frills or frivolities. There's just a bed, some small items of furniture and a tall cupboard in the corner. He said I could have whatever I wanted, that I just have to ask. What that constitutes, I'm not sure. It seems this is becoming a give and take relationship. Reward and punishment. I give him a body to play with, consume, which he takes, and then he gives me some attempt at love in return. The thought makes me snort as I watch the light from beneath the door peek into the room. Love, what a twisted sentiment for this endeavour of a story. I can't see the closeness others deem necessary for happiness, but there is still something. It forges a connection that seems disproportionate to familiarity, truer in its representation of intimacy. Whatever it is, it needs more than its current attributes if it's to go any further than this. It needs a strength it hasn't quite got yet, irrespective of its bond to my heart.

It takes me a while to slowly ease myself from the bed and drop my feet to the carpeted floor. Everything aches now the room is less heated. The pain has arrived, the same pain that was barely there last night. It's not like the first time he was inside me. This time it's enough to make me feel waves of sickness as I attempt standing. Assuming it's balance, or lack of my pills, or lack of fucking sleep, I try to sit still and let the sensation pass, but it doesn't particularly. It just carries on as I stare into the blackness and breathe deeply, hoping to right my dizziness. And then I try to push off again, but my calves refuse to cooperate in any way, almost sending me to the floor as they buckle beneath me.

"Stay still," his husky morning voice says, quietly. I turn slightly to look at him as he raises his frame up, the sheets slipping from his chest as he does. "I'll come and help you." Sweet. One could almost say romantic in some manner, like he isn't the reason for my agony in the first place. I nod anyway, confused about any sense of appropriate but thankful for the offer.

He walks slowly passed me, showing me hardly anything in the dim light. It makes me realise how little I know of his skin as I watch him go into the bathroom, which immediately makes me want to know more. It riles me that I haven't been able to peruse him as he has done me, worship his body if I want. I know nothing of it other than its effect on me. I want to savour it, trail myself around it and taste it. Learn every curve, every muscle. Choose which bit I like best, sense his response to me teasing him.

The thought makes me smile as I watch him wander back out and think of sausages, his cock firmly on display for me to lick again should I want to. I wish I could, but unless he brings it directly to me, I doubt I'm going to be able to do a thing with it.

"Try standing again," he says, his hand offered out to me as I stare into his eyes. I don't even know who he is, or why he is. Why did he stop teaching? Not that I could see him teaching young people, it seems so at odds with his bruskness, but why? Why anything, frankly? I'm here, naked, my body more bruised than it has ever been and yet I'm smiling at the thought. It's all fucked up, back to front, inside out even.

"Why did you stop teaching?" It's out before I think any more about it. If this is give and take, I want some answers. Starting with who he really is.

"It became monotonous," he replies, his fingers locking into mine as he waits for me to push upwards. I keep staring back, not quite happy with that explanation. "There's nothing else." The lie makes me snort as I grip hold of him and heave my weight up. He catches me the moment my legs weaken again, one of his arms pressing directly into the pain on my back causing me to groan out. "Painful?" The quirk of his lips isn't funny as I roll my eyes at him and snarl in reply. Screw him. Of course it's painful, everything is now painful, all due to him and whatever it was that hit me last night. I thought he said I was separating the pain. I'm not this morning, it appears.

"We'll have the truth, Blaine. All of it," comes from me as I slowly make my way to the bathroom with him, trying to stretch my muscles and ease into the motion of walking. "Or nothing else happens here. Always the truth."

"Making demands now?"

"I've earnt my right to know. That fucking cage was hell."

He doesn't answer that or give me any indication that I might have earnt anything, but he does smile as he leans me against the wall, starts the shower, and then ruffles his dark hair.

"Good morning," are the next words that come from him as he turns back around. Really? I think we've already spoken, haven't we?

"What?" He smirks and walks in front of me, his hands bracing either side of my shoulders as he leans in and draws his tongue straight over my nipple, the quick chew on it before he breaks away making me squirm.

"Good morning. You said you wanted dates last night, rewards. I'm presuming that means romance, ergo – pleasantries, like saying good morning?"

"Seriously?"

"Mmm. We might even do lunch, go shopping."

"Okay." My voice stretches the word out, unsure what the hell's going on as he drops his head down again and laves at the other nipple.

"Flowers too?" That's said as his hand lowers along the wall, slowly manoeuvring itself to my skin and gently stroking my thigh. "Candlelit dinners, sweet whispered words." My eyes close of their own accord, fascinated by the sound of his voice lulling me into a romance I've not heard from him before. "Moonlight serenades, a walk along the beach hand in hand." I feel the shiver descend, my body forgetting the pain it's in as he closes the distance between us and brushes his lips across mine. It's lovely, reminding me of proper dates, the sort I write about. Ones that enthral the heroine, making all wishes come true. A sigh escapes me as he pushes his hand between my thighs, widening them and flicking gently around the ache that's building there. "Hostile fucking and romance, is that what you want from me, Alana? The best of both worlds?"

The snatch inside me is so quick I hardly feel it happen. It pushes me up the wall as his other hand turns me away from him so my cheek's squashed into the tiles.

"Do you want me to hold you together or let you crumble?" His fingers splay inside me, the other set slapping at my arse and sending a rally of sensations to collide within my mind. He's so deep, like I'm perched on top of his hand and doing nothing other than waiting for him to continue. "Shall I just make all the decisions?" A twist of his fingers causes a yelp to come out of me, making me question the movement, but it's quickly replaced by another sigh as he winds his other hand to my clit and starts rubbing. "Your cunt needs the pain as much as your mind needs the romance, doesn't it?" I don't know. I can't answer that. It's a mess of emotions. I'm a mess of emotions, barely recognizing reality when I'm with him, only the quiet it creates when I let go of concern.

"Yes." It's all I've got to answer him with, the truth. It's what I ask of him, and what I'll give in return. This is all about truth in some ways, and the slow pull out and then forge back in as he pushes me into the wall only furthers that thought. I'm panting again from nowhere, needy. I can feel my insides quickening against his fingers, willing him harder, deeper.

"Tell me what you want," he says, his face hovering by mine, his words beginning to whisper into my ear as he increases his pressure on my battered spine. "Talk to me about your truths, Alana. Ask me to fuck you harder than I already have." Oh god, and now his mouth is nibbling my neck, teeth finding their way to my jugular again as his fingers keep rubbing, teasing. I groan. It's a groan brought up from the depths of me. Guttural in its pull as I press my arse into his cock and feel the weight of it pressing back. I'm lost again, any form of rationale disappearing into caverns I'm not searching a way out of. His chest hair scrapes the lacerations he caused, scratching them and reminding me of how weak I am around him. "Where? How deep?" Inside me, I want him inside me. Deep, so deep I can't think. And in my head, clearing it of any indecision of hesitation. "In here?" he asks, his fingers scissor again, then shove further as he pushes me up the wall again. "Ask me." I grab at his hand on my clit, wrenching it up my body towards my head, barely able to say the words, just wanting to show him. It's all the noise I want gone. He can do that. He makes it all quiet in there when he tries. It doesn't matter the effect on my skin, or his wants to decimate the flesh he analyses. It matters that he quietens my thoughts as he does it. That alone makes me feel safe in his arms, regardless of the fact that I might not be.

"Here," I murmur, guiding his hand across my forehead and letting myself rest into it. It's cool, and the scent of myself on his fingers makes me somehow feel coupled to his hand in a way I wouldn't have thought possible. "I want you in here." His weight relaxes a little, the sound of his breaths shortening as if he's uncomfortable with the words. "I want all the truths you have to give me, Blaine. All the stains, all the pain. It makes the noise go away. You make it go away."

I feel myself grinding my skin into his hand, suddenly completely focused on it rather than the other one that's still actually inside of me. It seems like a moment of clarity in the midst of unadulterated hedonism, my mind offering a solution to the conundrum that is sadism. Or masochism. Or whatever it is that we have become, are becoming. This hand here, this one holding me off the wall, providing a barrier between me and the harsh extremity of the tile's surface, is like a wrap of care around my skin. It protects me, keeping me close to him as long as I nuzzle into it and find a balance in all this.

"Have you done this before? Protected someone? Loved them?" It's whispered from me, filled with a fear I didn't know I had, because if he says he won't or he hasn't, or he can't, I don't know what I'll do. This here is my silence, it's the thing I need to find myself again and remember why I started writing in the first place.

His weight just keeps retreating from me, his fingers pulling back at the same time, leaving me empty, until the only thing left holding him to me is my head continuing to press into his hand.

It's an announcement of intent on his part, or fear of the untested, I'm not sure, but it's a movement that distances us immeasurably, making me yearn to close the gap again.

"You said you loved me," I say, still rubbing into his skin, my whole body leaning into it and waiting for him to man up, or bow out more successfully than he currently is doing. I'm here, naked, striped and bruised because of him and yet on the brink of feeling so fulfilled its unquantifiable. I can see it coming for me. The silence rumbles inside my mind as I smile into his hand, wanting him to lower it to my mouth, smother me maybe. Why do I want that? I don't know. I do, though. I want him wrapped around me again, consuming my thoughts with his, showing me another way. "Are you as scared as I am, Blaine?" I chuckle at the thought as I ease back a little, instantly feeling bereft without the contact so forging back to the comfort of it.

"Don't tell me you don't feel that." He must, he showed it to me first. Not the fucking, the fucking is only a part of it. This here is under the water, it's the space I found, the air he gave me without there being any to breathe. "There's more here than your needs, Blaine. More than what happened last night. Show it to me."

Silence carries on for a while, giving me nothing but the continued contact with his hand and the sound of the shower rattling water around the bathtub. It stretches forever until his hand slides around my waist again, slowly. The contact makes me smile, imagining a gentler man, one in love, one that might, if we're lucky, find a way through this all is to show me the man he really is.

"You're asking a lot of me," he says, his hand tugging my forehead back to him to lean on his chest and then slowly lowering until it too is wrapped around my waist.

"I'm hoping for something other than the norm for you," I reply. He gently manoeuvres me until I'm looking back at him, then moves until he's sitting on the edge of the bath, removing all contact as he does.

"You already have that, Alana." He stares at me for a few moments, a sigh coming from his as he thinks about something. "We should start at the beginning. I didn't realise you were already there." He frowns to himself, chuckling at something and then reaching for my face. "For me, not for you. You deserve that from me, you're right. Immersion without reward will confuse you."

"What? Last night was …" I'm not sure what it was, but I'm not backing away from it. It was the beginning, wasn't it? The start.

"Sit on the floor."

"Why?"

"That's why," he says, a slight smile on his face as he glances over my body. "You don't trust me."

"I do." Sort of. I wouldn't have done all that last night if I didn't.

"No, you don't. You never have. And why should you? I've given you nothing."

"But .." What is he talking about? "You said .. and last night we…"

"No. Be quiet and listen, for once, and without questioning." He raises his fingers to his brow, pinching it and shaking his head. "Just sit down."

"N… Okay." He smiles again and then sighs as he looks directly at me.

"Look at your skin, Alana." I do, it's bruised. No different than it was ten minutes ago, or last night before the second round started to increase the first lot of reddened markings. "Do you see what I do?" I'm not sure what I see. Cuts and bruises mainly, enflaming. None of it's as painful as it looks, though. Not now that I'm not thinking about it again, anyway. I'm more concerned with what's happening here than giving one damn about the aches of ten minutes ago. "I'll tell you what I see and then you can ask for that romance you want again. You want the brutal truth, you can have it without reservation."

"Okay."

"I see something to be beaten. I see something to be pushed and tormented. I see someone to be fucked and used until I've had my fill of it. This isn't a lesson in manipulation, nor a fragrant display of amusement, this is me. This is how my mind sees you, regardless of how my heart might be affected by you. I have already tested your weight, gaged your ability to run from me, and how long it will take me to catch you. The density of your muscles, your strength. I can tell how long you will be able to hang, how long you will go without food. I know which point on your body hurts the most, which section affects you most." Oh. "And for all the dates you ask, which you can have if they'll make you feel better, you can't think that the romance is real, not in the normal sense of the word. Sentimental attachment doesn't interest me. I don't feel it like others do. It means nothing to me other than a means to an end. It's not something I do."

"Don't be ridiculous. You're a grown man, Blaine. You must feel something …"

"I'm a sadist, Alana. That's all. One who may have curbed his appetite for a time, but still one who reacts on the basis of what it needs. I'm also an accredited psychologist. There is nothing I can't make you do should I choose to fuck with your mind as well."

"But …"

"But nothing. Do you even know what you're doing? Do you know that it's you that has agreed to this, or could it have been me that made you feel the way you do?"

"What?" I don't understand what he's talking about.

"Why are you here?"

"You asked me to see something, told me you loved me, and then .."

"And then you found me with 3 women, my hand inside one of them having made Delaney dispose of two of them. And all that after I choked you against the wall for fun."

"I don't understand ..."

"No, you don't. Where are they, Alana? Alive, dead? Did they ask, or were they forced?" What the hell is he talking about? I start standing up, ready to argue his points. Of course they're alive. He's not a murderer.

"SIT DOWN." Fuck, his tone sends me straight back down to the floor again, my arse hitting it immediately and causing pain to ricochet through my spine. "This isn't a fucking love story. I told you. I am unworthy of that, as is whatever you believe this is."

"But you told me you loved me, that I could have anything, that I just had to ask and ..."

"And you can, but it means nothing to me. Be aware of that. If you come with me, you come under your own risk."

"Why would you say all this? You're lying, you must be. You felt it in the water, and again in Priest's church. You know you did. You're the one that pushed this, not me. I was just writing a story. I was ready to leave you and .."

"I pushed being more than research for selfish purposes."

"Are you saying this is all just a lie? That you don't love me?" I feel the tears well inside me, chastising me for whatever we did last night. Whatever I took for him, I took for love. I stare up at him, hopeless sensations suddenly wracking through my nerves and warning me of impending storms. It makes me look away, feeling stupid, childlike in my search for happiness.

"It depends on your definition of a lie. What I feel is the truth, but it's not your truth, Alana. It never will be. I want the skin your body offers, nothing more. I love that."

I stare at the floor, dumbfounded and feeling as alone as I've ever felt as the tears start, regardless of his proximity. I haven't got anything to go back at that with, and I don't know why I should even bother if that's his true intentions in all of this. I glance over my own skin again, following the long scratch that travels up my arm and wondering what idiot would let that be done to herself if she didn't believe there was a reason for it. His words just can't be true. They can't. There's so much more in that brain of his than just a sadist. I know there is. There has to be for me to feel the way I do about him. There's a tenderness in his touch, a warmth. He holds me as if I'm the only person on the planet worth holding. That's love for me, not simply the skin covering me.

"You're confusing this. Confusing yourself," mumbles out of me, unsure of my own ramblings. "This must be more than sex, Blaine. You said you loved me. *Me*, not just my body." Although why I'm still trying to find a reason for any of this as I continue looking at my wounds, I don't know. He seems as unaffected by his own thoughts as a madman would mass murder, as I look back up into his face. He doesn't answer me, but he nods a little, his eyes completely focused on me as he slowly stands up. "Then, why all this? Love means commitment, trust, the possibility of more?" Still there's no voice from him, just a continued gaze at my body, perhaps hiding whatever he actually wants to say. "A life together?" Oh god I hope so. He made all this happen, didn't he? Made me see who he is and how I feel about him. I wanted professional. I tried so hard to maintain it. "You forced me to admit this, Blaine, to try it. You asked me to watch you. This was all you. I didn't want it, tried to stay away from it and…." I can feel my tears staining my cheeks as I try to figure out what he's talking about. What I'm talking about, even. He's just confusing it all. I did all this for him, or for me. I don't understand what's gone wrong or what's changed. And either way I don't stop the tears as they keep coming, a sob consuming my throat at the thought of more of them. "I don't get why you would … Why would you say all this?" Still he stands like a statue, not one ounce of interest or empathy on his face at the distress he's causing. I'm unravelling faster than I ever have and he doesn't even seem to care as I look away from him in search of comfort. "I don't understand. Why would anyone .."

"Because I can. You're mine to play with." What? I look back at him, sniffing in my tears and frowning at the thought. He sneers at me, tilting his head as I try to wipe my face. "I told you, Alana. I'm an asshole," he says, his sneer turning to a smirk as he shakes his head in amusement at my suffering. "One who seems to find your junkie cunt interesting enough to come in. It's your choice to accept that or not, Alana. I won't lie to you. I won't lie again."

What was tears becomes a gut wrenching flow as I replay his exact words in my mind and stare in shock at him. *My junkie cunt.* I have nothing to respond to that with as I swipe my face again, hoping to show him I have some semblance of control. But there's nothing to say. Nothing. Ten minutes ago we were lying in a bed, relaxing after a night of, oh god I don't even know what it was, and now I'm nothing but a junkie cunt to come in? It makes me look away from him, my eyes scanning the floor tiles for an answer they can't give as my hands try to cover my body. I don't understand what's happening. We were just there, together. I accepted what he showed me, stayed with him. Took the brunt of his hands and ... "Whether you want to like it or not, Alana, this is the love I have to offer you. It's all that I am. Full disclosure."

My eyebrows rise as I sniff in some of my tears again, perhaps still searching for a retaliation to his facts, but what's the point? I asked for the truth. All of it. This is apparently it. It's all he is.

The eventual realisation makes me move away from him slowly, my hope disintegrating as I lift my aching frame from the floor. The cuts barely affect me as I stagger, dazed by his confession and wondering what the hell I've been thinking. He doesn't feel the same. It's all a lie, or the truth, neither of which is any good for my happiness. I shouldn't be here, I should learn by this mistake and move on. As Bree said, learn what I need to from it and write, let it go as an adventure into the unknown. Let him go.

"I can make it quiet for you, though, Alana. If we start at the beginning."

The afterthought halts me as I look at the bottom of the bed, staring blankly at the dried blood on it and considering who the fuck he thinks he is. Why the hell I'm even viewing what he's just added onto the conversation as relevant in any way, I don't know. Perhaps it's because it's true, he can, I know that, but what does it come with now? Just fucking and pain again? No sense of anything more? I sniff in the last of my tears and snarl at them, then wipe them away for fear of more falling.

THE END

"Do you want to make it quiet for me?" I mumble out, my eyes flicking to my discarded clothes as I try to decide whether to just get in them and leave, or carry on discussing this horrendous plan instead. I don't even think these tears are really to do with him, they're to do with me and the thought that I have to go back to real life, cope with it. I'll need the pills again to manage it all. And the noise will start again, won't it? It'll all be the same endless goal with no finish in sight.

"If you want me too." If I want him to? I snort, sarcastically. It doesn't seem to me what I want comes into it anymore.

"Why would you bother," I mutter, defeated and exhausted with the entire topic. What's the fucking point anymore? There isn't one, not one worthy of love anyway. His hand grabs my wrist, harshly, spinning and pulling me over to a full length mirror on the wall to stand me in front of it, little care to my feet tripping the entire way.

"Look at yourself," he says, his voice back to the snap I'm used to. I struggle with the thought, hardly able to lift my eyes given the content of them at the moment. He just grabs my chin, lifting it until I have no choice but to gaze at my body. "You're beautiful. More than you believe. Your mind is stunning, and full of ideas you've supressed." It doesn't feel stunning, nothing does anymore. It feels drained and shattered, used and abused. Nothing but a lie in reality, a pretence, just like the man standing behind me. I wish I believed that last part, wish I could stop seeing the version of him I know is buried somewhere, but I don't. And I know it because as his lips connect with my shoulder, smouldering eyes not once looking away from mine, I feel myself falling back into a silence again. I'm just listening, letting his voice wash around my insides, strengthening them again, galvanising even, regardless of the words before. "I can help you, show you the way, but you have to trust me." I don't trust him anymore, not with those words he delivered. Why would I? "You have to trust me and forget your conception of love." He brushes my hair back, twirling the end in his fingers. "You could be so much more than you are now." I frown at my own image, scarcely noticing the reddened imprints or the state of my appearance, mascara blackening my eyes. "This is just a shell of who you've chosen to become. Let me find out who's in there." I'm confused by what he means as I stare at my hair, the purple stripes as lank as the blond they weave through. And his voice is so fucking soft again. It bleeds from his lips like satin as his mouth begins to wander across my back towards my other shoulder. "Who are you, little dove?" I don't know. He picks up one of my hands showing me my own fingers reflecting back at me, the stain of ink still prominent on them. "Where's this version of you gone?" I don't know that either. It makes me flex them in his hold, watching our fingers together, yearning for more than he offers. "You just have to let me have you, Alana. Just bow down and give in." I thought I was doing. I thought I'd made that clear last night when I let him use me. "No preconceived notions of something other than what this is." My breathing quickens as he lets go of me and then grabs onto my hip instead, pushing it downward slightly. "Just surrender to the help you need." My knees begin buckling under his pressure, the weight of them seeming too heavy to keep me aloft any longer. "Submission." Yes, I suppose that's what this all means, isn't it? "It's easier than you think," he whispers, his other hand rising to hold the back of my neck. "Just give in to it." I do, my knees finally giving up the small amount of resistance they were trying for. They give way as easily as a feather snapping in two, his hand no longer pushing me down rather just resting on my shoulder. "Widen your knees and look at yourself again." I do that too, slowly, trying not to question anything other than how the vision of myself makes me feel. I'm spread open as I nudge my thighs further apart, my crotch on display and the sight of my blemished skin reflecting back at me. "See, beautiful." I'm not sure about that. It makes me lift my hand, trying to make my hair look better than it does as I watch my trembling, blackened fingers move. "Leave it alone, take a good look at the state you're in." My frown comes racing back as his words penetrate the very core of me. *The state I'm in. A junkie cunt.* Lost is what state I'm in. I don't even know what I'm doing down here beneath his feet. I'm alone, that's what I am. My mind is blank of anything other than the sight of myself. My pale skin glows the colours he's delivered back at me, a small smattering of dried blood dotted along my left arm. I gaze at it, wondering what it all means. And then the tears start again, welling and racing through me as if I've got no control over them. They seem to erupt with no help from me as I watch them come. They fall for so long, as if they're from another time and nothing to do with here and now. I don't understand them, but I can't stop them, don't want to. They spill across my skin as a river would, travelling down my cheeks and falling onto my breasts. I follow one rivulet as it continues downwards, inching it's way around my nipple until it drips from the end. It's the single most cleansing experience of my life. I'm naked and not caring for the consequence of it. Protected by the man behind me, I hope, regardless of what that protection means to my soundness. He just seems, even now after his words, to sheath me by just being here and watching this unfold. Maybe he forced it like he said, I don't know, and I don't care either, because as the tears finally begin to dry, and as the thoughts start to creep back in making me question everything again, he walks in front of me blocking me of the mirror's reflection and showing me himself again.

"This is your reflection now, Alana," he says, his body lowering until he sits cross legged in front of me and gazes back. There's no smile, no smirk, not even a frown or a considered comprehension of care. He's just still, his face disimpassioned and his mouth a calm line of composed grace. "You'll only see me and what I can give you in return." My head tilts, hardly able to comprehend the meaning and not able to find any words to counter his. "It starts here, and it'll end when I say you're done." I think I'm nodding, although I didn't move my head that I'm aware of. "Good girl."

And then there's just silence again as we look at each other, me tracing his features with my eyes, hoping for enlightenment as I listen to his breathing soothe the moment, and him just staring back and letting me watch him.

"You're so handsome," comes from my mouth unexpectedly. I mean it, it's nothing to do with his physicality, more to do with the composure he holds. "Tranquil." That seems to cause a small quirk to his lips, not surprising given the word, I suppose, but that's what he seems to me in these minutes. It's like I've got a hurricane raging inside causing chaotic thoughts and he's the tower of light in front of me, guiding me to safer waters, regardless of him causing the chaos in the first place.

Charlotte E Hart
THE END

For the first time I feel a small sigh come from me as I blow out a breath and feel his words again. *Junkie cunt. The state I'm in.*

"No more pills?" I ask, quietly, my voice a mere breath of noise beneath my tears. He shakes his head slowly, his hand reaching for my face.

"No phone, no connections to your life, no pills, and no lies either," he replies, those fingers of his as soft as a feather as they land on my cheekbone and begin to stroke a thumb across it. "You'll do everything I ask, take everything I give you, and for that I'll show you the way through to the other side."

I rest into his hand, feeling his strength and closing my eyes. Whatever this will be, will be. Dates or no dates. Love or no love. It is what it is, and will evolve, hopefully helping me find me again by the end of it.

Chapter 3

BLAINE

I'd never stared at someone for so long, never been interested enough to do so. Yet I'd sat there in front of her this afternoon for a little over an hour, just watching her until she left her head looking at the floor and became comfortable with that process. It started as a means to an end, helping her prepare for what will become our ritual, but it ended with me being enthralled with the splendour of her, more so than I'd ever been before. The thought perplexes me as I continue along the coast road and listen to her softly humming a tune beside me. I've never heard it before, but it reminds me of old soul songs, bluesy notes highlighting flats and sharps rather than the monotone drone of pop culture.

"Put your phone in the console," comes from me, as I open the compartment. Her head spins on me, some part of her aggressive little brat saying no before her mouth utters the words. She catches herself before anything comes out, and I watch her dig around until she flips the thing into the console, a huff coming after the event. She stares away again instantly, resuming her song with little care to my demand. It amuses me, making me consider this whole fucking insanity I'm placing us into. I'm still not sure whether I want to save her or destroy her, but the fucking song coming from her lips seems to be lulling me into thoughts of happiness and comfort, a sense of companionship. "Tell me about your family," I say, surprising myself with my own curiosity in the thought. She stops her humming instantly and fidgets in her seat a little, her fingers grabbing at her dress to pull it down her thigh some more. "You don't like the thought of giving me that information?"

"I don't see its relevance anymore," she replies, dully, crossing her legs the other way to hide her thigh. I smirk at the move, pleased by what she thinks she can hide now that she's accepted my terms. She can't hide a fucking thing from me. It will all be dragged out if it needs to be. It will be raked across and dissected, queried until it gives me enough facts to recognise why she's become addicted to pills in the first place. Usually there are only three key reasons why people became addicts. Misadventure, anxiety, or abuse. This comes in varying combinations of physical, mental, circumstantial and emotional factors, considerably changing the dynamic of the key reason, proving the psychological or physiologic dependence on a subject or practice beyond voluntary. "My family isn't pertinent if there's no hope of more." She'd be surprised how relevant family always is. Underachievement anxiety. Fatherly mental abuse. Motherly dependence to the father, leading to criteria that explains a child's need to become non dependant on anything, and then drug dependant because of that continued anxiety. "It's not like you're ever going to meet them, is it?" Probably not. Although, I'd like to, strangely enough. "As you said, this isn't a love story anymore." I keep gazing at the road, wondering myself what kind of story this is becoming. It is a love story in some ways, one that confounds me, true, but there's no denying the way the little madam's mind infiltrates mine unlike anyone else's has done. She entices me for some reason, proving the heart inside my chest beneficial for something other than simple beating. "Can we just not talk about them? I don't want them involved in this, they deserve better than you." The remark cuts deeper than I could have imagined it would, making me frown as I remember the picture of her parents in her apartment. "They're good people, Blaine. This *thing* isn't something I want them associated with." And that remark pisses me off, deepening my frown to a scowl as I stare at the road. It once again shows a disrespect for my people, assuming they're unworthy of parental love. And it also negates the fact that this whole 'thing' is her fault, not mine.

"You want my help, Alana, you'll answer any fucking question I ask of you." Not that I care a fuck for the answer now, more that I want her to obey the principle of our dynamic and do as she's damn well told.

"What about yours?" she asks, her face turning away into the sun as she closes her eyes, seemingly unaffected by the malice in my voice. "Are they proud of their son's abilities in the bedroom?"

"Fuck you." The gravel of my tone shoots out of my mouth before I've got control of the words.

"Quite the emotional response for a psychologist. Aren't you supposed to be dispassionate?" She chuckles on the end of the statement, apparently amused at my reaction. "I mean, presumably they know about your predilections, or do you keep it a secret?" Both of their faces come straight into my mind, both of them smiling. And then the rush of my mother's arms around me as she'd congratulated me. Her perfume, my father's handshake, the way he'd spoken to the dean regaling him with stories of when Cole and I were young. "Actually, I don't know anything about your family. And if we're being truthful, you tell me first to get the ball rolling. You're the one that's asked me to trust you, aren't you? Are they proud?"

"They're both dead," I snarl out. It's the easiest way to move the conversation on. Her head spins around to look at me, both horror and sadness etched into her features. I only catch a glimpse of it, but it resonates nonetheless, making me feel the same sensations as the day I'd watched the plane crash on CNN.

"Oh, god. I'm so sorry," she says, quietly. I turn to glance at the sea running alongside us rather than look at the face that offers pity. Sorry? She needn't be, it's just one of life's curses. I don't need pity about it or someone to hold my hand. Cole might in reality. It would probably do the guy the world of good to be held and trusted, given a space to wallow in, but not me. "That must be awful. I can't imagine what that feels like to lose your parents. How did they pass on?"

What fucking relevance is that?

"I'd rather talk about yours," I counter, trying to nullify the memories that come with family.

"Oh, okay." She looks back out the window again, brightening her face ready to spring into conversation. "If you like, then. Well, they're in the UK, obviously. Both slightly overweight now that they've retired, with a little financial help from me. Mum was a hairdresser, Dad an engineer. He made the bits that interlink a plane's engine assembly." I roll my eyes at the thought, annoyed at the connection and yet somehow amused by it. "I'm an only child, apparently one was quite enough for mum to cope with." She shifts and looks back at me again, her eyes narrowing slightly. "You're sure you want me to discuss this?" I nod, trying to sink into her rhythm rather than mourn my own parents any further than I already have done. "I'm not sure what else you want to know, or even why I'm telling you."

"You're telling me because you want to take my mind off my own parents, it's called re-association. You're diverting me."

"Oh."

"Mmm. It's working, carry on."

"Right. Well, they're nice people. Honest. Trustworthy. They both worked hard to make sure I was looked after, safe. I don't have any Daddy issues or anything like that, if that's what this is all about. They're just Mum and Dad really. Decent, you know?"

"Do you miss them?"

"Yes."

"Why?"

"I don't really know. I suppose everyone misses their parents, don't they?" Her hand flies to her mouth again, eyes wide with her embarrassment. "Oh god, I'm so sorry, that was the wrong thing to say, again." I chuckle at her, charmed by her concern. None of which I deserve because of the dead body buried six feet underground, the one I put there. I sigh the chuckle away, scarcely enjoying the sense of contentment she's given for a few moments diversion.

"It all sounds idyllic. You've nothing to be sorry for."

"Do you miss them? Your parents?" she asks, quietly, her body turning to face me. I glance to look at her again, trying to remember a time that someone has asked me that. No one has, not even Eloise, although she had known better than to look into my mind. I smile at her as she screws her legs up into the seat, enchanted by how small she looks when she's being emotional. "I mean, you don't have to talk, obviously, but you can if you want to. I'll listen. Help if I can." The words make me sigh again and look back at the road rather than entertain that thought, nice as it might seem in some ways.

"This isn't about me, Alana. It's about you."

"Yes, but, it can be about you too, if you .."

"Want it to be?" I snort. "I've told you what I want it to be. You know exactly how I want it to be. My emotional health isn't part of that, not other than my predilections as you call them, anyway." I sneak another look, hoping to prove my point with a glare, and catch her face hardening instantly because of it, the lines of it becoming a mask again. "That doesn't mean you hide from me, Alana. You're the one that needs help, not me."

"I'd question that rationale," she mumbles, her face returning to its closed eye position as she twists her body away again. Would she? She needn't bother with that either.

Time ticks by, the coast road taking as long as it always does. I don't really know why I'm taking her home again. Perhaps it's because it feels safe there, comforting, but it's more likely the need to have her in the space I originally wanted her in. For whatever reason the need to have her in my own walls, protected by them maybe, is greater than the fear of having her within them. This, too, perplexes me as we travel on, the waves crashing the coastline as we go. I should be taking her anywhere but my home, regardless of the want to have her there.

"Do you ever swim in it?" she asks, her eyes still closed.

"What, the sea?"

"Mmm."

"Yes, often."

"Why?"

"What?" The question throws me off guard, perhaps digging deeper into the psyche of what it means to me rather than accepting the simple question for what it is.

"Why do you swim?"

"Why are you asking?"

"Because this fucking silence is deafening, Blaine." I snort out a laugh, charmed yet again by more odd things that shoot from her mouth. "I hate it."

"You told me you wanted the silence," I reply, a smile broadening on my face as the contradiction of her races home once more.

"Not when it's because of uncomfortable situations. It's the chaos I want dampening, not your conversation. Frankly, I could use more of it to understand what the hell I'm doing here with you in the first place. It might help, you know? You're unfathomable."

"I might want you uncomfortable." She smiles, her lips rounding into the glorious version that makes my guts churn, a wicked tilt to them.

"No you don't. If you wanted that you wouldn't be taking me to a place you consider home." She lifts her dress again slightly, sliding a finger along the crease by her knee and tempting me. "Come on, Mr Jacobs, or is it Doctor? Either way, by doing that you're opening yourself up to me, aren't you? Allowing me to prod at you as much as you want to prod at me. Uncomfortable would have meant going to Priest's Church, or staying in that ratty hotel room we were in." My brow raises at her thorough examination of the situation. "Bringing me here," she says, her eyes eventually opening as we turn onto the final stretch of the coastal line, "regardless of our conversation this morning, means you give a shit, whether you want to admit it or not. I don't need a psychology degree to know that."

I don't answer her nor look at her. The analysis is too close for comfort, and she doesn't need to know that she's right. It isn't any help to her at all to know that she affects me in ways I don't understand myself yet. Those types of confessions will only hinder my ability to aid her recovery, forging us closer than I need us to be. The whole purpose of my explanation in that bathroom was to distance her from me, to make her realise that she's on her own in this. Support, while needed for a time, is not endless here. I'm simply being honest, and in doing so will ensure she finds her way out of the other end sufficiently enough to guide herself onwards. With or without me.

"You're not quite the arsehole you think you are, Blaine." Oh, yes I am. I'm everything she should run from and nothing that she needs. I'm a selfish, twisted fucker, one who's using every technique to keep my monster at bay while I help her. "And I don't believe you when you say this isn't deeper than the superficial you're trying to portray. You're a liar." Liar? Not entirely. Not this time.

She just waits in silence after that, the rest of the coast road seeming to take hours as she looks out of the window away from me. It gives me time to ponder everything, analyse it, find a sensible solution to her problem, and mine. Mine being that no matter how hard I try to hold this monster in, I'm constantly bombarded with anything but the help she asks for. It's sickening even to me on occasion as visions corrupt the already corrupted, tempting me, goading me. I'm even irritated she's in as high spirits as she is, perhaps wondering why she's not in tears again from my words, or constantly wriggling from the agony the wounds on her back should be causing. The concerns make me focus on the road solely, trying to dislodge the sense of shame and elation that collide together. It's been so long since I've had a toy to play with. And this one next to me, she's everything I want. Vigorous enough to challenge me and durable enough to take my response to the challenge. It's a match made in hell, one that waits for me to burn it to its end.

Eventually the house comes into view, breaking me from my analytical progression along routes no sane person travels. The image of its sleek white lines brings my peace with it again, causing me to smile as I wind the window down and smell the air. Home. Calming and bolstering. It protects me from the world as much as it protects the world from me. But not anymore, not now I've brought her here.

She gets out immediately, presumably not caring for my opinion on what she can or can't do. It amuses me, lightening my considerably heavy thoughts. So I sit and watch her for a while, gazing at the way the wind picks up her skirt as I take her phone out and put it in my jacket pocket. She seems to blend into the wind's grip around her, her arms opening to it rather than shuddering from its incessant breeze. Perhaps she's more ready for me than I thought previously, more in tune with her body's needs than I've given her credit for. It's like the Daddy conversation all over again, her mind engaging enough for her to forget this is different and accept it as normal. The visual hardens my cock, making me imagine the kind of fucking I've dreamed of and only recently found, with her.

I smirk at the connotation of romance, flicking my eyes down to the beach and considering a walk there rather than the den I was thinking of moments earlier. Would that alleviate the ache she causes, or will it just further the abandonment coming?

She makes the decision for me, as I watch her begin walking towards the cliff steps to the sea, her footsteps as unhurried as the breeze she drifts through. It only takes one small glance from her and my stomach flips like a twelve year old's, a wry smile attached to her nod at the water below. The sensation both pisses me off and excites me, leaving me with little explanation for either. And then she's off, her feet hurrying her along the frontage, her arms already unwrapping the top she has on. I climb out of the car, not sure whether to strap her up for using her own judgement on what she can do, or kiss her for challenging any discipline I have to offer her. The problem makes me frown as I slowly walk in her direction, the sand kicking off my shoes as I go and reminding me of my harmony here. Nature is always such a confusion. My fucking beast inside might be desperate to initiate its desires, ones I've suppressed for too long, but it's now being disordered with the juxtaposition of meaningful situations. Love, I assume.

"I love you." I mouth the words to myself slowly as I wander down the steps and watch her walk away from the bottom of them, wondering what the words mean. I do, though, on some level that's attached to the base of me. Perhaps it's an instinctual bond, something that tears the monotony of the 'usual' from my guts. Or perhaps it's just that I can come in her, the action giving her a piece of me that few others have managed. Either way, it's as real as she believes it is, regardless of my attempt to make her see otherwise. She knows, and she's right. It started in that pool and has grown from there, whether I've tried to stop its path or not. It's as rickety as these steps I traverse to get to her and as dependable as the sea ebbing in front of me. Constant. Irreversible.

"Are we going in?" she calls, a brief glimpse back at me as she carries on forward anyway. I'm not, the only time I go in is to try drowning myself in the heavy undertow, and today, for once, I don't feel the need to bother. Today, and because of her, I feel like living and trying.

My smile broadens as I realise I haven't stopped smiling at her. Seeing her here, unbound and nearly unclothed, is freeing in some ways. It replaces the other memory attached to Eloise's form doing the same thing. She'd never been as animated as Alana is, her smile never as vibrant, but she did walk these beaches too, alone, and never with me following her. She wanted to drown as much as I have since her, wanted the life sucking from her so she could forget it and move on to the next place, but nothing about the woman in front of me now wants to drown, she wants to be saved. Protected.

The realisation makes me take my jacket off as I watch her feet getting closer to the water's edge, my shirt buttons quickly following as I quicken my steps a little. And a panic begins to race up my own throat, an anxiety. I feel it quickening my guts, making my heart speed, too, as I frown at her knees being lapped by the water she's crashing into.

"Don't go in any further," I shout. What the fuck am I thinking? She must be able to swim or she wouldn't be so stupid. Regardless, my hands begin to grab at my belt, unbuckling it to get to her. "Alana, don't go too deep." It's too late, and the wind flowing in the wrong direction, casting the words back at me rather than towards her, means she can't hear anyway. The vision increases the anxiety ebbing inside of me as I watch her discarded clothes flutter by in the wind, making me walk faster to the water regardless of my trousers still in place.

The waves keep coming as I zone in on her form and watch her swim out into them. They're small by the coast, showing nothing to be concerned about, but I know these waters like the back of my hand. The current is strong, devastating in some circumstances. I've swam in them enough, letting the undertow take me further out or surge me into the cliffs face.

"Come back in," I shout. Nothing comes back at me but the sound of light laughter drifting through the air. "Don't go out too far," I call instead, hoping that will make a difference to her continued splashing around. It doesn't, she just keeps swimming on, occasionally diving under the water and disappearing only to pop back up again in the spray. And the fucking panic keeps coming, too, making me feel sick in some respects, something I've never felt before. It yanks at my guts, making them cringe in fear about something.

I look down, distracted by something and realise I'm knee deep in the shoreline. It makes me laugh as I toe my shoes off and let them drift away, not caring for their demise. The woman out there is of more concern, the one who's asked me to save her. But when I look up again to find her, she's gone. I wait for a few seconds, expecting to see her bob up again, but she doesn't. The odd sense of sickness forms as bile, my throat almost strangling me as I wade out deeper, dragging the water with my fingers, to search for her in the cresting spray.

"Alana," I yell, the ground beneath me starting to disappear as the waves pull back and forth. I tread water for a second, watching and waiting. "Alana?" Nothing still, so I swim towards the last place I saw her, my trousers tugging me in the swell. Fuck. Panic grips harder, making my arms speed through the water to get to where she was. And then when I get there, there's still nothing but the rise and fall of the waves, my body being battered about within it. I dive straight down to search below, grabbing out at anything that looks vaguely solid, but nothing sinks into my hand other than more water, so I break the surface again, immediately searching for her as I shout her name over and over again. Where the fuck is she? I won't have another death on my hands, can't. One was enough, and that was one I didn't love. I'll fucking kill myself trying to save this one rather than live without her.

I look back at the beach, checking the shoreline in case she's been washed up, but nothing's there either. True fear grips, making me drag in a huge lungful of air before diving straight back down, hands grasping like mad, clawing at anything in hope that it's her body. It's just a sea of fucking murk, nothing presenting itself other than more waves and crashing breaks. I struggle against it, pushing through the gloom, for once wishing for clear fucking water rather than this obscurity that I linger in so often, and then finally my fingers grasp at flesh, heaving it upwards as I kick to the surface to eventually break through it.

"Fuck," I splutter out, yanking her frame to me to find her face. Her hair is slathered across it, half of it embedded in her mouth as I tug it out of the way and wrap her into my hold to keep us both aloft. *Fuck, fuck.* I tuck her in, my hand instantly slapping at her cheek to wake her or try to get her to cough out the water. Nothing happens, her body just lies limply alongside mine as the waves crest again and nearly take us both under. Fuck. I grab tighter, gripping her so hard I might break her. I couldn't give a fuck. I'd rather her be broken than dead. I'm getting her back to the shore, making her breathe again, broken or not. I'll fucking crush her ribcage to start her lungs again if I have to because I'm not losing this before it starts. I'm not losing her.

"Alana?" I shout, spluttering out the cold water as I gulp in salt. "Jesus Christ." Still no answer to stop the bile wanting to launch from my guts. Nothing at all other than a lifeless form being towed, as I pull for all I'm worth to get us both back to dry ground.

The moment my feet touch the sand I run with her, her body becoming heavier the moment the water's surface leaves her. It makes me trip, her near naked form slipping from my hold and tumbling onto the shallow waters. It's enough though, just enough for her mouth to be above water which spurs me over to her, my hands already tipping her chin up and opening her mouth as I lower my ear to her. I can hardly hear anything over the waves that keep coming and slapping my back, certainly not breath, so I hit at her face again, hoping to wake her out of her daze. Nothing happens but her head lolling sideways, her hair slicking the sand as she turns.

"You'll fucking wake up," I snap, as my hand moves down to her chest, the other following to start pumping the water out of her. One, two, three, four, five into her ribcage, and then my chest moving across her to breathe into her lips. Nothing but my breath blowing her own chest upwards happens, so I do it again, and again, repeating the move until fear and fury made me slap at her again. She just lies there, her lax body being washed around in my hold by the sea. "Alana?" Nothing. I start it all again, furiously pumping her chest in the hope that I can bring her back to life. She just has to breathe. Just one breath. One breath followed by another. I can feel it happening inside my own body, huge lungfuls being pulled in as if I can somehow give them to her. My lips wrap over hers as if it's the first time I've kissed her, blowing the breath in hard until I've got nothing left inside me to give. Still nothing. No movement. I bind my hands into her hair, tugging at it and leaving my lips where they are, covering hers until my own soften into a kiss. It brings with it a feeling of tears travelling through me. She can't die, not here, not yet. We haven't started yet. We've got so much to see together, so much to do now that I've found her. Rage wells again at the thought of loss, my body rising away from her to gaze at the lifeless form, which forges my hands to pick her head up and knock it against the sand, shaking her and shouting her name. And then another slap, her face tumbling away from the contact.

"Fuck you, Alana," I shout, my hand hitting her face again, and again, fear and terror charging my body for a firmer hit. "I love you, wake the fuck up."

Still nothing but a lifeless body, one I clamber over, my knees either side of her as I pull her up into my hold and clasp her into me.

And real tears come then, they fall from my eyes, anger or dread, defeat maybe, sending them into her hair as I hold her close and begin rocking. *Fuck you.* It repeats itself over and over, causing me to become so infuriated violence rages. My hands grip her so tightly I feel her muscles grate against each other, bones constricting on themselves. *I love you.* That keeps coming too, fuck you and I love you continually swirling as my lips rest on her forehead hoping for an answer.

No, it's not happening. I push her body away from me back to the sand again, my fingers finding her breastbone and beginning to drive downwards again as I stare at her closed eyes. "Fuck you, wake up." I pump again, my mouth descending the moment I've finished the compressions. And then again, and again, and again until I hit her chest cavity in fury, vehemence fuelling the move. She instantly twitches, the muscles in her chest heaving at themselves and forcing another movement. So I turn her, pushing on her ribcage at the same time, hoping to force the water out and up her windpipe somehow. And then comes the cough, she sputters it out, water spurting out of her lips as her hand moves a little. *Fuck you.* I snarl the thought, still infuriated with her, or myself, or whoever's fucking fault this is as I stare at her coughing it up.

"Get it out," I yell at her, my hand still hitting her back as I hold her on her side.

She does, repeatedly, her body convulsing as she rolls herself onto her front and braces her hands up to help the water fall out of her. And then a breath, she sucks it in, her mouth open wide as she heaves and I watch her lungs inflate. It's all I can hear, the sound of her pulling in breath after breath dispersing the noise of the waves, near nullifying the wind still battering around us.

I back away and rest on my knees, giving her room to do as she needs, not sure if I should hold her close or beat the shit out of her for petrifying me. The sensation's worse than it was with Eloise. It isn't fear of guilt or reprisal this time it's sheer terror associated with the loss of her, something that drives me inwards for fear of what that means to us, to her. I just kneel and watch, a sneer developing at the sight as my heart rate continues to thunder away inside. Fuck you, still. She's done this, wound this up, made me feel emotional, and in doing so has drawn us closer together than I want us to be. I'm not worth it. She's worth more than me. So much more.

Eventually I get up, choosing to keep my mouth shut rather than announce anything as I begin walking away from her. She can fucking stay there, learn by her own mistake, chastise herself for stupidity. And then I stop and turn back to look down at her instead, still unfinished with whatever it is that I'm trying not to say.

"Fuck you," I shout, my fucking hand wiping hair from my face. She looks up, her body still heaving in air and coughing out water. "What the fuck was that?" She looks down again, her eyes searching the sand for something as she braces herself out, purple fucking stripes falling around her too fucking beautiful face. Maybe she's looking for answers down there, who fucking knows. "Don't' ever go in that fucking water again, do you understand?" She coughs again, her head only nodding a response as I start pacing around in front of her, barely able to contain my own fury. "You scared the shit out of me." Another nod as she tries to sit back, her body wavering around the move. I rush forward, reaching for her before I get around to controlling the fucking impulse. "Jesus Christ, Alana," I snarl, grabbing at her body and hauling it up into my arms for fear she'll drift out into the ocean again. "Are you trying to kill me?" She snorts, another rally of coughs following the sound as she grabs onto my neck. The sound makes me feel like dumping her back onto the sand again, leaving her there to wallow in her misadventure, scare herself by it, hopefully teaching her a valuable lesson in safety at the same time. Fucking stupid bitch.

"There was a wave .." she attempts.

"Keep it fucking closed until I calm down," I cut in, still struggling with the concept of dropping her, drowning her, or fucking any breath she's regaining out of her. Fucking woman. Fucking emotions. I fucking hate it all. Other people do this shit, not me. I walk on muttering and snarling, grabbing her closer and furious with myself for the need to. "You're this close to getting the beating of your life."

She nods again, trembling a little in my hold as we cross over the beach towards the steps. Good. She should be trembling. She should be frightened for her fucking life, terrified, because now I've felt that, now I've sensed a fear associated with her leaving me, there's nothing stopping me from taking this exactly where I want it to go. Whether she wants it or not. She's not going anywhere, not until I've had my fill of her life.

Chapter 4

ALANA

I've been dumped on a black leather couch in a room I've never been in. He didn't once put me down as he struggled with keys, nor did he release me as he went and found a towel to wrap around me. He only let go when we got in here, at which point he almost threw me at this leather I'm sitting on, huddled and freezing cold. He then proceeded to glare at me for a few minutes, watching as I fidgeted about trying to get comfortable under his gaze, and then he left me alone. No words, no conversation, and most definitely no sense of compassion or love. He's pissed, furious even. I don't know why, it's not like he's the one that nearly died, or is still coughing up salty water. If anyone's supposed to be angry surely it's me. I mean, he could have told me the undertow was too strong to swim in. No one should be swimming in that water. It's beyond dangerous.

I stare out at it through the floor to ceiling French windows, watching its persistent crash against the shoreline I was on a while ago. It drives its crests at the beach like a torrent, not giving a damn for anything that gets in its way or the affect it leaves there. What was I thinking? I could have died out there. Although, it didn't look like that when I went in, or it didn't seem to at the time. Now, though, it looks like a living, breathing rage of hatred as it batters the sand and cliffs. Beautiful maybe, no doubt about that, but certainly not for swimming within. It was alive, full of malicious intent and doing nothing other than exposing its power over me, proving my limited ability within its arms ineffective.

The sight makes me huddle further into my towel, peeling off my soaked clothes underneath it and trying to get some more warmth into my bones. I'm so cold, and this room doesn't help. Doesn't he have anything in this house with any sense of comfort attached to it? It's all so barren. Neat, yes, but sparse, as if it's been deliberately kept to feel cold and unwelcoming. The house in Manhattan wasn't like this, it felt homely in some way, cosy even short of its lack of furniture. This place, though, especially this room and the other one I was in when I was here last time, is nothing but walls and a few basic pieces. Large plain, light grey walls, built in cupboards lining one side of the room, another cupboard on the other and then this couch I'm on. No curtains. No frills. Only what I suppose are necessities.

"Put these on," his voice says. It makes me jump a little and turn to look at him as he walks in and throws what seems to be a tracksuit at me. "They'll be too big, but they'll have to do till Tabitha gets here." Tabitha? Great.

"I could do with a bath," I reply, knowing that no amount of blankets or clothes are going to warm me through.

"No. You'll suffer the consequence of your actions in here."

"What?"

"You're damn lucky you're not doing it from your knees, Alana. Put the fucking clothes on." I frown at him, wondering what's made him so mad, as I slowly unfold the towel from around me.

"Why are you so angry?" I ask, quietly, slipping my arms into the hoodie and then beginning to put the bottoms on. "It's not like it was you who nearly drowned."

"Rather than question me, again, perhaps a fucking thank you would be nice for a start?" Oh, haven't I said that? Shit. The thought makes me look back at him, really look for a second or two rather than just remember what happened out there. His brow's furrowed, his hair still wet, the trousers on his body still soaked. He hasn't even changed or dried himself yet. He's that furious that he can't even feel the cold in his own bones. I tilt my head at him, trying to hear whatever he's thinking about, but as usual there's just a wall of nothing looking back at me.

"I'm sorry, and thank you for saving me." It comes from me with little emotion attached to the words. It isn't because I don't mean either of those things, I do, it's just that I don't want to give the emotion over to him anymore. As he said, liar or not, there's nothing here but a process to get me off the pills. He's showing that loud and clear with his aggressive attitude.

I turn away and pull my knees up, huddling into the oversized tracksuit, his I assume, and look back out of the windows again, choosing that over the anger he's portraying. I've got no interest in an argument or trying to prove something that doesn't exist. I nearly died out there, and that only happened because I chose to believe that if I showed him some fun, showed him that this could be so much more than just a process, then maybe we could make something else of it. But this reaction here, the one he's delivering with as much malice as the sea out there, well, it's not worth my effort. He was right this morning, we don't feel the same way. It might be love on both our parts, but his sense of the word is far removed from mine. Perhaps he just doesn't know what it is, or perhaps he doesn't want to. Either way, I'll just do whatever it is that I need to do to gain help from him and get off these pills, and then, after that, I'm done.

  He moves in my eye line, his hand dragging along the long line of cupboards on the opposing side of the room. I don't look or give him any more impetus to make him think I'm scared or intimidated because I'm not. That scared me, that sea out there as it pulled me beneath it and whipped me around. Blaine is nothing compared to that sense of battery against my skin, even if I do get the sense he could be if provoked. I remember its pull on me as I went under, remember its effortless hold on my frame as it tugged and wrenched, no care to how my death came attached to its force. It just swallowed me, churning me over within until all my air evaporated and there was nothing left. And, in some way, after I'd finished kicking for my life and clawing for breath, I accepted it and let it whirl me around, not caring for my own death either.

  The thought makes me glance at him, then back towards the ocean, wondering how similar the two of them are. I mean, he lives here next to it, allows it's collision on the sand to mirror his own thoughts, perhaps enhance them even. And his mood currently is as black as the ocean out there, the sneer on his face as rage filled as the sea that nearly killed me. My own sneer develops at the thought, my eyes heading back to the sea again. I'm thankful to him for saving me, no doubt about it, but I'm not going to be humiliated or shouted at because of it. All I was trying to do was prove his love for me, make us closer than he wants to keep us, and if he can't see that, or doesn't want to acknowledge it, then so be it. I'm done trying.

There's a small bleep then a quiet whirring noise, and as I notice the wall of cupboard doors start to move, I turn to gaze at its movement along the floor. He follows the vertical line as it draws backwards, his feet padding backwards as the doors somehow sink into the wall at the far end of the room. It's not until the final click of the mechanism that I look up at him to find a still scowled face staring back at me.

"Dates," he says, quietly.

His tone makes me linger in the word, turning and searching his face for a meaning as we're not on the same page as far as romance's concerned. Nothing changes on the sculpted brow staring in my direction, not a flinch. He just stares as I watch a droplet of water crawl from his hair, my eyes following it along to his jaw, seemingly fascinated by it. Quite perversely given my current state of loathing for his mood. "Get some sleep, Alana."

And with that he swings his body away from the corner, his hands unbuckling his belt as he leaves the room, softly closing the door behind him.

"Sleep."

The word murmurs out of me as I continue staring at the door he left through, wondering how the hell he thinks I'm going to sleep. There's too much running through my mind to sleep. It's chaos in there again, perpetual concerns zooming around, my body quaking and shaking, still from the shock presumably. It's a laughable thought. In fact, I'm becoming more and more convinced by the second that this whole thing is laughable. Love and near drowning. Twice. Both times my life saved by him. I snort out, my head swinging back to the sea again for guidance, or answers on why the hell it wanted to kill me, but I'm halted in my tracks by the vision of the open cupboards as my eyes scan round for the first time.

The gasp that leaves my lips is uncontainable as I flick my eyes around, nervously looking over the veritable array of objects on display. My body attempts cocooning further into this tracksuit, presumably trying for escape. Jesus. Although, Jesus very clearly has nothing to do with what is in front of me. Rows and rows of implements, contraptions, ropes. Drawers lined beneath them, no doubt full of other apparatus and riggings. And something mechanical is clicked upright, maybe a bench, or a mechanism for fucking torture. Who knows? Where the hell am I?

I'd like to say I'm rigid against the leather I'm sitting on in the middle of this room, but I'm not. I might be shaking, my body still fluttering against the cold, but I'm actually reasonably relaxed given the content I'm looking at, inquisitive now that the immediate surprise has worn off. So this is him, is it? All of this in front of me is what he wants to do, what he wants to use. On me, at that.

My feet are up and starting me towards the collection of possibilities before I've thought much more of it, more interested than I perhaps should be. There's no denying it, though, is there? I'm addicted in some way. Either to him or the pain that we create together.

It makes my own brow furrow at the thought as I try to remember the last time I had a pill and watch my hand reach for a tasselled leather whip. I'm shaking still, not sure whether it's the images in front of me, the fact that I've nearly drowned, have actually drowned, or the lack of pills. Bree was right, I am shaking a lot lately. And it's only highlighted as my inked fingers try to grab hold of the thing in front of me and I watch the throngs wobble delicately in response. I snatch my hand off of it, disgusted at my inability to control my fingers and irritated at my dependency on drugs. Whatever this is, and whatever it might become, I do need off these pills if this is what I'm turning into because of them. Quickly too.

I scan over the entirety of the cupboard again, detailing the lines and implements hanging in it, storing the information with no clue how to organise it in my mindful anarchy. I feel pathetic, unorganised. It's pitiable to be so needful of something. To not be able to survive without amphetamines is truly mortifying in some ways. My shameful mind feels exhausted trying to manage the clutter coming at it again. I shouldn't even be here. I've got deadlines to keep up with, times, meetings. I should at least get my laptop and start writing some of this down, try to attempt my story again. Sleep? Not a fucking hope. My mind's buzzing too much, confused, that much is most definitely true, but now that this wall is looking at me, asking me things, taunting me with thoughts I don't know how to prepare for, I'm wide awake and ready for an argument. About what, I'm not entirely sure, but I'm not hovering around in this room waiting for him to make decisions about my life without any insight from me. Him having my phone is irritating enough. I mean, how am I going to arrange things, answer emails?

He's certainly not going to. He'll just leave it there in his car, unconcerned with the entirety of my life. Screw that. I'm important in my make-up. I'm what I am because of how I've become, who I am. He knows nothing about me, psychology degree or not. In fact, have I just been following his lead with no thought on how I should be behaving? Good lord. I'm so weak. Flawed is what I am. Faulty. Malfunctioning. Where have I gone? Where's my sense of rationale or validation? It's like I'm lost in a sea of Blaine, diving under its water in pure hope that he'll lift me out of it in time when he can be bothered to try. *If* he can be bothered to try. Enough, frankly. If he's not going to enjoy a sense of love, let it become part of whatever this is, thus improving the odds of me letting strange behaviour slide, then he can damn well explain himself. Or, at the very least, explain the process of his rehabilitation ideas, if that's what one can call this method of withdrawal. Fuck.

I'm yanking on the door and storming down the corridor instantly, no idea where I'm heading to and not really giving a damn either. I need answers, ones that he's going to give me. Either that or he can take me home. I'm tired, tired of all this secrecy and oddity. Just the truth. He's said I had to give it, well so does he, and here's where it might as well begin. Right now.

"Blaine?" I call out, my feet still freezing against the marble floor. "Blaine?" There's nothing in reply as I keep going, glancing into rooms searching for him. It's all as sparse as the other room. No homeliness, no relaxation, just stretches of cold marble and grey walls. It's contrasted to the man inside him, I know it is. No one kisses, fucks, or holds someone like that unless there's more than just teaching.

THE END

"Where are you?" Still nothing as I arrive in a large room and stare at what should be the end of the house. There's nothing there but an entire open wall, the wind whipping in through it as the faint light of the sun begins to descend on the horizon. I creep forward again, scanning the room's interior for him and finding nothing but a large bed, its grey covers neat and tidy, and more cupboards and wardrobes. "Blaine?"

Why is he never here? I feel like I'm constantly calling for him only to get nothing in reply. I fucking want some answers. I'm asking for them. In fact, I'm just asking. He said that all I had to do was ask, so I am. And I don't want the answers that show the sadistic arse side of him that he delivers so efficiently. I want the other side, the one I know is in there regardless of his need to hide wherever he is. "Blaine? Will you fucking answer me?" Christ I'm riled. Truly. It's like the only way I'm going to dampen it is to have a bloody good row, one that shouts and screams and swears into the night, hoping for resolution and not caring if it doesn't get it.

My feet pad me over to the open end of the room as I squint my eyes to look out into the dusk. He's here somewhere. I know he is because I can feel him. I don't even know how I know that, but I do. It's intrinsically laced inside me somewhere, just like he is. I can still feel his come burrowing through me even though the sea should have washed it away, and I can still feel his lips on mine regardless of the frigid chill that lingers in them. *He's* inside me. Deep inside.

There's nothing on the terrace as I walk out. Nothing in the immediate gardened area either, just a table and chairs and a large glass terrace bracing around the edge. I walk closer to it and gaze toward the ocean again, searching for him in the cliffs. Maybe he's out there walking off the need to do something deplorable, or perhaps he's sulking somewhere, brooding over his sadism and chastising me for foolishly going for a swim. Fuck him. Telling me off for trying to show him love? He can go suck a fish. He brought me here, offered me a slice of his home rather than take me to some dive of a back alley strung out with degenerates and reprobates. Anywhere we could have gone, anywhere, but oh no, he brought me here, to his home. Could he be more fucking confusing? "Where the hell are you?"

That's me getting into a little temper tantrum, I think. I can feel it building, as if it hasn't been released enough. In fact, I can't remember the last time I let loose at anything. It's all business talk and professionalism. Either that or containment. The thought makes me shake my head, trying to control the tirade that wants to come out at anything. I never used to be like this. I was reactive. I reacted on the spot, levelling my reaction from my guts rather than finding the acceptable response to things to make people feel comfortable. I'm not even sure if it's Blaine I want to yell at anymore or if it's just the world in general, that sea definitely.

My breathing's hitched and uncomfortable, making my stomach ache and convulse. I feel sick, waves of angst rising through me and desperate for release or dulling. I'm confused as I stare out, my eyes still narrowed as I watch the sea crashing eternally onto the shore, my fingers grasping onto the rail that borders the terrace. And I still can't stop the fucking shaking that racks my hands. It's continuous. Enough so that I look down at the brushed stainless steel rail in my fingers and feel like screaming at it too. How did I get to this? Where did I go wrong? It's all so disjointed and inharmonious. Nothing feels combined or even in sync with itself. One side of me wants to scream, the other wants nothing more than to crawl into a ball and cry for days. And the only thing I know with any sense of clarity, the only thing that seems barely plausible, is that when I'm in his arms, no matter what he's doing or how he's doing it, it's quiet, regardless of the pain.

"Tell me you love me," comes from my lips. It's mumbled into the wind, not loud enough for anyone to hear it and hardly loud enough for me to believe I need it, but I know I do. I need it to make the ache go away. And I need it to give this more purpose than just drug rehabilitation and his idea of fun, no matter how much I do need that, too. But most of all, and because of the way he looks at me, I need it so that I can relate all this onto paper and show the world that these people are beautiful in their own way. That he is.

"Not sleepy?" his voice suddenly says behind me somewhere. It jolts me around to look at him, my hands instantly grasping the stainless rail again. "Pissed?"

"Yes." No. I'm not fucking sure anymore.

"Why?" Because you're an arsehole.

"Because .."

"You can't get what you want?" I don't know what I want, and the fact that he's naked isn't helping my cause to remain attentive to mental conversations about love. "Life isn't about perfection, Alana. It's about creating an equilibrium." What the fuck does that mean? I'm too snarky for intelligent conversation. And where's furious Blaine gone? I need him at the moment, not intelligent condescending arse. "Something you've bypassed as unusable." What? My mouth opens to disagree, but I don't quite know what I'm disagreeing with. "Too many stories about a perfect coupling, perhaps forgetting that happy ever afters are just for the stories' sake?" I frown at him, irritated with his analogy. Happy Ever afters do exist. They do. People get married every day, living with each other until the day they die, loving in their own ways and settling down. "I don't want that from you. And I can't give it to you either. Stop asking me too." I'm not asking for a fucking thing.

The initial thought makes me glare at him, but it's quickly replaced by some kind of pout as he raises a brow in my direction. It pisses me off, reminding me that I am still a fucking wreck of a junkie, one who's searching for him to make me better. He sighs and walks over until he's resting on the rail near me.

"But ..." Nothing. But nothing. But if he'd just acknowledge this as more than he'd like to admit, maybe give it a chance to develop into something more, then we could be ...

"No, Alana. Take the clothes off."

"What?"

"You've come here for an argument, haven't you?"

"I .." How does he know that?

"Honesty. If you want an argument with me then you'll do it naked so you can bare your soul at the same time." I don't even know what that means. Argue naked? Unlikely. I huff out a breath, annoyed at his superiority in the midst of my dishevelment, and flummoxed as to what I'm trying to damn well say anyway. It's all the noise, it must be, or my lack of pills clouding my judgement.

I snatch away from the rail, choosing to bypass him and head back into the house. Arguing naked. That's as laughable as telling me to sleep. What idiot would even do that? I'm at my most vulnerable naked, it's certainly not a time when I'm happy to let rip, my body wobbling about as I do. Fucking stupid. This is all stupid. He's right. "Get your fucking ass back here and strip. I'm in no mood for tantrums."

His tone halts me, and I suck in all the swear words that want to launch back at him. Who the fuck does he think he is? I can't do this shit. It's … "Shall I start it?" I swing round, eyes narrowed and a snarl forming, my body humming with its own need to explode again. "Or shall I finish it before it starts? Your choice."

"Fuck you. You're right. You are a fucking arsehole." It's out before I've got full control of my faculties, or perhaps I just don't give a shit anymore as I grab at his hoodie and begin yanking it over my head. "You're a fucking arsehole and a liar." He stares at me as I throw the thing to the floor, calm as fucking day with a slight twitch of his lip. Naked? Screw him. What? He doesn't think I've got the balls? "I mean, what is wrong with you?" I glare back, already pushing at the tracksuit bottoms to get them the hell off my legs. "Do you think I'm too weak to argue back? I can assure you I'm not. I'm not scared of you, Blaine. I never have been." Fuck him. Fuck all of this. "I'm not the liar here. You are. You want me all on display," I shrug the bottoms off, kicking them sideways and continuing to glare with as much malice as I can muster. "Will that help your honesty?" How dare he be so controlled when I'm so livid? "There. Fuck you, again." I'm seething inside. Shaking angry. Not at him, or at me, or at anything in particular. Just seething, like the whole world can go screw itself. It's shock, or fury, or confusion. "Why the hell are you making this all so hard? Why?" He just stands there. No fucking answers. No questions. No retaliation or forward steps, not even any backwards ones. He's like a block of stone. "What's that? Are you trying for impassive?" Still nothing. "Please tell me I'm not just going to get a beating because you haven't got the words to combat a real argument. It's time to man up, Blaine. Prove why the hell I should trust you with anything?" I don't know where that's come from as I step towards him, nor do I give a damn. It's about time I said it like I feel, about time I stopped being the one who's lost all the time. I want proof. I want to know that this has a purpose, an end if it has to have one. "When does it end, Blaine? When is the grand finale to this story?"

"When I've finished with you." The fucking words leave him so calmly it riles me further, whipping me up into a rage I've never felt before. And then he steps into me, closing the distance, his whole body a wall of muscle and sinew. His eyes darker than I've seen them before, regardless of his demeanour. "When you're finished, Alana." What the hell does that mean? When I'm finished? Like dead? I glare some more, unsure what words I can use to inflict enough damage to force him to answer questions. Or even what damn questions I want answering anymore.

"Fuck you." It seems that's all I've got, that and my body moving into him, the damn thing still humming with the impending explosion that wants to hit out at him, something, anything. It's consuming me, making my whole frame vibrate along with my hands. I grab at them, twisting them about in my fingers to control whatever energy wants to leave them.

"No," he snaps, his body suddenly in front of me, his own hands slapping at mine to stop them twining with each other. "Let it out." What? I yelp as he pushes me, enough force in the shove that I trip backwards across the empty floor, barely keeping myself upright. "Or kneel on the damn floor. Make a fucking decision before I do it for you." And now it's me standing and staring, unable to process which is the better option as he lowers his head slightly, reminding me of him crouched over that woman. "You count it down. Ten to one." Count? To what? What's he going to do at one? I snatch a glance at the open doorway, not knowing what I'm hoping for and not really understanding why I'm looking. "You do remember how to count, don't you, Alana? Ten."

"Oh, I'm not damn well doing this. This isn't a school ground."

"Nine. Floor or argue."

"I just want some honesty, Blaine."

"Eight. I'm not saying them aloud anymore."

My feet back me away a step, my head looking around for the doorway, and then casting back at the floor in front of his feet. *"It's easier than you think."* That's what he'd said, and it was in that ratty hotel. It really was. The smell, the air around us. The mood. But I wasn't this angry then. I was desolate, upset, alone. And all because of him. Now I feel energised and enthused, confident again. Arrogant even. Oh shit, what number are we on? I look up at him again, sharply, wondering what's coming at number one and trying to understand why my knees are giving way regardless of my anger. He looks so damn beautiful. Why? He's everything I'm confused about. But the way his peaceful mouth lies in its flat line, the way his shoulders seem to flow into every other muscle, charging them, highlighting the calm before the storm, it's a display worthy of art. I could write the lyrics to a song by just looking at him, angry as I might be. He's so in tune with who he is. So fucking superior about how everything should be, rightly so, it seems.

My knees have lowered me to the floor before I've realised it's happened, my head dropped into the position he put me in last time. Not that he physically did. I did it myself, but I did it because I heard his sigh when I achieved the correct posture for submission. It had felt so strange, so at odds. Yet within minutes it had become like an old shadow had returned, blanketing me with a shroud of comfort. My arms had lain just as they do now, my thighs widening slightly - just as they do now - and my hands had lain against those thighs, uncomfortably at first and continually shaking, until they finally stopped and I heard that sigh from his lips. It was as astounding to me then as it is to me now. It's reassuring. Calming. Soothing. Enough so that my own sigh let's all the tension go, throws it away, not caring for any questions I had anymore.

"How do you feel?" he asks, his frame lowering in front of me until he's mirroring me again, just as we did before.

"Calmer." It's the best response I've got to give at the moment. I'm not at ease, nor completely comfortable, but it's more relaxing than the screaming venom that wanted to leave my mouth minutes ago.

"Good."

THE END

And then he stands up and walks away, leaving me staring at the floor. I eventually close my eyes and listen to the rhythm of my breathing rather than deal with the commotion still raging inside. I did that this morning, too, as I looked at the floor. I let his gaze of me guide me into it. Lull me. It dried the tears up completely, made them go away. It made all the noise disperse. Long slow breaths, just me and my own noise. No one else's to deal with. No other sound interfering, no notifications or chaos, only the occasional crash of a wave, which seems to ease the rhythm rather than interrupt it. I feel the tension start to evaporate. It leaves my skin bit by bit, as if it's pouring from my muscles and seeping out through the surface of me, quieting the noise further with every exhaled next breath.

Music starts somewhere. It makes me twitch, the tone of it at odds with my current calm. It's gloomy. Melancholy, but alive somehow. I'm not sure what it is. Not quite classical. Not operatic. Just a piano, its notes dull and long, rhythmic. The flats in the song making it feel eerie, haunting. It's warm, though. Not cold or sharp. And I can hear the breathing of the pianist as he plays, the intakes make me react to them and alter my own breathing to join in with him.

"If you're a good girl, we'll do your dates tomorrow." I could almost laugh at the words, knowing that none of that means anything anyway. Instead, I smile slightly, allowing the calm in his tone to envelop me further as I feel his hand wrap into my hair. "You're sure you don't need to sleep?"

Maybe. Who knows? I'm both exhausted by my near death experience and my argument, and yet energised by the unruffled composure this positioning provides. It's juxtaposed. At odds. And I'm suddenly completely at ease with both.

I shake my head as he begins to wrap his hold tighter, not knowing what he's about to do but somehow understanding it'll be done for the right reason, whatever it is. I have to trust. I have to. He gave me the option to fight and I folded to my knees instead, not out of fear, but because my mind wanted to. He's saved me twice now. He'll do it again if I need it.

The yank on my scalp doesn't come as that much of a surprise, nor does my body being slowly dragged across the polished floor. It doesn't bother me, or make me feel scared. It doesn't even hurt, the pressure on my hair having been applied to its entirety to cause the least pain. I just lie here, letting the sound of his bare feet lull me further into my silence as I watch the ceiling above me go by. I feel small, insignificant. No, weightless. I feel like there's nothing but air inside me, keeping me light as a feather, as if I'm actually gliding across this surface to wherever I'm going.

I end up back in the room I was in earlier, my frame still prone on the floor which makes me stare at the ceiling again as the lights dim.

"I'm going to see how much you can take," he says, his beautiful face arriving in my eye line. Is he? Okay. I'm so peaceful I couldn't care less what we're going to do. I knew the last time he manhandled me I'd be alright. I got lost in whatever he did to me, presumably enjoying myself even though I can't remember much of it. I will this time, too. "This is the best time for your pain threshold to be tested." Is it. Fine. Everything's just fine. "Do you understand what I'm saying?"

THE END

I nod. Yes.

Chapter 5

ALANA

The lights lower further as the minutes go by, until only a dim glimmer of daylight streaks across the ceiling. It's as gloomy as the music I'm listening to, and as peaceful as the sound of his feet padding the floor quietly around me. I focus on both, letting the sounds merge into one as I realise he's moving to the beat of the sound, making it more rhythmic rather than more chaotic. It's mesmerising in some ways, as lulling as his eyes when he gazes at me. I'm not scared or anxious, neither am I inclined to move in any way. I'm just here, relaxed. Calm after my outburst.

A quiet cranking sound starts behind me. It's mechanical, scratchy to my peaceful state. It interrupts the gentle ebb of melancholy, making my anxiety rise again. My fingers grab at nothing, hoping to feel the ground beneath me, find some solidity to hold onto like it did with the bedframe last time. There's nothing there, though, only the polished floor I was dragged across. And then my body's lifted as if it's as weightless as I felt ten minutes ago, his arms moving me somewhere.

"What are you going to do to me?" I ask, suddenly a little unsure of what's coming.

"Hurt you." My mouth opens as I look at him and he lays me down on a padded bench. "Test you." Anxiety races through me as his words finally begin to seep into my mind and reality comes back in earnest, but I can't find the word 'no' anywhere. It doesn't want to come out. It's somehow retreating regardless of my attempt to get it through my lips. "You're going to let me play with you without the ability to ask me to stop." I frown at him, wondering what he means as he holds up a strap. "There are no safewords with me, Alana. You have to trust me to know when you're done. I don't want to hear your voice." He raises the strap higher, showing me the entirety of it. It's a muzzle of some kind, a large ball behind a leather mouthpiece. I frown at that too, suddenly understanding what he means. I won't be able to say no at all. He lays it on my stomach, letting me stare at it as he begins walking around me, softly putting my wrists into cuffs I hadn't noticed before. "I want you to ask me to put it in your mouth. Gag you." I'm not sure what that means.

"Why?" it slips out, almost mused rather than asked. I don't know why it does, but I couldn't stop it. Maybe I don't trust him as much as I think, or maybe I just need to know what it does for him to not hear me. I tilt my head at the black leather, wondering what's wrong with my voice.

"That's why. That question. I don't want you questioning me anymore." He says that as he clicks the final cuff around my ankle and stands at my feet, his frame filling my eyes and his torso seeming bigger than life itself. I gaze at it, somehow making my breathing join with his as his chest inhales and exhales, then crawl my eyes up towards his face, longing to search his eyes for truths. "You're going to give yourself over with no capacity to stop me." I suck in a breath as I watch his eyes narrow and his hands land on my ankles, slowing pushing them apart, the bench appearing to separate between them. "In fact, I want you to beg me to put it in that filthy fucking mouth of yours." Oh.

My own eyes narrow, not that I'm able to fight whatever he's tied me into, but the thought of not being able to speak, to say stop if I need to, to scream for help? "Stop searching for help, Alana. There's none here apart from me. We're alone." *Apart from him. Help.* I squirm, my body trying to get comfortable with the thought, or maybe it's my mind. I don't know. "Start begging."

I squirm again, barely able to comprehend the thought of not being able to question him, let alone scream for help should I need to.

"But …"

"No. I want no but's, no why's, no anything other than - 'Please put that gag in my filthy mouth, Sir'."

The sound of Sir coming from his mouth makes me glare back at him, annoyed that he'd make me use a term I only ever use out of disdain. "I'm waiting, Alana. Make it good."

My fucking fidgeting continues, my peaceful security obliterated under this scrutiny as he looks down at me, his hands applying barely any pressure to my skin. And his stare penetrates all my fears, making me more fretful rather than the relaxation he offered before. I force myself still, unhappy with my sense of nerves and trying to remember the silence I had minutes ago, but it's like the calmer he seems to become, not one ounce of happiness on his face anywhere, the jumpier I'm getting.

"I want …" What do I want? I want to scream if I need to. I want to shout at him, speak. I want to let my fears out, not hold them in. He raises a brow at me slightly, his body relaxed and completely in tune with what's around him, me included, it appears.

"What do you want?" I want my peaceful back. I close my eyes to him, asking myself that very question, because that's why I'm here now, isn't it? I put myself in his hands, submitted. Told him this is what I wanted. And I so want that quiet back that I had when he dragged me in here, his fingers guiding me along the floor without any permission from me. I want fields filled with endless thoughts, ones that I make, not ones that other people force me into. "Just ask me for it, Alana. Beg."

"I want … I want you to put it in my mouth." They come out as shakily as my breathing feels, perhaps driven forward by the tremble in my fingers as I keep gasping at nothing and squeeze my eyes tighter shut.

"Tut, tut." I snarl at myself, shaking my head and trying to pull up the courage to mean the words he wants to hear, rather than a simple citation of them. I can't fool him anyway. There's no lying for me here. He wants the guts of me, the very heart of my fears, so he can pull them apart. He said that about me when he said he'd help. "Try again."

"I want you to put it in my filthy mouth, please, Sir."

"And again, Alana. Look at me as you ask." I open my eyes as he finishes the sentence, allowing myself the freedom to just look and stop questioning him. He's right, but I feel so afraid of letting him have all of me, of tearing up my insides with no promise that he'll be there for me at the end. There's nothing here, is there? "Ask."

"Please, Sir. Put the gag in my filthy mouth. Silence me."

There's a smile that comes after that. It's one I've never seen before, perhaps more chilling than I've ever seen, but yet still laced with the same sense of hope he gave when he first kissed me. It's like a sunrise, or sunset, making everything else in the room dissipate. There aren't any words in reply, just his body moving to the side of me, his hand dragging up my thigh as he goes until he lifts the gag from my skin and offers it towards my mouth. He doesn't ask me to open my mouth, he expects me to do it of my own accord, and I do. My lips widen as I ponder his tranquillity, wondering what will come next and maintaining my stillness. Still - that's what I want here, as he moves the leather into my lips. That's what I'm going to get with him if I trust him. I know that much. I know he'll find it in me one way or another. Perhaps he's not offering the love I know is here, but he will help, whether through self-satisfaction or support. I don't know, and am beginning to care less and less about it.

The strap tightens as he lifts my head to accommodate it. It ratchets snugly, and then squashes my cheeks inwards further as I try to stretch my mouth around the ball. It's hard plastic, giving me room to move slightly, but no ability to speak or squash into it. He moves away again, the clattering of metal immediately sounding as he reaches into a drawer and then turns to face me.

"The beauty of pain comes from you allowing it inside without fighting it," he says, his hand slowly pushing one of my legs wider, then twisting something until my knee lifts a little. "If you fight it, it becomes debilitating to your senses, overwhelming you passed your mind's capabilities." I flex my hands in the cuffs, trying to get a glimpse of what he's holding. "Pain is something your mind needs to enjoy before you can truly appreciate the hedonism of it." Is it? I narrow my stare of his waist, part enjoying the muscle tone but still more interested in the metal I heard. "Do you think you can compartmentalize the pain I'm going to deliver, like you have everything else in your life?" I frown, wondering how he knows that. "You can't contain and be free, Alana. You have to let go. When you're with me, you have to let go."

   I stare for a few minutes more, watching the way he moves around me, his fingers applying pressure here and there, tugging me occasionally into a new position. It's calming somehow, lulling me back to how I was before this started, even if my mouth struggles with this ball in it. "You've used the amphetamines to speed you up, keep you organised, I assume. I'm going to slow you down again. You're going to learn to value your time, enjoy it." The more his mouth speaks, the more the tone ebbs into me. It's like velvet again, smooth and meandered as he muses his thoughts, his hand never leaving my skin. "Do you like that thought?" I don't know. I don't know what I like other than the sound of his voice like this. It's stunning as it deepens and growls the endnotes, pacifying whatever argument or fear I had, making me feel secure again as I lay here. "Does your cunt need me to hurt it, Alana? Ask me to hurt you?" How, I can't speak? I stare at him as his eyes turn and slowly bore back into mine, my mouth moving around the ball, my body fidgeting again because I can't get the words out. He smiles and lifts his hand above my stomach, about 5inches, and just hovers it there. "Reach for me," he says, his smile broadening as I frown again. "Squirm. Show me your need for my hands." I lift slightly, my body rising into him, my muscles straining to get higher regardless of the strange embarrassment at his words. "Weak little brat. That effort deserves a caging." My frown turns to a glare, desperation making me try harder to get to his hands as I shunt about. He suddenly slaps down on my stomach, sending a sharp sting straight through me. It makes my eyes water, my back scrabbling around to get away from the sensation. "Try harder," he snarls, his hand back to hovering again, taunting me. But no matter how hard I reach, how hard I push my body towards him, my hips thrusting upwards, I can't reach, he won't let me. I fight, every inch of me forging upwards, desperate to get to his hand so he can calm me again, but nothing makes me get there.

My body eventually slumps in defeat, hardly able to move for the exertion I've put it through. "See, your mind gives up first. It makes you unable to continue because it's focused on not relishing the feeling." I don't know what that means, and the panting I'm doing through this fucking ball irritates me, enough so that I close my eyes in frustration. It's only when he moves and I hear the metal again, that I open them and find him between my legs. "Pain is a good thing for brats like you, Alana. You need its focus to realign yourself." Oh, for god's sake, what the hell does that mean? I shake my head as I watch him lift his hand again, hovering it once more. "Let me help you reach what you need."

Pain instantly assaults me between my thighs, a tearing kind, making me lever so far off the bench I think I'm going to fall. Whatever it is pinches in to the side of my vulva, inflaming it with an agony that makes me scream into the ball. "See?" I can hardly draw in air let alone see. My eyes are wildly searching for any escape from the pain, my back's arched and twisting to get away, swift intakes of breath trying to stem the pain assaulting me. And then another sharp stab of pain joins in on the other side, wrenching me further away from the padding, my feet and shoulders keeping me aloft, pushing me upwards. A muffled scream sounds from my own lips again, saliva pooling and making me swallow rapidly as I snort air through my nose. "You're so beautiful when you try. Look, focus." I suck in more air, using the pain to forge more strength to my muscles, and squint towards him through watering eyes. He's blurred, the outline of him merged like a shadow, but I see the hand resting on my stomach as I squirm. It makes me halt my tempestuous struggle, somehow finding a stability in his hold rather than concentrating on the pain. "You reached me, Alana. Proved yourself." I whimper into the ball, both pleased with myself and embarrassed at what's happening to me. I'm like a fucking child, somehow begging for a damn compliment. "Keep showing me." I frown again, not knowing what he's after, then see him lick his lips a little as he rubs his hand lower towards my crotch. It makes me widen my legs without thought, the pain down there near forgotten as I focus in on his eyes and let them guide me. "Good little brat," he muses, rubbing my stomach again and then lowering. The sensation makes me crazy as he carries on, my back still holding me aloft, my arse slowly sinking back down to the bench so I can widen even further. It makes me ache, the intensity of the pain turning dull as something tugs and pulls at me. I need something inside me. Something hard, something driven in to make the throbbing subside. I need him and whatever he chooses. Hard and heavy. His hand, his cock. Anything to make the void that's arrived feel filled.

I try to speak again, beg even, forgetting the gag, and mumble instead, hoping he hears me. There's another sharp sting, his hand joining the other one between my legs. This time it isn't as intense, or maybe it is and I'm too lost in this shadow to give a fuck. It just throbs, all of it. It makes my insides pulse, grabbing for him to be inside me. And then he loops a chain around his waist, one side of it tugging me widen open, until I see the end of it. It's a clamp, crocodile clip, something, and I realise that's what the sensation is below. He's put clamps on me, ones that pull me open more as he sharply tugs the chain again and snaps it in his hand. "Dirty little brat, hmm?" The sight makes me squirm again and widen my eyes, unable to process what the fuck's going on, but relishing the feel of the dull throb nonetheless. "You want me inside your cunt, little brat?" I whimper again, desperate for exactly that as I feel the last of the clamps bite in, tears welling as I move into the pain rather than away from it. He chuckles, his hand skating across my clit, and all four of the clamps suddenly engaging. I try to focus again, blinking the water out of my eyes away, and find him leaning backwards and forwards, his eyes trained between my legs, watching me open and close. "This is true beauty, Alana. Fucking and grinding, giving in to what's inside of you."

He lowers, his body disappearing as I prop myself up a little to gaze at him, the chain slipping up his back to around his neck. It slides around his neck as he moves, linking me with him as he inspects and probes at me, his fingers beginning to forage their way inside. The moment one does I sigh, the miniscule contact already bringing with it a sense of relief as my head lolls back, and then another joins in, prodding and pushing, opening me further than I already am. I rattle my cuffs, impatient for the ache to be taken away, only to hear him chuckle again as I shove my hips towards his face. And then one long slow lick of his tongue lands just above my clit, his hair rising up my stomach towards me. It yanks on the chain as it goes, his shoulders moving to let the metal fall around him. Teeth begin nibbling as his hands work their way inside. A third finger, a fourth maybe, and then a shove, his knuckles grating on my bones, searching for a way in. "Open that cunt up, Alana." Oh god, I can't breathe, or think, and no matter how wide I stretch my legs I can't open anymore. But I want him deeper. I *need* him deeper.

He keeps pushing, his lips and teeth roaming my body, his other hand slowly making its way across my skin up towards my face. And when it gets there it yanks on my hair, ripping it sideways, making me snivel and scream into the gag again. "Tell me you like the pain." Do I? I don't know. I just know I need him to fill me up, to give me something to make the ache go away as he keeps forging his hand in deeper. It crawls in slowly, the slippery sides of me slowly giving way to his continued demand, and my body moving to accommodate it. "Your body is begging for it." He's right. It is doing. I am doing. I'm shaking my head still, frantically, my toes curling with need for something I can't get. And I'd scream for him if I could. I'd shout pleases into the air, hoping to give him quicker access, crack myself open wider somehow. He's so far into my screwed up mind, teasing it with nothingness and silence, taunting me to break through this last barrier. He's just not far enough inside my body yet. I know that, I can feel him missing from me. I'm still empty, regardless of his continued forage, void of substance. We're not together.

The pressure suddenly stops as quickly as it began, his hand withdrawing slowly, his mouth backing away from my chest as he runs his fingers the length of me again. It makes me catch my breath and close my eyes, taking them away from him, perhaps feeling wretched to have disappointed him so much. That other girl managed it, why couldn't I? It's as troublesome a thought as the very act I'm participating in. Disappointed? I'm strapped down, gagged, bare of clothing, clamps of some sort pulling my genitals apart, and I'm bothered about disappointing him? I feel the tears prick my eyes again, their flow nothing to do with the pain anymore, more the sense of loss I feel because I couldn't do what he wanted, or confusion over why the hell I'm doing any of it.

I end up turning my head to the side, embarrassment or humiliation taking over rational thought given the context of what's happening. I can't think straight again, but I'm mortified nonetheless, ashamed even. They're both emotions I've not felt for so long. They're awkward to me, making me cower to the side, trying to hide my face in the padding of the bench somehow.

"Look at me, Alana," he says, a quiet lilt to his voice as I feel a sharp tug on the clamps again. I shake my head, dulled to the pain and still embarrassed. I don't even know how to find my power again. It's gone, as if I've lost all strength because of this thing he's made me do. I feel small and pathetic, inadequate. Not worthy of whatever his hands can do perhaps. It's black here. Black and cold. It makes me internalise everything, the gag in my mouth preventing any eruption I'd normally deliver, questions too. Not that I can see any answers, and not that he'll answer them. "Alana, look." Still I don't turn, the thought of his displeasure too overwhelming to contend with in my current state. *His displeasure.* All I can hear is the word Sir being banded around in my head, as if my feelings mean nothing other than cause and effect. Sir's displeased. Sir's mad. I couldn't finish what he started. It just causes yet more internalisation, until all I've got is a black hole in my mind, one as empty as the cunt he couldn't fill.

 A hand slaps my cheek quickly, barely giving me a chance to linger in my own thoughts about what's happening to me. It lands hard, shocking me and fostering more tears to come, but they're from the sting again, from the pain. "Don't you lose yourself yet." I don't know what that means. Lose myself? I'm not lost. I'm alone and tired. So fucking tired of trying to achieve everything for everyone. "I'm not finished with you yet." There's another slap, followed by my body being yanked towards him, my arms stretched back in the cuffs as he pinches his fingers in. I just lie here and let myself be dragged, still with my eyes closed and my head turned away. I can't face him, don't want to. I've let him down, let myself down.

 His fingers dig in again, the crunch of my thigh muscle turning over in his hands as he pushes and pulls. It's mesmerising in some ways, slowly drawing me from my thoughts back to the present as I churn my teeth on the ball. There's an authenticity in his hands, a focus to bring me back from wherever I'm heading. They're warm, tactile maybe, even in their excessive grasp. They're real.

 "Blaine." His name mumbles out of me, the gag preventing any volume as saliva builds around it. It makes me choke and cough as the spittle slides down my throat, causing an anxiety to build again. "That's it, come back, little dove," he says, a hand sliding behind my cheek to lift my face back to him. Little dove? I like that. It's dreamy, sweet. It reminds me of Noah's ark, being rescued.

My eyes slowly open as I feel his fingers pinch in around my cheeks and hold me so that I'm facing him again. Dark, brooding eyes stare back, not an ounce of disappointment etched into them, only a glimmer of the love he denies. He's so still, like any minute he might erupt or explode. A calm before the storm, ready to decimate what's in his hands if I'll let him. And I will, I'm here, laid bare and open for use, ready for him to push himself inside and find all my hidden secrets if he wants them. He's right, I do want all this. I want to ebb down inside myself and find who I used to be, perhaps swim his current for a while, get lost in it.

I mumble into the ball again, trying to get his name past it. Not Sir, Blaine. He smirks. Just slightly. It's barely there really, but I can see it hiding behind the scowl. And I can feel it in the way he watches me trying to shake my head at this restriction in my mouth, his grip holding me still. He's enjoying my degradation, playing with it, arousing himself with every whimper that comes from me. So I give him another one, my legs opening further as I push myself as far down the bench as my wrists will allow, hoping he'll put himself inside me again to fill the void. I don't want alone and cold. I want to join. Be joined.

"Mmm, better."

It's the only words he gives me as he slowly releases my head and drags his hand down my body. He just gazes then, the occasional pinch to my nipples, another tug here and there on the clamps, causing yet more whimpers and howls to try breaking through the gag. And then his finger rubs my clit, sending shockwaves racing across me, my back arching immediately and causing the ache to become near unbearable. He just keeps teasing it, neither giving enough pressure to cause explosions nor allowing me to retreat from it. It just keeps coming, flick after flick, followed by another tug on a clamp. I writhe, trying to induce my orgasm, or maybe trying to back away as he keeps smirking and taunting. I can't keep up. It's painful. Raw. The sensations bite and twist, rubbing me the wrong way and making the hole inside near weep for attention as I scrunch my eyes away from him again. The slap happens instantly, and it's so hard tears spring into my eyes.

"Try fucking harder," he growls, his chest moving down towards mine, his tongue licking my stomach as he gets there. "Earn my cock, little dove." Oh god, it's all I want. I want it shoved into me, forced. No niceties, no preparation. My insides burn to have him there, to feel the skin rubbing against me, to feel his heat there. I'm desperate, desperate enough that I scream into the gag, begging for him to fuck me. I want that pressure he won't let me have. I want it consuming me and driving us together again. "Say it again, ask for me."

I shout louder, my voice trying to elevate itself over the blockage. Spittle pools again as I suck in breath, ready to stammer back into it, my hands battering about in the cuffs. Please springs out, followed by more begging and pleading. I'm actually grovelling for the fucking he's withholding. Desperate for it. Over and over I beg as he keeps taunting and goading, his hand gently dabbing when it should be ramming in. I don't even know where I am anymore as madness takes over. I'm just so fucking desperate, and I can feel him in there even though he's not there yet. Please, I just keep chanting it, mumbling it, desperate for the sensation to go away or get stronger, harder. He's all I need. Him and this fucking hole he seems to own.

The gag suddenly falls from my mouth, saliva falling away with it as it goes. And the first words that spring out are the ones I've been reciting.

"Please, fuck me. Please Blaine…. Please." He licks again, something hard finally rubbing at the aching hole that screams for him.

"Keep begging."

"Please," what more does he want. "Please, Blaine, please." I can't even find any other words and he swipes that cock across me again and starts to nudge at me. Please, that's all I have. Please and the need to feel full. It makes tears weep out again. Makes them erupt as my legs shake and quiver, my wrists grinding into the metal to give me more pain.

"More."

Then the shunt comes, hard and fast, forged in to maximum depth. It widens every nerve I've got, sending a ricochet of nerve endings spiralling out of control around my skin. It electrifies everything, rendering my mouth open and no more words left to say as I sense him settling in. I'm just immobile, lingering, my back still arched and my spine feeling like it's on fire. I can't breathe, can't move, and I so wish I could grab onto him, my own nails grasping for air, hoping to embed into his skin.

"Please," it comes from me again, no longer knowing what it's begging for. Pace, speed, harder. I don't know. I just look down at him as his mouth climbs up my body, his lips sucking on my nipples as he passes them. They keep coming, elevating whatever desire it is that I'm travelling through, sucking and licking, biting down, making me gasp and groan as his hips move a little at last. The relief is almost immediate, another shock of pleasure following the one I'm trying to claw onto. "Fuck me, Blaine, Please. I need you. I need the .."

The rear back and slam in makes me scream, my head tossed back again before I've got a chance to suck in air. Pain hits the end of me, merging with all the other sensations coming at me, creating something new, something barely sane. It's a mess of reactions, all converging and causing exhilaration, something to be chased, reached for. My hands screw tighter onto nothing, making me squirm and writhe again, until I feel something touch them and widen their grasp. It makes my eyes fly open and find his mouth hovering over mine, his fingers linking into mine as he climbs onto the bench and moves my weight with his knees.

"You're a rare thing, little dove," he whispers, his breathing ragged as he hovers there, watching my mouth pant. "A gift."

A gift? Oh god I can't breathe. His mouth is just there, taunting me and showing me a sense of passion only he has to give. He moves, settling over me, his hands tightening in mine, holding me still as his hips grind, the tug on the chain inducing more pain to counter the moment. And then he shifts backwards again, causing another pull on all the clamps and he surges his cock further in. "This is everything I need from you." He does it again, the same move, over and over, causing yet more whimpers and moans to come from me, his own stare trained on my eyes as he makes them happen. "Fucking with courage," he muses, his lips gently brushing against mine, somehow managing to maintain his composure in the middle of my disarray. I'm lost to the pain, riding it and finally finding a sense of ownership in its tormented pull on my skin. It makes me sigh into his mouth, ready to let him deliver anything he chooses to as long as his lips stay with me. A swipe of his tongue has me reaching for it, my mouth searching for it so I can suck it inside me, make it belong to me. And he gives it to me, his lips smirking as he pushes it towards me, and finally allows me my reward. I'm on it like a dog in heat, my hips rolling into his, the feel of his cock as incapacitating as his weight above me as he speeds slightly. And my orgasm climbs inside me immediately as he roughens his movements, giving me more friction to press against, the continued tug and yank of the clamps becoming more severe with every push and thrust. It's blindsiding, sending me delirious as I suck at his tongue, inching forward to make our lips meet again and trying to get us closer somehow. We couldn't be any closer, we're bound in a way I've never been bound before. Our skin slick with sweat, our breaths joined somehow as I hear his ebb and flow, ragged in their haul. I'm so full, so full of everything I've never felt before. It's hot, sticky. His fingers tightening on mine, the sweat between them making everything glide and groan together. I can't begin to stop the climb as it races through my body, his hips continuing to grate against mine in, his lips rolling more and more kisses to suck me into them.

"Blaine, please." They're my last words as I break away, trying to gasp in air. It's all I've got left to say. There's nothing else but him and these sensations driving me over the edge of sane and into a new place, one I'm never leaving. He's right, I'm like him. Just like him. I want more of all of this. I want him fucking me, holding me, giving me some purpose, exposing me. I can't hold it any more as I feel him swell, the increase in his drive a sure sign of him coming. It's all I can do to scream my orgasm into the air, letting it guide me through whatever the fuck he's made happen here. It's explosive, deliberately shattering every nerve ending I've got and making me jerk and spiral, gasping for breath and trying to find something I can hold onto. There's nothing but his hands, them and the mouth that finds mine again, snatching me back to him and proving his feelings whether he wants to admit them or not. I lose myself completely in them, allowing whatever he wants as I feel the pain turn to a pounding weight on me, his heartbeat escalating against my chest as his teeth rip at my lip. That's all there is left, just a heavy weight and a sense of friction, the shattering elation of my orgasm still riding my skin as he does the same, connecting the sensations into one. It's all one. One mind. One body. Me and him. Savage growls and grunts, spit flying. A sense of blinding clarity being washed through two bodies as metal clinks and clanks, merging us into one. Until all there is left is him inside me, him all over me. Him and the thought of love quaking my insides, defeating my last fight.

Chapter 6

BLAINE

"Alana, get up."

Still she hardly stirs. Part of me couldn't give a fuck. I'd watch her lie here all day if I could, probably ramming my hand inside her again while she slept for the fun of it, but I can't, not if she wants her damned dates anyway. I check my watch and snarl, wondering if the dates matter as much as I want them to, anyway. They don't in reality, not with regard to my feelings for her. I'd stay in these four walls forever if I could now, just pushing her body further with every new session and indulging in the luxury that brings me. But they matter to her. They're her reward for good behaviour, or for putting up with my heavy hands.

The thought makes me chuckle as I gaze out towards the sea and remember her walking the beach before she went for her eventful swim. I turn back to gaze at her body again, wondering whether she should go wade herself through it before we leave, salt the wounds, but the cream I've applied for the second time since last night should do until tomorrow. If it doesn't, so be it. I'll go and wade with her, wash the fucking stains away with my own hands, because no fucking way is she going down there by herself.

THE END

I snort at the memory of her wrapping her hand into my hair last night, as I sneer at her face. She's inside me now, weeding her way in deeper and forging every reaction I don't want to give. She's as good at it as my magician is. Virile in her ability to cajole and caress. It's annoying me. Pissing me off. Making me needy for her. I hope to fuck she's writing all this down on paper, immersing herself in it. It's clever. Intricate and sophisticated. She's so damn manipulative. She counters every move, somehow looping herself around me no matter how hard I push her. And now she takes it all too, enjoys it as I try something that usually scares even the bravest of subs.

Thumbing through her phone again, I send some holding emails in reply to whatever seems important to calm their scream for more from her. I've been doing it for days now, my replies getting shorter and less obliging each time. Editors, publishing contracts, more editors and then some tripe about marketing and finance. She's on fucking holiday. That's the response most of them have gotten for the last few days, as if written from herself, politely requesting more time. Anything relevant will be done via email, it always is. I sigh and drop through her messages again, finding nothing of relevance other than more seemingly tetchy demands from someone she's labelled as fuckwit the 3rd. The sight makes me chuckle as I toy with the idea of responding, then snarl at the tone of the texts. Fuckwit needs a beating of his own by the looks of these demands on her time and energy. I scroll back on the texts, more anger levying with each one I read. Every fucking day there's something new, hotly pursued by asking to take her out for dinner soon. It's all too fucking personal. Too close. And it makes me fucking jealous now I'm thinking about it. Furious.

Although, she's quite clearly avoiding actually making a date with the cunt. I'll see what he sends tomorrow before I reply, perhaps go see the fucker if he proves annoying enough to my plans.

I tuck the phone back in my pocket, more interested with the woman softly groaning in her sleep. I'm not sure if it's the strapping she took last night, or the thought of this crap in her phone. It makes me scowl at her idiocy. Allowing this to take over her life has been a waste of her energy, and fucking detestable to her talents. It's caused a never ending decrease on her ability to write well. I know now because I've had the words in my hands. Ordered and bought them so I can read the way she's failed herself, and help her find the route back to herself again. The first one and her most recent. The last of which is sappy, hopeless, romantic garbage. Repetitive and unexciting. Such a waste of spirit. She's right when she says there's too much noise. This endless stream of diatribe, relevant or not, would make most people lose their minds let alone their ability to write well. No wonder she's groaning next to me now. I would be too if I had to deal with this amount of garbage daily. I've barely looked at her social media. I couldn't give a fuck. And the amount of accounts she has for different platforms is stupefying. No wonder she's lost. I doubt she even remembers who she was before all this fucking constancy.

Time to wake up and remind her.

I wander into the bathroom and stop the flow of hot water, switching it to cold and going down the hall to the lounge to put some more coffee on. The old typewriter on the table greets me as I flick the switches, the ink inside reminding me what she originally came for. It seems so irrelevant now, regardless at my attempt to realign her mind.

THE END

Nothing here is happening for the purpose of a story anymore really, not on my part. Try as I might to continue this charade. I'm not even certain I want her to leave this house, let alone remind herself she has a life outside of me. I've never wanted someone so much in my life. Whether it's her or the surface she provides, I can't quite quantify, no matter how much I've scrutinised my own thoughts on the matter. Perhaps these dates will evolve my thoughts on that, giving me a sense of realism over my world of sin. Dates. Not that I'm sure what constitutes them. I'm delivering what should be seen as one, an element of romance to fulfil her need, before the filth she's going to deliver for me. Fucking romance.

The thought is as disconcerting as my thoughts about her. I can feel her burrowing her way in with every breath and moan she makes, asking me for more than I can give, and now she fucking kneels on the floor again out of choice rather than fight me. Why does she do that? I don't want that from her. I want that fire in her eyes, the spit and venom. I want the vitriol that flows so freely she shows me a glory in her temper tantrums, wounding me with them. It's as fascinating to me as the touch of her fingers the first time we met. But the kneeling, the way her body gives in, offering me everything to play with yet again, that makes me feel shame and remorse for the visions that keep coming. It makes me want to hold her, be close. It's invariably why I choose to take her and hurt her all the more, testing all her limits simply because she still, even in that position on the floor, challenges me. Bitch. The fact that that pain continually turns into something unexpected, drawing me deeper into her, isn't something I've come to terms with yet. Nor is the fact that I want to tell her I love her in the midst of our rampant fucking. It's yet another thing I can't quantify or measure. It is, still feels, enlightening. It's beyond my usual realms of fucking and torture. Quieting.

The sound of something makes me turn to the doorway. She's there, looking at me and hovering at the top of the steps leading down to me, her body draped in my fucking shirt.

"I should get some writing done," she says, her head nodding at the typewriter as she crosses her arms and leans on the frame.

"You should take a bath, you look a fucking state." Not that she does, it's just my insidious little way of making her feel alone. I don't know why I'm fucking doing it, I just am. I'm riled by her again, pissed. She grounds me, making me question things I don't want to question. She only has to stand there looking at me with that arched brow of hers and I can feel all that sense of responsibility again, haunting veins I don't care for. Looking at her is becoming like looking at my sea, all the time trying to work out whether I want it to drown me or float me in its maniacal crest.

"I thought you liked me all stained and messy?" she questions, her feet stepping her down my fucking steps as she walks into *my* space and starts undoing *my* shirt. "You're the one that put all this on me, aren't you?" If she says Daddy I'll beat her ass so hard she won't sit for a week. She's got that look about her. The holier than thou one that I hate to admit to adoring. "Don't you want to look at your handiwork, Blaine?" The buttons keep popping, the slight bruise beneath her breast starting to emerge as she begins stripping the material from her shoulders. "It doesn't hurt, if that's what's bothering you." It fucking should be. It irritates me. As does the sight of her hands as they calmly move lower, the shake in them barely present anymore. "It feels warming, like I can still feel you on me even when you're not there. I should write that, don't you think? It's good. A good representation of submission. The readers will understand that." Screw the readers. Screw anything but the madam that's still slowly covering the ground to get to me. I clench my fists, attempting to remember that this is her date time as I turn away and pick up my coffee. I offered that, said I would do it for her. Nothing is going to persuade me otherwise at the moment. She could sit her ass on that chair and spread her legs and I'd still make her get in the bath. "What's the matter?"

"You need to have a bath, we're going out."

"Hmm?" I turn back, watching the way she lifts the typewriter and smiles to herself about something as she fingers the keys. The sight makes me sigh as I watch them flitter across the pads, each day passing evaporating the toxins within her system. It makes me wonder how long I can keep her here in that guise, thinking she needs me for those reasons. "I don't need to go out." Fuck that. I do, as does she if she wants to continue walking. "Where can I set this up that's a little less in your way? I need to write."

"No you don't. You need to have a bath and put some clothes on," I reply, as I walk over and look at her, examining the marks on the base of her bottom lip without touching it, enjoying the way the bite mark still lingers there. "You can choose a room when we get back." Preferably one that's far outside of these walls so she can stop interfering with every fucking thought I have. "Or you could use the summer cottage out back." Why the hell did I say that? The mental image troubles me immediately as she looks at me, the thought of her being outside my private space more confusing than comforting. "I might clear it out if you beg well enough." Her brow rises again, a slight challenge associated with the smirk that appears.

"Beg?"

"You're good at it."

"Only when I need to be, Blaine. It gets me what I want."

That it does, and exactly what I want, too.

Her smile broadens, illuminating the fucking room as she picks up a lock of her hair and twiddles it around in her fingers. "I'm not doing it out of love, you know that, right?" I take the lock of hair off her, tugging her over to me with it and withholding the need to make her tell me she is. She doesn't squeal or groan, she's becoming accustomed to my handling, hardening up. Regardless though, she's doing all of this for love, and I'm allowing it because of love, irrational as it might be. I stare at her, a snarl forming as I consider this date I've arranged and begin letting my cock talk me out of it. "Where is it? This summer cottage?" she asks, her mouth continuing to smirk as I tug the hair again, wrapping it into my hold and chastising myself for every fucking thought I'm having. Fuck going out. We should stay here all day, all month. Just stay inside these rooms so I can play with her, relax with her. Walk around naked and enjoy the smell of her cunt overpowering my desolation. "Is that supposed to hurt?" The words filter into my mind, making me smile as I sense her comfort in the pain I'm causing. It's not much, she's right, only enough to remind her who's holding her, but not many others would find the tension acceptable, no normal human anyway.

"Go have a bath," I eventually reply, letting go of her and turning to walk out. "Wash the stains away for the day. We're doing something you asked for. Take it before I rethink the immaturity of it."

I don't stay around for an answer, rather walk in the opposite direction and out of the front door to get to my sea, perhaps searching for its calm to regale rational thought into this senselessness. Love. It's biting in more efficiently now. Her words, the sweet sound of her challenges, the way she moves, making me question everything I've ever understood. It's all absurd, twisting my insides around and making me think of things I don't deserve, irrespective of whether I'm taking them or not. It happened last night too, part of me wanting to rip the skin from her limbs and the other needing to stop myself from doing it and hold her instead.

"Blaine? Why don't you have one with me?" her voice says. I close my eyes and keep facing the sea rather than turn and acknowledge the prospect. If only she knew the confusion she causes as she crawls through my skin, her breath as close to a direction as I've ever found. There's nothing I want more than her fingers stroking me, perhaps her lips travelling over my throat as I bury what's left of my fight for decency and let her have all of me.

"I'm dressed, Alana, and waiting. Get a fucking move on." The words come out as I shove my hands in my pocket, hoping to alleviate their incessant grab towards her. It's as galling as the love I feel for her, as troublesome. It once again makes me question what happens to sadists in love. Where they go when the lines blur and emotion takes over. It's interfering in my process, guiding me along roads I haven't travelled before, weakening my methods of control. And that's something neither of us needs to happen.

~

"I still don't understand how she knew my size," she says, as she climbs out of the car and looks around her. I do, it's the same ability I have to gage weight and muscle resistance. Tabitha's in tune with her surroundings and what she is, purposely focused on the only thing she desires. "I mean, the whole ensemble fits perfectly, the shoes too. How does someone know what size shoe someone else is?" It's called a foot fetish. Tabitha has one, much to Delaney's enjoyment. "I'm not sure I like her, though. Something seems weird about her, or perhaps it's just her aura, being a submissive." Tabitha's far from a simple submissive. She's a rare commodity, not dissimilar to Alana. She hovers on a border for people such as me, neither needing guidance in her potential demise nor caring for the eventuality of it. She just breathes each day, perversely excited in any option that might present itself to play under. She might be with Delaney, but she's far from owned by him, a situation that suits them both.

"You're just not ready to understand her yet. She's closer to you than you think she is."

"I doubt that, but I'll take your word for it for now." She wraps her arms around herself, stepping out onto the tarmac, her coat shielding her from the wind as it whips about. "Where are we anyway? And why am I dressed like this in the middle of the day?" My eyes skim her legs again, appreciating the slit that runs the length of her thigh, opening the form fitting black material with each step she takes. Tabitha made a good choice. High patent, red heels that arch the foot stunningly. The dress as tight as it should be, one shouldered and flaunting every curve Alana's got. It's the sort of outfit that should make the entertainment drool for her and ensure her movement's not hindered by restrictive ratcheting for now.

"Dates, Alana. Your reward."

"You've brought me to an abandoned wasteland for a date?" I smirk at her and check my watch, seemingly unable to stop walking over to her as I watch the sky and wait. "What are you looking up there for?"

"Look, you'll see soon enough." She huffs a little, giving me enough reason to put her ass back in the car and forget all of this is worthwhile in any way. "This is nice, though. This thing we're doing. It's different." I look at her as she slips an arm through mine and stares upwards. "Proves you're not that arsehole you keep claiming to be."

"You don't know where I'm taking you yet," I reply, for some reason unlinking her arm and stepping behind her, my hand wrapping around her waist. "I could be kidnapping you again, fucking with your mind. It could just be a rouse to get more of what I want." She laughs, her fingers finding their way into mine as we both look upwards.

"You don't do rouses, Blaine. Not for me, anyway. I know that about us. If you'd wanted that I'd still be in the house, gagged and bound - again." She turns, her body brushing against everything that fits perfectly. "This is you accommodating me," she says, her lips moving towards mine. "Listening to me. You're showing me a snippet of that person you refuse to let me see, aren't you? The one who called me your little dove." The thought, or the way she softly lands her lips on mine, makes me smile into her, amused by her analogy of all this. But this is the easy bit for her. The show my magician produces with little care once he's engaged in the performance. She's doesn't understand how much of the real me she's already seen. She's seen my temper, my frustration, something few have ever produced nor will ever see. She's made me move forward into her with just those two emotions, breaking through barriers that shouldn't be broken as she did. Little doves or not, she's far from understanding me yet. "This is one who loves, isn't it?" I growl back at her, pissed that she won't let it go and ready to show her why I can't love anything, not as she does. "It's only three little words, Blaine. You've said them before." She brushes her lips on mine again and wraps her arms tighter around my neck, deepening the kiss into territories best left for hedonism. My cock instantly remembers the thud of her skin as I struck it, and the sound of her squeal as she took another clamp, but my mind seems to disperse into the unknown with her, just as it did last night. It allows her access to places I haven't been before, maybe letting her tongue guide me elsewhere as I increase my grip on her hipbone. It's bemusing, confounding. I feel the tension inside me increase, a sense of anxiety attached to its escalation as she keeps the kiss loose and soft, not allowing me the pressure I crave. The whole fucking thing makes me want to sink to the floor with her and fuck, not for pain's sake, but for sensation's sake. To just feel her again, feel her around me. For once I want slow fucking. I want to ease in, taking my fucking time and letting her mouth guide the moment onwards, not caring for the come I'll eventually spill. The whole fucking episode clouds me and makes me sigh into her, my hands slipping lower and grabbing at her arse, barely restraining themselves from going further. And then she just slows us more, gently leading me into more misguided delusions of making love like normal people do, of fucking for the pure enjoyment of being inside someone. Loving them. Until, eventually, all that's left is a millimetre of space between our lips, her panted breath as consuming to me as the moon descending each night over my sea. "Why won't you let me in enough to say them again?" she whispers, soft fingers stroking the back of my neck and her mouth a barely parted void of expectancy. "I'll give you everything if you let me in." She'll fucking give me everything regardless, yet her voice makes me consider the connotation of the words more absentmindedly, letting sentiment linger in my heart rather than the simple mechanics of owning something to play with. It's enough to make me gaze at her lips as her hands stroke purposefully across the back of my neck still, calming me or fucking lulling me into dreams and horizons I shouldn't be privy to.

"You already are in, little dove." My own fucking words come out unrehearsed and without thought. They bleed out of me with less than honourable intentions, sin and devilment forging forward into her self-indulgently, and yet they're filled with a substance I can't comprehend, nor am trying to. We're both becoming lost in my sea, her demise as worrisome as my own. "You're just in a wonderland you can't understand yet."

The heavy, dull, quickening of sound in the air behind us breaks her from me, her body spinning her frown away from me in surprise, as the sound gets louder. I can do nothing but stare at her as she walks away from me and looks up into the sky, her lips still lingering regardless of the fucking distance. It's all so true. Factual, irrespective of my annoyance with it. I'm falling deeper into the fucking rabbit hole myself, barely comprehending the way she makes me feel and more afraid of the drop with every next kiss.

"A helicopter?" she calls, her voice hardly audible beneath the drone of blades that keep rotating. I'm still staring, not caring for inane questions or the futility of this date. It's her I want, with or without clothes, with or without her smart ass mouth, and with or without torture. I'm as ready to sit on my beach with her as I've ever been, and happy to dwell in the sea's calm lap on my skin. I don't know why, I wish I did. It's something inside of me I've not felt before her, a fucking epiphany that has no base reason for existence. I can't categorise it with any sense of clarification or psychological evaluation. It just is. Fucked as that might be.

I chuckle at the thought, watching as she giggles a little and wraps her coat further around herself, her body naturally backing its way into my hold again with little resistance. "You're taking me up in a helicopter?"

"No, I'm taking you dancing. We need to get there."

"How exciting. Real relationship dates." Hardly, but as long as my cock's rubbing against her cunt before the end of the night, I don't care. If this is what it takes to keep her with me, to make her comfortable with what we'll become, then I'll do it, hardly caring for the pointlessness of it. "Aren't you the charmer when you want to be,

Mr Jacobs?" I smirk and drag her back as the chopper lands, giving it room and shielding her from the worst of the wind and dust.

"I'm only charming when I want something, Alana. Just like you with your begging. You'd do well to remember that," I say, chuckling at the thought of what the evening holds in store for her, and then moving us forward as the chopper settles. "You'll work hard for your treats tonight."

She frowns again, her mouth opening ready to fly into a tirade, no doubt, but she seems to take stock of herself before releasing it, and shrugs my hold from her to walk away. The move leaves me amused at her internal battle as she struggles with it, the war between love and sanity clearly playing with her as much as it does me. But for now she needs this strength from me, not my overly emotional response. She needs me to be unaffected by her, bored even, because until she's ready to trust the very floor I walk on, or until she no longer needs me at all, my other responses are of no use here. I'm not in control while they haunt me, and not wanting to try either.

"Still making it bloody difficult then?" she says, sulkily, her arms folding to put the barrier between us again. Difficult? I could slap her for childishness. I grasp hold of the door to open it and hold out a hand to her, unable to articulate how accommodating I'm actually being given other toys I've played with lately.

"You've got no comprehension of difficult, Alana," I snarl back, my ears near deafened by the continued whirr of the blades spinning above us. She sneers, that look of disdain raising her brow and riling up any blood I'm keeping at bay. "You're being a fucking brat again. Perhaps you'd like to see my difficult, try your chance at scrutinising it under pressure?" The blades keep blaring above, the dull thud of them continuously whisking her hair about as the sun hovers behind her. It's as irritating as her sneer, and as fucking beautiful as my damn horizons. "Well?" I snap, my hand still offered as if begging her to take the damn thing. It's annoying, she's fucking annoying. "Take the damn hand and get your ass on the chopper, or I'll take you home and teach you some more manners instead." She smiles slightly, the corner of her lip lifting rather than any sense of fear shining through her features. And then she chews the fucking thing, raking over the cut I've put there, her eyes focused on mine and not backing down one inch from any ounce of Dominance I might be providing.

"Temper, temper," she says, her hand stretching out to mine. I've snatched the fucking thing before I've thought, hardly giving her time to move a leg before I yank her into the step. Bitch. Infuriating, rude, churlish, and apparently now amused at my temper rather than scared of it. Christ, I need a drink. "There's no point in it, you know?" What? That's fucking annoying too, my inability to understand her next move succinctly. She confuses me, going off kilter with her questioning. It makes me push her into place, hardly able to stop the need to fuck her ass as she leans over the seat. "You can't hide it, Blaine, not from me." More expletives want to come from my mouth. They want to raise hell into the air as I calmly fuck about with straps and latches, ratchetting the buckles into place and thinking of anything but dancing. I'm part admonishing her for being as self-satisfied as Delaney, presumably, and part blaming her for the pain she's pushing for. "You can't run from what you instigated, Blaine. It was you on those steps at the church, not me. You asked." I keep looking at anything but her, my stare unfocused as I turn back to my seat and begin my own process of buckling in. Bitch. She might be correct, she might even be rash enough to try this full tilt, allowing me my fucking freedom as she does, but she's the one who asked for my help, not the other way around. "And, if nothing else, I won't let you lie. You told me you wouldn't lie to me."

I stop and close my eyes to the torment as I knock the security screen between us and Mac signalling that we're ready, all the time listening to her chuckling as the chopper lifts and we start the journey. Unfortunately, she doesn't seem to have stopped her mocking laughter by the time I glance back and see her smiling out of the window, her eyes crinkling under her amusement as we travel on. It makes me stare at her, part infuriated and part bewitched by her casual behaviour. She's nothing like Eloise was with me. She's stronger, less inclined to capitulate to my moods, but perhaps that's because we're adults, not adolescent beginnings who don't give a fuck about consequence.

"You never have been in love, have you?" she says, out of nowhere, infuriating me further as she continues to gaze at the fields below. "You don't know what to do with me, do you?" And still she smiles, her body slowly turning back towards me, crossing her legs and reaching her fucking exquisite heels towards my shin. "Are you terribly perplexed?" Yes. The question makes me smirk before I contain the reaction. "Daddy's confused about baby girl, isn't he?" That just widens my smile rather than contain it any. "What does Daddy need to make him admit his love?" Daddy needs her to shut the fuck up before she gets dangled out the window for amusement. "Big, bad Daddy's got his cock in a knot, hasn't he?" Bitch. Cock in a knot? I stifle the laugh that wants to come out, too irritated with her inexplicable abilities to get inside my head with little fucking effort. It's refreshing in some ways, entertaining, and my magician is more than ready to fuck all over her condescending attitude, but I don't want that. For now, and for her, I'm enjoying this lilt she has over me. It causes reactions in me, ones I don't know how to handle. They need investigation and research.

"Why do you ask so many questions of me, Alana? What do you hope to achieve with them?"

"Honesty. You're lying to me." She says it with a fierce determination, flippantly raising her brow as if I'm stupid for not understanding her concept. "You said you wouldn't lie." I won't.

"Would you like me to say I love you because you need it, or because you think I do?"

"What?"

"It's a simple question. Answer it." She frowns at me and crosses her arms again, flummoxed by the question.

"I .. Well, you need to say it for you."

"Why?"

"Because you're lying to yourself."

"I'm not lying to anyone. Certainly not myself."

"You are if you can't say the words out loud." I smirk in response to her statement, proving my own point even though she hasn't got the guts of the problem yet.

"That would mean you need me to say them for you, little dove, not for me." She opens her mouth instantly, ready to launch something back at me, but stops before letting rip with any intelligent thought she might have had.

"No, it's because you …" I raise a brow, waiting for more and wondering where she's going to go next. "You're not acknowledging this between us."

"I'm not?"

"No, you're denying it. Making it something difficult to feel."

"I would assume you can still feel me all over your cunt." She frowns and tuts, admonishing me for crude reasoning. Fuck her. She won't win this in any way. And the main reason for that is because I'm right and she isn't. She's the insecure one here for now, not me.

"That's not the point. You're rejecting this, killing its forward momentum."

"You're saying I'm going backwards?"

"Well, you won't say it …. And … That makes it difficult to go forward, doesn't it?" And now she's fucking pouting, beautifully, drawing up any sense of adoration I might have for her and tripling its clarity. Still, she's not winning a battle with me any time soon.

"For whom?"

"You. Me. Us, as a couple."

"A couple? I thought I was helping your junkie cunt."

"That's …I don't like that."

"Don't you? It's what you are. Say it."

"No, you're avoiding the topic."

"And that is?"

"That you're a liar, Blaine. You're lying. Trying to deny me my feelings."

"Listen carefully, Alana. You're feelings are yours to assimilate. I said I would give you the world if you asked, as long as you gave me your body to play with. I also told you I would help remove the toxins you've shoved into your system through your lack of ability to manage yourself. At no point did I give you any indication of a coupling going forward. That would offer a life I can't give you. I'm a sadist, Alana, not a self-serving masochist."

"But …" I wait again, becoming amused by her continued aggravation and brattish behaviour. "Well, what the fuck is this then?" I raise a brow again as she fucks around with her skirt, more irritation creasing her face. "You know, your mouth, the dreamy haze on your face when we kiss?" She flicks her gaze to my lips and licks her own. "You hold my hands, Blaine. You smother me, make us closer than we need to be if it's all just help." Sadly, the fucking directness of the statement as it rushes from her mouth confuses me, my mind struggling to find sensible thought as I imagine that haze she talks of. And why do I hold her fucking hands? Why? I've never held anyone's hands but hers. Cole's maybe when I was younger and he needed me.

"It's a chemical reaction to my come spilling into you. It's edifying to me."

"Fuck you."

"Watch that dirty mouth of yours, young lady. You're unknotting my cock." She's eternally unknotting the damn thing. Irritating it. Winding it up. Making it think of something other than the damn battering it normally intends.

"No. I'm not having this anymore. In fact, go screw yourself, because you won't be doing it with me anymore. I don't fuck liars." I chuckle at her and turn to gaze out of the window, watching the ground go by and wondering how she'll feel by the end of the night.

"Mmm. Let's see if you keep that vow by the end of tonight."

"Why, what's happening tonight," she snaps.

"A date. It's what you asked for."

Chapter 7

ALANA

Days seems to have passed, weeks even. I don't know where I am or even what time it is as we fly onwards. He has me in an unknown routine every day. Sleeping at odd hours, getting up when it's dark, going to sleep when it's light. Some part of it is disconcerting. Strange. Like I'm being tossed from pillar to post, unable to make my own decisions about even the most basic of things. Other parts are clarifying, somehow teaching me that my quiet is in there, him guiding me through without me having to think at all. It's become a blur of kneel, learn, write, eat, sleep, repeat. After that first night when he dragged me by the hair and put clamps on me, my first time of kneeling of my own volition, it's been a trial of new and unencumbered sensations. Day after day. Hour after hour. Until I get a reprieve and am allowed to sleep and eat. Who knew orgasms could be so exhausting. They are. And I ache, everywhere, regardless of this perfect outfit and my hair looking like I've just been preened by a salon. Underneath all this I'm a mass of bruises and marks, ones I appear to stare at daily with a smile on my face. He makes me do that too, makes me linger after the acts and stare into a mirror as he stands behind me, apparently so I can appreciate the sensation and learn to trust it, trust him. And I do, with everything but my heart. He just won't let me into his enough to know this is real. It feels like an obligation on his part, occasionally fluttered with an act of kindness, or a nice word to lift us from the distance he still keeps me at. But when he comes inside me, when he uses his lips on mine and breathes the moment through us, he's as close as I've ever felt anything be. He can't hide that behind facades and walls. Not from me.

I gaze out at the clouds, watching the skyscrapers come into view and wondering what's coming next. I don't know, and part of me doesn't care. There isn't much left he can do to my body. He's had his hands everywhere, in everything. Put me through hours of torture, something called edging, getting me so close I'm screaming into the wind, only for him to deny me anything and make me write again. And the story flows so well because of it. It pours from me as I gaze at his beach, the winter's rains starting to change the landscape around me as the sea crashes constantly. All I see is him when I look at it. Sometimes calm and enriching. Sometimes furious and dark. And it's best at night. In the near black. When all I can see is the last crash of a wave against the shore, or the moonlight showing me the tranquil waters further out.

Why can't I reach him out there?

I've mused all this shit the entire way here, having hardly spoken to him because of whatever that was a short while ago. I've mused it and become more and more exasperated with his lack of love, denying me the very emotion I need from him to make this truly happen.

"Where are we?" I ask, sullenly, as the helicopter lowers to a rooftop. The whole thing makes me want to cry and scream and yell, both at him and at myself. I just can't get a handle on my feelings. I can't switch them off like he is doing, if he ever had any to begin with.

"Dates." Screw him and his dates. I stare out the window again as the blades begin to slow, the view nothing but rooftops and skyscrapers. A date constitutes something worth dating for. Nothing here is worth dating for, irrespective of what my heart tells me. I should have adored this journey. Enjoyed my first flight in a helicopter and been content, perhaps held hands with him. Apparently that's not what this is, though, regardless of the endless sessions we've had together. It's just fucking. This is just a clinical procedure to him. A test case. I'm obviously something to be prodded and poked, played with. Love in his world, it appears, does not involve loving. "What you asked for."

I turn to his, rather unfortunately, still handsome face and begin taking the buckle of my belt apart, part wanting to slap him and part needing to kiss him. How does he do that? It's a thing I need to write more of to find my way through, a problem that needs further expansion. And he looks so fucking smug with himself as he sits there in a three piece suit, no doubt proving that no matter what he suggests, I'll follow that lead. I'm not sure I will any more. He might be able to help me, might even be able to show me his path, but without more connection from him it's beginning to mean nothing. It's solitary, irrespective of him always being there. It confines me in a veil I want him under with me. It makes me feel alone.

"Tell me something personal about you," I snap, my hands batting the belt away as the door opens beside me. He smirks. It's something I'm getting sick of. Bloody smirking. I'd rather the frown that descends every time I get close to pushing a button he doesn't like. Or the thrill of his intoxication when he comes inside me. Or the benevolence that settles when he lets his hands roam my skin.

"No."

"Wanker."

That's all I've got as I swivel away from him and try to avoid breaking my neck in these heels, lovely as they might be. Christ knows how Tabitha knows anything about my dress size or shoe size, but she does. It's all perfect. Lines skimming exactly where they should. The fit dressing my breasts to precision. A long purple fur coat. One I'm hoping is fake. Even the jewellery matches my skin, a dark purple stone on the choker matching my hair too. It's all as irritating to me as my mood is, the one he's provoked by being an arse.

I walk on as I get down to the floor, not bothering to shield myself from the slowing blades as they keep spinning behind me, or wait for Blaine. I don't know where we're going, but I'm assuming through those double doors is a good start. I'm greeted by another random man who holds the door open as I arrive, his eyes looking anywhere but at me. Perhaps he's not allowed to look at me, or perhaps he's eyeing up the good looking arse who's following me. Who knows? Who fucking cares anymore. I don't even know why we're here. We might as well have stayed in his house and fucked ourselves stupid until I had no energy left at all. Then I could have slept through these slight tremors still riding my skin a little. Eventually ridding myself of them completely. Job done, and with no need for this damned adventure that becomes more ludicrous with every passing day.

"Alana?" he growls. It's all low and possessive, the same tone he used last night when he made me beg for him. I snarl again, then suck in some air before I swivel back to him, only to find him looking too damned glorious for words to explain as he stands there. It makes my insides melt. Maybe it's something to do with the fact that I can still feel him in there. His cock, his hand, his come. It's infuriating. He's infuriating. What sort of man doesn't love, or perhaps know how too? "This is what *you* wanted from me."

I spin again and walk through the door towards an elevator, very nearly telling him that this is absolutely not what I wanted. Then swish myself straight back around to face him again, my feet striding forward with little care to my actions. I want love, not whatever this is.

"Why the hell did you bother rescuing me if this is all I get from you?" I yell, barely able to contain whatever emotion is halting me from just doing it like he said it had to be. "Hey? Why not just let me fucking drown." He stalls, his mouth opening and then shutting. "Seriously, what the hell is the point in you and me, short of your perversions?"

He glowers, his eyes flicking to the guy who's still holding the door open. What? He's bothered about someone knowing? Idiot. I laugh. I adore his fucking perversions, doesn't he know that? My own mouth stops mid rant, my brain catching up with what I've just thought. I look at the floor, trying to assimilate the information, find a place for it. *I adore his perversions.* It makes me look at my wrists, until I move the bracelet entirely and check the bruise that's defacing my skin. It glows a slight purple hint at me, reminding me of the rest of them that I found this morning in the bath. I'm covered in them, my bits in particular, although nothing hurts, not with any real inclination of pain anyway. It's comforting in some way, soothing perhaps, reminding me of him with every step I take.

"Finally finding yourself, Alana?" he says, conceitedly. My head snaps back up to him, confusion and irritability still waging a war inside my mind. Screw him.

I'm whirling and wandering off again before I can process anything, the fire in me dowsed by his superiority. I don't look at him as he arrives beside me, his finger reaching for the elevator button. I just narrow my eyes at his hand, watching it move calmly, a sense of righteousness about its glide through bloody air. "If you beg you can have some more. I never have fucked on a rooftop." He's not about too either. Not with any sense of willingness on offer, anyway. Still, the damned hand is as attractive as ever, tempting me with thoughts I shouldn't be thinking. It makes me sigh, or huff. I'm not entirely sure which reaction I'm offering. It's not consent, though, I know that much as the door pings and opens. That's a definite. Arse.

The short pitch of the elevator seems endless, the small box around us reminding me of confines, ones that involve the straps he put across me last night to hold me down. The thought has a smile creeping across my face before I've contained it, regardless of my irritation. Memories flood me. The taste of him, the smell. The way he gripped my skin, the way he whispered all the words, taunting me with the next drive inwards. And I can't stop my eyes meeting his in the reflective mirror because of it, wanting them to join again. He stares blatantly, as if he holds every right to do so. No smirk, no frown, just a relaxed face as he keeps looking into me.

"Why did I save you?" he asks, a slight tilt of his head as if he doesn't know who he's asking the question to. It's as confusing as my own mind is.

"Probably because I would have drowned without you," I eventually reply. It's true, even if it doesn't offer anything other than facts. It's just yet another clinical decision making process on his part, I'm sure. "Because it was practical to do so."

"Mmmm." That's all I get, as he breaks our locked gaze and stares at the door instead. No rolling sentiment of love. No show of desire or romance. Not even the slightest hint of care. It was just practical to do so. I'm just something he saved so he could maul me again. That's all.

The doors open again and he steps out, leaving me behind. I stare after him, wondering what I'm supposed to do with those thoughts. It makes me look at my hands, noting the tremor that's subsiding with each passing day with him. I don't know how he's doing it, but he is. Or perhaps it's just the fact that I'm not putting any speed inside me anymore. I've not even really had what I would consider withdrawals, not that I know of anyway. It makes me consider if I need his help or not. Maybe I can do this without him. I could just go home. Find my own path.

"I won't let you go, Alana. Not yet," he calls back, his brogues clanking the tarmac as he walks towards a car that's idling by the side of the road. "I'm not finished with you."

He holds his hand out to me as he keeps walking, offering me that side of him I'm so desperate to see. He doesn't even turn back to me, probably because he knows I'll follow. My knees lock themselves, wobbling me on my heels, some part of me fighting the momentum that still wants to travel after him regardless of all this angst inside. I wish I could say I don't want to follow him. Wish I could keep this venom inside going and let it show me my own route out of all this, but it's a lie to try. I know it. I can feel it in the way my heart keeps trying to push me forward again. And I can sense it in the way my body screams for more of whatever he wants to deliver to my skin. I miss it already, perhaps rebelliously tormented by this new found need for pain to be applied.

He just opens the door of the black car when he gets there and waits, one hand resting on the top of the frame, his suit falling in its impeccable cut. He doesn't look back. Doesn't flinch or move. He just expects me to arrive at some point, yielding to whatever he requires. And it's ludicrous I know, but my legs propel me to him without much more thought. I might have tried to stop them, might have tried to apply rationale to matters, perhaps trying to save my heart the breaking that's coming for it, but it doesn't work. Nothing appears to. I even try to huff as I wander forward, chastising him, or me, but that's a lie too because I'm smiling quietly. Seemingly enjoying this strange union of ours.

"You're not boring, Blaine," I say, ducking under his arm and sliding myself in to the back, refusing to look at his face. "I'll give you that."

Silence carries on again as the car begins to travel, nothing more than hearts beating and the rumble of ground beneath us as night begins to fall around us. It's heady, making me consider a drink, something to take the edge off my irrational emotions. A glass of Sancerre would be nice, followed by a truck load of gin.

"Make yourself come," he says, quietly. My eyes shoot to his, astounded by the way he just says it so openly in the back of a car when there's a driver in here. He's just lounging there, his eyes relaxed as they gaze at me, his mouth soft and ready for a kissing he doesn't deserve. "Just do it, Alana."

"But .." I snatch a glance at the driver, then look back at Blaine, nodding my head in the driver's direction. "He'll be able to …"

"See you? Yes. And hear too. But that's not your concern." He leans forward, his fingers reaching towards my ankle and picking it up. "Spread your legs and make yourself come for me." There's a slight fight in my reaction to his handling, but it's as much of a lie as it was when I tried not to walk towards him. "You want free, this is how you get it," he says, a damn smile spreading on his face as I keep tugging at him. "Or we could keep fighting. You'll do as I want in the end either way."

Arrogant fucking dick.

Unfortunately, he's probably right, and I know it because my leg's weakening, almost wanting to open for him as he tightens his grip a little. It's not the show of strength, though. It never damn well is. It's something instinctual in me, something at my base core, telling me to yield. It makes me give in, or maybe just accept his wish regardless of my fear. And he knows it the moment I widen my crotch to him, the ankle in his grip going lax to accommodate his tugging me around. "Better," he says, as he releases me and waits for me to get on with it. The tension makes me falter, hardly knowing if I can even achieve that in here. It's not something I've done before, and the thought of the driver being here makes me nervous, but my hand travels my skin anyway, all the time keeping my eyes trained on the man that's making me do this. And within seconds the rest of the damn car seems to disappear, tingling sensations taking over and guiding me onwards. My hand lowers further and slides the slit open on my dress, searching for access to the place he wants me to go. It's comforting somehow, giving me a direction to stop me thinking about all the other confusions he causes, quiet again once I focus in on the task at hand.

"Inside you," he says, his tone turning to the one I love, its texture like a blanket over me in the midst of this hedonistic delight. I slide downwards again, my fingers wandering over the boned corset I'm strapped into and inching into the black lace of my g-string. He moves suddenly, the speed of it causing me to jerk in response, wondering what's coming. The slight lift of the corner of his mouth makes me frown, my nerves getting the better of me, and my legs clamping closed at the same time.

"Oh no you don't'," he says, picking up my legs and lifting my arse to grab hold of the g-string. The sides come down my thighs as quick as a knife through butter, removing the apparently offending item as they do. He pockets it and sits back to watch, the curve of his mouth still in place at my look of panic. "Carry on." Right. I shake my head a little, struggling to get my mojo back and looking back at the driver. "No, Alana," he snaps, making me swing back to him. "Where do you look?" At him. That's where I look.

I pull in a long breath and begin, letting myself be lulled back to him, my heel lifting to bend my leg up onto the seat as my fingers tentatively travel again. He just keeps looking at me, directly at me. There's no wandering of eyes as I let my fingers caress my clit, trying to wake it up. No deviation so he can see what I'm doing. He's focused only on my reactions to myself, like he's trying to help me with nothing but his eyes. It makes me swirl into their chocolate brown depths, imagining his hand on me instead. The thought makes me smile and then gasp as a shudder descends, my insides beckoning me towards them.

"Both hands," he says, still a vision of calm as my breathing starts to escalate, my legs widening. "Fuck yourself with them." I roll my eyes back at his words, letting my other hand join in on the party, my fingers dragging my thigh to reach as I lean back further. Nothing else exists in this car as I keep rubbing, my own calm beginning to come as I hold myself open, teasing the edges and prolonging the climax that's coming for me. It makes me moan at my own torment, as I slowly start pushing two fingers in, letting their grate upwards tease more elicit groans to escape my mouth. Oh god, it's so dark in here. So full of Blaine and quiet. Nothing else is in here with us. No noise, no interference. No sense of threat or consequence. It's just our little world filled with fun and torture, the world outside passing by in a blur.

I smile at the words in my head as my breath hitches, my fingers pushing in deeper as my other hand starts rubbing furiously. The whole fucking situation elevates my groans to broken gasps for air, the heat swelling around me and making me desperate to come. I open my eyes to watch him, knowing it'll help me find the final shunt I need to make it happen, and find him looking at my hands, his mouth slightly open, his eyes narrowed. He's so fucking handsome as he near death stares the thing he wants most. It makes me groan, wiling him to take over for me, make me come in his own way. One damn touch and I'd explode. One slide of his thumb. One grip of his fingers. Anything to help me over this final hurdle. I gasp again imagining it, my eyes fluttering closed as the heat builds, my stomach muscles clenching around the orgasm that's chasing me. It floods me with images of the time we've spent fucking. The church. His bed. That bench I'm coming to love. Oh god, I can't breathe all of a sudden, and yet I'm wanting nothing but his hand over my mouth, his weight on me, holding me down.

"Stop," he snaps, a sudden sharp pain on my ankle. My eyes fly open, my hands continuing of their own accord regardless of his order. Screw that, I'm nearly there. I pant out, still feeling my insides as I clench around my fingers furiously. "You will stop, Alana, or you'll regret your decision to defy me." My brow furrows, my fingers slowing a little at the thought as he smiles, and rolls his finger over my ankle. "Make a choice." The clenching continues inside, my breath wanting nothing more than to stop so I can carry on and finish what he made me do, but he's got that look. It tells me he means it this time. He's not playing. There won't be anything nice about his punishment for this if I challenge it. It reminds me of the feeling when that belt buckle hit my bits, causing all sorts of pain to collide inside me. Or the damned cage I despise. That thought alone is enough for me to slow my hands to nothing and pull them away altogether, hoping to appease whatever monster was beginning to appear.

It leaves me aching as he watches me carefully and continues rubbing my ankle softly, until he eventually turns away, a small lick of his lips signalling the end of our sexual conversation. I don't turn away this time, rather stare at him, wondering what the hell goes through his head sometimes. Was that for him, or me? Was I supposed to learn something from the experience, other than feeling empty and unsatisfied? I let his hand soothe me to some degree, feeling the gentleness in his fondle pull me back into normality again.

"What was that about?" I ask, not understanding a bloody thing.

"A lesson in control." My brows shoot up. Well, I suppose I did stop my orgasm, stupidly given my still aching crotch area. The thought makes me huff a little and glare at him, irritation lacing my every bone because of my lacking orgasm. The huff causes him to immediately dump my ankle back down on the seat, breaking our contact. "About who owns whom."

"You think you can frighten me into doing what I'm told?"

He doesn't answer that, rather looks back out of the window again as the car pulls up, clicking the handle the moment it does and getting out. I stare at the back of his suit as he waits, his hand on the frame as usual, waiting for me to follow. So I huff and clamber across the seat, rubbing my crotch on the seat one last time for some form of relief from my non-orgasm and then getting out to stand in front of him.

"Where are we then?" I ask, looking around and waiting for him to educate me to what this date is all about, because so far it's been fucking appalling.

He doesn't answer, he just looks up, scanning the skyscrapers and then starts walking off in the direction of a building.

THE END

  The door looms, dark red in colour as I, yet, follow blindly, not at all sure why I'm bothering. I mean, I can't even have orgasms now? That's not acceptable, especially after all the crap he's given me. The pain. The snarls. The fucking cage. I'm going mad. That must be the reason for all this. I'm utterly insane.

  "Read or White?" he asks, as we walk through the door and head our way around some corners, a small man scampering alongside us the moment we reach another doorway.

  "Mr Jacobs, Sir," he says, his head bowing. The formality surprises me, regardless of our attire. I've never seen anyone bow and scrape around him, even in that first innocuous venue I met him in with all of its submissives dotted about. "Where would you like her?" What? Who? Is he talking about me? Blaine keeps walking, his footfalls as calm as clouds drifting by as I hurry to catch up, the mere thought of me going anywhere in this place without him totally alarming.

  "Red or White, Alana?" Blaine asks, his hand coming back for me and clasping mine before I could decide if he deserved it or not.

  "What?"

  "Wine?"

  "Oh, red, please." He nods and continues on again, towing me with him until we arrive in a large foyer. I stare up, half stumbling, amazed at the majesty of it given the bland outside of the building. "Wow." That's all I've got. The ceiling is around 40 feet up from us, a huge cascade of stone work elaborately decorated with bosses and intricate carving. Botticelli paintings lay between the buttresses, lining routes to heaven and hell. "That's incredible." I'm so lost in my musings I don't really feel his hand leaving me, or notice him wander off as I spin in circles underneath the art work, slowly drawing my eyes over the imagery.

"Miss, if you could follow me," the man's voice says. I look back at him, wondering what he's talking about, and then look for Blaine, who's disappeared.

"What do you mean?" I ask, stupefied and desperately scanning for Blaine again.

"The show, miss." Oh, right. "Where's Mr Jacobs gone?"

"He'll be waiting for you, miss." Okay.

I follow the man as he begins walking off, scanning the lines of corridors and doors off the room, all elaborately decorated. It's like I'm in the Royal Albert Hall, gold leafing and gilding everywhere. It's beautiful, reminding me of sophistication and manners, something our other 'dates' have been sorely lacking in, given the venues.

We eventually turn into a small door, the heat hitting me the moment a door opens.

"Ah, come on, come on," a hassled looking man says, his yellow outfit as garish as his clearly very homosexual flamboyancy. "I've been waiting for you. Did you get caught up in traffic?" What?

He appraises me, his eyes travelling over my body, roaming it and then nodding to himself about something. "Yes, oh yes, this is lovely. Did he pick it?" I have no clue what this man is talking about, so much so that I look behind me, wondering if he's talking about someone else. "I think you'll do just fine like that." I'm sure I will. I rub the sides of my dress down, unconcerned about whatever he thinks of my attire.

"If you could just point me in Mr Jacobs' direction I'll take my seat for the show," I say, confused about what's going on as I look around at all the maniacal people rushing around.

"Oh, no, no. They watch, you perform," he replies, his hand swinging a set of handcuffs around as if they're part of an outfit.

"What?"

"The stage is set, your audience awaits."

He says this as if there's no question about me performing. As if no matter how much I look at the door behind me, aim for it, or even run for it, I will still be made to entertain in some manner. I glare at him, confused with the thought as he wanders over to a curtain. It makes me realise I'm back stage in a theatre, opening up my mind to what it is that I'm being asked to do. "I hope you've brought your best with you," he says, smiling as he tips back the curtain a little to have a look. "We're quite full." What an idiot. If he thinks I'm going to be doing anything to entertain anyone, he's mad. I don't know why I'm here or who the hell this fool thinks he is, but it's not happening. I swing myself round, aiming for the small entrance door again, only to find the first guy standing in front of it, blocking my route.

"Move please," I snap, frustrated with the whole bloody thing. I'm very clearly in the wrong place.

"Oh no, darling, one doesn't leave. The only way out is off the stage, Alana." I swing back to him, wondering how he knows my name. "Or there is the dungeon, of course. Harold, did we get rid of the last lot?" he asks, tipping his gaze to the man behind me. The man at the door shakes his head. "Still rotting in their chains then. We really don't have time for this. Are you ready?"

"What for?"

"We want to see you shine. Fuck the crowd for me. Make them beg." I'm aghast.

"I'd rather damn chains and a dungeon, frankly."

"Easily arranged," he replies, swinging his cuffs around his fingers. "Harold, if you could. One of the other girls will have to entertain our special guest."

"Who's that," I snap, slapping out at Harold's hands as he reaches for me.

"Your Mr Jacobs, of course."

"Special?"

"Do you know nothing, young lady? Oh good god, I do not have the time for this. "Merry, get yourself ready," he shouts, slapping his hands together and discarding the cuffs. "He'll need the black corset, thigh highs. And get your choker on." I stand, bemused as I watch the kafuffle of bodies suddenly rushing around. And then a woman walks out, her legs ninety miles long as she zips up some black latex boots. I stare again, still unsure what the hell is happening around me. "Yes, lovely." She strips off her top, revealing perfect breasts and a minuscule bra. "Oh, no, that won't do at all. Lyra, get the Stalin corset, the one with steel studs."

"I don't unders…"

"Ssh, ssh," he flutters his hands at me, his body walking over to the woman. "Harold, get rid of her until later. Hair up," he says, pulling a clips out of his pocket and fiddling with her auburn tresses. It's just a whirlwind of movement. Corsets coming out of the wings, making mine look tame. Spray being sprayed. Lipstick being wiped from her face and what looks like a thick dog collar being strapped around her neck. I turn and physically shove Harold off me, my wrist wrenched from his hand again as he tries to manhandle me somewhere.

"Is this all for Blaine?" His hands shoot to his mouth, surprise etched into his face as he spins on me and narrows his eyes.

"Say that again?"

"What? His name?" He nods excitedly. "Blaine."

"Oh, it's divine. It falls so beautifully from your lips, too. When did he start letting you call him that?"

Oh, I've had enough. This is all utterly ridiculous. These are the strange people I met in that club originally. They're nothing like me, or Blaine for that matter. What happens between us is deeper than this, it's more .. I don't know what, but it's more than whatever this charade is.

"Look, I'd just like to get back to Blaine and then you can all carry on doing whatever it is that you're doing. Odd as it might be."

"Well, that's out of those curtains darling," he says, slipping around behind me and taking the coat from my shoulders. "He's out there waiting for you. The boys are ready whenever you are."

What boys? He flicks his hand at the other corner of the room, showing me two men sitting there, the pair of them eyeing me up as if I'm something to be played with. "Now, let's have a look at you." He prods at my waist, his fingers grabbing me and twirling me round on the spot until I feel sick. "Did he put you in this?"

"No. Get off. Jesus, stop it, will you? I don't know what the fuck this is but get the hell off me."

He stops his faffing around and comes back in front again, his finger on his lips, one hand on his hip.

"You really don't, do you?"

"What?"

"You don't know where you are, do you? At all."

"No. I thought it was a show. I'm on a date." Although, this is barely resembling a date so far. Still, I glare, hoping to show superiority above all this chaos around me.

"A date?"

"Yes."

"That's interesting. Are you special? What talents do you have?" Writing is my talent. Other than that, nothing as far as I can tell. "You must have something special about you for him to be so infatuated." Not that I'm aware of. And infatuated? Hardly.

"Well, never mind. We haven't got time anyway. Let me give you a quick rundown of what's happening so you can get on with it," he says, his body spinning from me again and walking off in the direction of the curtains. "This is my cabaret, look." He tips the curtain, waving his hand at me to make me look. "It happens four times a year. The room out there is full of sadists, ones who come together to watch whatever show I put on for them." I peek out, looking at the array of guests, all dressed immaculately, just as people were at the party we went to. Old ones, young ones. Men, women. "Your prestigious Mr Jacobs has only been here once." I look around for him, not seeing him anywhere. "I'm hoping to impress."

"Why?" He looks at me aghast, as if I'm a moron of the highest order.

"Because he's the monster." Really? I frown. He chuckles and looks at me, his eyes scanning the length of me. "One you clearly haven't met yet, young lady. So, I have to entertain. You, have been added. What can you do?"

"This is horrendous. I don't even know your name and you want me to go out there and do something for you?" He nods, his fingers sweeping the curtain back closed as he smiles. "And I can't do anything, anyway."

"Can you come?" Oh my god. They're all fucking insane. Although, yes I can, and it probably won't be too hard given the non-orgasm that happened a while ago.

"That's none of your business," is my tetchy reply as I back away from all this insanity.

"Tango?" he asks, two women hurtling behind him and holding up wigs and outfits for his perusal. He turns and looks at them, fluffing his hand at the first and grabbing a wig from the second. "So, Alana. Tango? Yes or no?"

My feet continue their backing away as he smiles, wholly unsure what the hell he's talking about and wanting nothing more than to run. This really is wonderland, and I have a feeling I'm about to get very lost in it.

Chapter 8

ALANA

"Boys, tango."

That's all he says. It's enough for the two guys behind the women to stand and begin looking through a rail of clothes, one of them immediately pulling out something red. I stare, not knowing what it is that I should be saying or doing. I'm here to entertain a room full of sadists? Part of me is infuriated at the very notion, and still backing away from the madness, but the other is becoming more and more fascinated by the second as one of the men starts stripping down to his underwear. It's appealing, making me halt my feet and remember the feeling Blaine gave me in that back alley. Something inside me is shifting to the slut he asked me to be then, perhaps engaging this new predilection that seems apparent every time he uses his dirty mouth. I wander over to the curtain again and pull it back a little, searching for him and wondering what the hell he's playing at by doing this to me. No warning. No conversation. It's expected of me. Like I should just do it with no argument brooked. It's true submission and Dominance, isn't it? The thing I came to him to learn about. Not dissimilar to me making myself come in the back of the car, something I wasn't allowed to achieve. Or any different to me kneeling, I suppose. *I ask, you do.*

I scan the crowd again, nerves swirling around at the thought, hoping that at least if I can see him it might show me some reason why my brain's nearly considering this as acceptable. I find him eventually. He's propped at the side of the room, a small table beside him as he leans on the wall and sips a tumbler of something dark. There's a woman at his feet, one who's kneeling with a tray in her hands. She's scantily clad, a bodice of some description ratcheting her breasts out of her outfit. He's as calm as he always is, not a hair out of place or fidgeting as he looks at the other side of the stage rather than at her, disinterested in her presentation. Others are quietly staring at him, whispering about him by the look of it as they tip their heads at him. Some frowning, others swinging their heads away the moment he turns his own head towards them. It makes me scowl at them, irritated that they'd be discussing him in any way for some reason. I don't know why. Maybe this just all seems less private than we've achieved before. Less private than he'd like. I know that about him. Something about him just doesn't seem to fit here, irrespective of the status he's apparently got. Just the two of us seems so much more intimate, loving if one could call it that, regardless of his non acceptance of that fact.

"Who are you?" I murmur at him, regardless of the fact he can't hear me. He's asked me that, asked me where I am. Who I am. Told me he'll help find me again. And the more I stand here gazing at him, seemingly seeing a different man than all these other people, the more I want into his mind. I want that version he keeps just for me. The one that comes crawling out of him when he least expects it.

I want to help him too.

"My name is Oliver." What? I turn sharply, the garish yellow suit assaulting me again as he stands there with a comb in one hand. I didn't mean him. I'm not interested in anything he has to offer. It's the man out there I want. Apparently through these curtains.

"Right, well I don't care. How do I tango?" He looks slightly affronted. I don't care about that either. The only person I'm remotely interested in pleasing is the one who seems bored with what's going on around him. The one who's waiting for me. "And I'll need a mask. I'm not going out there exposed." He smiles, a look of surprise suddenly etching itself into his face as he chuckles and walks away from me. I follow, snatching a glance at my boys, who have miraculously transformed themselves into something resembling an Argentinian eighties porn flick. "And they look utterly dreadful, make them change into something more suitable." There's another chuckle, this time rising to a laugh that makes me smile too as he hands me a red cape from the rail, his hands swishing away a girl that appears at his side

"And now I see why he's infatuated," he says, as my fingers run over a long blue dress. "Not many would question me." The long legged girl arrives, her studded corset now in place, her hair piled up into a high ponytail.

"She's not even his type." I don't know how I know that, but I do. I'm his type. I tempted him forward into me. Woke him up again. She's not me. It's me he's waiting for. Nothing else will garner a reaction from him. "You know nothing about him. Tell her to go away. She's absolutely ludicrous. He'll think you're useless if you give him that."

"You're a goddess," he says, still laughing as he looks me over again. I huff out, glaring at the woman who dares to glower at me in response. I can't even be bothered with her enough to respond.

I spy a mirror and head towards it to do my make-up instead, wondering what the hell I'm letting myself in for. He follows me and holds a mask over my shoulder. It's pretty. Lilac swirls of taffeta falling in soft tails around the edges, a flash of black around the eyes to match my dress. I nod, swiping a thin layer of clear lip-gloss on and clicking my head around to quell my nerves. He reaches forward and grabs some pins, then starts slotting them into my hair to hold the mask in place.

"I could use a drink," I say, looking at a bottle of champagne that's on the next table. The woman sitting there stands and brings it over, her red clawed nails wrapped around the neck. She smiles and wanders off, not bothering with offering me a glass. I pick it up anyway, glugging from it like it's my next drug of choice. Jesus, what the hell am I doing?

"You will be something to watch, I'm sure," he says, across my shoulder, his hands working with the precision of a trained hairdresser.

"I'm not sure about that," I mutter, taking another swig and staring myself down in the mirror as he dusts something on my shoulders. "I can't tango to save my life."

"Baby, they're not here to watch you dance. They're here to see you scream." I frown behind the mask, knowing that's not true, not of Blaine anyway. He can watch that in private. Has done. He's brought me here for me to learn something about me, not to entertain all those other people out there. "Is there anywhere the boys need to stay away from?"

"What?"

"Broken areas?"

The words make me realise they intend on touching me, hurting me even. I don't know why I didn't realise it before. I turn and look at them, travelling my eyes down to their hands to see what damage they can do. It doesn't scare me, but it's not the same sense of anticipation as I'd have when Blaine holds me. It's actually revolting in some way, making me feel queasy. I swing back and glug some more champagne, hoping to dislodge the sensation.

"Not inside me. Anywhere." Christ knows where their hands have been. At least if they're on the outside I can pretend it's just dancing, get lost in the music maybe.

Raucous laughter streams from in front of the curtain suddenly, making me gulp down yet more champagne. Jesus. I'm really going out there? Stupid. Utterly and categorically insane. What on earth is happening to me? There isn't any version of Alana who would do this, either before the person I am now, or the one I have become. I cling onto the table, hoping reality kicks in at some point soon to whisk me away from all this. It's got nothing to do with writing, nothing to do with who I was when I was young. I'm fucking lost in a whirlwind of emotions, neither knowing what I'm doing or seemingly caring for the outcome.

"Ready?" he says. No. No, I'm not ready. I'm a mess.

"You're a beautifully twisted mess, Alana Williams."

I stare into the mirror, remembering him saying the words and trying to dismiss all the sound around me. It only takes a few seconds to see him reflected at me, just as he asked me to do. His face is calm, his mouth soft and ready for kissing. His eyes, still with that semi-permanent scowl attached. I smile at it, listening to his breathing, perhaps trying to regulate my own with it and find our rhythm together. My fingers soften their grip as I imagine his hands on me, the corners of his lips lifting slightly as he listens to my moans. He's here with me. Even in this chaos that's happening around me now. I can feel him.

I look at the reddening around my wrists, perversely enjoying the way it shines back and reminds me of him. I can feel him everywhere when I shut everything else off. On my skin, in my thoughts, inside me. I blow out a breath and close my eyes, letting his image linger inside me as I stand up and turn. I just need to keep him here with me, ignoring anything else that might get between us, these other two men included.

"I'm ready," comes from me, my feet walking towards the curtain in some sort of trance I've created for myself.

"Just let them lead you, Alana." I nod, barely able to discern his voice above the continued sound of Blaine inside my mind. He's all I can hear. All I want to hear.

The two guys arrive beside me, their porn star outfits replaced with smart looking suits, akin to proper dancers. It makes me look at Oliver, amused that he listened to me. He smiles back and nods at the curtains as a heavy Latin beat starts around us, drowning out the bedlam further as the lights dim to pitch black. Tango.

THE END

I suck in a breath again and leave my head looking at the floor as one of the guys wraps his hand around the top of my arm, his grip less solid than Blaine's could ever be. The other one chuckles, making me snarl at him. If either of them think I'm scared, they're wrong. There's nothing they can do that I can't handle, and if there is, Blaine will stop it. I know that. I know that because he said he'd help. I trust that about him, even if I don't trust his heart completely.

The beat starts low and gravelly, dragging its edges around the melody. It makes my foot tap, seemingly linking me into the sound as it begins to escalate. I'm turned to face guy one, both his hands gripping my upper arms. I don't see him, though. I'm still seeing nothing but Blaine as I stare into his bland face and let the music ebb and flow. He sways me, left and right, the rhythm making my head nod from side to side, my hips joining in without care. I smile at the thought, listening to the darkening notes as they take me away and ready me for sensations only Blaine has provided before. And it's still pitch black as I watch the guy smile and tighten his grasp on me, one of his hands lowering to my backside. I don't care. They're not his hands, not really. They're Blane's. I can feel them as I start moving my feet, a light suddenly cascading down on me to illuminate us. I'm twisted and turned, my body pushed across the floor to the other. I spin, my feet tripping a little at the sudden rush that happens. It causes a ruckus of chuckles to come over the music, presumably at the poor little fuck toy on the stage. Screw them. That's not happening here. I'm doing this for me and him, no one else. I search for him in my mind again, letting guy two maul me with his hands and trying to feel Blaine's again, but it's not coming. Nerves are interfering as I listen intently to the beat and feel fingers gripping at my waist. And then one hand drags up my leg, the touch of it on my thigh making my breathing escalate quicker than I would have thought. It makes me aroused, my legs widening without thought as I finally find Blaine's hands again and let them guide me.

Forwards, backwards, the twirl of me continuing as I sense more hands touching me and making me hungry. I can't explain it, it just washes over me as the music intensifies, Blaine's voice inside my head telling me it's alright. I sigh, letting the hands keep mauling, letting them paw as I land heavily against one of them, the thud of my body reminding me of Blaine's weight on me.

"Bend over," one of them says, my body suddenly being halted and forced forward into the other one. He catches my head, his fingers gripping my chin and asking me to go downwards. I do, too engrossed in the sound that's floating around my mind to bother with who's holding me. It's all Blaine, as I sense something touch my lips and gasp. I open my eyes to see a leather crop, perched by my mouth, his fingers asking me to open up. I do that, too, happy to let the leather embed itself. It reminds me more of Blaine and the straps he put over me, the gag around my mouth. It's gripped tight between my teeth as I'm shunted upwards and spun, guy two's hands spinning me away to the beat of the sound. It's all so beautiful. A dark and echoing room, filled with nothing but sways and sighs. I can hear moans over the music too, now. A revel of chorus. Women's and men's. Accompanying grunts. The occasional sharp scream coming to join my own melody. And my feet are finding themselves, finding a true cadence to cling to as I twirl and turn in their hands.

THE END

I stretch my arms out to the other one, enjoying the melodic dark that cascades around the rhythm, temping me into whatever this will become. I'm like a butterfly being batted around, willing to land on whichever thing presents itself next. It's freeing, a sense of lightness about it, regardless of the dark encompassing us.

I'm suddenly halted again, something sliding around my neck at the same time. It doesn't make me gasp in fear, or worry. If anything it warms me, making me hungry for what's coming next. Enough so that my legs widen in response to it, seemingly urging something inside me that's not there to take. But I ache so much. My breathing's pitched and hassled, my arms feeling lighter than air, but as heavy as they've ever been. I'm exhausted and yet ready to take more. It's all contrasted, a fighting of two halves ready to have the argument driven from me by anything that dare.

I feel something buckle and look out into the audience, searching for Blaine so I can comprehend what's happening to my body. It's all over the place, my mind falling back into its jumbled mess as the leather tightens more than before. Each notch is like a viper constricting, like another layer is being taken away. And yet my frame's so calm as it happens, my arms being held out to my sides, my hips still swinging slowly to the staccato music.

"Kneel, pet." One of them says. I frown at his voice, unconvinced by its tone and needing to hear Blaine's there instead. Nothing happens. I don't go down, my body won't let me. It stays upright, my eyes still searching for Blaine in the crowd. "Get down you little slut." That causes nothing but disdain to level my face, my hips still moving, my shoulders joining in. One of their hands slaps my face, an order of a kind, I suppose. I grin at it, remembering Blaine's hand and wanting nothing more than him to come and show these two how to do it properly.

"Blaine," comes from my mouth, quietly.

The crop falls out as I mutter his name, hoping he'll come and do this instead of them. He doesn't appear, and one of them starts shoving at me, making me bend at the knees by slapping it with the very thing I dropped to the floor. It stings, its biting sensation sending a riot of sharp pain to buckle me to the floor. Still I stare out into the crowd, waiting, a slight snarl on my face as I keep looking for him. I just need to see his face, let him reflect back at me, but he's not there to find. I'm alone. I'm alone and gazing into a sea of peering eyes, ones who are laughing. Some smile up at me, one masturbates even as he stares back at my face and sneers. It seems to snap me back from my lulled trance, my body becoming rigid as I start fighting the guys grip on me to get away. What the fuck is going on? He's left me alone to deal with whatever this is? I can't do it alone. Don't want to.

"Get off me," snaps out of my mouth, my wrist wrenching at his grip.

He just tightens again, a laugh coming from his own mouth as the other one hits me across the back with the crop. I shout out at the impact, tears springing into my eyes at the assault of it. It immediately sends me scrabbling upwards, my heels trying to gain purchase against the floor to get away from this craziness.

"You'll stay down, pet, if you know what's good for you."

THE END

I don't know which one said that. I don't fucking care either. I'm twisting and turning in their hold as hard as I can, levering all my weight at them, trying to make it difficult for them to hold onto me.

"Get the hell off of me," snarls out of me again. "I don't want this. Fuck off." Laughter booms around the room, the entire audience jeering at my performance as I keep tugging and yanking on them. "Piss off," I snap, my nails finally finding something I can scratch into as I free one of my hands. The guy growls and slaps out at my face so hard I tumble to the floor, my one free hand hardly gaining purchase before I hit the wooden boards.

"Fucking bitch," he spits at me, his fingers instantly hauling on the leather that's wrapped around my neck.

I struggle again, desperately trying to get away from the sensation, my fingers looping into the leather to stop it strangling me as I'm dragged. The instant presence of Blaine in my mind is a welcome reprieve as I remember the same scenario at my apartment, making my legs stop their fight. It halts me regardless of my momentum, my mind trying to find some comfort in the image of his face again. But it's not Blaine doing this, is it? I need him here. I can't do this without him. This is the unknown, a man who might harm me beyond my threshold. Someone I don't want near me. It rallies my legs back into kicking, their fight for freedom as angry as I've ever felt them.

"Stay down, brat." *Blaine.*

My eyes snap open as the tone of him washes through me, their search for him as instant as the calm that settles and stills my legs. I find him immediately, as I pant on the floor. He just stares at me from the shadows in front. One hand around a glass as he picks up a chair and turns it to sit astride it. He leans forward and rests on the back of it, watching closely as I open my mouth to spit venom at him and arching a brow. The man holding my neck tugs again, making my body move like a rag doll as I stare in confusion at Blaine and watch him gaze back, a slight lift of his lip forming. He wants this, doesn't he? Wants to see me do this for him. In fact, he's damn well ordering me to give in to them. I frown again, wondering what thrill he'll get from seeing me like this, although just the thought of him watching sends a chill through my mind now I've found him again. "Let him play with you. Do as you're told."

I'm hauled upright at that request, my body placed roughly over a table face down. It makes me struggle again as I lose Blaine's face in the whirlwind of movement. It's only seconds passing before I feel the zipper on my dress being pulled down, exposing the entirety of my back and arse as the material falls to the side of my body. The scenario makes me close my eyes, praying that whatever happens doesn't hurt too much. And then I feel clips hook onto the side of the leather at my neck, my head being locked into position so I can't move at all.

"Turn her towards me," Blaine's voice says, still full of that arrogant calm.

The room immediately starts to spin, the table being manoeuvred so I can look at him. I grip onto the edge of it as it turns, panting and hoping desperately that he will make this sensation of fear go away. Perhaps I'm desperate for validation, or security, or just a sense of realism. This is like the fucking rabbit hole he talked about. It's not even lucid. I feel like I'm dreaming, the world blurring by until

THE END

I get to him again. And the instant I'm there pain ricochets along my back, making me yell into his open face. He smiles, a look of satisfaction, pride even, settling on his features. He just taps his hand to the noise, his fingers creating a rhythm of his own as he drums them on the chair and watches me. This is my performance, isn't it? This is for him, no one else. That's what I offered when I came out on this stage in the first place. Whatever is coming is coming because I said yes and he asked it of me in his own way.

My chin gets comfortable against the wooden table, my hands finding calm beside it as I stare at him and watch his smile increase. He is proud, happy. This is making him happy. Me being here and taking this, offering it, is making him happy. It warms me, softening my temper and making me gaze into his eyes for comfort. They're full of love as he stares back, watching nothing but my eyes and letting me slip into him. And just as I'm falling, getting lost in them, another stabbing pain lands, shunting my body forward with the impact of it. I grit my teeth to the feeling, remembering the pain he delivers and knowing that nothing is going to hurt as much as that. And it's quiet here now anyway. I've become acclimatised to what's happening because I can see my reflection in his eyes. It's just the two of us. Proving ourselves.

Blow after blow comes down on me, weakening my resolve to stay focused on him with every landing. Eventually it makes me mumble, begging for it to stop, or carry on. Either way, it makes me ache to have something inside me, filling the void he left open by not allowing me to come earlier. The thought forces a sneer from me as I sigh out, imagining his cock buried in me as this carries on. I grip the end of the table, thinking of the way he fucks into me or touches himself. It helps me concentrate, or get further lost in his self-indulgence.

He smirks as another thwack hits my arse, making me squirm and buck, my neck yanking against the constriction it's under as I groan and think of him. I'm drooling before I've rectified the sensation, my arse raising ready for the next impact as I imagine him pushing himself into my mouth. Oh god, I want to come so bad, and the sight of his tongue licking those lips, my eyes focused solely on it as it travels across them, is making me desperate to release. My fingers curl over the table edge, gripping on for dear life as I try to rub my clit against the table, force an orgasm to happen.

He nods, I'm not sure what at. I'm too fascinated by the face in front of me to care, too engrossed in the sound of his breathing changing as I arouse him, even though I can barely hear it above the din. I want too, though. I want to be so close I can feel his breath on my cheek as he grunts and groans. I want his arm curled around me while he does it, his hand grasping my hair. And I want this fucker behind me to spank me, or hit me with something more powerful than the crop he's been using. Its sharp sting hasn't held any weight to it. I need blunt force, like Blaine's. I need heavy and undiluted, a sense of ownership on me, around me. Not this weak teasing. It's useless, making me frustrated with a lacking depth to the sensation. I'm dirty, truly fucking filthy. Blaine has always been right. I've been lost in a world of clichés, just as he said, not truly fitting into them and frantic for something new to reawaken me.

THE END

Another blow lands, this time embedding itself with more fever. It's thicker across my skin, its landing area wider. It's like a blanket over me, covering me. It eclipses all my skin, warming it and readying me for orgasm. I grunt out again and close my eyes, letting the pain intensify as another lands and sends me delirious with need. My body bucks and squirms. My thighs tremble. My skin is on fire as I writhe, trying to gain more purchase against the surface and rubbing.

It's all just becoming a haze of need again. A frantic search for release. I need something inside me. I need Blaine inside me. I'd do that in this minute, fuck for everyone to see. If he came and got on top of me now and drove himself inside, I'd let him, not giving a fuck for all these people. Maybe if I beg he'll do it. He likes me begging. Likes my little moans and mewls of need, likes my screams of pain too. Perhaps Daddy needs a little waking up.

"Fuck me," the words come out softly, barely audible really, surprising me. They're so quiet, in fact, that I can't believe I've said them aloud in front of all these people. The guy behind me knows, though, because the blows stop instantly. My arse rises again, hardly able to stop itself from presenting for more as I open my eyes and stare at what I want. He's still there, completely focused on me. "Fuck me." He gazes back, his hand coming to his mouth, slowly, deliberately antagonising me with it as he wipes it across the mouth I want. "Baby girl's desperate, Daddy. Please, fuck me."

The slow spread of his smile is glorious, making me writhe my arse about more, flaunting it to him and begging for what he's got. I'm so far in love with this man I couldn't care less anymore. Whatever he wants, he'll get. If this is it. If this is normality for him, then he can have it. Screw the dates. Screw anything other than fucking and smiling. We'll find our laughs in here, where dirty floors and submissives meet, gladly.

He stands, his tongue licking his lips as he walks over the front of the stage so we're eye level. I don't look at anything but him. I couldn't even if I wanted to. I'm transfixed. Locked. We're together irrespective of the distance separating our skin. None of the rest exists anymore. No viewing guests. No concerns other than him. Just us in this room full of air and darkness. He tilts his head, lowering it to get beneath my gaze of him and look up to me.

"Are you asking for something?" Oh god, yes I am. I'm asking for everything. My arse bucks again, my fingers stretching for his skin as I try to widen my legs, regardless of the fact he's in front of me. I can feel him there already, feel it in his gaze of my lips. "Beg again for me, little dove."

I hate that I'm doing it. I do, but it doesn't stop the need, or the ache.

"Please."

"More."

"Please, Blaine." He smiles again, the crinkling of his eyes warning me of a love I shouldn't think of, let alone want more of.

"More. Here. In front of the crowd. Say it louder for me." I feel the tears come. They scream up the back of my neck, begging for their own release as much as I'm begging him to fuck me. I need him. Or I want him. Or I can't do anything without him. It's a horrendous feeling, evaporating normality, tearing it to shreds and making me desperate for him inside me. My fingers reach again, my whole body straining to connect our skin.

"Please. What do you want?" I scowl at him, the snarl landing through shear frustration. "Take me. Please. Do it. Fuck me. Please."

There's a pause, his brow raising as he stands back upright and looks over to the left of the room. My body instantly rakes at the strap around my neck again, trying to lift my body away from the table. I'm not even embarrassed or self-conscious, I'm furious. Enough so that I snap my teeth in fury, my arse and frame still thrashing to get off and prove my frustration.

"Stay on the table," he says quietly, his head nodding at something in the wings.

"Why, so you can have more fun? Screw you." It spits out of me, venom laced and ready to kill anything within ten foot of my body. The grab at my chin is so fast, and so sharp, I yelp in response to it, my body instantly stilling itself. He crouches again, his eyes coming so close to mine I back my head away for focus.

"Don't you make me show them what they want, Alana," he murmurs, his fingers digging in sharper to warn me of what's going on. It makes me snatch a glance back at the room, my breath stilted through my exertions and my insides going crazy now he's on me again. "They don't want to see you pleasured. They want me to provide a fucking show." My mouth opens, the reality of what's happening here racing back to me as I glance at the crowd again and really see them again for the first time. I've been so absorbed in my own hedonism I forgot, or didn't care, maybe I still don't. I look back at him, letting the ache between my thighs embed itself further and remind me of his touch. It's still as solid as it always is, still as dependable in its own way. *Whatever he wants. Whatever we need.* The words linger as our breath mingles and mine calms, our eyes connected and me falling further into them with every passing second. It's our rabbit hole to fall into, isn't it? Our wonderland. Mine, anyway.

"I love you. Do whatever you want," I say, my voice trembling around the thought. "There isn't a thing you could do to make me love you less. Do this."

He backs away, a confused frown descending to replace the anger that was pitched at me. Good, I'm glad he's confused, because this fucking room and whatever I'm doing in it is all for him. He might have brought me here for a lesson of my own, might even have thought this would show me something, but this writhing and bucking, this ache, it's all about Blaine and the way I feel for him. It's about us.

Chapter 9

BLAINE

The words shake from her lips as I watch her and snarl at her reasoning. Love, it's a fucking ridiculous notion for the pain this crowd want from me. The pain my body wants to inflict on her isn't for this room. It's for my den, or my beach. It's for the private confines of my mind, should I wish to show her what she's asking for. This damned love interweaves us. It confounds the show, makes it seem insolent to touch her here, no matter how much she begs me for it.

I growl again and listen to the music starting, ready to attack the room for being here in the first place. Nothing is private here. Nothing has any sense of seclusion. Oliver's show might be renowned, important ostensibly as it glorifies us all, but regardless this wasn't supposed to be the outcome of her learning. She was made to show herself for her own benefit, so she could understand her need to submit, not so that I would fall at the first hurdle and want nothing more than to tear skin from her bones. The thought makes me sigh and remember the feel of my cock in her as I watched her scream and pant, the rest of the crowd grunting behind me as they watched on. That thought conjures up more visions as I keep staring at her body, the rise and fall of it as elegant as it always fucking is, making me want to force anything to hand straight into her.

"Please, Blaine."

Please, please, please.

I flick her chin away from me. The sound of those words drive me insane with need, my hand tightening in my own pocket as I glare at her ability to reach into me. She tears the fucking heart out of me, wrenches at it as if it's nothing but paper to be shredded as and when she chooses. I despise her for it. Loathe her. Fucking adore her.

I close my eyes and try to let the music remind me of my ocean, let its ebb and flow clam me back to something resembling human formation. But all I can hear is her voice now across the clipped nuances of notes, begging and pleading, pulling me back to who the mob want from me.

"Let her up," comes from my mouth, my hands still clenching and releasing.

I hear the commotion rather than see it as her heels scatter the floor. It's enough for me to let my body walk me towards the steps to the stage, her noise becoming part of me no matter how I choose to deny it. It pulls me to her, egging me into something that neither of us should choose.

"Blaine?" Oh, the fucking sound of it. It has a luxury tied to its frustration. A relief. It causes visions of fucking and pleasure-seeking, of decadence. Just her voice and I'm shaking, regardless of my outward sense of composure. None of these others need to see this, and yet, one part of me wants to show them that even sadists like me can love, that we have that ability if we find a mate who dares brave us. The indecision makes me smile and open my eyes as I walk up the steps, knowing I'll find her waiting. The result of her body hovering in front of me, the back of her dress still open as she hovers there, is debilitating to sadists such as I. She glows again, the mask hiding nothing from me as she stands tall in her new found self. She may care less now for these people than I do, perfectly content in her need as she stares back. Whether it's because of a true sense of love or not is questionable, irrespective of her belief it is, because it wasn't me that wound her up on this stage, it was these other two bastards.

She doesn't say anything as I move across to her, nor does she kneel, she simply pants and scowls. It makes me consider the best thing to do with her as the music carries on, its dark notes elevating our desire to an unachievable merit here. Perhaps a dance would be best, something to drive us closer and improve the show for these other fools. I'm not fucking her here, no matter how she begs. I'm not sharing her cunt with anything. Ever.

I move around the back of her, watching her body still further as I gaze at the marks on her shoulders and ass. Good little Brat. Slight stripes, reddened imprints, nothing that will scar like my own still lingering beneath this corset. I lick my lips at the image of them, remembering her cunt in clamps and the way the pitch of her yelps were different for me. It makes me want to see her on display, all of her. I glower at the thought of the audience, almost forgetting they're here. Fucking sadists and their little shows. They're as irritating to me as the occasional screams of their subs, annoying my eardrums and stopping me hearing Alana's breath. They're nothing but a damned pit of disrepute, willing us all into our darkest needs. It's the reason I've only been to one before, perhaps choosing to cage my magician after the first time, let him be stagnant and dormant. Still, it doesn't stop me moving into her and take hold of the dress to remove it, feeling the instant shiver that descends across her frame. In fact, in some ways, it drives me closer into her, wanting to forge the bond I keep distanced from her. Disband the room around us possibly. I smile again, enjoying how relaxed she's becoming as she helps me take the material from her. It peels slowly along her arms, showing the room her flawless skin as she moves to accommodate me peeling the other side too. And eventually all that's left is the body of a goddess, wrapped in heels, a mask, and a fucking corset. My cock instantly hardens again as I back off to gaze at her, the surge of desperation to deliver pain sweeping through my body, readying me for fucking and torture.

It riles me, regardless of her perfect posture and submission. It wakes the cantankerous primate who waits inside, priming every instinct, calling it out to play as I gaze on.

"I love you," she says, quietly. The sound of her softens the need, making me smile again and remember coming inside her. Soft and wet. Her nails digging in. The feel of her lips pulling me into her. And then she turns, her body twirling as if it floats rather than walks, all heaviness removed from the sound of her heels. "I do."

What I should do is beat her for announcing such a personal thing in a room full of idiots, but what I want to do is tell her I love her too. I want to hold her and show her there's a decent reason for loving me. Neither of which I will.

"Bend over," I say. "Show yourself to them. They're our guests." She frowns as I tap her ass, making it clear what I want this crowd to see. I couldn't give a fuck for their thoughts on the matter, only that she'll do what's asked when I ask it. That's what I need to maintain the control I need for her, not that I truly care for its pleasant attributes. She shunts sideways, still frowning at me but putting her cunt and ass on display for the room as she lowers her hands to the floor. "Do you feel that sensation?" She shudders as I run my fingers along her spine. "That's greed, Alana. You're greedy for them to see you. For me to see you." She grunts as I slap it, the sound reverberating around the theatre space. "You've got a gluttonous little cunt, haven't you?" She shivers and shakes again under my fingers as I drag them back along her spine, making my own sense of gluttony ache for her all to myself.

My hands pick up hers of their own accord, perhaps desperate to alleviate the tension in them on something softer than the round of her ass. It's a stirring few seconds, making me think of dancing again as I consider how long it actually is since I've danced a tango. At least all those years in private schools weren't wasted completely. At least something good comes of a sadist tamed.

"Dates," comes from me, as I gaze back into my ocean of blue seas. She smirks a little, still with that frown defacing her beauty. "It's what you asked for, isn't it? Or we could carry on with this crowd fucking you instead."

She shakes her head sharply as she beams back at me. It's an honest, open smile, one I don't see from her enough. It makes me think of love again, as our bodies begin to sway, not sure how to contain everything I want and give her love too.

"Interesting date," she mutters, her feet beginning to move with mine. I suppose it is, but then nothing with me will be as it would normally be. Nothing will be average or usual, not the typical version of it anyway.

"You've been a brat." She snorts, making me fucking smile as I lower her and flick her back up to me. She shouldn't think me entirely amusing. I'm pissed beyond belief that others have heard her howl, regardless of how fucking arousing it might have been. We turn again, the music beginning to flow into me as it had done all those years ago, the feel of her in my arms welcoming me into the home I refuse to need with her. "Teasing all these other men is dangerous for your health." She gasps as I tighten my fingers into her back just to fucking remind her who she belongs to.

"You put me up here, Blaine."

"No, you put yourself up here."

It's the one thing I wanted her to know about herself. It's why there was no warning, no conversation. I enabled her by denying her an orgasm, but she's the one who's been strong enough to show herself. She's strong enough for anything without me. She doesn't need me. Who fucking would? She just needed a small shove into finding herself, one I've given by keeping our distance. The thought riles me further as I spin her, aggravated with my own lack of abilities in love. It makes something ache inside me, levelling the feeling against the pain in my cock, as I let go of her hand and wrap her closer to me.

"For you," she says, her face slowly returning to mine as we turn again. She pants, the sound of it as infiltrating to me as the feel of her skin on mine. "I did it for you, Blaine."

THE END

We stop, or the fucking music does. Either way there's nothing but her face in front of me, stirring up something that damned well doesn't deserve to live here. I glower at her lips, warning them to stay the fuck away from what they're asking for, but nothing fucking changes. It's as desperate a plea for smothering as her whimpers when I make her come.

I shake my head at her, still feeling her crippling advance into a heart that merits nothing. There's nothing there worth loving. I need her to slow down. I can't control this. It's fucking freefall into an intemperance I can't contain. It boils inside my blood, heating me along with the sparks coming from her body. She doesn't know what these hands have done to another who loved them. I need submission, the correct route forward. Quiet control. Obedience. But this damned heart just keeps lurching for closer contact, enjoying her challenges, making me want to reach inside her and rip her apart for daring love.

I just keep staring, bemused as to what to do as her bones undulate in my hold, for once in my life juxtaposed in my own hesitation. Move forward, or deny yet again? I'm so consumed with the question I don't realise she's frowning and squirming for a moment, until she shakes in my hold and tries to move. Jeering's coming from the crowd, embarrassing her, I suppose. It makes me snarl at the lot of them and hold her tighter, unconcerned with what they think.

"Say it again," I snap, wanting nothing more than to hear her mean it so I can make a decision.

"What?" she says, her body trying to get away from me. Fuck that. We're not going anywhere until I quantify this feeling inside and do something with it. "Blaine, you're hurting me." I don't fucking care about that either. My fingers just bite in deeper, to the point of pushing her downwards.

"You want this, you fucking own it." I snarl, as her knees hit the ground beneath me, her face looking up at me in shock, purple fucking stripes framing her. "Say it again."

"What? That I did it for you?"

"Yes." I don't know what the fuck I'm asking her for now. Just something. Anything to make this whole fucking ache in my chest piss off.

"Why are you angry?" she says, her lips trembling, her body beginning to vibrate as I crouch down and glare at those fucking lips again. "Where have you gone? We were … What have I done wrong?" Been fucking perfection. That's what she's done. It's what she fucking does wrong every damn day. She glances at the crowd again, her face falling to the floor as they chant for more of my sadist to appear. They can fucking have it in a minute unless she owns herself, me along with her. This is what she needs to own. This version of me. She needs to lift her fucking eyes and tell me to stop. Tell me she loves me irrespective of this monster inside, the same one that's waging a war I can't win on my own. "I don't understand."

I sneer at the words, my fingers reaching for her chin to pull her back to me.

"Try harder."

Still she trembles in my hands, her feet scrabbling away and winding up my thoughts. It would all be so easy to just move forward now, just unleash myself and let her skin take the brunt of me. Everything's here. All the fun of the fair. My magician could revel in itself, enjoy her tears for a while and tow the monster along with it, but my aching heart longs for those fucking words again, something to tame me, form me into a person who deserves more.

"Please, Blaine." She glances around again, her eyes looking anywhere but at me. It pisses me off. She can challenge me on every other occasion but not on this? "I don't …" Screw her. And screw all this. I flick my hold of her chin away, infuriated with her lack of self-assurance and search the back of the stage for something to enthuse her mouth.

"Please what?" I grumble, as I return with a paddle and some hooks, kicking out at the table as I go to send the wheels skating towards her. "What the fuck are you asking for?" She shivers there, her arms tucked around herself and a look of undiluted fear gracing her features. That pisses me off too, reminding me of what I want to do to her when she begs. It confuses me, making my mind seem senseless. There's no quiet here, no feeling of calm descending to lose myself in. It's manic. A fucking riot of thoughts and images. "Fuck you." It growls out of me with as much fury as I've ever felt, seemingly elevating whatever fucking monster wants to play into a damned demon.

I've grabbed and dragged her up onto the table again before I've thought much more of it, uninterested with the concept of discussions. She'll say it when she's riled up, when she's forgotten all the noise around us and focused in on the only concentration worth merit. She's said it before, she'll fucking say it again. She'll say it when she's yelping and screaming, and she'll beg me to carry on as she does, owning the fucking air I breathe because of it.

"Look at them," I spit, my hand levering the clips to her collar again, the other holding her neck in place as she struggles. "Look at them and remember me." She fights at the restriction, her hands lashing out at my legs, trying to get grip. I give one of them to her, happy to have her hanging onto me, suddenly wanting nothing more than for her to grasp onto me for eternity if that's what she chooses. "You learn what this means from me. I'll expect a fucking answer by the end of it."

The paddle lands hard and awkwardly, cutting into her hipbone rather than the flesh I aimed for. Stupid brat. She bays into the air, her yelp exciting the morons in front of us. I glare at the buck that comes back at me, watching the instant pinking of her skin and attempting to contain my own mirth at the fact. She should say still, give me a prone body to play on. Be a better landing surface.

The second lands just as hard, the angle of it against her thigh enough to make her yell out and then silence her noise. I feel it instantly in her hold on my leg as she loosens her grip and sighs, drifting off into her private space as I let another one land on her. A heckler dares to laugh in the audience, aggravating my mood. It makes me spin on the noise, my fingers holding her firm, grounding her against me as I let my blood boil on for the man that dares laugh.

"One more laugh and I'll come find you. Use you instead of use her."

There's an eerie hush after that. It makes me glare into the dark and wish it was a man beneath my hands for a second, but then her pulse quickens in my fingers, pulling me back to her again. A whimper escapes her, her mouth trying to form words. Nothing comes, though.

Only another small whimper as I send the paddle home again and wait for more enthusiasm to come. Nothing this time. No sound. No affirmation of pain. Even her neck relaxes in my hold, her body giving way to the treatment it wants as her hand lets go of me entirely.

I move back and trace her legs, feeling the raised welt that's erupting already. If love was a consideration beforehand, it's now a desperation as I watch her body realise its need. It corrals every instinct inside me to offer her a home, a life, my fucking heart on a plate if I can relax within this every day. And I can't stop my roaming fingers from inching between her spread thighs, needing to feel her arousal on my hands, needing to taste it as I take some from her and lift it to my lips. It glistens and glints in the bright light above us. Showing me how wet she's become, how ready for me she is. And fuck do I want inside her. I ache for it as much as the hole in my chest beats for her to stitch it together. The thought makes me scan her again as I lick my hands, considering the fucking I said I wouldn't do.

"Please," she says, more reverent whimpering following the plea. "Love me."

My smile breaks through as I let my finger suck out of my mouth, my heart wanting nothing more than to love her. She says it so sweetly, as if it's the only thing she wants. Love her. Yes. I can do that for her. I can love and cherish her. That's what the priests say, isn't it? They talk of commitment and oaths of trust. Bonding. Lives spent together searching for destinations, perhaps aimless wandering beneath my stars. "Just say it, Blaine. Let me have it all."

Not here.

THE END

I look at her lips moving as she stares into the mob, a continued chorus of words coming from them. Mused, barely coherent. Certainly not audible to the crowd, but I can hear them tumbling from her. She talks of love and passion, lust, fucking and sleepless nights. She might as well be reciting my mind's untidy ramble, creating order within it. They all make me look at the leather around her throat, suddenly realising its worth in my community. It swells an emotion in me I haven't felt before, forging sentiments of honour and truth. Enough so that I let my magician rise again, willing him to decimate the connection before it's too late for her to live free of me.

"Please, Blaine. I need you."

I force my eyes away from her, skimming the floor I'm standing on rather than let any other thought take hold. She deserves so much more than I've already inflicted, but the rise of her ass as I try not to look, the way her body lays here patiently, it proves her being. It acknowledges her need, making me lift my eyes to the rest of the mob, knowing any one of them would taint her without any care. She'll search for it now, be desperate for these sensations again whether I let her go or not. Responsibility and self-indulgence mingle inside me, collaborating this sense of love into an all-consuming hunger. It has no rationale, no application of psychology. It's as instinctual as my need to fuck into her. As tempering as my need to evolve.

"Who do you belong to?" I ask, my body weaving around the table again, errant damned fingers apparently incapable of staying away from her skin.

"You."

I could tell her I feel the same. I could give her that thought, but I won't do it here. Instead I unhook the clips and point at the floor, needing to see her agreement, acknowledge its true worth in this world of mine. Not that I truly care for its pronouncement. Only that I need to know she does. It's intrinsic in my guts, a part of who I am. A part of what we'll need to survive this storm she's creating in me. She looks a little startled for a moment, as she raises to sit on the table, but does exactly what my little dove should do before she gets a punishment. She drops to her haunches and lowers, gracefully accepting the position and giving me that part of her she fights against.

"Crawl for me," growls out, as I start walking away, partly amused by the notion that she'll follow on her knees wherever I ask. The humiliation of it in front of this crowd should remind her who I am, give her a sense of my wants. But the feeling of watching her as I pick up her dress and she begins following, her ass high in the air and begging to be fucked, proves the sentiment of humiliation incomplete. I'm not enamoured by the humiliation, I'm enamoured by the way she moves. Captivated by her trail after me. It stirs more feelings of love as I watch her frame come for me, the position of it as decimating as the burden she'll carry for me.

Good little dove. Charming.

There's noise in the room again as I walk to the curtain, hooking it back for her. Hollering and cat calling, an uprising of jeers and disappointment at my lacking show. I don't hear it, nor care for its opinion on what I am becoming because of her. She softens this monster of mine. Contains him somehow. Perhaps smooths his explosive edges to a more familiar breed of respectable. Either way, we're going on a date of her choosing. A place she can see differently because of this bond we have created together. She can have her dinners and her wine. Drink until she's drunk and show me who she is that way, rather than me forcing it though my magicians tricks. We can be honest with each other. Attempt a consideration of respectability.

"A little disappointing," Oliver says, his yellow suit arriving in my eye line. I've backhanded him before I've recovered from the insult, my other hand letting the curtain fall back behind Alana's ass. He tumbles away clutching his face as I turn and glare at his rudeness, ready to deliver another blow to rowdy fucking mouths who do not get to judge me. No one here gets to judge me. Only Eloise's dead eyes have that right, and perhaps this madam kneeling at my feet should she choose to play with that thought.

"Enough? Or another to prove my worth?" I snap, buttoning my jacket up as I do and holding a hand down to Alana. He snarls as she takes my hand, his face a picture of contempt. "You can get up now, little dove."

"Really, Mr Jacobs. What am I supposed to do with them now? You've left them baying for blood."

I'm not interested in blood. For once, I'm interested in anything but blood unless it's seeping out of steak and accompanied by a good Beaujolais.

"You can go back," Alana says, her hand wiping at her knees. "I don't mind." We both stare at her as she rises back up, astonished at her superiority given her crawling 30 seconds ago. "Finish the performance with something that will enjoy it." She takes the dress out of my hand, her smile a picture of refinement in this back stage bedlam. "I know you want too." She looks at Oliver, a sneer embedding onto her features. "And if it's so fucking important to his little performance then .."

"No," I cut in, pushing Oliver out of the way. I don't want to. I want dinner and dates. I want what she asked me for. I want to revel in this feeling she forces into me, perhaps dance some more then go home and fuck until she bleeds. I don't give one fuck about the crowd. "We're leaving." My hand reaching for hers without thought. Oliver throws his arms around, proclaiming something that's of no interest to me or the woman in my hold. We're gone from here. This is all as desolate as the place I used to live in before her. It's lonely here. It reminds me of times I don't want anymore, memories I'm not wanting to reside in any longer.

"That was brattish," I snap, dragging her along behind me as she reaches for her bag and snatches a bottle of champagne as we go. "Oliver has power here." She laughs, the bottle going up to her mouth as we keep walking through the throng of bodies. "It was rude of you to chastise him." Rude enough that I should beat her for her insolence.

"Fuck Oliver," she says, another gulp sinking down her neck. And that certainly was. Although, the sentiment's correct, and my smile just keeps spreading regardless of the filth in her mouth.

"That deserves a beating."

"Good. Because, honestly, if I don't get to come sooner or later I'm going to fucking explode."

The tone of her makes me laugh as I duck through the hall, searching the corridors for somewhere useful to let her come in. "And fuck you, too." That makes me halt and spin on her, considering just doing it here for the damned world to see. She raises a brow and lifts the champagne to her lips, challenging me with all she's got.

"Be careful, little dove."

"Please? Does that help? The begging? I can beg again if you want," she says, her fingers hitching her dress up as she leans against a wall, like my good little slut. "Just one little orgasm, please?" I smirk at her as she shakes her hips and widens her legs. "Baby girl's desperate. Needy."

Good, baby girl can fucking wait for her treat then. I drop her hand and snatch the champagne to throw it in the trash, amused with her brattish behaviour, but not giving her the reaction she wants.

"You can't wind me up that way, little dove," I say, leading her out through a quiet entrance of the building. There's only one way she can get what she wants out of me, and it's to do with her reaching inside me and pulling my heart to pieces with those nails she owns. "Do you know how many brats I've tamed?"

"No, don't care either," she says, sullenly, her hair flicking in my face as we arrive at the car. "You don't want a tamed brat, Blaine. You want a brat who you can tame on occasion." I smirk, opening the door for her and watching her slide in, slapping her ass as she goes. She laughs, making me smile wider. Which pisses me off as much as the analogy she's foraging her way through in an effort to find what I hide. "You could have any of those other brats drooling over you the entire time, I'm sure." True. It's as monotonous as the tedium life was in before her. "You want someone to know when's the right time to submit, and when's not, don't you?" Bitch. Loathsome, exasperating, beautiful bitch. "You want a woman to argue with, fight with." I slide in beside her, turning to face the font of all fucking knowledge as she fucks around with her dress and reaches for my hand again. "And whether you want to believe it or not, you want to love."

    Bitch.

Chapter 10

ALANA

We've danced all night, slowly, to music I wouldn't have considered his type of style. It's been refreshing, offering me a side of him I've only seen on a few occasions. He's been light hearted. Sweet even a few times. I've not paid for a thing, not been able to open a door on my own, and not even been able to go to the loo without a chaperone. It's been rewarding in some ways, like I've been offered a reprieve for my behaviour with him. Been given my date. Been shown who he is without the force attached to his hands. It's also been clichéd, something that's made me realise this isn't him. It isn't us.

We're sat in a restaurant come club, two bottles of red wine on the table as I stare across them at him, and something akin to the Tango we danced to going on in the background. The whole place is full of dramatic theatre, not unlike the place we left earlier, but far more luxurious. It's high end. Full of other people wearing expensive clothes and expensive suits. A small band's playing the music while a woman sings her heart out to no one in particular. And waiters scurry around, their uniforms as pristine as the venue itself is. It's lacking in something, though. Lacking in dirt maybe. It's as beautiful as it should be and yet so cleansed of filth it makes me want to run back to Oliver's cabaret. This is the kind of date I went on before him. Wined and dined. Subtle gestures of appreciation. The occasional brush of a hand, a smile, the last of the red poured into my glass before he orders another one. But it all seems redundant, as if the very heart of me wants nothing to do with its dreariness.

"Ask me about my life," he says, breaking me of my mused thoughts.

"What?" I look at him as he shrugs out of his jacket and lays it down beside him, the tie coming loose as he tugs at it.

"Anything. I'll tell you."

I stare again, unsure what someone asks of a man like him. It's odd all of a sudden, like I'm uncertain if I even care about his past anymore, or what he's got up to in it. Everything seems so clarified lately, like there isn't any reason to be muddled. Well, apart from working out Mr Jacobs, anyway. I laugh lightly, thinking how it all seems so long ago, as if the last week or so has taken a lifetime to achieve, but the impact of him has been so profound it's changed everything. I sigh out, not knowing how to word the conversation I really want to have about where this goes from here, how I return to normality without him once my stay is over. It's barely plausible to imagine myself in my own apartment now, the creams and light tones echoing a life I thought I knew. I should be there now, writing. I should be like Bree will be. Nose down, mind driving me onto another chapter as I attempt to get lost in a character. Instead I'm here, blissfully unaware of the texts, notifications or emails that usually keep coming at me, and contemplating my future with a man who's shown me something I knew nothing of. A new kind of life.

I shake my head at the thought, a small smirk lingering on my lips because of it, and grind my sore backside into the chair.

"Okay. Why did you stop teaching?"

"I do teach," he says, reflecting my smirk. Arse.

"No, you know very well what I mean."

He takes a sip of his drink and lowers it to the table carefully, his hands clasping together as he looks at me. Something about the move makes me question if the truth's going to leave his lips or not. He might as well tell me it all. He's got nothing to hide from me. It doesn't matter. Nothing does really, only the feel of his skin on mine, or the smell of his aftershave as he leans over and fucks into me. Everything else is becoming a blur of nonsensicality. I'm not even sure what I've been doing with my life before him. The thought of going back now, of doing what I did, of trying to achieve those deadlines and targets, feels like it's a million miles away and slipping further every day.

"Something happened that made it an impossibility to teach in that way anymore."

"Like what?"

"That I can't tell you."

"Can't or won't?"

"Won't."

"Why not?" He cocks a brow at me, his smirk disappearing to produce a look of confusion, one that suits him less than the look of sorrow I get on occasion.

"Because your opinion of me will change, Alana. I'm not ready for the outcome of that change. I'm not finished with you."

He says the last of it with such finality I know I won't get it out of him, and I don't really care anyway. It's not like he's a killer or anything. And I'm doubting men like Blaine molest anything underage. Anything underage would break in his hands. What use would that be to someone like him? The thought sickens my stomach, turning it over as I gaze at questioning eyes, wondering if I should ask anyway, just to be sure. I shake my head at the outlandish idea, relegating it to the back of my mind as I drink down a glug of wine to cleanse the thought. It's horrendous, frankly.

"When will you be done with me?" He smiles, nothing more. No answer, no gesture of time constraints, and certainly no offer of the commitment I'm still after from him. I sigh at the lacking result, unsure about bothering to push the conversation. He's clearly not in the same place as me at all. Or if he is he's not going to talk about it until he's ready. "Okay, well your turn, I suppose," I say, not able to form another question in the myriad of questions I've had for weeks.

"What made you dye your hair?" I laugh slightly, stunned at the question.

"Of all the questions you could ask, you ask that?"

"Yes."

"Well, I guess I got bored. Needed a change perhaps." I twirl a lock of it, snorting at the colour and wondering why I chose purple in the first place, then remembering him picking up my first trilogy. The thought warms me as I stare at him, recalling how much passion was in those words all that time ago. "You don't know what my life is like in the real world. It's just a continuation of the same day after day. Same words, same love story. Same meetings, same offices. It's why I started this story. A new pen. Fresh perspective. I needed the change of direction."

"And I'm a change to your monotony, am I?"

"Oh, you most definitely are, Mr Jacobs," I reply, amused at the concept. He pulls in a breath and leans away, his eyes looking to the dancefloor and over the rail we're behind as if he's offended. "I didn't mean you were a one off, you know? I'm not saying that this is .." Oh, I don't know what I'm saying anymore. And he's the one that said he'd fuck the monotony out of me. He has. Well done him. "I didn't mean that you're a fling." Or maybe I did. Maybe that's exactly what this is, regardless of the love I feel.

There's no movement from him as he carries on gazing downwards, his body leaning into the rail. He smiles, enough to make me wonder why he's smiling at all given my frenzied ramble. I look down to and see an older couple dancing. The man's hands placed carefully, the woman perfectly balanced in his arms.

"You think they knew, all those years ago?" he asks. Knew what? "They're married. They've been dancing in this building for years, regardless of the two generations after them who run it for them. The atmosphere might have changed, but they remain. Still dancing to the same beat."

"What?"

"Mr and Mrs Renovevi," he muses, nodding his head at them. "I've watched them dance here for years. I always wondered how they knew, if they knew."

"You've come her often?" The thought bothers me. I don't know why. Perhaps because I thought he didn't do dates. He told me that. Why would you come here to eat alone? Especially given the first place he took me to eat. Which was nothing like this opulence.

"Never on a date, Alana. Don't be brattish." He chuckles and leans back into his seat, presumably amused at his own acknowledgement of the word. "My parents used to bring us here when we were young. Teach us our table manners." He sits back and gazes at me, his fingers reaching for the wine again. "Cole would behave like a brat and produce a face similar to yours now. Stop it," he continues, pointing at me from his glass. "Clearly our Mother's swatting didn't work on him. Mine will on you."

"You lived around here?"

"Mmm. In the hills. Penchley Estate. This is my home town." The thought makes me grin. He might not have parents who are alive, but we're here in his home town. It's akin to introducing me to them, making me realise that all isn't quite as it seems under that thick skin of his.

"You brought me home, Mr Jacobs."

"I guess I did, Miss Williams." He chuckles quietly and gazes at me for a minute. It's a sweet moment, filled with feelings neither of us are saying. It still seems so strange that we can't talk about this. All the things we've done. All the holes he's been inside. All the tension he's put me under. Saving me from the sea only to cause more pain again. And yet here, now, there's an uncomfortable air from both of us. "So, what do you think? Did they know they'd be together forever when they met?"

THE END

I look down at them again, smiling at the vision of the two of them in their old age. They're so in tune with each other. Her feet moving along with his, not one part of her faltering or changing direction until he shows the way. The sight highlights Blaine's hands on me, the way he holds me together, regardless of the direction he chooses to take me in. The pain he causes.

"I'd like to think so. Wouldn't everyone?"

He stands up abruptly, making me frown at him as he smiles back and offers me his hand.

"Shall we?"

"Again?"

"Yes, again." I chortle and put my wine down, moving the tablecloth to get out and stand next to him, his hand linking into mine before I have a chance to fathom why he wants to keep dancing. Not that I care. I'd dance with him all night, all year even, just to feel the heat of him and sense of ownership around me. I smile at him as he leans in, his mouth filtering a soft kiss on my lips, his other hand tugging a lock of my hair gently. "As much as we can, Alana, before I take you home and forget this part of me exists."

He turns and walks on, his hand towing me with him, a part of me in a daze at his words as I try to figure out why any of this needs to be forgotten. This, him being like this, is as much a part of him as the other version. I just need to get to know him better, need to feel this around me. He needs to show it to me more often, let it become normal for him.

"You don't have to, you know, forget him I mean. I quite like this side of you." He tugs me to him as we reach the dance floor, a vicious pull that snaps my body into his, my chest bouncing on him as I collide with it. It makes me grunt with the force of it, air puffing out of me as he wraps a hand around my back and holds me close to him.

"But your cunt needs my mouth on it," he whispers, "It still needs teaching its fucking manners."

And there he is again, reminding me of the man who wants to hurt me just for pleasure as his fingers grip into my waist. It's nice in some ways to have him back. Soothing. It causes the shyness to seep back inside of me, his to disappear completely, making me okay with what's happening around us again. It's calming. The air between us on a level playing field again maybe. It makes me lean my head on his chest and look at the older couple who dance the same rhythm, imagining his beach at home, perhaps wondering if I'll walk it forever or just for the next few weeks. I wish I had more answers than he'll give to me, because this isn't about my book anymore. Or the amphetamines that disappear more with every passing day. It's my love story, isn't it? It's my Once Upon A Time. It's a journey I've yet to see the end of, let alone understand if there is an end for. This man holding me, his breath filtering into my hair as he tempers his hold a little and lets me lean on him, is becoming the entirety of my life. He's skin deep. Heart deep, no matter the way I try to keep my beating blood away from tales of love. He's just there, here, his hands continuing to cajole me, his lips warming me, and his mind warping into mine, joining us. Keeping me strong. Keeping me quiet.

~

THE END

The wind whips through the trees as I gaze at an old house, its perfected gardens covering the space around it. It's a huge wooden place, the white boards neatly running the outlines, countering the solidity of the brick structure around them. It's beautiful. A place I could imagine children running in and pets playing. A real family home. A rich family's home at that.

"You grew up rich," I say, wrapping my fur coat around me to keep the cool evening chill off my skin. He snorts, apparently disgusted with my question.

"Still am, if you choose to count monetary value as worth."

He pushes the gates open and walks in, instantly making my hand grab at him. What the hell's he doing? We can't just wander into someone else's home.

"We can't go in, Blaine."

"Why not? It's mine," he says, glaring at my hand on his arm. I slowly pull it away, startled by his reaction to me touching him given the last few hours. "Mine and Cole's anyway. It was my parent's house." Oh.

"You still own it?"

I don't know why I said that. Perhaps it's just the hope at conversation again, because that seems to have stopped ever since we got in the car to come here, as has touch, it seems. He doesn't answer me as he keeps going, his fingers dragging through some tall flowers on the way up the drive. It makes me think of him when he was young, imagining him playing here with his brother, enjoying their life. It's not something I can see at all. No images of him smiling or being free. No thoughts of happy families. No sense at all of him being hugged by his parents or given gold stars for good behaviour. It's like, to me, that version was lost a long time ago, or perhaps he never had it to lose.

I walk after him slowly, keeping my distance as I look at the surrounding grounds and wonder who keeps it all so neat.

"How often do you come out here?" I ask, hoping that might spark conversation again. He looks at the house for a minute, tracing the lines of it and then begins ambling again.

"I haven't been here for years," he eventually replies, still wandering and now smiling up at the windows. "I think Cole comes more often, stays on occasion when he fucks something of no importance. The town is full of meaningless encounters for him."

He seems melancholy after that, his body weaving through paths to get us around to the back. We end up in a large formal lawn, a stepped terrace down to a wishing well sitting in the middle of it, more flowers surrounding it. He just stares at it sadly, as if it holds some memory he won't let me have. So I move in a little closer, hoping to get it from him, help him maybe.

"I used to throw my money in here," he murmurs as I reach him, "wishing for things to change." I frown, wondering what that means. "Cole would spend all his. Girls he took out. Bikes. Computer games. All I did was keep throwing mine down there, wishing I could fuck like everyone else did. Wondering what was wrong with me."

I move in to put my hand on his arm, but he flinches, making me feel unwanted in his gloomy mood. So I back away again, leaving him to his musings and turn to look at the house instead. Whatever's going on in his head, he's not letting me into it for the time being.

Perhaps it's not my memory to have, and presumably emotion isn't a thing he achieves well.

I sigh and look up at the windows. 18 in total, three levels, all framing a huge set of doors that lead to this terrace in front of me. It really is grand, but in a homely way. It reeks of love and informal meetings. Warm fresh bread. Sunday morning brunches. Those back doors thrown wide, two small boys racing out of them and into the grounds as guests come round for drinks and the like.

"Tell me about your mum and dad," I say, trying to break this sadness that seems to have descended. "What did they do?"

"Politicians. Mother was. Father was her marketing agent." He snorts directly behind me, surprising me as he slides a hand around my waist and looks up at the house with me. "He made more money doing that than she did trying to feed the poor. Interesting perspective on wealth."

"You don't sound like you like it much," I reply, gently placing my hand on his, wanting nothing more than to connect us this way if he'll let me in. This is what we need to move on from the rules he's applied. I need this, as does he.

"I don't like people who use it to fund irrational behaviour and self-indulgent whims," he mutters.

He slides his hand away after that, his body moving away from me in the same instant. It makes me frown, bothered at the thought of all of his distance as I watch him go up to the back door. What was the point of showing me this if not to open up?

He pockets his hands when he gets there and stares again, looking at the doorknob as if it's the last thing he ever wants to touch.

For the first time it makes me consider his upbringing, really consider it, trying to comprehend what made him the way he is. Did something happen to change him, something that maybe caused this sense of anger?

"Is that why you chose Psychology as a profession?" I call, my arms still wrapped around me. "Did it help?" Still he doesn't move as I try to find the right words. "I mean, did something happen with your parents? Did they screw you up?"

He swings back towards me so sharply I falter backwards, his eyes coming at me as quick as his steps as he crosses the ground.

"Don't ever fucking speak ill of my parents," he snarls. I stand my ground, raising my chin to meet him. Nothing frightens me about him, not anymore. I've been under those hands, dealt with them. And he would never hit me out of venom or frustration anyway, regardless of his needs. It's not his style. "They were good people, Alana. They did nothing to me but show love." The words break my heart for some reason, wondering if that's the whole reason he's so closed down on emotions. Perhaps a little boy lost just lost his sense of love when he needed it most. "I'm the damn failure here, not them."

I gaze at him as he glares, never once removing my eyes. If he wants to stare into someone's soul, know that he has that to fall on if he needs to, he can. He can gaze at me forever if he chooses that comfort. If he needs it. I just need some more words from him, something to make me believe it entirely rather than this paused attempt at momentum he keeps inflicting. The thought makes me smile as I keep looking back, tracing the contours of a face that's softening with every second that passes. He needs me. He needs this version of me that hasn't flinched as he came at me. I stood up to him, showed him he doesn't scare me. It makes him glance away eventually, his head turning back for the door, then coming back to me again. His fingers reach for my face, another thing I don't flinch at nor move away from. He rubs the sides of it, a slight sigh coming from his mouth as he does.

"It's okay, Blaine. It's fine. Be who you need to be." He grinds his teeth for a minute, still twirling my hair, then turns for the door again and leaves me to follow.

"You still think something happened to make me this way, don't you?" he grumbles.

"Yes." There's no point in lying. There's no route forward with lies between us. I don't want them. I don't want lies, or deceit. It's the only way I'll survive the storm he is. I need all the information, all the fear, tantrums if he'll give those to me, too, because without it what is this? What am I? That makes me just someone he can beat when he needs it. I'm more than that. I wouldn't be at his family home if I was any less.

"Think you can fix me, do you?"

"Do you need fixing?" He chuckles at that, his fingers finding some keys and inching one into the door. "As far as I can tell, you're perfectly fine the way you are." He pushes the door wide and walks in. "Short of the asshole behaviour on occasion." I might have mumbled that last bit.

"I told you I was," he says, dumping the keys on the small mahogany table as I walk through a large informal lounge. It's as perfect as the outside, making me gaze around at it. Cushions neatly placed, presenting themselves against the opulent furniture and fabrics.

Wallpaper adorning lavish decorative walls, the doors covered in mouldings and gilt edges. They really were wealthy.

"Do you want a drink?" he calls.

I turn to find him gone, the echo of his voice resonating against the interior.

"Yes. Brandy, please." I think I'll need one for whatever's coming.

I chuckle to myself as I wander out, looking around the hall and then turning my head to stare up at the landing. It's beautiful, all of it. As if it's been created with care and attention to detail, showing that loving family home the outside suggests.

I end up slipping my coat off as I walk to wherever the sound of him is coming from, occasionally tinkering with a photo here and there. They're all of people I don't know, none of them resembling Blaine. But then I reach one of a couple and recognise it immediately. It's the same one Bree showed me when she searched for Blaine. Archibald Jacobs, his hand wrapped around what I presume must be Blaine's mother.

"This is your father?" I ask, picking it up and carrying on along the hall. I study it as I go, trying to find a similarity between their faces, see some genes that unite Blaine with either of these two. There's nothing that I can see, apart from the fact they're both handsome men.

He's looking straight at me by the time I enter another room, the sound of clinking glasses leading me into it.

"Why do want to know all this?" he asks, a sulky haze gazing back at me. It makes me frown at him. Because that's what people do.

They learn about each other, find things they can help with, guide even if need be.

"Perhaps because you've had to ask that question, Blaine." He takes a sip of his drink and points at another one he's placed down by a sofa, the crinkle of his own brow mirroring mine. "You told me a while ago that I could only see you as my reflection for a while, that you would help me. I suppose I'm trying to do the same."

"I don't need your help, Alana. That's not what you're here for."

"Why am I here then?"

"What?"

"How is this helping me?"

"Dates."

"You haven't brought me to your family home for a date. You've brought me here for some other reason. It's something you need, not me. What is it?"

He hovers, his face stone cold, a glower forming to annihilate the slight frown that was there, before downing the rest of his drink and storming from the room. Seems pushing and needling is, for some reason this time, causing him to back off rather than move forward.

"Coward." It's mumbled from my lips, along with a few other expletives that shouldn't follow as I stare into space and sip my drink. But fuck it. I'm tired, and still very much in need of my damn orgasm. I've done all this for him and he can't open up? Idiot. We could be so much more than this façade of rehabilitation. I'm not even sure I need it anymore. Nothing shakes, not other than between my thighs, anyway. That still throbs with unknown depth, making me fidgety for finality. For him probably.

I snort as the brandy sinks through me, perhaps slightly tipsily given the amount I've drunk this evening. Not that I care. I deserve a drink for dealing with his moods. And, God, I want to laugh with him. Really laugh. That's what drinking should be for. I want to see him smiling and chuckling, showing me a part of him he keeps reserved from the world around him. I don't even know why I want it. Most people would run a mile at such treatment, not me, it seems. I need him like he's the other side of my coin, the sea that flows across my beach.

"Why do you keep pushing?"

I just tip my glass to my lips again and wait for whatever else comes from him. Perhaps I'll get another spanking for disobedience. Frankly, I couldn't care less. What is there to lose? In fact, now I'm imagining the thought, I'm quite turned on again as I take my next swig. He just huffs behind me, hovering in the doorway. Fuck him. I've not pushed anything until today. I've been obedient. Calm. I've taken everything he's delivered and learnt from it, made it relevant to my story, to my life actually. I've changed, become something happier than I was in some ways, and all because of him. But this lack of honesty from him. This refusal to acknowledge the very thing that made me accept any of this in the first place, it's fucking farcical. Annoying. Downright irritating to the skin he's plundered. I'm here, waiting for him. Following him wherever he leads.

"Oh, sit down for god's sake. Talk, Blaine. It's not hard." I swirl my drink again, staring at the ice cubes and wondering if his heart lives in them. "You brought me here, what for?"

"You're a mouthy little brat," he snaps, clearly infuriated with my tone. I turn my head over my shoulder to look at him, instantly remembering the feel of his hand on my arse because of his glare.

"Yes I am. I was the day we met, and I will continue to be so, regardless of your," I raise a brow at him, "...help." Screw him. Beautiful bastard that he is. "Will me begging and calling you Daddy help?"

"It's stupidity to rile me," he mumbles.

"No, it's just the only damn way I can get you to be fucking honest with me," I spit out, suddenly pissed at the whole situation he refuses to move onward with.

He looks as shocked as I feel given the venom attached to those words. But screw him. This is becoming intolerable. It's hot and cold. Day and fucking night. Spankings one minute, my arse on display to a room full of sadists, and then a date and bringing me home to meet mother. Well, not quite, but the sentiment's there.

"Why Blaine, why won't you just fucking say it again? You're going to lose me."

He frowns and backs away a step, his feet showing me the damn distance he's trying for again. Well, not this time. This time he'll move forward, I'll push him there if it's the last thing I do. I'll keep moving into him until there's nothing but a slither of air, and then I'll push in again.

"Say it," I snap out, the last of my drink slipping down my throat as I turn into the hallway and follow his backward steps. "Just damn well say it."

"No." For once the word makes me smile, knowing it was coming as I walk another step and watch him retreat again.

"Don't know how to?" He snarls at me, his feet still continuing away. The glass tumbles from my hand, something like a blank haze taking over from the care I should offer myself. It swirls inside me, begging me to make him move forward rather than the backward steps he keeps taking.

"Fuck you and your snarls. It's all here, Blaine. You brought me here. Show me. Tell me." He stalls his movement, his eyes boring into me like he's ready to kill. Good, at least we'll lay it all on the line that way. "You're fucking terrified of me, aren't you?"

"No." Liar. I don't know how I know this, but I do now. It's the only reason for these continued steps away from me. He loves me. Needs me. Is lost in his own conundrum of what he should do with me. Well, I'll show him, teach him for a change. Make him show me.

I keep going as he retreats up the hall, the shadows looming behind him as the sweep of the staircase comes into view and highlights dark corners at me. Perhaps it's a fucking ascension to heaven from the confines. Perhaps it's the view I need to get me out into those deeper waters of his.

"You're terrified of loving me and showing your heart, Blaine. Admit it."

"No." Oh, he is. He's petrified of me getting in for some reason. I know that look in his eyes when we fuck, and I know that slight hitch in his breath when I kiss him. This is all so much more than he wants to show.

THE END

"You're a liar, Blaine. A coward." He growls at me, one hand held up as a warning. Of what? There's nothing left he can do. No punishment. No other cruel intention he's got to offer. I've taken them all. I've felt his wrath already, let it resonate on my skin, in my mind. I've taken it, thought about it, let it come out through my still fucking blackened fingertips and written it like it bleeds from me.

"Stop," he says, true anger levelled at me. I shake my head, my heels slowly moving again as I begin to unzip the back of my dress. One way or another we're doing this. Right here. Right now. "Alana, don't do this." I smile, listening to the words and watching the way he looks behind him. He's got nowhere left to back away to, has he? Nowhere to hide. "Don't make *me* do this," he snarls out, his head shaking slowly back and forth. I laugh as the dress slips from my shoulders, emboldened by this sense of power travelling through me. He made this happen, brought me to this point, and when I don't overthink it, when I just concentrate on what we need, the forward momentum into him is easier than anything ever has been. No fear. No concerns. No worries about what he'll do, how he'll do it. He's built me this way. He's done it for whatever this reason is right here. Shown me how to not fear him. To trust him.

"You're right." He holds his hand up, stopping me. "I am afraid." He looks away again, then scans my body, his tongue licking across his lips. "You want the fucking truth, you can have it." The sense of relief that flows through me is instant, making my body sag a little in triumph. He takes a step forward and solidifies his weakened frame, taking my strength with the action. "You deserve it." Visions of happiness and longing erupt in my mind, ones filled with his beach and this strong man who I adore for my own reasons. Not that the rest of the world could even comprehend why. I'm not really sure I do most of the time. He's mine, though. My oddity. My quirk of nature. I smile at him, wanting nothing more than to hear what it is that stops us being completely bonded. We should be companions for life, he just needs to let me walk beside him and hold his hand. Show him he's loved. Endure him. "I'm afraid of killing you, Alana."

My mind stops, flummoxed at the words as my momentum falters, all thought of my own sense of comfort slipping away with the dress I've nearly abandoned. He sighs and blows out a breath as his eyes return to mine. "Just like I did with Eloise."

Chapter 11

ALANA

My mouth moves around feelings I can't assimilate into functioning thought, let alone words, as I stare at him. Eloise?

Who the hell is Eloise?

And why is he talking about killing her?

"What?"

My hands clutch at what's left covering me, his words making all this seem weird, not real. It's a dream. It must be because this isn't happening here. Not one part of him backs away from me or the statement that's left him. He means it. I frown in reply, my mind exploding with frantic questions again. He can't mean it, though. He can't. It's not possible. I shake my head at the thought, my eyes searching his for a retraction of the words. Perhaps he's just trying to scare me away again. He must be. That must be what's happening here. He doesn't give one, though. No retraction. No withdrawal. Not even a look of sorrow attached to him. Nothing about him says this is a lie or fabrication to scare me. It makes me take a small step back from him and frown further, the realisation finally finding some bedding in the pit of my stomach. Oh, god. It's the truth, isn't it? He means it. He's done that to someone.

It makes me gasp eventually, the held breath puffing out of me and fogging the few steps left between us as another foot away from him happens. He's killed someone. A woman. Eloise.

"Alana .."

He doesn't finish whatever he was about to say as I keep moving backwards, my hand hovering in front of me as a warning. I want to run, run this hall as fast as I can, but I can't take my eyes off him. Why can't I do that? I need to run. He's killed someone. And I'm here in this house with him, alone. No one knows I'm here. He could do it to me. All those hours with him. All the bonds, the handcuffs, the rope. Oh god, he could have killed me already. I could be dead now.

I snatch a glance behind me and look around the hall, trying to remember where the door to freedom is. Where the fuck is it?

"Alana.."

"No." The word snaps out of my mouth, its deliverance fuelled by the chaotic response my mind's trying to fight its way through. It's a rally of words and intents I can't process as I scan the doors, no matter how I try to order them. They're just there, rattling around and making me scream inside, but the scream won't come out. It won't leave me.

Both hands come up as I swing back to face him and see him take a small step forward, one hand stretching towards me. "Don't you fucking dare. You stay away from me." He halts instantly, for the first time showing some emotion on his face as his hand lowers again. It's not sorrow, though. It's not a beg for forgiveness or a show of contrition about the act he's admitted. Its anger, shown by his scowl descending, probably because of my language. It makes me pick up a vase, ready to defend myself should I need, my heels beginning to trip over themselves as I go.

    I turn into the next room I get to, hoping it's the right one, but the moment I'm in it I realise it isn't. It's an office. I've spun and looked at the doorway within seconds, only to see him there blocking me, his body filling the frame like it always does.

    "Move," I snap, the vase still in front of me as if ready to attack.

    "No," he says, calmly, now smiling as if I'm amusing. Nothing about any of this is funny. Not one fucking thing.

    "Get out of my fucking way. I swear I'll …"

    "You'll what?" he cuts in, crossing his legs and leaning on the frame, still smiling. "Kill me?" I scan the room quickly, looking for an object to make that happen should the need arise, because this fucking vase isn't going to cut it. "Sit down, Alana. You want it all. Here it is."

    "Fuck off."

    It's out of my mouth before I've got any thought of controlling it as I stand here, vase in hand. Sit down? I'm not sitting down and discussing this as if it's acceptable. It's not. None of it is. I thought we were getting somewhere, getting closer. Thought I was pushing him into loving me, making him admit it. And now? Now we're going to have a conversation about him killing someone? That's not going to happen. I'm leaving is what I'm doing, and he's going to let me so I can process whatever the hell this is. There's nothing here for now.

Nothing to discuss. Nothing to talk about. Nothing to deliberate. There's no excuse for this. None. I'm done.

"Get out of my way so I can leave." I'm leaving. I am.

"Sit down, or I'll make you sit down."

I pull in a long, slow breath, trying to calm myself and find some order. I can't beat him physically. I'm not even going to try. He's going to let me leave because I'm asking to. That's everything he's always said to me. I only have to ask. So that's what I'm going to do. I'm going to calm down. Settle myself, and then I'm going to leave so I can think, form an opinion on my own without his interference.

"No, Blaine." I look at the vase in my hands, for some reason now seeing it's absurdity in the middle of this, and move to the desk to put it down. The sight of the desk makes me smile for some reason, its leather laid top intricately carved into the wood, papers neatly piled and organised. "Is this your father's desk?" Why the hell did I ask that? I don't care. I don't.

"Mother's." His voice softens a touch when he says it, straight to that damned level that makes me do anything for him. It's disconcerting, making me feel flustered again within my thoughts of leaving.

"I suppose she'd be happy about you holding me here against my will, would she?" I spit out.

There's no response to that as I turn back to face him again, still keeping my breath coming in and out slowly. I'm in control of this, not him. I have to be before he makes killing someone sound okay or forces me to listen to things I don't want to hear. Because that's what he's going to do, isn't it? He's going to tell me about this Eloise and make me listen to the thing that keeps him distanced from me. And for once, as I look at his brown eyes, the ones still pulling me into them regardless of this conversation that's not going to happen, I don't want to hear that answer. I don't want it tainting the thing I thought I was becoming, or the person that was helping me become it. The words he delivers now will change us, destroying the heart of what I thought I was beginning to understand. I would rather walk out of here and remember the man I thought I knew rather than even try to comprehend the one he's about to tell me of. He's right, he can't give me what I want from him. He never could, could he?

"I want you to move so I can leave, Blaine. I'm asking you to let me go." It shakes out of me, my heart breaking in two as I say it because I know it'll work when he tells me, won't it? I'll fall into his hands again, finding some resonance in my mind that makes this tolerable. "Please." It isn't tolerable. It's wrong. There isn't any circumstance that makes killing someone alright, especially not within the grounds of this community that bases itself on trust.

He frowns and stares back, not one inch of him moving from the frame he's still filling, but he has to move. If nothing else he has to, to show me that my opinion is worth something in all of this, because if it's not then this was never anything more than fucking anyway. If there's any chance of me understanding this, forming a solution in my mind about how I feel, then he has to prove the whole theory of this. For once, he has to let me be me without his mind altering my course on it. I can leave whenever I want, make my own choice. That's how this works. That's what he's shown me through all this, what he's taught me.

Charlotte E Hart
THE END

I raise a brow, challenging him and waiting for him to do the right thing. Nothing changes as he pulls in his own breaths and then sighs them out. Nothing but the two of us locked in an internal battle that he can't win unless he lets me have my choice. It's the only way.

Eventually he backs out of the doorway, giving me the space I need to get passed him. What should have been a confirmation of respect annihilates my heart completely as I watch his feet step away. It feels like he's giving me my freedom with one hand and yet stripping me in two with the other. I hover, my feet refusing to follow my own thoughts, and then force them to move through the gap he's created by leaning on the opposing wall. I'm going. I have to. And the fact that I shiver as I move passed him has to mean nothing for now. I have to make it mean so little that I can think rationally without him. Life is not just about Blaine and his needs, nor his wants. It's also not just about this fucking love that won't let go of me. But something inside screams at me as I try not to look back, the hallway suddenly feeling like a tunnel I can't escape from. It wrenches and pulls internally, challenging everything I thought I would do in this situation. Nothing is logical inside me. It makes me need to look at him again, for some reason needing to see even the slightest contrition from him about it. I shake my head at it, furious with myself for giving the emotion credence as I keep travelling and looking into rooms.

I grab my coat and bag from the one we drank in, then turn and start moving again because I am going. Without him. I'm going home where I can think, perhaps sleep, on my own. Wake on my own. Find my own routine without him dictating the ebb and flow of it anymore. I can do that. I can. I don't need this shit in my life.

THE END

"Alana?" I close my eyes to the sound of him, finally finding the right doorway to freedom and opening it to get out into the night air again. Home. Safety. Away from him and his killing hands.

My steps feel like the longest ones I've ever taken as I trail the path around to the front of the house, then traipse down the drive. They're heavier with each clipped footfall that tears me away from him, trying to make me wait, or stop, turn around again even and go back inside to listen to his reasons. It feels visceral as I tug the main gates, fighting the impetus trying to lever me back at him. It's a fucking instinct I can't deal with at the moment. A predisposition that has no right to live within me given his admittance of murder. I won't turn around, no matter how much something makes me need to. I am my own person, with my own thoughts. He does not rule me.

I stand outside the gate looking down the road, wondering how the hell I'm going to get anywhere at all, then make my feet keep me moving down the hill we originally came up, bypassing the car we arrived in. Stupid maybe, but I need to do this on my own, find my own way. I feel like he's led me so far down his fucking rabbit hole I can't remember my way out of it, or see the light at the end of his tunnel all of a sudden. Its blacker here than it is when I'm with him. It feels as alone as I've ever been, somehow relinquishing me to a pile of bones and ash, burnt from the knowledge he's given me. It's ruined this. Broken it, me with it.

I tuck my arms around myself to ward off the cold and keep going as houses blur around me, their white picket fences signalling happy units of love. Fuck all of it. Happiness doesn't live around here. Murderers do. Sadists who kill with their errant hands, debasing and humiliating someone before doing it. I snarl at my own lack of ability to let the thought of those hands go, still remembering the tenderness of them after his acts of need. Monster, that's what Oliver called him. I'd screwed my nose up at him, not knowing what he meant. This is what he means, irrespective of the man I've come to love. Did they all know in that audience, were they waiting and hoping the monster would appear, ready to do its worst on my skin? The thought embarrasses me, making me tighten my arms again to protect myself. And yet, it doesn't make any sense to me as I think about it, wandering aimlessly in hope of help. I can still see his smile tonight as we danced, still feel his heartbeat in my ear as I'd lain my head on his chest, wishing for more answers than he'd give. He was there with me. Alive. We were breathing as one unit. Falling further in love. Well, I thought we were. Maybe we weren't. Maybe he was just pushing me further into his decadence, ready to kill the next one presenting itself as available. At least I've got the reason for his distance now, for the separation he continues with. And I suppose, much as it might confuse me to think about it, with a truth like that hiding in the background, he couldn't ever be close, could he? He was trying to keep me away.

Keep me safe.

"I'm an asshole."

He's damn right he is. A murdering one. So why can't I truly believe it?

I don't know where I'm walking to as the ground keeps travelling underneath my feet. Downhill is all I know. At some point I took my shoes off, choosing to feel the pavement beneath my soles rather than keep up the pretence of elegance. It grounds me against the tarmac, giving some sense to the haze I'm walking through. It feels like hours passing by as I trudge on, hoping for a route to follow, almost as if a fog has descended at some point and made the roads indiscernible from the next. Not that I know where I am anyway. I'm lost in reality. Lost on the streets, lost in my mind. Visions and images assaulting me. Hands softly sweeping across my skin one minute and then causing pain the next. And the pressured moments are clouded with screams now, too, but they're not my screams. They're not my howls of passion. I don't own them anymore. They belong to someone else's voice. Someone else's tears, fears.

    I stop at a junction, looking left and right into more haze, barely caring for which direction I take. Home is all I want, my home, my sanctuary, and I can't find it. It's out there somewhere and I can't get to it. The thought makes my eyes tear up, my nose sniffing the effect back before they erupt and leave me less able to make decisions than I already am. But, try as I might, I can't make them stop. They won't stop coming. I swipe at my eyes, trying to make them clear, but they just come with more force, their power coming from my guts as they race through me. It all aches so much, leaving a forsaken hole inside my heart that can't be fixed. It's his fault. He did this to me. And he'll keep doing it to me, won't he? This pain will keep travelling the inside of me, tearing at my heart, opening it and making it weep for something reality can't give it. He is that monster he professed to be. The man I know doesn't exist. Perhaps he never did and I made it up in my head, hoping for a fucking dream to save me.

    My knees buckle under the strain of the thought, their weight seeming to crumble with visions of my apartment again. It's no fucking home to me. His house has felt more like a home than mine could ever be. His routes, his directions. The ease of everyday without having to think about the whys. It's all been so easy to conform to. So tranquil, regardless of the strikes to my skin. My knees hit the tarmac, the skin on them cutting. I barely register the feeling as I hug myself tighter and try to see through the tears. Oh god, why? Why? I can't do this. I'm alone again. Lost. I couldn't manage before him. It was a mess. And it will be again. I can't do it now I've seen straight with him guiding me. I can't go back to that. I want his home, and his arms, and his voice calming me down. I need it.

Tears splat the ground beneath me, the wetness seeping into the drab grey, blackening the surface and reminding me of oceans I've near drowned in. I just want that view back again. I do. I want its crash and its turmoil swirling, the same turmoil that leaves me with a sense of wading deeper in, losing myself within its pull to get to the stars he offers. I can cope with that, did cope with it, but losing myself out here in the dark when I'm alone, no stars to shine down on me? I can't.

My fingers run circles in my own tears on the dirty street floor, searching for his reflection in them to help me see sense. I nearly reached those stars. It was becoming seamless, a flow of energy between us, deepening us into something filled with honesty and intent. Commitment. Perhaps I actually did reach them, made him ascend with me to the actuality I pushed for. I asked, didn't I? I asked and he told me. He proved the reality of why he is who he is, showed me his reasoning for his behaviour. Showed me the truth.

A man suddenly flops down beside me, the heavy thud of him making me jump and topple to the side as his hand hits my leg. I gasp out, scared at what he might do and trying to scrabble away from his advance.

"Fuck me," shoots out of me, my feet scrambling the floor, legs staggering me away to the safety of a lamp post as I glare at the prone body.

"Thankfully not this time." It's Blaine's voice. It makes me jump, too, instantly looking into the shadows behind me for me.

"What's that? Have you killed him too?"

"No, saved you. It appears to have become my job lately," he says, walking into the light and kicking at the lifeless looking guy's hand. A knife knocks out of it and tumbles, highlighted by the glare above us, its metal glinting. I swipe my fingers over my eyes, trying to focus on the knife and realising what nearly happened. "He was going to attack me?"

"Everything wants to attack you, Alana. Me included." He reaches down and grabs the knife, his other hand reaching for the fucker's neck. I stare, bewildered as to what he's doing, then realise he's checking the dick's pulse.

"Really?"

He nods at himself and then puts his foot on the hand of the guy, crushing it, seemingly without any care. I wish I could say it bothered me, but it doesn't. In fact, I will the crunch of the bones, disgusted with the idea of what might have happened. I just clutch this fucking post instead, trying to process what the hell's happening to me, why Blaine's here at all, and why the fuck I care so much about the fact that he is.

"Saving your shoes, too," he says, reaching over the man and picking up my heels, chuckling.

I don't even know what to say to that. I swipe my eyes again as he stands there, not knowing what to do or say next. I'm terrified of what might come out of my mouth all of a sudden, my heart flustering around the vision of him in front of me again. He's too handsome. Too big. Too – in my face. I can't function with him here, can't get my thoughts back together again. Not that they were.

"Thank you," is the only thing that ends up springing to mind. That's safe. Nothing else has to be said than that. It's polite. Sensible. Thank you and goodbye. Nothing else.

"You're welcome, Alana." His mouth around my name makes me gaze at him, perhaps searching for those fucking stars he just tore from me with his admittance of murder.

"Were you following me?" Why did I say that? No conversation. None. I need to go. He's making me say these things somehow, probably using his psychology degree to infiltrate my mind.

I shake my head and tug my coat tighter as I let go of the lamp post, hopefully shielding myself from any thought of togetherness. There isn't any. I need to be gone. To leave and process the murderer who's moving closer to me.

"I let you go, little dove," he says, more fucking steps headed in my direction, his hand putting my shoes on the floor in front of him. "I'm far from letting you leave, though."

He just stands there, three feet from me with his hands in his pockets, forcing me to run my eyes over his face. Oh god, he's beautiful. Even with this knowledge I've now got inside me. It's dark here and the lamp light just bounces off his cheekbones, somehow softening the fact that he's killed someone. I want to reach out and touch him, let my fingers wander his body, let him pull me into him and hold me.

"What the fuck does that mean?" I snap out instead, still trying to fight the thought. I have to.

"Language." He smirks, the very movement slowly widening into that happy face of his that weakens every resolve I've got. It makes me want to do it too. Makes me ache to walk into him, let him lead me through this. I don't.

"I'm still leaving." I clench my own hands, grasping my shoes from the floor and clinging to my coat in the hope that he stays where he is. "I don't want to know anymore."

"Yes you do," he says instantly, his eyes boring into mine. "Don't lie to yourself. You pushed me for this." The fucking smile's still there as he watches me and then turns his body away to walk to the kerb. "Push, push, push."

I snatch glances around, wondering if I should run. But where to? I'm still as lost as I was ten minutes ago, not knowing where to go. It makes me snarl at myself, irritated at my inability here as he nods up the road at something.

The car comes then, the rumble of it approaching down the road highlighting the very real possibility that I'm about to be taken against my will. I see it coming for me and wonder if that would really happen, its black outline an image of the darkness he creates. But he's never forced anything before, not with any legitimacy anyway. He's only ever forced something when I needed the extra shove, and he's always been right. I've always enjoyed whatever happened next. Always learnt something about myself because of his guidance. And I'm still in fucking stall as I stand here, flicking my eyes between his back and the car. I'm even chewing my thumb, my heart racing at the impending information that he'll impart if I get in that car. It's concerning. I mean, will that make me an accomplice in something? Would I be aiding and abetting in some way? Still, it doesn't stop this impetus inside me from continually propelling me forward towards him, driving me to the very thing I should be running from.

"Life with me is not the rainbows you're after, Alana," he says sharply as the car pulls up alongside him, his errant fingers clicking it open before it even stops. "This mind of mine you want into? You'll have to follow me further to get it all. I'll show you when we get there." Get where? "It's always been your choice to make." My feet have stepped forward before I've realised it's happened, making me halt myself from further stupidity and snatch more glances around. For Christ's sake. What am I doing? "You asked me for this, come and find out why." He just stands there, his back still turned away from me as he holds the door open. It makes me look at the gap between his arm bracing it and his body. There's just a dark hole waiting for me to enter it, darker than the sky above me, darker even than his sea at night. There aren't any stars in there, no flickers or glimmers of light. It's just pitch black, his arm framing the entrance to it. "Come."

I chew on my nail, still deliberating what the hell I'm even thinking about. I should be getting home, writing, doing things to enhance my career. Meeting Bree even and apologising again, finding a way to build myself back up on my own. Or I should be screaming at him and running, making sure I don't vanish into a hole I can't get out of. Wonderland, that's what he called it. Alice does not live in that car. And this little dove is becoming frightened of the hole she's wanting to fall down.

"Not pushing anymore?" he says, quietly.

I want to say no. I want to tell him that I'm not doing this, that it's over, that I need to think and find some sense to all this, but I can't stop the next footfall that happens in his direction, or the one after that. And I can't stop looking at him through the fog my breath's creating in the air, his outline as clear as day regardless of the mist obscuring him. He tilts his head at my advance, his arm crooking a little to give me access.

"Blaine?" comes from me, not sure what it is I want him to say, or even if I want him to say it. He turns slightly, showing me his cheek, but nothing other than that. No contrition still, no show of affection, no love to guide me in. He just waits as he always does, waits for me to show my agreement to his forward momentum, the one I asked for. "Is this forward?" The corner of his mouth curves upwards before his face swings away from me.

"We go backwards before we go forwards, little dove. For you, we go backwards first."

I walk on, emboldened by the statement, although I don't know why. Backwards seems dysfunctional, useless to me. My backwards is a mess of chaos and commotion, irrespective of how I portrayed my calm at the time. I know calm now. I know its effects on my skin, on my mind. He's shown me it, let me linger in it with no consequence other than pain.

THE END

There's a moment as I duck under his arm and look back at him, a moment I don't know how to describe. It's haunting, like I've seen him before in another life, dwelt with him somehow. It just hangs me in one place, needing to stay locked right here. It warms me, making some part of me want to let him take over completely. Brown eyes so murky their depths seem fathomless, like his sea. A constant churn of controlled havoc just waiting for the storm to whip them up. Whip me up.

"Get in the car," he murmurs. It's so soft now, lulling me quietly, making me forget everything other than the black hole my body seems to lever me into. I don't even know if I want to get in really. I'm just going, perhaps lacking the ability to stay out. "Good girl."

I close my eyes to the sound of him and lean onto the door as I sit, not knowing what I'm doing but too exhausted to fight my feelings anymore. I can't run. I've tried. It doesn't work. Every thought I try to employ just makes me turn back to him, makes me want to fall further into the dark with him. I'm alone without him. Lost. He makes me feel real. He makes Alana feel alive for reasons I can't compute or organise effectively. He makes me want to dream and find the stars in my words.

"You'll hate me before you love me again," he says as the car pulls away. Hate him? I couldn't hate him if I tired. I should maybe. I should be able to sit here and detest this monster he's told me of, should be able to despise the essence of any human that kills, but I don't. That fact is proved by my body being in this car with him still, regardless of my shudders at the thought.

THE END

I don't answer his statement or look at him as we begin driving. I can't. I've got nothing to answer that with. I've got nothing to tell him yet, regardless of knowing my own feelings on the matter. At this precise moment, and perhaps because of my fear of what I'm about to find out, I need quiet and peace. I need to let my mind wander, hopefully finding some ability to organise myself in the time it's given to let go of my initial response. That's one of the main things I've learnt since I've been near him. My initial response is often not the deep seated one. It's not the true Alana from times gone by. The one who breezes and dreams, who lingers in time and finds passion. I need this new ability I've found because of him, I need to let myself go.

And that's what he gives me for the following journey as we travel on. We don't speak as the car arrives back at the hotel lobby we left from. He doesn't speak as we climb up in the elevator towards the roof. And he doesn't speak the entire flight back to the abandoned strip of ground we first took off from. He just behaves like the perfect gentleman as he opens doors and helps me climb into things, climb back out of them. He shows me that Blaine that I danced with earlier, his heart almost on his sleeve as he looks at me and occasionally smiles. It's become a sad smile, though, one that I can't stop reflecting back to him. No grinning, no beaming. The glimpse of that I was getting from him now relegated back to its closed borders. I suppose it's tainted with knowledge now, changed. It's become something that makes a love derived from filth and learning, appreciation from new found sensations, now an irrevocable bond of trust. It's a commitment in some ways, a binding that's deeper than the love I was pushing for. It's something I'll always know, something I'll always have to know.

And he still shows no repentance for his act as we cross to the car to get in, but he does radiate a sense of discord because of it. He seems uncomfortable as we get closer to his home. His movements becoming less fluid with every mile we inch through. Perhaps it's just because I know about it now. Or perhaps he's anxious about what's coming.

I chuckle slightly as I watch the now familiar roads go passed us on the way, more out of the same sense of dissonance as he shows. Blaine Jacobs in disarray. What a thought. It forces me to imagine what happened to the woman he spoke of, the one he killed.

"Tell me about her," I mumble, for some reason needing to hear about who she was, what happened maybe. Nothing changes in the air around us. No answer. No change in breath as he eases us onwards. So I sigh at the dark night, searching the horizon for my stars and not finding any there.

"Not yet," he eventually replies, quietly. I watch as we turn onto the highway, bypassing the route we should have taken to get back to his house. "First you go home and you think." I frown at him, wondering why he would say that. I mean, I got in the car. I followed him when he asked me too. I don't need time to think. I need answers to my questions, an explanation. A way of finding a route through this, if there's a route to find.

"But I ..."

"Give me time to do the same," he mumbles, his head shaking as his hand reaches over and drops my phone into my lap. I look at it lying there, its dull screen reminding me of life without him. "I need time, Alana. So do you. I didn't expect this."

I frown at him, watching his face turn from passive and calm to something akin to concern or worry, and then that eventually turns to one of depression as we keep driving. I physically see it change. His body language becomes smaller, weaker maybe. The lacking eye contact as I bore mine into the side of his face, hoping for boldness to make this seem easier to bare. He seems sullen, morose even, sighs leaving him with every rounded corner of each further mile we go. It becomes worrying at some point. I've never seen him like this. It's unlike him. Strange. And it makes the air around us uncomfortable, more so than the word 'killer' does.

Chapter 12

BLAINE

My hand launches the chair at the wall, the other one hauling the table in the same direction. Everything follows, a fucking riot of bedlam and destruction, all thrown at anything it'll break against. Everything needs to break. Everything always does eventually, no matter the containment around its shell. And I don't fucking care as I heave and tug at a line of more worthless objects, throwing them in the same direction, fury levelling each lob of hatred. No physiological evaluation of the facts. No considered approach or assessment and calculation. For now it's just me and these walls of inadequacy, fuelled with a love that screams for acceptance from her. It breaks me in two as I snarl at myself, listening to her words flood my insides.

"Don't you fucking dare touch me."

Fuck her. Fuck her to hell and back. She pushed and twisted me, turning the thoughts over in my head until there wasn't any other answer in here to be found. Now she's tainted my home, saturating me with reminders of her and her fucking perfection as I scour the walls for clarity without her.

THE END

I lob another fuck knows what at the glass doors and pick up the bottle of scotch, glugging it to prove my own fucking point. Nothing's left here. Fuck all good resides inside of these walls or me. I'm an asshole, one who's just given her everything she needs to decimate what's left of me. I might as well fucking top myself now, just wade into my fucking sea and let it do its worst. I'd rather that than the grating pull on my heart that she keeps trampling in.

The final slug of drink has me glaring at the bottle, rage at its shortfall fuelling more fury to vent. It erupts inside me, finding its way straight to a thousand dollar painting that I couldn't give a fuck about. Fucking money. It's all worthless and insignificant, barely registering as usable in my life as I lie my way through it, containing my needs for the better of others. Fuck that now. Fuck this excuse of a shell I've become. Fuck her. I'm nothing but a casing for gunpowder, eternally restricting the flow of its explosion. I'm fucking tired of it. Tired of its continual grate on my mind. Tired of its hesitance. Tired of its pleasantries and niceties for society's sake.

The painting is lobbed with little fucking precision to its landing, my arm reaching for more to grab at as I storm passed the drinks and swipe another bottle. Fuck, it feels good to be drunk. Good to be alive and free for a while. Fucking place. I snarl at it all as I stamp through the hall, bored of its fucking grey interior and its ineffective content. It makes me turn into the den, hoping for fulfilment from its sadistic arsenal, but she's not in here to brighten it. It's as fucking empty as the rest of the building, as useless.

I glare at its desolation, suddenly unable to stop myself kicking out at the furniture that had her lying on it. It's disturbing to me that she's all I can see or think about. Provoking. So I keep fucking drinking instead and turn back out, content with the thought of just releasing more of my monster at this interior, colouring it with something other than the calm I've lived in to cage myself. Fucking caging.

I'm sick of it. Sick of its unsettled resonance. Sick of its repression and suffocation around me. Sick of its dishonesty. She's my fucking honesty. It lives in her, waiting for me to breathe life into the feel of it again. It rides my skin whenever I'm near her, galling me with the possibilities of love and honesty. Fucking love. Fuck her. Fuck all of it.

My hand launches the bottle at the wall of glass as I walk into the bedroom, fury expelling from me with it as I imagine her naked body there. It halts me, my mood faltering as I stare at the bed and let this fucking drunken haze gaze at her. Beautiful. Sinful. Sexy as fuck. Her skin covered with my bruises, my stripes, her blood. Fuck that tastes good. It's like a fine wine coating my tongue, bringing with it a relief that no drug counters. And her cunt, the same one that envelops me in its heat and promises me release. It's fucking divine. It tastes of her and her alone. Unique, and only enhanced by the combined taste of my come inside it, leaking out and letting me lave at its nectar. I'd fucking lose myself in there forever, let it guide me home, bring me back from this mayhem into a more manageable version of monsters who lurk in the gloom. I smile at the imagery, picturing her running on my fucking beach, fear in her every panted footfall as I chase her down.

And where the fuck is she now I need to expel these thoughts? She's where I fucking drove her to. Back to her lacking life.

Fucking decency.

I crick my neck and turn for the door again, ready to get more drink, but become distracted by my sea this early in the morning. It's as beautiful as her, as mesmerizing as it laps the edges of my shore gently. I stagger in its direction and aim for the handle, wondering if drowning seems a good idea today. Perhaps it is. She knows about Eloise now, doesn't she? She won't come back. No one would with that knowledge inside them. The only fucking reason she got in the car was because she couldn't get home without me. That was fucking stupid of her. I could have done anything to her in the mood I was in, especially given her foul fucking mouth and its effortless tug on my soul. Fuck knows how I didn't kill that fucking pervert that was going to attack her.

I should spank her ass for that, all of it, make her cunt bleed for being so reckless.

My throat growls out in distress as I ratchet the lever, desperate for more alcohol to fuel this panic ridden hatred of myself. That's all this is. I know that. It's fucking rage and indecision. A barrage of self-loathing and repugnance, one confused and trapped in its own irrational behaviour. The psychologist in me would tell me to quieten down, fucking mediate or some shit that holds no sense in my world. The monster in me? He's ready to rut hell into anything that will take me, just so it can imagine her face and abandon the last drops of my resistance into her.

Bitch. I hate her. Abhor her ability to do this to me. And yet I would throw myself into a fucking fire to ensure her survival. She's engrained into me. Embedded. She's like a worm I can't pick from my skin, burrowing under it and eating her way to my heart, wakening it from self-imposed desolation.

"Blaine?"

I halt and swing my head, wondering why I can hear her voice. She's not here. I took her home. I snort, amused with the fact that perhaps I'm finally losing grip of reality. Finally seeing the fucking light and going completely insane from the constant pressure to cage myself in. I ratchet the lever and head out onto the deck, ready to walk myself down to the sea. My fucking sea. My chosen despondency in the wilderness. I can't get anything here, can I? I'm not tempted by fine young things dressed in summer skirts that flaunt themselves in my face thinking pretty thoughts of love. That's why I stay here, never bringing anything here, never playing with anything on my own. Never contemplating anything more than just this emptiness. Never smiling, never laughing. Never fucking crying like other humans do.

The sigh that leaves me at the thought has my mind running back to Eloise again as I stumble on, my feet travelling the same sands she had laboured through. It makes me see her image in front of me, her voice echoing back as a ghost, laughter filtering through the sun's rays.

"Come get me, Sir."

She used to say that all the time, her pretty little voice belying the monster inside her too. I can hear her now. *Come get me, Come get me.* It calls me further down to the water, the shadows around me barely registering as I stumble through the dunes, searching for a fucking answer to all this. There's only one, and it all fucking rests in the hands of Alana and her acceptance. A woman who will, with any luck, never come back to curse herself further than she already has done. She'll die here with me. She'll fall into these hands, giving me her flawless skin to fuck with, and then she'll die. I'll kill her like I did the last.

My knees give way to the visions that assault my mind, my hands not bothering to break the descent that's coming. What the fuck does it matter? I'll just crawl to the sea instead, find Eloise in there. Let her take me to where I should be so I can fuck her forever in Alana's place. Death would be so much easier to manage my thoughts within. Nothing matters there. I could fuck anything, strangle anything, cut it open and lick its open weeping wounds till it drains dry.

My fingers scratch in the sand to turn me over, now needing my sea more than ever. It's not far, just a few hundred yards and I'll be there. It's clear as fucking day to me as the sun rises and another small splash of waves draws me to it. Beautiful rays, beautiful sea. It's all beautiful. Free of limitation. Free of mayhem. Free of guilt. I just need to keep crawling, need to keep pulling my nails through this sand. Just get there and then this will all be over. It'll be done.

The salt of the water feels like a fucking fountain of life as it slips down my throat, the crash of another wave bringing it in. It makes me try harder to get in deeper, my feet pushing my clothed legs onwards. I can hear her calling me, telling me to come in, to come get her. She's like a fucking angel out there, her voice mesmerising me to follow and finally be free. Fuck love. This is where love takes me. It takes me here because of Alana, to save her, protect her. Love isn't a fucking fairy-tale for me. Perhaps it never was. I'm undeserving of its effect on me. It's nothing but a descent into hell. A place that will welcome the likes of me.

I'm deep now, the water beginning to envelop me as she does. It trickles across me, wrapping its fucking arms around me and letting me float in it. It's relaxing, soothing to me. I'd only need the dark and it would all be fucking perfect. I can just close my eyes here, let the waves pull me out, drown my forbidden fucking soul into the depths of it so I can finally breathe easy.

Something grabs at my leg, twisting me over and yanking me backwards. I struggle against it, irritated with whoever the fuck it is that's trying to save me. Save me? I don't want fucking saving. Never did. I need to drown. I need to, to save Alana. She has to be free of me, and I need to be free of this mind of mine. Take it off this fucking planet and give the world a chance without me in it.

I kick out at whatever it is, my legs thrashing and turning, trying to get the fucking thing off me as white crests crash my face.

"Fucking idiot," comes growled at me, something hitting my jaw in the same instance. It sends pain straight to my brain, knocking it around my skull as my head goes under the water. I struggle again, blowing air out of my lungs and trying to kick my way out of whoever's holding me. But it keeps dragging at me, wrenching me backwards and away from my fucking sea. And then fingers grasp into my hair, yanking on my scalp and reminding me of Alana again. It breaks my fury of murderous thoughts, suddenly helping me see clearly beneath the water.

I'm pulled up, my mouth immediately hauling in a breath of air as I turn to face my attacker and try to stand. It doesn't work as

Delaney's face flashes in front of me, in fact, he helps hinder me by pushing me back down again, submerging me before I've got a chance for decent breath. It forces panic to set in, a rally for life perhaps as I challenge the hold keeping me down here, propelling me upwards as I find my feet. I lever against it, all my muscles racing back for use. Fucking saviour. Who the fuck does he think he is?

My fist comes through first, instantly connecting with something hard. Nothing changes though, the force on my head just shoves me back down, a leg sweeping mine from beneath me. And this time it pushes down with such weight behind it that my face mangles the stones on the sea bed, the crunch of it opening my eyes to the salt water. It burns as I look around, my hands grasping out at a rock so I can destroy the fucker with it. But just as I'm about to kill him, just as the murderous intent comes racing back to me, the weight vanishes. It leaves me staring into the water, letting my body rise of its own accord as I search for answers again. My fucking sea. Mine.

My mouth slips over the waves, a breath being drawn in as I gaze out into the ocean and wonder what the fuck I'm doing. Drowning, living, existing? I don't know anymore. Nothing's clear or focused. It's all as murky as it is beneath my ocean, still as dark as it always was. Still as out of reach. And the sun keeps rising in my eye-line, the vast expanse of the water diminishing around the globe of yellow coming into full view. It focuses me in on it, for once choosing to stare straight into the light as I let my feet land on the seabed again, let its rays penetrate me.

"You done?" Delaney's voice asks behind me. Done? Done with what, killing myself? Probably not, but for now, yes.

THE END

I turn to him and find him waist deep, his hands idling the water around him as if it's his divine right to come save me. It makes me snarl as I wipe the water away from my face, eventually nodding to acknowledge the help in some way, and then walk passed him to make my way back to the house. I didn't need saving, still don't. He's got no right to be here, no reason either. Why the fuck is he here? "You can thank Alana for saving your ass," he calls as I hit dry land and peel my shirt from my body.

I snort, amused by the fact that she's had anything to do with my salvation as I cough out some water. She's the reason I'm here. She's the very reason I crawled out there in the first place. He doesn't understand, still, even after the conversations we've had. Men like Delaney Priest don't know how to understand, close as he might be to me. They play, amusing themselves with toys of affection, pushing a boundary every now and then with something able to take their sadism, but they don't want to cross the line. They just manage the situation, knowing the line's there and never endangering because of it. They achieve true dominance because of it. I don't, not deep down. I simply don't have the want too.

"Christ, Blaine, use Tabitha for an hour or two if it's that bad. Let off some steam," he calls after me.

I look up at the house and see her standing there waiting for me, her body resting on the wall as if she has no care in the world for what my hands could do. I could, I suppose, let some of this angst and confusion dissipate onto skin willing enough to endure it. The thought makes me scan her over as I keep walking, each step heavier than the

THE END

last. She smiles at my perusal, rolling a lollipop in her mouth, willing me into her with each passing second.

"Did she contact you?" I mumble, not able to stop blue eyes haunting the vision in front of me, for some reason telling me to stop myself.

"Yes."

"Why?"

"She was worried about you." The thought makes me smile and gaze back at the sand, regardless of the fact I nearly killed myself for her. It makes my heart ache again for something I shouldn't have, don't deserve.

He jogs up to my side, the sight of his shoes in my space making me want to kill him for his interference in my plans. I stop and face him, wondering why she was worried. I did nothing to provoke concern, I was level headed, calm. I gave her the space she needed to begin understanding what I'd told her, thinking about it.

"You think she can't see inside you?" he says, a smile creeping up his face as he strips his t-shirt off and slaps me on the back. "The right ones always can, Blaine. It's what made me let Flick go." He nods at Tabitha. "The wrong ones don't bite in the same." I frown at him, searching his eyes for more information. He doesn't give any, just winks and walks away from me, his body as calm as day, like nothing happened out there in my sea ten minutes ago. "You're fucking welcome, by the way."

Fuck him.

THE END

I turn back and gaze at the ocean as it taunts me back to it, the calm swell of it ebbing and flowing, tempting me to go back in and find my peace there instead of using Alana for it.

"Any drink left?" Delaney calls. "We've got a conversation to have."

The thought makes me sigh, a slight smile rising at the thought of hours deliberating facts and truths with him. We've done it so many times already. Fucking involved sometimes, other times just a drink until we're shitfaced and basking in our own debauched glory. It causes a sneer to descend at Tabitha's proximity to our truths. She's not welcome in them, not now that I can see Alana in my mind overwhelming her.

I turn and head back again, ready to have conversations about subjects I don't comprehend as usual or agreeable, and give Tabitha wide enough berth on my way passed to let her know I'm not interested in her kind of help.

"Tell your pet to go," I snap, weaving my way passed him and scanning the chaos I've caused in my own home. "I don't want her here." The only woman I want here I've forced away. She's miles from me and seemingly still thinking about what we should be. She's as fucking lost in this as me now that she knows what I've done. I've made her that way, given her the truths she wanted, and left her with them. Left her to deal with the horror of it on her own.

"Blaine, you could calm down if …"

"OUT." It roars from me, her fucking voice interfering with my visions of a woman I want near me. I swing back at her, making her frame shudder and scamper away from me. "Fuck you. Your cunt is of no fucking use to me. Get out before I force you out."

Delaney's hand lands on my shoulder instantly, making me snarl at it, near ready to shove him out of the door too.

"Leave, Tabby cat," he says, slowly putting himself in front of me. She smiles over his shoulder at me, tempting me with the fury that's rising. It's sickly sweet and full of an intent she's got no fucking clue about. I glare at it, and then at Delaney. "Where's the drink?" he asks, pushing me backwards slightly. Drink, yes. Get fucking drunk and let all this confusion dissipate, let it rest.

Tabitha begins walking away from us, her body as tempting now as it's ever been irrespective of my own inner dialogue. I can feel it in the sound of her heels clipping my pristine floors, and the way she keeps looking at me, still smiling as her fingers twirl the lollipop she's got in her mouth. It reminds me of Alana's eyes again as she glides passed, not a care in her debauched little world of fun. My little dove doesn't look like that, she has eyes that draw me into them, one's that make me want to hold on as I devastate her, go with her even.

"Quicker, Tabby cat," comes from Delaney, his fingers gripping my shoulder tighter now as I watch her leaving. Leaving. Maybe she shouldn't go after all. Maybe Delaney's right. I should lose myself for a while, enjoy the offering she's giving me. I lick my lips at the thought, my cock remembering it's alive and willing to indulge itself as I follow the madam's movements.

It swings me round to her, her ass calling me to take hold of it, use my den for some time, put her in the ropes I've barely used with Alana's naïve frame. What would it matter? She's offering. Delaney's offering. I could indulge these fantasies, make them a reality again and set them free. It makes me smile at her as she gets to the door, tempting her back to me again. It takes nothing for her to stop in the doorway, her head tilting to question my moves as she runs her tongue over the ball of pink in her mouth.

"Drink, Blaine?" Screw the drinks. I don't want a drink. I want to breathe life into the slut making me greedy for pain she knows nothing of. I want screams and howls, begging. I want the fucking silence after the begging's stopped. I want the lights dimming until there's nothing left but prone flesh for me to play with, revive if I choose to. "Blaine?" I shrug his grip from my shoulder, my feet moving without thought to anything other than the here and now. Fuck it all. I was about to kill myself, I still can, but maybe after this rather than before. In fact, I could take her cunt out there with me when it's over, let her drown and know the feeling she pushes me for in that way.

Delaney's in front of her before I've got chance to move forward any further, his body protecting her like a good little Dom should. Fuck him too. Saving me? For what? So I can keep doing this to anything that gets in my way? He's not saved me, he's fucking condemned Alana. That's all he's done. He's enabled me. Given me another chance at it.

I pull in a breath and watch him watching me, his brow rising in challenge, some fucking authority or concept of friendship I should be honouring. Fool. The psychology professor isn't here anymore. He's gone. Abandoned because of the little slut sucking around her sweet, her eyes looking at me, taunting me towards her. Friendship and loyalty don't live in my monster, they hold no relevance to his needs.

And Delaney can join in anyway if he has too, see what happens when he lets himself loose rather than the façade he uses to cajole and please his subs.

"One more step and we'll both leave, Blaine." I snarl at his words, irritated with his weakness for the skin that hovers behind him. "Let me help you." She doesn't want to go, she wants to stay and play, good little cunts always do when I smile at them. She wants to feel me on her, just as she always has done. Constant little remarks each time she's seen me, occasional touches when Delaney's not been nearby, the glances, the lip licking as she's watched me. Fuck, she was even there the first time I sank myself inside Alana, watching the way I fucked her, panting for it to happen to her, too.

"Your little cunt's interested, Delaney. Don't fucking kid yourself."

"She might be, but not in this fucking mood, you don't," he says, backing away from me as I advance on them. "You're not killing mine."

He pushes her backwards, his body acting as a continued shield as they both disappear out of the doorway. *Not killing his.* It halts the unrelenting footsteps I was going to take after them, shaking me from whatever fucking cloud had begun descending and making me scan the room again.

Debris from my expulsion litters the floor, broken ornaments and paintings, upturned chairs and trashed tables. It's a volatile reaction, one that makes me smile into it and remember the way she causes such aggravation with nothing but her fucking mouth and her unrelenting push.

"Push, push, push." It falls from my lips as I reach for a shard of ceramic, the edges of it sharp enough to slice skin with. It's cracked and sheared, the half section only barely resembling the piece it once was. Cracked and sheared, splintered in two. Only part what it used to be. Fragmented by a substance more significant than the sum of its own original quantity.

I smile wider as the answer hovers in the distance somewhere, beckoning me with songs of love attached to moonlight wanderings. I'm broken in two. My monsters and my professor, both so distanced from each other, unable to form coherent thoughts within themselves. I lower to the floor, searching for a matching part to pair the two back together. Unite them maybe, find a balance. I keep pushing her away, don't I? Keep making her think for the sake of her own health. Maybe it's time not to anymore. Maybe I should just let it be whatever it evolves into, no thought to the consequence of the inevitable fall. She fucking knows now. Knows what she's got in front of her, and still she was worried enough to phone Delaney.

"You calm?"

"No."

I'm a riot of emotions, ones that chase and burn through me, limiting my professor's response to situations such as these. Fuck, I can hardly breathe as the answer finally dawns on me and I see the other side of the ceramic under the cupboard. I should just show her it all, just let her feel it and be done with any recrimination that occurs because of it. No more hiding from my little dove. No more protecting. We'll just fuse, like an idiosyncrasy that does not conform to anything but each other. We'll become the imperfection that enables the perfect, loses themselves within it.

Getting up I reach for the other half of the pot, smiling as I slot them back together and then frowning at the flaw that remains in place, one small piece still missing from the joint. I don't want any cracks or flaws. I want joined and merged. I want every thought that passes through my mind to be able to speak freely and be accepted as standard. I want her mingling with those thoughts.

My eyes rise up to look around again, scanning for the last remaining piece of my jigsaw puzzle as I stand up.

"Where is she?" I snap, my fingers unbuckling my belt and dragging the sodden jeans down my thighs as I keep searching the floor. "I need her."

"Need?" I glare up at Delaney, warning of the temper that's still resonating regardless of my softened fucking heart. He holds his hands up and backs off a step. "At home when she called me." It's not her I want, not the actuality of her, anyway. I want the last fragment of my vase. That's what I'm searching for. I need to see if it fits and slots the pieces back together, completes them.

"Why did she have your fucking number, anyway?" I mutter, my clothes discarded as I turn furniture upright, glancing underneath it and scanning again.

"I put it in there, just in case she needed a confession." Needed a confession? More like fucking.

I scatter the bed sheets, ripping them from the mattress and up ending the frame to look under that too. Nothing is there, nothing like my missing piece, anyway.

"When?" The muttering continues from my mouth, regardless of my disinterest. It calms me down, focusing me in on finding what I'm looking for, perhaps alleviating the strain on my mind.

"While you two slept in my bed, which you never thanked me for." I stop and swing to him, a look of continued irritation settling over my features. Thank him? Fuck that. He holds his hands up again, a smirk lingering around his mouth as he watches my frantic search. "The fuck are you looking for?"

"Answers." I walk away from the bed towards the doors, searching the floor there for it instead.

"You're looking for answers on the floor?"

The thought makes me mutter on, barely hearing his conversation as I keep examining and turning things over, ordering my mind as the events unfold, until I eventually see it laying by the ottoman. It makes me sigh and blow out a breath as I stare at it. It's so small in comparison to the rest of the blue ceramic. Just a simple shard of detailed pot, a sliver of a section, but it's the missing piece I'm desperate for. I don't move for a minute. I just find myself frowning at it, trying to process the information and allow it's credence within my own disarray. It's just there, slightly out of reach, tempting me with its fucking mesmerising gleam in the sun.

"Blaine?"

I don't hear whatever he's saying. I'm disinterested. Unengaged with anything but that slither of ceramic telling me something about myself, or about her. It's indecipherable. A contrast of imaginings I can't find a route for. The jumbled mess inside me narrows my stare, focusing it in on the one thing I'm looking at and blurring the outside around it to indistinct obscurity. The aim eventually drives me towards it, my fingers scooping it up as if it might shatter, and then squeezing it within my grip until I feel it cut in. "Blaine?" I glare at him as I sit on the bed and begin pulling the three bits together in my lap, slotting the portions in place on my thigh and hoping that, when I open this hand, the section inside will still be in one piece. He stares back, a look of confusion on his face. Of course he would be confused. He doesn't know this significance inside. He never will. Never feel its throb within his veins, never feel it's depth of fortitude or determination.

"Look," comes out of me, as I swing my head back to my hand, watching my fingers unfurl to show the missing piece. "It didn't break. Perfect."

"What are you talking about, Blaine?" The vision makes me smile as I gaze at it, the shard still intact as it mingles with my blood and shimmers through the liquid. I lift it out and brush it down, slowly drawing it up towards the top of the pot. It slots into place effortlessly. No sound, no effort required, the blood helping ease the section to where it should be.

"Dates, Delaney. I'm talking about dates. About love."

Chapter 13

ALANA

I don't know when Priest put his phone number in my phone, or why, and if I hadn't been scrolling to find my publisher because of my emails I suppose I never would have found it, but I did. Then I couldn't help but phone him, ask him to check in on Blaine, make sure he wasn't about to do something horrendously stupid. He'd seemed so odd on the drive back to mine. His mood changed from gentlemanly and quietly reserved, to one that became sullen and depressed. I'm not even sure how I felt it, but I did, and that had caused enough worry for me to text him hoping he'd respond. He didn't. It caused, still is causing, an unease I can't put my finger on. I'm worried, anxious to hear he's okay. Love, I suppose, continues regardless of the information I now know. He might have killed her, but he's a killer I have feelings for, irrespective of the rights and wrongs involved in that thought process.

That was over two hours ago, and the time keeps slipping by as I attempt to busy myself with notifications and emails I've no interest in, all the time trying to work out what Blaine's been up to with my emails. I'm backtracking constantly, trying to follow the path of his replies to people, follow the thread to make my responses sound sensible. It's made me smile the entire time, the thought of him ensuring my career doesn't fail because of my 'holiday' somehow comforting to me, as much as it's surprising. I thought he'd let this slide. See it as ineffective and intolerable. Ignore it all. He hasn't. He's been completely on top of it. Kept it flowing without my help at all. When and how, I'm not sure, but he's taken control, allowing me to not think about anything other than him and writing. Every day he's ensured fluidity, interspersing professional emails with ones that answer questions and add a hint of joviality. I didn't realise, didn't think he'd be so thoughtful. And he's fucking brilliant at it, using my tone, but using it more effectively than I could ever employ. It's like he has been me, pretended. The only thing he hasn't been able to do for me is send the actual words to the people who want them. I snort, amused with the fact that he's even given his opinion on my latest covers, telling the designer to change the graphics. He's right to have done as well. He's done just what I would have wanted.

So now I'm just answering and renewing what needs to happen, find my path back into this again. Not that I want to. It was easier with him doing it, less worrying. Still, it needs doing after my sabbatical into finding myself under his hands. A few make me smile, readers telling me of how they enjoyed something I've written, glowing feedback from edits that are in on one of my latest works, but there's nothing from Bree, and she's the one thing I've been searching for. I need her now. I need her guidance, her ability to say it straight and lift me from this fog of confused thoughts. She might not understand completely, and it'll take some explaining to her, but when she gets it she'll help me find the sensible answer to this, or she'll give me the momentum to just go for it and throw caution to the wind entirely.

Picking up my tea, I stare at one of her profiles, checking she's been online and still alive. She is, although her posts are more sporadic than usual. It makes me frown at them, checking for signs of emotion involved. There's none, typically Bree, she just delivers precise content, sales information, occasionally interspersing it with a joke to pull the readers in, but nothing more.

I scroll to my last text to her, the one she never answered, and thumb out another one asking if she wants to meet. Nothing comes back. Nothing at all. So I chuck the phone on the sofa and stare up into my apartment, wondering what to do with myself. Perhaps I should go out and walk the streets, be free for a while and let Manhattan enthuse some words from me. I snort at myself, knowing exactly what I need to enthuse myself. It's got nothing to do with Manhattan's pavements. It's all to do with Blaine and his way of surrounding me. I miss that. Miss that sense of ease under him, regardless of tightening fingers. It makes me look at my own and scan the remnants of black ink still tracing my nails, amused that they no longer tremble. The staining from the old typewriter seems less embedded now, or perhaps it's so engrained it has sunken through and changed the colour of my blood instead, blackened it to match his.

It makes me chuckle a little, remembering the first uncomfortable clunk of that old machine and the harness he strapped me into to use it. We seem so far passed that now, like it's now more natural to me than the laptop that lies in wait in my office. And I haven't even thought about my pills since I've been back, even though they're littered around this apartment. In fact, whatever he's done he's done so effectively I stand and start heading to all the places I keep them in, ready to empty them down the sink. I don't need them anymore, do I? He's done that, helped me away from them. It didn't even seem like he tried.

My phone rings as I'm emptying the last of them, making me run for it in case it's Bree, but as I pick it up Fuckwit's number flashes, his piggy eyes instantly coming to mind as well as the number. Fuck. I pull in a long breath and keep staring at the number, remembering the 19 texts Blaine's already ignored over the last however long. It's the only thing he hasn't responded too. Like the sight of Fuckwit wasn't worth bothering with. But I don't suppose he knows who Fuckwit is, or how relevant he is to my career.

I sigh out and lean back in my chair. I can't do it anymore, can I? I have to get back into this, be Val again. Pretend Barringer is of interest, enough to keep my contract in tow anyway. Still, I throw the phone down again and look towards my office. I could write. I should. And the notifications don't seem as insane as usual, or maybe less chaotic somehow. I'll get back to it. Yes. Perhaps after a few hours writing I'll be able to face conversing with Fuckwit the 3rd and realign my career, find a path through its irritations. It's the writing I want after all, and Blaine's helped me see that again. I can finish this story he's helped me find, use its dialogue to keep me focused enough to put him out of my mind for a while.

Priest would have called if there was a problem, wouldn't he? I nod at myself, knowing he would. He said he would so everything must be okay. Nothing to worry about. Focus, Alana. Christ, I wish I had my stack of papers that's currently sitting in Blaine's house, the same ones that contain the entirety of my story, because without it I'm lost as to what comes next.

~

By the time I look up I realise it's turned dark in the space around me, the evening apparently coming long before I realised it had arrived. I snort, trying to remember the last time I was so absorbed in my story that time simply slipped away as I wrote it. Months, years even. Well, other than the time Blaine made me write. I smile at the thought and check the clock, then listen to my stomach as it growls at me, instantly reminding me of Blaine again, not that I've been able to ignore his interference. He's everything this story is. Bold, considered, unabashed in his deliverance of words. He's the epitome of a hero, one drenched in dirty words and endless orgasms, something that is as true to him as I could ever write. It makes me smile wider as I push myself away from the desk and wheel away to my folders, hitting print as I go. I still don't have a title for this, nor a pen name. It's still such a change from my norm that I can't find the right words to describe it. Certainly not a name that hints at its plausibility. It might even be that it needs to be another male author writing it, not a woman. I don't know. Maybe I'll know when I write the end.

I wander out into the kitchen and open the fridge to find some food. There's nothing in there. I don't know why I thought there would be. I haven't been here, haven't been shopping. I haven't even got a pint of milk. I drank the tea black earlier, strangely enjoying it for some reason. So I pick up my keys and jacket, swiping at my bag as I go. Shopping it is, perhaps it'll help me focus in on something other than Blaine, who continues to linger in my mind.

I'm not sure what to do about it as I keep going out the door and down to the streets below. He's so present in here, like he's here beside me now as I stare at the traffic and walk towards the deli. I can feel him, just like I could in his home. I can feel his hands on me, his voice in my ear, and his heartbeat on mine as I keep walking. It makes the noise around me become a distant cacophony rather than the chaos it should be. Almost like a blur of muffled rebounds, not the sharp sounds I normally reside near.

My phone bleeps at some point breaking me of the comforted smile that's still attached to my mouth, so I reach for it and scan the message, not caring for its content.

- Where?

It's Bree. The sight of her name makes me sigh in relief and stop to send a pleading response. Anywhere she likes, at any time she likes. I miss her. I miss her banter and her charm. I miss the way she just says it straight, cutting right across the bullshit and offering precise answers to questions I fumble around. I miss the closeness of her.

She comes back reasonably quickly as I carry on, saying Bluties in about an hour, which makes me check out my attire. It's atrocious. Black jeans, a brown t shirt and my green leather jacket. It's as drab as the mood I returned in, one that had me thinking of nothing but Blaine and what I should do with the thoughts he left me with.

Charlotte E Hart
THE END

Think, that's what he said. Him and me. That we should think. In reality, no matter how much I've thought, nor diverted my thoughts, it doesn't seem to matter to me. The information is all there now, waiting for me to find out more if I choose to. I got into that car. I followed irrespective of the knowledge he delivered. And I still want to, don't I? I'm still willing to travel down that rabbit hole, learning more about him with every mile we fall. I want to know more. I want to feel more. I want those waters to be calm on top, no matter the ferocious intent beneath them.

Whoever he might have been before me, I don't believe that man's still there. For all his heavy hands and bitter words, his heart beats in there. It thuds with its own cadence, one I can still hear against my ear as I keep going towards Bluties. I need a drink so I can fathom explaining this to Bree. She needs to understand so she can help me organise myself, form an opinion that isn't just based on the area between my wayward crotch and my heart. I need her logic for a while, her sense of rationale on the outside of this world I've slipped into, no apparent care to my well being involved.

Screw the shopping.

I fluff my hair around as I carry on along the pavement, shaking it about and heading straight for the person who can help me find sense in this. I'll apologise for the last meeting, or leaving as the case might be, and then talk. I'll talk my arse off at her, explaining it and giving her a base to work from. No wonder none of those other submissives I talked to in the beginning could explain it. It's not logical. It's inside me, something most people can't relay with words, but I can. It's my job. It's what I do. I turn emotions into words so people can understand them, find sense in them. I can do this. I can. And then she can help me understand why, even after the knowledge I've got, I still want him around me. Inside me.

It's only ten minutes before I'm turning into Bluties, my bag discarded onto the nearest available table. I'm enthused by the thought of seeing her again, joining back into the reality of the normal world maybe. Everything looks so new here, as if it's somehow changed from the place I once came too. It's not just this venue either. It's everything. I've noticed stupid things on the way here. The way the light glints as the afternoon sun cascades down on it. The way the occasional tree whistles above me as autumn winds whip them around. The sounds embedded in other sounds. Not the top line noises of everyday life, the ones beneath the surface. The ones that complete all the other noises somehow, making them deeper than they are on their own.

I smile at the waiter as he comes over and order a coffee, one hand reaching for a chair as I think about those noises and differences. It's the way I used to write. I used to find those small differences, use them to explain something. Not because I searched, but because they came naturally to me. I suppose it was the whimsical Alana in me. The version of me that daydreamed and let the little things be so much bigger than they were. He's made me see them again somehow, hasn't he? I don't know how. I don't even know if it's entirely him, but they're here again regardless.

"Lana." I look up, shocked out of my musings.

"Bree." She just stands there, her arms folded and her bag still firmly clamped under her arm. "Are you going to sit down?" I ask, as the waiter delivers my coffee.

"Thinking." Oh. I smirk a little, amused by her attitude. She deserves it. I've got no right to have a go. If she wanted to walk out of here right now and never speak to me again I'd understand, much as I might hate the thought.

"Please, Bree," I say, as I pick up the coffee and look at her. "I'm sorry."

"What for?" she snaps, no movement in her frame whatsoever. The question throws me for a minute, making me wonder what I am actually sorry for. I'm not sorry for going with Blaine, but I am sorry for making her feel like her opinion didn't matter. It does, did.

"Please, Bree, just sit. I need to explain this to you so you understand."

"Are you still with him?" My head nods, irrespective of whether I am or not. I will always be with him in some ways. This is a part of who I am now no matter how much I think like he's asked me too. I've felt what he's shown me, let it change me, or take me back to who I used to be. "No fucking point then," she snarls, her body swinging away from me. I stand up instantly, my fingers reaching for her without thought.

"But I need you too, Bree. I need your levelling. I need your help to work it out." She tugs my hand from her, her feet backing away almost immediately.

"No, Lana, you don't. You proved that by getting in the car with him." I sigh, wondering how the hell I'm going to make this work.

They're poles apart as humans, each with their own way of being themselves.

"But Bree …" She dumps her bag on the table and glowers at me.

"I mean, how fucking stupid are you?" Her words make me wince and raise myself back from her as she sits. "The fuck, Lana? What the hell is wrong with you?"

"I …"

"And don't give me any of that submissive shit." She glares, her body leaning across the table at me as she snatches my coffee from my hand then starts drinking it. "Jesus Christ, what's he done to you? It's not real, Lana. You damn well told me that yourself." But it is.

I sigh out again, shaking my head at myself more than her as I stare at the table, near defeat setting in before I've even attempted explanation.

"Bree, you need to let me …"

"I don't need to let you say shit," she snaps, leaning back into her seat and still maintaining her glare of disdain. "I need to get you to a shrink." I snort, tickled by the thought.

"Blaine is one."

"Great." The sarcasm in her voice, as I creep my eyes back up, is loud and clear for me to hear. She rolls her eyes in response, huffing a breath from her lungs. "Whippy dick's a sex god, too, presumably." Well, yes. I smile a little, letting thoughts that shouldn't be in this room encroach into my mind. His hands, the way they move across me. The clamps I endured. The rack. She just rolls her eyes again, digging into her bag for something. "Still, the fuck are you thinking? You could have been raped or some shit." I tilt my head, acknowledging that not only have I just about been anyway, but I actually encouraged the thought in my own mind. How the hell do I explain that to someone, her? "At least tell me where you've been before I beat the shit out of you for stupidity." Where have I been? Down a kinky rabbit hole, that's where. "And order me a decent fucking drink. This coffee is disgusting."

"His house. The beach," I reply, remembering the sand beneath my feet, wishing I was back there again with him. Preferably not drowning, though. I smirk and raise my hand, signalling for the waiter again. "Then Boston. A latte please for my friend," I ask him, as he comes over, hoping the sentiment still rings true after what's about to leave my mouth. He disappears again leaving us to our conversation. "Normal stuff, Bree." I lean in, my voice dropping to a whisper. "And then I was on a stage in front of a room of Sadists, tied down. I whimpered and moaned, Bree. I gasped and I panted. In fact," I raise myself back to upright again, suddenly unashamed of what I'm explaining and happy for the world to hear should they choose to eavesdrop. "I was begging to be fucked, from my knees. And after that I crawled after him, desperate for a fucking orgasm he wouldn't give me." Both her brows raise as she still hovers over the drink. "And then we went to his parent's house."

"Dinner?"

"Hardly, they're both dead," I reply, remembering the words that came from him in that house and how much they affected our perfect night. I blow a puff of air out of my mouth, wondering how I deliver that next piece of information when I don't have the facts about it. "We had an argument instead."

"Wow, busy few days," she eventually says, a snort coming from her nose. "Sore are we?"

A slow smile breaks across my face. At least she's smiling again. That's a route forward I can use, her too. I nod at her, barely feeling the welts and bruises that are under these clothes. It's not them that make me sore, it's the continued ache that's under my skin because he's not here to touch it. I should feel free of him, ready to be who I was before. Instead I feel trapped again, regardless of the open air of the city I'm in. It feels suffocating to me in some way, like the sea isn't here to open the horizon anymore.

I stare at her, trying to find more words to help explain the sense of ease with him when we're together, the application of emptiness maybe.

"I need him, Bree, and I need you to understand that." She shakes her head.

"I don't."

"What do you do when it's all too much?" I ask. She frowns and takes the coffee that's offered to her from the waiter, her other hand pushing mine over to me. "You must feel it sometimes, the panic?"

"I guess I sleep." She shrugs and sips her drink.

"You don't sleep, neither of us do," I reply.

"I do, maybe not on the US's normal time zone but …"

"I haven't had any pills for days, Bree. I haven't wanted to take them. And I sleep and work seamlessly, no concerns. Nothing."

"Okay."

"He made that happen, don't you see? He makes so many things happen in my mind. It's like he changes me into someone else, or maybe a repressed version of who I became." She stares, less than convinced with anything that's coming from my mouth. I huff out in exasperation, mainly with myself. This isn't working. Why can't I find the right words? "I can just ... I see clearly now, Bree. It's quiet with him."

"Right." She draws the word out, a look of uncertainty on her face. "Because I'm doubting that with the screams that must come from your mouth." I snort again.

"The screams are the silence, Bree. They come from a black hole inside me and when they come out, they take everything else with them. All the notifications. All the madness. All the deadlines and unachievable things I've placed myself under." I twist, focusing on her and finally finding some way of relaying this. "Some notion of achievement lead me to this place we're in, Bree. But some *'thing'* happened to me along the way. The stories got lost. Or became dead. I don't want dead stories, Bree. Do you? I want life breathed into them again. I want the ocean and waves. I want the freedom that gives me to let go, not just another story, you know?" She looks confused. I'm not surprised. It's becoming more and more chaotic in my own head with every next word uttered. "Oh god, I'm failing at this. I need you to get this, Bree. I need your help with something."

"What? Sounds like you've got it all sussed out in your mind." She snorts cynically.

"I need to search for my words again, Bree. Don't you get that? I need to find them in a fog, not have them leap to me without thought. He gives me that grey area I lost."

"By beating you?"

"No, he .. Yes, he does do that, but it's not like violence," regardless of the pressure. It has a foundation beneath it deeper than any normal application of love, giving a sense of purpose maybe to the entirety of being with him.

I flick my gaze away from her and look out onto the street, hoping for inspiration to help me explain. It's so murky in his world and yet clear as day in some ways too. Why can't I get that out?

A woman walks passed, her face smiling in the window to check her lipstick as she goes. It reminds me of the woman he claims to have killed. "And he's confused me now with something." Well, not overly confused. I mean, it's not like I don't want to go back. "He's …" Killed someone by doing the very thing I'm venturing into, wanting? Fuck. I can't tell her that. Even I don't know if that's okay yet. Tears well up at the thought of it all, taking me back to walking that street in Boston and feeling so alone until he arrived behind me again. "Oh god, he's just so different, Bree." I swipe at my ridiculous tears. "The other subs were right, the ones I first interviewed," I continue, still swiping and trying not to look at her. "It's an inexplicable sensation." One I can't get out of my own mouth, let alone tell her. "Life with him would be so altered from what I have been."

"Then you stay right where you are, Lana," she says, her hand reaching over and grabbing mine.

I look at it, knowing there's more to the statement than just staying in Manhattan without him. She means her too. She means staying with her and within this life I've create for myself. She means going back to the old me.

"I don't want too, Bree," I eventually say, still looking at our hands and wondering what I mean. "I don't want any of that anymore, not unless I can find a way of doing it without going mad anyway. I'm not coping like you are. I'm done with it." She sighs at the same time as I do, both of us lost with what the hell to say. "I am sorry for what happened by the way. I never meant to ..."

"I know. I was bitchy." She cuts in, waving me off from finishing. "He is hot as fuck by the way. Smug fucker."

"He kinda has every right to be."

"Sounds it. He got any sisters lurking about? We could double up."

I laugh, her words breaking my used thoughts on him as I fiddle with my cup. That would be good. Bringing him into normality with average people and their everyday lives might make things seem less removed, maybe joined up somehow.

"I don't know. He's got a brother. I don't really know anything else about him, but I want too, Bree. I do. I want everything with him." I shuffle on my seat, strangely unused to the words coming from my mouth. I've never had to explain them to anyone before. I've only ever thought about them while he does all the things he does. And I've never loved before him, never chatted with girlfriends about giggly girly moments, sex, the want or need for more of someone.

"Does he want you?" She suddenly asks.

My eyes shoot up to hers, my mind instantly catching up with the fact that I don't know. I hadn't thought about that lately, not in any real depth. He just told me to think about things, to go home and really think. That must mean he wants something more than just fucking, mustn't it? He told me about the thing that's been keeping him distanced from me and then told me we'd need go backwards before we went forward. That he'd do that for me. That must imply trust, love.

"I ..."

"You don't know, do you?" she says.

I stare at her, wondering if he's at home now ridding himself of me. He could be. He might have sent me here with the intent of never darkening my door again, or brightening it. It could just be his way of finishing us. The thought makes tears come again, which instantly brings on visions of him wiping them away and sucking them into his mouth.

"I need a drink," I spit out, my feet having me up and walking to the bar before I've had any thought of stopping myself. Perhaps if I get plastered it'll all make some bloody sense, because this feeling of insecurity is not getting me anywhere at all.

"Why?" Bree asks, her body sliding up to mine at the bar. She bumps shoulders with me as I look back at her sharply. "Why, Lana? Why would you need a drink if you love him and life is happy?" I scoff, turning away and focusing on the alcohol bottles for direction.

"You don't understand, Bree. How could you?" I'm not telling her the whole truth, am I?

"You're damn right I don't. None of this is like you," she says. "Where has the other you gone to? The one who's self-assured, forward moving. The one who knocks out books like a fucking queen and doesn't let anything stand in her way? I've never even seen you cry. Didn't know you could." I roll my own eyes at her, exhausted with trying to find words I don't have to give.

"I can't explain it, so let's not bother. We'll get drunk instead, go dancing. Forget it."

"Because that's going to fix it, isn't it?" she replies, disdain levying her tone.

"Fuck you," I snap. "You've no idea what it is to be me. No idea of the pressure or the constancy of it all. You sit there in your office, never meeting anybody, never dealing with having people pressure you for more. You do it because you've got nothing else, Bree. No life, no sense of responsibility to huge publishers." I signal the barman, pointing at the Jamesons and nodding, twice, then turn back to her. "You've no right to judge what I do or do not do, or who I do it with. You have nothing but screens and whatever you choose to do with your time, and yet you waste it holed up in your 8x8 box getting lost in other people's dreams. I want reality, Bree. I want dreams to be real. I'm fucking tired of living everyone else's. When is it my fucking turn, hey?" She just stares. No emotion. No response. "What?" She raises a brow. "I just want my fucking turn at it. Is that so hard to comprehend? I want to look up at the sky and see a reason for all this. Not rot in a hole pretending I'm happy with everyone else getting their fix of happy ever afters I can't find myself. You go for it, though, rot away. Hide from the world as much as you like. Carry on pretending you're straight. How's that working for you?"

"Fuck, you're a bitch sometimes, Lana."

"Screw you." Screw it all.

"Screw you back."

"Whore."

"Slut." My smile creeps back in as two glasses of Jamesons lands in front of us, a puff of air coming from the expulsion of rambled rubbish from my mouth. I don't even mean it, not some of it, anyway.

"Cunt," I snap out, a smirk breaking through.

"Ooh, good one," she says, her brows raised as I laugh and watch her smile coming back, a snort following it.

"Yeah, he taught me that one too," I say, lifting my glass, clinking it with hers. "Cheers."

We both down it, our eyes peering over the glass at each other, until she drops hers and begins to walk away.

"Let's go do cocktails and dancing then. Fuck it, yeah?"

"Good call." Fucking perfect as far as I'm concerned. I won't have to think when I'm drunk. I won't have to acknowledge anything. I can just get hammered, dance, grind on something of use and let myself drift off into any place that'll attempt the silence he manages. I'll just get lost for a while and forget.

Chapter 14

ALANA

It's the beginning of my favourite song. I can hear it in front of me somewhere, or all around me. Who cares? I'm just looking into the vast room of writhing bodies, trying to keep myself from becoming entangled with the next set of waving arms. I'm not even sure I care about that much, as my hips begin moving. It's so loud in here. The beat thumping into me, the bass booming. I think we're in a new high end club, some place that Bree said we had to come to. Or we might have moved onto somewhere else. No matter. It makes little difference to the concoction of drinks inside me, or the way it's making me forget everything and just feel.

I don't know where she's gone, or care for now. She was with a woman, I know that much, and that's good enough reason for me to have left and moved into this thrumming mass of limbs. A body glances off the side of me, her arms locking with mine, fingers mingling for some reason. It's surreal, making us join in with a rhythm as the room seems to move up and down. Up and down, my knees pushing me along to the tune, the bounce of them in time with the bass thundering on. Everyone's moving like a tidal wave, smoke cresting on the top of them, a distant blur of fingers and hands in the air. And the strobe lights. Oh god, they're so vivid. Greens, blues. Flashes of pink shining onto people's faces, highlighting their smiles and laughter. It's turned into fun riding this wave, letting it take me out and away from my thoughts. Forget. No intensity, no orders or instructions. No pain. No love, for now, either. There's nothing but freedom and music, a sense of not caring for tomorrow or what it brings. I could do anything here. Be anyone.

I close my eyes at some point, listening to the sounds around me and letting them ebb in, my body still moving with little care to what people think. It's been so long since this feeling was inside me. School days, college maybe. It's wonderful, uplifting. It makes me raise my arms higher, letting them join in with the others and soar. That's what it feels like as her hold gets tighter on me, like we're flying, a dreamlike state becoming near orgasmic in this atmosphere. And I'm so aroused. I can feel my insides wanting nothing more than fingers inside them. They ache along with the rest of me for touch, for someone to slide over me. No force, no being held or pushed into position, just a gentle glide of touch.

It's all so far removed from what Blaine achieves, but that's what I need in here. A myriad of my dreams, lifting me into them, reminding me of happy ever afters. I need soft lips and a gentle caress, something to prolong the ache in a different way, making the build less dramatic. These hands in my fingers would do. I could put them on me now, let the world blur into something intriguing and stimulating. A smile grows on my face thinking about it. I don't even know who they belong to, and it's something that might seem odd outside these doors, but in here, now, it feels natural. A progression maybe. I don't know, and don't damn well care either.

I'm aroused, my arse writhing onto whatever's behind me, my breath bouncing back at me from whoever's in front. It's all so close, so hot. There's no space here, no room to escape what my body's craving. And why should I? I'm different now, aren't I? Perverted by him. I could just let this happen, make it happen. Use what he's shown me about myself to learn something new.

I tug on the fingers, bringing them down around me and putting them onto my hips. I'd fuck here. I would. I want everything I've never felt before him. Filth and sex, fucking against toilet walls. I want the grime he's shown me I can excel in. The garbage bins spring to mind as the fingers start inching closer to the crotch of my jeans, the memory of my mouth around his cock embedding further than it ever has. I want that sluttiness again. I need it.

It makes me grab at the hands wandering my body, teasing me, and pull them to exactly where I want them. My own hand stays on top of hers, guiding it, putting the pressure on the area that I crave. I couldn't give a damn who it is or even why I'm doing this. It's what I want and I'm taking it. And the music just keeps its relentless hum going, its thundering bass pulling me into it and making me moan as the fingers dig in harder. It's not going to take much either. I'm close, desperate for an orgasm, but I need the fingers touching skin, not this separation. I want them inside, making the ache disappear entirely.

My eyes open at the awareness and scan to see if anyone's watching. No one is. No one cares. They're all too busy feeling the same sensations I am, getting lost. So I turn and close my eyes again, not wanting to see the person who's doing this to me. I don't need to see. I don't care. It's happening regardless of who it's happening with.

She's so close, so close that I brush her breast. It makes a blush rise through me, my hand hovering around the area, momentarily unsure what to do with the thought. Fuck it. It's as hot as I am, the feel of it in my hand an enticement I can't refuse as I let my mouth move in again. I rub at it, gently teasing the soft flesh until I find the nipple through thin fabric. And then lips are on me, their impact as mesmerising as the music.

I'm lost in them before I know it, wiling her hand further into the jeans she's hovering around. It causes a groan to echo from me into her mouth as our tongues begin swirling, chasing each other around and heightening the mood. It's all so damn sexy, riddled with sin and connotations of fucking. It's just like him, dirty and full of passion. And her hand inches in as I keep grinding, travelling along the fine down carefully, perhaps not sure what it's doing either.

I push my pussy into it, moaning into her mouth again as I feel the slight contact with my clit and welcome it. Nothing's stopping this now. Nothing. We're sandwiched in, surrounded by a room full of bodies grinding on us. I don't care if they're watching, joining in even. We should all do this. Fuck ourselves stupid until nothing's left but heaving bodies and primal need. And then something changes in the hands holding me, they become bolder, tightening all over me and dragging me into them. It causes another gasp and groan to come from me as they do what they want, slowly pushing further in and finding that sweet spot inside.

THE END

"Fuck," comes from me, as I break away from the lips and tip my head into the music again.

I open my eyes and just stare upwards, not wanting to know who is doing this to me and not caring either. I'm just here, flying in the hands of a woman as another tune bangs into the air, blues, greens and pinks flashing through the air, my mind churning along with it all.

It's mind-bending as my orgasm starts crawling through me, making me want nothing more than the fall at the end. And the sounds keep coming along with the rhythm of her hand, a momentum building because of it. It makes my legs tremble, weakening under the pressure of what's happening.

I grab out at something to hold onto behind me and lean into it. Hands are quick to wrap around my waist. I don't know who they belong to either. What does it matter anymore? It doesn't. Nothing does but this orgasm that's coming.

The hands are firmer than the woman's, harder. A man's I should think, not that I care. They'll do. Anything will. They grope at me, my breasts being squeezed and tugged, fondled as a mouth latches onto my neck from behind. And then it leaves me, pushing me back towards the woman and leaning over me. The vision of her face as I'm pushed at her comes too late for me to do anything about it. My orgasm's coming too quickly, the gentle pounding of her hand driving me into it as our eyes meet for the first time. *Bree.*

I gasp, shocked, as she locks lips with the man over my shoulder, too involved in the moment's escalation to stop it and too wound up by the sudden vision of her kissing someone to really care. It explodes inside me, sending my body lax between them as she keeps rubbing and he holds me up, our combined bodies still moving to the rhythm around us. Oh god, Bree. And who the fuck is this guy? I'm not sure if I care or not. Maybe I don't. I don't know as he begins running his hand down my body too, his fingers heading towards hers still moving inside me. Fuck, what's happening? It's all strange, perverse. It's Bree. I can't …

His lips come back to me again, the feel of them on my cheek as mesmerising as hers. I stare at her, dumbfounded and hazy about the whole fucking thing as she draws her hand out of me. Bree. I shake my head at her, not knowing why I am doing. Perhaps it's him on me, or the fact that it's her. I don't know. And he fucking pushes on me, guiding me away from the crowd. I snatch at Bree's hand, unsure what the fuck I'm doing but knowing I'm not going to stop it. No way. And Bree's coming with me. She is. I want her there. If this is going to happen, she's coming too. I need her. We started this, we'll finish it together regardless of who this guy is.

Everything seems to flash by as we move, a blur of lights and bodies zooming passed as my feet keep moving, the rhythm seeming to propel them onwards. Is this what I've become because of Blaine? I'm insatiable with the thought, almost leading him rather than being pushed. And I'm heading for those toilets I was thinking about, searching the walls for directions and madly barging people out of the way. Jesus, what's wrong with me? And his lips are fucking divine on my neck, still nibbling occasionally, chuckling at my impatient hustle through the throng of revellers. Bree's still with me, I can feel her fingers in mine, following me as if she wants this too. Why? We've been friends, nothing else. I don't understand. It's foggy, a mess in my brain, but it feels good, right. I can't process it, nor do I bloody care at the moment. If this is me, if this is what I want, then I'm taking it without thought.

I feel like this because Blaine's made me see it, don't I? It's as liberating as him. Freeing. I feel bold and unabashed with my decisions as I push another woman out of the way and finally see the arrows pointing to the place I want. I hurry on, dragging Bree and turning to see him for the first time. The flash of him shows me half his face. He's handsome in a pretty way. Ruffled blonde hair, a sexy as hell smile, blue eyes that remind me of Blaine's sea. Fuck. It makes me greedy for him, for Blaine actually, but he's not here. This one is. And he reminds me of him in some way, perhaps around the eyes or that smile. I can hardly see in this light anyway. I'm drunk. She's drunk. We're all damn well drunk and who gives a fuck anymore. I'm behaving like a slut. I might as well enjoy it for a while, no regrets or recrimination involved. It's a one off.

"Left," he says, his hand pushing me into a doorway as he opens it. It's not the toilet, it's a store cupboard we all fall into. It's rammed with goods and bottles of cleaner, barely enough space for the three of us to stand in. He doesn't give me a chance to think about it, nor Bree, as the door closes and it goes dark again. His mouth is on mine instantly, my own fingers dragging him to me in the dark, feet tripping over something.

"Lana," Bree says. I barely hear her over my desperation to fuck, my hands beginning to rip at his belt. It's insatiable. Voracious. It's like nothing's finished here yet. It's not completed until I've got everything from the moment. I'm taking it. I have too. It's like I have my own power here. I'm in control of it. I've never felt anything like this need before, unless it's been with Blaine, and he's always in control of everything. I need to know this is me too, that it's not just his influence. "Fuck, Lana. Stop for a minute." My mouth tears away from him to look at her as she pulls on my arm, my fingers still yanking at his jeans.

"What?" It's panted from me, my mouth wanting nothing more than to latch back on, have her get involved in the kiss too.

"Look at him." What? I back off a little, pushing his chest away from me. What's wrong with him? I scan his body, looking for issues, there's nothing to see. In fact, in this muted light, he's still hot as all hell and I'm gagging for him. It's ludicrous how much I want him, actually. "Really look, Lana."

"What?" he says, his hands grabbing for me again. She moves behind me, sounds scattering the quiet space. "Come on, ladies. You're not fucking stopping this now." No, quite right. It's happening. The light suddenly flicks on, momentarily blinding me. I raise my hand, trying to stop the sensation interfering with my flow.

"Christ, Bree," I spit out, flummoxed by her sudden halting of proceedings.

"Lights on is fine by me," he says, his fingers pulling me towards his crotch as he leans in to kiss me again. It's fine by me too. Bree can leave if she wants. I don't care anymore.

"Look at what you're doing," she snaps, her hand wrenching me away. "Or who." I stumble back, the force of her pull making me stumble over something beneath my feet and collapse to the ground. I look up as I scrabble to my knees, catching the glimpse of his hands undoing his jeans before carrying on to his face. "Look, Lana." He sneers a little as he looks down, impatience etching his face, and the instant he does I can see exactly what she's talking about, even in my drunken haze. He looks like Blaine, his jaw mirroring the exact same lines, his eyes boring into me with his frustration.

"What's your name?" I snap up at him.

"The fuck does that matter?" he replies, hitching his jeans around as I watch sweat run along his cheekbones. Oh god, he really does look like Blaine. "You wanna suck it?"

"No, she doesn't," Bree cuts in, her hand on my arm to haul me up. I just stare up at him, letting Blaine's eyes look down on me, their power as strong as they've ever been when he looks at me. Oh god, what am I doing? I'm here with a stranger, and Bree. "Get up, Lana."

"Who are you?" I snap out as I clamber to my feet. "Name?"

"The fuck's wrong with you two?" he says, a confusion coming over his features, changing his whole face to one I don't know. He looks like a lost schoolboy suddenly, hardly anything of Blaine remaining because of it.

"NAME." It shouts out of me as I move into him, fuelled by my own edginess probably, or my insatiability to mate with men in store cupboards. God, I'm a slut.

"Fuck," he says as he backs off, his eyes looking between the two of us, his hands in the air. "Cole. What's your problem?"

"Surname?"

"Jacobs."

The air puffs out of me, my feet stumbling back at the recognition. It causes realty to come racing back, the sex driven drunken haze evaporating at the same moment. Christ.

"Come on," Bree says, quietly. "We're out of here." I'm still staring, unable to process the fact that I nearly had sex with Blaine's brother, let alone the fact that Bree had her hand in my knickers, or is even in here with us.

"No you don't," he says, his frame blocking the door. "You don't do that and then just leave. The fuck is your problem?" My eyebrows shoot up at his tone, amused perhaps at how similar he sounds to Blaine when he's frustrated.

"You sound like him," mutters out of me, a slight slur attached to the laugh that follows. Christ, this is utterly absurd. I look down at myself, noticing my undone jeans and laugh some more as I pull them back together and zip up.

"Who?" he replies, his hand trying to reach for me. I bat it away, still giggling around in my thoughts as I look back at Bree and smile. This whole situation is bizarre. And if he thinks I'm even slightly scared of him he's got another thing coming. I've been under his brother, these schoolboy fumblings mean nothing to me, regardless of how good those lips felt.

"Your brother." Good god, I need to get out of here. Regain some bloody control over myself. For a start, have a conversation with my best friend about why we just did what we did. "Get out of my way, Cole." He stares back, his face a picture of confusion, which just makes me laugh again as he stands in front of my exit out of here. "Or can you do what he does?" The thought intrigues me for a second or two, making me wonder if he's into the same thing as I scan his features again. "Can you?" Because I might carry on if he can.

Bree coughs, probably at the thought, or me. Even without Blaine I'm doing this. I'm searching for it in Cole's eyes, wanting nothing more than tightening hands and something to tell me to get on with this, forget my own confusion. Nothing's there, though. He's empty of Blaine's commands and dictations. He's simply out for a good time, ready to fuck the next thing that offers itself, I'm sure.

A sigh comes from me. I need to go home, sleep whatever this is off. Try and rationalise it in the morning maybe. "Cole please, just let us out. This is done."

He still stands there, probably as perplexed as I am. Although, I'm not getting high grade intelligence flowing from him, more a sense of baffled bewilderment. It makes me chuckle as I look at him and remember Blaine's dark eyes and scowl. He's so different from the Jacobs brother in front of me. Grown up, perhaps. Older, wiser. Nastier. Dirtier. The thought makes my insides clamp around nothing again and snarl at myself, wishing he was here to deal with this fucking ache I can't do anything with now.

I end up pushing him out of the way, grabbing Bree's hand as I do. Whatever this has been, it's over, and Bree and I need a chat, or another bloody drink. A large one. He lets us go as I turn out of the room, clinging to Bree as if my life depends on it. The feel of her in my hand makes me shake my head at myself and giggle, as I wander through the crowd again, leading us towards a bar. Perhaps we don't need to chat. Perhaps this is just something that I'll do now. I've been turned into something I wasn't before, enjoyed it. Why should it need explanation or discussion? I'm not even convinced I want to discuss it.

The thought has me smiling wider as we creep through the throngs, my fingers feeling comfortable in hers. Maybe this is just who I am, who the real Alana is.

"Hey, you're the girl, aren't you?" a voice shouts behind us. I swing round to see Cole following, his body cutting through the crowd. "The one I crashed into?" I turn from him again, still with a smile as I continue aiming for the bar. What a night. What a morning. Everything changed that morning. I didn't know it would, didn't know my whole being would change because of Blaine, but it has. For the better, I might add.

He suddenly arrives at my side then slides in front of me, a warm smile on his face as he looks at me and runs a hand through his hair. He seems dishevelled as I smile at him, still searching for similarities. Brother. What a strange thought. Blaine seems so alone all the time, distant from the world around him.

"You look different. Your hair's down," he says, reaching for it. I pull away and twiddle the purple tips of it, trying to envisage Blaine in this guise. Friendlier, happier. Cole looks almost contrite, a boyish charm in his uncomfortable posture, nothing like Blaine ever does. I stare again, wondering what I could ask him, if I should even. He must know so much about who Blaine is, why Blaine is. "He wouldn't let me see you after. Said he'd kill me if I went in your room." The words make me snort and smile, imagining Blaine in his irritated mode, his eyes levelling antipathy at anything that dares defy him. "Let me buy you a drink to say sorry," he shouts over the music that's building again, his frame leaning into me. I raise a brow, wondering what for. I'm not sorry about any escapade I nearly got involved in. Not really, only that it was Cole. I'd still fuck now if his brother was here. "Not for that, you two are hot as fuck. A man has needs." He smirks, which makes me laugh as I watch the crinkle of his eyes, the lines of them the same as his brother's. "I mean the crash. We could talk," he points at the bar. "If you wanted too. No fucking involved." He holds his hands up. "Promise." Talk.

Bree squeezes my hand behind me, making me turn to look at her. She nods, then pulls me into her.

"You need this, Lana," she says into my ear. "Go with him. Learn about that man who's got you all fucked up." I'm not fucked up. I know that much without any guidance. I'm alive and finally beginning to feel it again. "We can talk about this another time."

She smiles at me as she squeezes my hand again, letting me know that whatever this was, it was okay. I know that too. Odd, perhaps. Different, yes. But it's okay. I nod at her, accepting that I absolutely do want to know more, and if Cole can give me something that will help organise what I do about Blaine then I'll take that information from him. Besides. I am thirsty.

"So," Cole says behind me, as I watch Bree go. I turn back to him, tilting my head at what exactly he's going to offer with his 'no fucking involved' statement. He hovers there, his hands sliding into his pockets nervously as he glances around.

"You're nervous, Cole," comes from me, amused at his change in temperament from the man ten minutes ago. "Do I make you nervous?"

"Anything to do with my brother makes me nervous," he replies.

I smile, as he pushes alongside me, clearing a path to the crowded bar and hailing a female bar tender. She's there instantly, her boobs aimed at him without much thought. He leans across and orders something, kissing the side of her face as he does. Seems he's on a winner after we've done our talking. It's another thing that makes me smile and chuckle to myself, amused at his affability. He's nice, happy. Cute even.

I end up wandering back into the masses while he waits there, my body not caring to stop with whatever partying it was joining in with before. It's all so happy in here. No worries, no concerns. Nothing to think about or tax myself with. I just let my frame mingle again, the occasional bash from someone welcomed really as it reminds me of carefree abandon.

"Drink," he calls.

Drink and words. Conversations about someone I'm trying to deal with, a life I'm trying to fathom. It causes a slight sigh to leave me as I turn, the weight of my fears coming out with it. He tips the tall glasses of clear liquid at me, his smile a reminder of the very man I'm trying to process, and then waggles it as he moves towards the side end of the bar. I follow, bracing my hands to my side, perhaps hoping to knock this free for all Alana out of myself and concentrate on serious matters, but I don't want to, not really. I mean, why should I? Why should I let this relaxed nature dissipate into fogs of trying to understand a man who is indecipherable on most occasions? Perhaps I should just accept the fact that I can't have everything I want with a man like Blaine, and maybe that's the fucking point. It might just be that his strength around me lies in the fact that I don't see his fears, shouldn't.

We keep moving, the music becoming less raucous as we weave our way through more people towards a corner at the back, until we eventually reach an anti-room of some kind. It's full of people milling around, leather seats and long couches dotted around, barely clothed women lounging on them in their state of disarray. He walks over to one girl, who's about passed out on one of them, and turns to hand me our drinks before lifting her and moving her somewhere else.

"Wasted," he says, gruffly, the beginnings of a snarl directed at her prone body as if it disgusts him, his hand brushing the seat off for me. It amuses me more given the cupboard we've all just been in, our own minds near as wasted as that poor girl. "Sit." Oh, harsh.

"That sounded like your brother, too," I say, as I find my way into the area and take a seat.

"I'm nothing like my brother, which I'm sure you know all about," he says, reaching for his drink in my hand and smiling again as he takes it.

"True," I reply, as he sits next to me. "You look nothing like him either."

"No, we never did." I don't doubt it. They're so different, both in looks and nature.

"So, what are we talking about?" I've no idea really. I can't even process how one starts a conversation about Blaine, or even if I should in reality. It seems rude in some ways. Uncouth.

"How is he?"

THE END

"What? He's your brother. Wouldn't you know?"

"I don't know anything about my brother anymore. I just worry about him." The admittance makes my brows rise, wondering why. "He's been distant for a long time now. Changed from who he used to be. I don't know what happened between us. You're the first woman he's shown any interest in for well over a year or so. I just thought you might know how he is."

"He's okay," I reply, quietly. Assuming that what I know is as okay as Blaine ever is. Although, how would I know? He's the only version of him I've ever known.

"Is he? Really?" Cole seems genuinely concerned as he asks the question. Probing, as if I should understand everything he doesn't. But I don't know the answer to that question, and I also don't know how much I can say to him about anything anyway.

"The last time I saw him, which was yesterday, he was fine, Cole. Just Blaine. Normal."

"Hardly normal." I smirk at that, bizarrely happy about the fact that he is in no way normal, and neither am I now by the looks of my behaviour ten minutes ago.

"He's normal to me, Cole. It's the only way I've ever known him."

He fidgets about and smiles, a slight frown descending as he thinks about something for a few minutes. I just sip my drink and stare off into the crowd again, smiling at all the exhausted bodies lying around, wondering if they've all fucked themselves stupid tonight.

"He never used to be like that, you know? He was larger than life." I turn to look back at him, intrigued with whatever's coming next.

"He used to play tag in the gardens with me, show me how to do stuff. He was a great big brother. Fun." Fun?

I snort out, drink spluttering from my nose, trying to fathom a picture of Blaine being anything close to fun. I don't know what to say to that. I just gaze at him as he flops back on the sofa, his head lolling back as if he's tired of everything, certainly this place and what it has to offer. I smile at the move, wondering when men like Cole grow up and find a family, for some reason knowing that Blaine will find this type of lifestyle completely unsuitable. Although, it's not like Blaine's exactly settled down is it? Christ, the man can't even say I love you successfully. "But it started changing in college, and then conversation stopped completely about a year or so ago. I tried, but he wasn't interested in talking at all. Still isn't. Do you know what happened?"

My eyes widen at the directness levelled at me, his face a sudden mask of his brother, pushing for answers I absolutely will not give him regarding dead women. I pull in a breath and twiddle my straw around in my drink, unsure how to avoid the topic if I want more information myself.

"Why would I know anything, Cole? I'm just writing a book. He's teaching me. That's all. Giving me information about his lifestyle. It's just research. I wish I could help, but I can't." Won't. I won't. Not at the moment, anyway.

He nods and stares back into the room again, a look of acceptance all over his features as he flops back again and gazes at the ceiling. It is annoying, though, now I'm thinking about it. Perhaps Blaine should give his brother more than nothing. At least something. Guidance maybe. Help. That's what families are for, aren't they?

Support. Happiness. A sense of home to run to when you need it most. It's what mine is for, anyway. Perhaps if he did then he wouldn't seem so alone.

"I don't even know your name. Lana, isn't it?" He turns his head towards me again, his hand signalling a bartender, who's walking about collecting drinks, and ordering two more drinks. She disappears off again, grinning gleefully at the wink he gives her. "He wouldn't tell me that either. He's so fucking secretive about everything, don't you think? Never lets anyone in."

I laugh, snorting my drink out again and trying to regain composure as I lever my jacket off and settle in for a long discussion about the man I still damn well love. Fuck it all. Regardless of whether we stay together or not, Blaine needs his brother in his life. He does. It's the only family he's got left. And from what I've seen of Cole so far, a little lightening up would do Blaine the world of good. Chill him out. Make him laugh on occasion. Relax. Be happy.

This is a conversation that's happening, minus the dead woman part.

Chapter 15

BLAINE

The wind whistles through the trees lining the avenue, as I gaze around the desolate place and keep walking on. It's getting cold now, late autumn's air bringing a sense of the winter coming at me. I barely feel it, though. Not here. I've got no right to feel anything here other than guilt and remorse, something that settles deeper in with each footfall towards her. I can still sense her in my fingers, the taste of her as prevalent in my mouth as it always is when I'm here. It's the same every time I come, some resonance of hatred guiding me into her, hoping for forgiveness maybe.

I weave the stones as I scrunch up my sleeves, not caring for any other corpse beneath my feet as I trample them. There's only one soul in here I'm bothered about, only one I need to talk to again. She won't answer. She never does. I made sure of that by putting her here in the first place, but she does help me see clearly on occasion, perhaps giving me some form of clarity between my wants and needs. She stops the inclination to decimate, reminds me what happens when I let the sensation roam free.

Scanning around again in the low moonlight, I consider how many of these deaths were natural or forced, not that it matters. I'm one of those killers, though. I took life. Played with it and mocked it. Treated it like my own private adventure into the sordid and disgraceful. She's here, 6ft under because of me. I still don't know what I hope to achieve with these roses in my hand, but I bring them each time I come. Blood red, their thorns still on. It seems laughable to remove them given her want for the pain I applied to her skin, the same pain she begged for. As if removing the spikes would inhibit her progression to the afterlife, making the place too soft for her to land in.

I half chuckle at the thought as I walk passed the tombs littered with angels weeping, their hands offering prayers to some needed expectation of gods. Fuck gods. Gods wouldn't have made me this way. They wouldn't have let these internal beings inside me build to uncontainable, wouldn't have allowed their progression to fruition, let alone excelled them to their final decadent reckless abandon. Gods and demons exist here. Right here on this planet. They exist in the money makers and charitable ventures. They reside in the human condition to behave and conform to other's wishes, not least shown by the exhibition of monetary gain from those charitable ventures. Pockets lined with corrupt earnings. People starving while kings sit on thrones, their crowns slanted at jaunty angles to show their unmoveable disposition.

The thought makes me growl, uncomfortable with my family's association. Perhaps I would have been a better politician than a psychologist. Perhaps I should have followed in mother's footsteps rather than Cole, made a difference to this fucking planet by bullying and charming, rather than attempting to help and guide. I could have used this inside me then, forced compliance in other ways, controlled it.

The thoughts continue as I get closer, some semblance of order trying to pull together both Eloise and Alana in my mind, complete the jigsaw I created with that smashed vase. One's nothing but flesh and skin, the other a torrid mixture of feelings and emotions to challenge what I believed empty and unreachable. It causes a sickening sensation to rise in waves as the grey marbled slab comes into view, some connotation of remorse for my wants etching home to rival the sense of love she calls for. I do want it for her, though. I want it enough to stand this sickness inside, weather it forever should she choose to stay now she knows it all. But I want her to come here first, to stand in this place I'm nearly at and lay her hands on what lies beneath the slab. She will need that to understand what she's involved in. She needs to feel the cold of this grave and comprehend its meaning to her body in my hands. I won't lie, nor hide this from her any longer because love, a life with me, will forever hold this possibility for her.

I stop as the grass shortens and gaze at the long slab of marble, tracing the edges of it like I've done hundreds of times before. It's as barren of Eloise as my heart is of her. Nothing more than a façade above her which encases her bones. The similarity forces a chuckle through my lips, remembering her arms around me at night, her head on my chest, perhaps hoping for something she would never have achieved. She holds more of my respect and acceptance because of her positon now than she ever would have found in life. She was a body. A toy. A plaything to dabble in and test myself on. And now she's a corpse because of that arrogant escapism of mine, one left to putrefy with the decadence of the moment.

I lower and start clearing the area, my hands brushing the leaves away as I put the fresh roses to the side. For what it's worth it seems necessary to clean her. I always do, perhaps hoping to cleanse myself in some way of the sin. I never did in life. Never once did I bathe her or offer support for the wounds I caused. I amused myself with her pain, languished in the look of her as she winced every step she took towards the sea. And then I made her take more, my fingers focusing in on the areas that already hurt the most, pressing for more of her agony so I could celebrate their sound.

They come back to me as I keep swiping away the dirt, the tone of them so different to Alana's. They were juvenile in comparison to the ones she honours me with. Simple, like a child's weep, tantrum even. Long continued howls, all the time filled with tears and pleas for help. I didn't help. Wouldn't. Helping her like I should have done would have meant releasing her back into society, using my mind to guide her. It's what my professor should have done, what my monster refused to do, and what my magician entertained himself with.

He came from her. Learned his craft through her petulance and irrational behaviour. No one teaches that in school. No one shows a sadist how to manipulate or weave his web effectively, the beginnings already coming from school yard pranks and jokes. We learn it through trial and error after those, influencing our decisions based on the best outcome for our cock's wayward endeavours. We smile when the pain lands, laugh when the weeping continues, become more aroused as the screams come. We fuck raw and hope that it hurts like hell, not caring for the eventuality of breaking the very thing we're fucking into. Our minds, my mind, wants the inevitable ending. It claws for the humiliation and continued cry of agony. Fucked as that might be. It's what I am, what this fucking monster needs feeding with.

"I'm in love," comes from me, quietly, perhaps hoping she'll hear it from 6 feet down, tell me what to do. I am. Deeply in love. I'm as lost in Alana as Eloise was in me. She doesn't answer, and even if she did she'd be jealous, petulant. She'd sulk, make me chain and beat her for her reaction. It makes me rub my fingers together, trying to feel her in my hold and gage that thought, wonder if it's something I need from Alana. "What should I do?"

I don't fucking know why I'm asking that. Some need for approval maybe, some guide to tell me moving forward into this is acceptable. Delaney would say it is, that I should just let myself go, let my little dove take whatever I give and see how that works out. Cole would push me into families and children, tell me that will make me happy. It won't. I know that much. I'm not interested in paternal longings or sentiments of containment for the children's sake. Marriage be damned. I just want my beach and her on it, purple fucking stripes and ink stained hands forever washing into the ocean in front of her. I want skin I can bruise, arms that can wrap around me when I chose to have them there, and a life free of doubt and accusation. My mind wants to be clear, accepted. Allowed as moral in some fucked up way, honourable. I want those dates and my aggressive thoughts blending, finding their own equilibrium with no one to condemn or judge. For once, and because of little doves, I want all the things the average human appears to want.

Charlotte E Hart
THE END

I stand up after fuck knows how long, not sure if I want to walk away or sit on this slab and ponder life's merits for more of my time. Part of me wants to leave, get to Alana and show her I am capable of her request. Another wants to bed in here. Lie on top of Eloise and let the winter coming freeze me to this spot. Let myself die on her tomb and watch as the birds above fly free. Let Alana do the same with them. *Without me.*

I look up, searching for birds in the night sky, hoping to see their path, show me mine. Nothing is there. It's empty but for a few dull clouds drifting across the moon, one that's descending slowly into the ground the longer I'm here. I smile at it, some visage of understanding because of its emptiness. For all the mental turmoil this place gives me, it does provide a sense of companionship still. Always has. It's the very reason I banned myself from it, hoping to tame this monster of mine back into its fucking casing. Force it away rather than have this place remind me of his wrath. There's a hope here, a warmth, a memory of someone who knew how to allow me on them and welcomed that sensation. She loved me for it, gave me her heart because of it.

Stupid girl.

I turn, annoyed with the thought of her corpse suddenly and irritated at my feelings of sadness associated with that thought. I should leave. Let this go and move on. Move on from Alana. Move on from Eloise. I should continue with existence without either of them, relax within that and let my monster quieten again. Be bored again.

It's an infuriating thought, rendering my heart as dreary as it was before the little madam arrived and woke the fucking thing up.

THE END

"Chase me, Sir." Eloise.

My smile grows wider as the dead roses rustle in my grip, the dried up petals crunching between my fingers. The thought encourages more sneers to come from me, remembering her skin in my fingers as I begin scrunching them to feel their texture. They crumble, just like she did, the petals and leaves disintegrating onto the slab below. I watch them scatter, their fall some reproduction of her tears as the wind blows them away. She took it all from my young monster. She pleaded and begged as the blood ran across her skin, bellowed her screams of pain into the night. She wept and choked, gagged. Every sordid capability I could think of, she ventured into without care to her safety. Pretty skirts and tanned legs, the bruises covered with make-up each day to avoid gossip in the classroom. And she fucking teased me all day in there. Batting lashes, licking lips. She pushed and goaded me, knowing what would come in the evening when I got her home.

I can remember the sound of her skin splitting even now, as if it's still here with me. She'd taunted me with a guy in class, showed me that she could leave me if she chose to. She couldn't, and the resulting night brought more pain than she'd ever taken before. Flesh tore exquisitely, the slash of it as enticing to my eardrums as the fresh scent of blood that came from the gash. Pretty knives, serrated blades. Blood that drips and pours. Screams that resonate. The dull thud of flesh once it stops struggling in my grip. The silent pleas for less, more. Fists full of torture, and a mind full of countless possibilities, all because of her disobedience. She brought that out of me, gave me that avenue to play in, toy with. It was the first time my magician got involved with my monster. The first time all of me worked as one. And the first time she nearly ended up under this slab.

The image of Alana clouds my mind as I finally turn from the grave again, my feet trying to find the route away from temptation. Sick and twisted. A sadist in love with no ability to veil the once adored route forward. Life has become a never ending riddle of complications and challenges, puzzling me rather than the once simplistic view I coveted. I'm tainted with hopes and dreams now because of her. Fucking writers of stories, their resonance rubbing off on me somehow, willing me into happy ever afters I do not deserve nor believe in. This story will have nothing but a black cover and words written in fountains of crimson blood, her blood.

I wander after that, barely knowing where I'm going nor giving a fuck. Around this graveyard is probably the best place for me, continuing to lull in my maudlin thoughts until some correct path booms inside of me. Clarification is what I need. Factual insight. A case study that denotes evidence and preferential parenthesis, dependant on the subject matter at hand. Time spent analysing and evaluating the present acute data. Fucking feelings have no connotation of representative facts here. Feelings muddy waters. They lift too much dirt from the floor, saturating facts with inconvenience and counter-productive attributes.

I snort, glaring back at her grave as I walk the circumference of the grounds. She made this happen. Made me question myself and wander these entangled thoughts. Had she not have been part of my life, I would have been just one. I would have let the monster come, let it ravage and feed on victim after victim, not caring for the eventuality of death nor pain. Instead, she's halted my escalation with her death. Tamed me. Provided multiple sides to challenge themselves and cause confliction.

The thought makes a laugh come. She fucks me over in death more than she ever could in life. She'd be amused by that. Find it funny. She'd giggle, and then she'd run my beach. She'd run for her life knowing only too well the outcomes of finding a route inwards.

Perhaps this is my penitence for her death, her revenge. I've become my own test case. My own evaluation of merit, or lack thereof. Now, rather than her, my magician fucks with itself, amusing itself with my continued turmoil and split personalities.

Bitch.

The gates come into view, my car waiting for me behind them. I head towards it slowly, all the time wondering where my little dove is now. Sleeping probably. Just as average humans do at this time of night. I sent her back to average. Sent her back to deal with the knowledge she now knows, hoping for her acceptance of those facts. I should go to her, hold her. Show her she is worth more than this graveyard I'm in. I'll come back again here next time with her right by my side, if she still wants to come. She can make her decisions here, bring her hope and dreams with her and judge me over Eloise's body. She deserves that. Needs it. There is no forward without backwards. No progression without acceptance of the past. There never is. My psychologist knows that, irrespective of my magician's denial of facts and restriction of truths. This love she chooses to bound on with comes with repercussions. It comes with eventualities and consequences, ones that mean a life she knew nothing of before me. Fuck, it could even

THE END

mean an initiation I'd never considered as beneficial to my life in any way. Love's curse is, I suppose, one that requires absolute honesty. All truths bared.

Chapter 16

ALANA

Cole and I got kicked out eventually. Apparently it was four o'clock in the morning and they needed to clean. I hadn't even noticed the time, nor had I cared in the slightest. I'd been too fascinated with hearing everything there was to know about the man I love from someone who wasn't like Priest. Into 'it', I mean. That's what Cole had called it all night, as if that was the only explanation of needs and wants he could manage. I'd giggled and laughed a lot, my feet curled up onto the couch, perhaps sensing parts of Blaine in his character and enjoying their lilt on me. It made me think of what Blaine could be, imagine the way he might have been had he not have become the monster he talks of.

The cab slowly rounds the corner as I keep stroking his head, wondering why he's even still in the car with me. He's taking me home apparently. Being a gentleman because Blaine would kick his ass if he didn't. He's not. He fell asleep, or passed out two minutes after we got in here. I don't care. For once I'm happy to dwell in this nothingness as he leans on my lap, his hair running through my fingers. I can hardly feel him in all honesty. I'm too busy imagining Blaine's hair in my hands, Blaine's weight on me. He's all I've thought about most of the night, some resonance of him coming through Cole's lips as he talked of growing up, of living together and being brothers. It was all so far removed from the Blaine I know. Cole made him seem happy and contented, a boy who loved freely and helped with every instinct he had. No games, no mind fucking, only shenanigans and fun. Years, it seems, of running neighbourhood gardens and smiling, occasionally getting caught. Two cheeky youngsters having the time of their lives, enjoying it. Where's he gone? Where's that man run away to?

I sigh out and watch the federal hall's columns creep past beside us, part of me trying desperately to piece him together in my mind as I remember his words of killing. That's not the boy Cole talked of all night. That teenager wouldn't have killed anything. He would have loved and honoured everything, helped it, guided it through anything. Cole even told me of Blaine beating the shit out of him for treating a girl badly and making her cry. I'd snorted at the time, remembering all the things he's done to me in the pursuit of his needs, but now, looking back on it, there's a significance in that story.

Cole snuffles to himself on my thigh, his cheek rubbing against me as he drifts deeper into sleep. Christ knows what I'm going to do with him when I get home. I don't even know his address to send the cabbie on with him. He'll have to come in, I suppose. He's barely capable of speech, let alone instructing a cabbie where he lives, or he wasn't when he drunkenly fell into the cab. Maybe he'll wake up at some point and decide that for himself. I don't know. If not, he can come in and sleep it off, wake up in the morning and we can chat some more. Or not.

THE END

If I'm completely honest with myself, I don't even want to go home. I want to stay in this car and idle, or have it take me to Blaine's house so I can walk that beach and let all this settle in my mind. I feel lost in my own apartment, like it's empty of meaning. I don't understand that other than it being missing of him. I feel like there's no order in it anymore, or too much of the wrong kind of order. It doesn't even feel like a home. Blaine's house feels like home. I hate that. I hate that I've lost something I thought I knew, had it taken from me maybe, but I also can't deny its calming effect on me.

"Cole, we're home," I say, shaking his shoulder as we finally hit the main street leading to my apartment. "Wake up." Nothing. No movement. No more snuffles. Only a stream of drool that falls from the corner of his mouth and pools on my thigh. Nice. I roll my eyes and shove at him a little more fiercely. He splutters and coughs, then turns his head into my crotch, breathing deeply. Ewww. One Jacobs brother between my thighs is quite enough, regardless of the near mistake I made earlier in the evening. Store rooms, for god's sake. What was I thinking? Which reminds me, I need to talk to Bree. Christ, lesbian happenings need discussing. I'm not gay. Or maybe I am. Screw it. I don't really care what I am anymore.

I slap at his head, both hands helping him wake up as I try to scramble my crotch from his face.

"Cole, wake up for fuck's sake." Jesus. He splutters again, more drool pouring from him as his lips smack about together. Attractive. "We're home." My home. House. Apartment. Whatever the hell it is. "Come on, up, out."

THE END

    I fling some money at the cabbie, who doesn't appear to want to help in the slightest as I eventually just get out of the car and let Cole flop back down onto the seat. My lips blow out a breath as I glare down at him, part wanting to slam the door on his head. Idiot.

    "Right, come on then, you," I say, heaving at his shoulders to get him out. He weighs a tonne, not unlike his brother, I should think. Still, I heave again, and again, until he half falls onto the pavement face first. Well, that should wake him up. It doesn't. And the fact that the god damn cabbie just drives off as I close the door, neither giving me any help nor change, really pisses me off.

    "COLE!" I shouted that. I don't care. It's late, or early, and there's a flight of stairs to get up before I can get into my apartment. Nothing happens, other than more lips smacking and his body curling up into a ball on the pavement.

    "Cole, Jesus. How much did you drink?" I'm not sure why I'm bothering with questions.

    I end up heaving at him again, pulling him towards the doorway. At least if I get him there he's out of the way. I might even leave him there if he doesn't wake up on his own.

    "Cole?" Still nothing as I tug his weight. "Cole, Christ." Still nothing. "I bet if I got my boobs out you'd wake up," I mutter with another pull. He stirs, words mumbling from his lips. "Yes, boobs, Cole. You want a feel?" I chuckle as he mutters something else. "How about cunts? You like those too?" His feet move at that word, which makes me laugh. Seems he's more like his brother than I thought. "Cunts and boobs, you want a blowjob too?" His eyes flicker open, a smile rising on his face. "You'll have to get up for it, Cole," I whisper, my lips close to his ear as I reach for the keypad on my door. "Chase me. Can you do that, baby?" I'm trying for sexy through my giggling fit, hoping it works. Bloody men and sex. It's pathetic. "You want me to suck it for you?"

"Fascinating." Fuck. My whole body freezes over Cole, my insides flipping over as Blaine's voice drowns out any other noise available. I'm not even sure how this looks. I've just been talking about cunts and boobs, haven't I? Did he hear that? Balls. "Moved on with my brother? He'll disappoint you, little dove."

"No," I snap out, hoping for superiority. "He's drunk. That's …" Words stop as his shoes come into view and I scan the floor around them for inspiration, their highly polished surface reflecting in the street lights above. "I just. I'm trying to get him …" Oh god, this looks bad, doesn't it? This looks really bad. He tells me about his privacy, then sends me away to think about that very thing, and I end up drunk with his brother talking about boobs and blowjobs? That's bad. I'd be really pissed if I was him. Furious. I slowly creep my eyes up his legs, wondering what the hell I'm going to find when I eventually meet his eyes. Anger, rage? Possibly a slap. "Blaine, it's not like you think," I blurt out, desperate for him to calm down if he's wound up.

"What do you think I think?" I have no idea. I glance at the door rather than at him, my fingers fumbling with the pad to open the damn thing as I continue supporting Cole's head.

"Suck it," along with something about babies, comes slurred from Cole's mouth. Jesus.

This is horrendous. I could use another drink to deal with this shit. I laugh lightly and try organising Cole again, before deciding I should just leave him and drop his head to the pavement. I mean, his brother's here now. He can deal with him, can't he? I should leave before the argument starts about me fucking a brother I had no intention of ever fucking. Well, not after I realised he was a brother and zipped my jeans back up. Oh god, I'm leaving.

"Never could hold his liquor," Blaine says, his presence getting closer to me. "And wouldn't give you what you need if he was sober, anyway." He's smiling by the time I work up the courage to look back at him over my shoulder. It's small, but it's there nevertheless, showing me his humour at the situation he's found us in. "He knows nothing of fucking like we do. You'd be unresponsive after the first slide into your cunt." Nice. My mouth gapes at the comment, my hand half holding Cole's shoulder still as I let his tone ebb into me again. Just the sound of those words bring every thought I've had over the last god knows how many hours flying into alignment. Love, respect, a position beneath this brother. Amusement even. "You going to try him on for size, little dove, see if average still works for you?" I frown at him, flicking my eyes to Cole's prone body. "You can. I'll watch, wait until it's over and then listen to you beg for a decent fucking after."

"That's disgusting," splutters out of me, the thought making me feel a little nauseous. He raises a brow and chuckles, his feet stepping over Cole's frame to decrease the distance between us.

"Yes. Slutty. Have you been a slut again?"

"No." My face screws up a little as he keeps looking at me. "Well, maybe a bit."

"With my brother?"

"Sort of." And Bree. I'm not telling him that. God knows what that might produce from him. He smiles, his frame closer still. "But I didn't know he was your brother." His hands come out of his pockets, both of them slowly bracing the wall next to my head, forcing me back to it. "What are you even doing here, Blaine?" And why can't I think all of a sudden?

"Do you want to carry on, little dove?" What does that mean? I frown again as I stare up at him and watch him lick his lips. I'm not fucking his drunken brother. That's screwed up beyond words, even for him. "You can tie me up, have your wicked way. Fuck with something while I gaze on, helpless." My mouth opens, nothing comes out. I can't even comprehend that thought. Him tied up? That's just odd. It feels strange, although it would give me time to wander that skin of his if he was tied up, which makes me flick my eyes to his chest and ponder the thought. He closes in again until there's nothing between us at all apart from a rigid cock and breath. "You want me inside you again?" Yes. "Want to imbed yourself again?" Fuck, yes. "You can have that. If you want it. Unlock your door. Just ask to take what you want and then we'll go backwards."

"But what about Cole?"

"You want both of us? Greedy girl. I'll get him hard." He smirks as he drops his eyes to my mouth. It's all kinds of wrong, making me check my own inappropriate thoughts.

"Yuk." I really wish I thought that with complete honesty attached, but Cole is cute. Seriously? I'm revolted with myself. He chuckles and leans his face into mine, his lips brushing over mine so softly I moan out in torment. "He's your brother, Blaine," I mumble.

He just keeps kissing me, little concern to my statement until he backs off and stares downwards at a muttering Cole. "That's too screwed up even for you." He just smirks again. "I mean, have you done that?" He shakes his head slowly, his feet stepping over Cole again to move around him. "Then why would you? Look, he's annihilated. That is not appropriate, Blaine."

"I'm not the one that wants to fuck him, little dove. You are." Oh, that's not fair, and not entirely true either. I look back at him lying there like a baby on the pavement, his mouth moving around the snores emanating.

"I do not want your brother."

"Yes, you do." He says it with that tone that brooks no argument, the softer side of him disappearing into the ether as quick as it came. "Honesty."

"No I don't. He just .. Well, he just … And he was there, you know?" My hand flicks around, unsure how I explain this given my euphoric dancing come storeroom incident. I don't even know if he's angry about it or happy. Do sadists share like that? I shake my head again. We're talking about his brother. It's a horrendous thought. He must be furious. "And you weren't, were you?" I'm backing away now as he keeps coming at me, my head glancing around the road. "Which is not my fault, is it? You sent me away to think. You weren't there, Blaine. You left me on my own to think. So, I was thinking."

"About fucking my brother."

It's not a question. It's a statement. It's also true. Bloody hell.

I look back to find him smiling quietly, making my fucking heart melt. It wasn't about Cole really, it never was. It was about this man in front of me and the way he's changed me, made me feel myself differently. It's all about him and his mouth, or his thoughts.

"No, Blaine. I was thinking about fucking you." He grins, his feet planted with no thought of moving them. "But he was handy. You weren't." That seems to increase the smile to the one that's full of sex and sin, its curve as tempting as the twitch between my legs because of it. "Bree was too." And that just changes it to an amused smirk of unknown proportions. Fuck, why did I say that? Although, it's a beautiful look on him, enough to make me want to fall to my knees.

"Good. She's appealing."

"What?"

"Your friend. Fuckable." My eyes could have popped out on stalks. I can't believe he said that. Who says that sort of thing about your best friend? Possessiveness immediately floods me, filling me with selfish thoughts and bitter meanderings. "But you're right, I shouldn't have left you alone." No, he's right he shouldn't. I don't want alone. I never did. But seriously, fucking Bree?

"What the hell was that?" I snap out, hands on my hips. He keeps smirking, his fingers reaching for my door again as he steps away.

"Stop it, Alana. You're being bratty," he says, as he leans over Cole and begins heaving him around. Bratty? Screw him. "And you could have a very different reaction from me than the one you're getting." I narrow my stare of him as I watch him manoeuvre Cole towards the door, knowing that's true. This could very well have resulted in fury and rage. Still, him thinking about sleeping with Bree is not okay. "Open the door, little dove. Or would you rather I took this degenerate home?"

"I'd rather you left, but you can both come."

"Can we?" There's an irony in his voice as I stab buttons on keypads again, barely understanding anything anymore. I'm too tired for all this. Too exhausted all of a sudden.

"Oh, fuck off."

"Mouthy," comes from him as he drags Cole across the threshold. Whatever. I'm so over worrying anymore. I should just say exactly what I think, at exactly the point in which I think it. "You're asking for a fucking you can't walk away from." He's laughing as he says that, seemingly finding my confusion hilarious. If I didn't know better I'd say he was drunk with the amount of amusement that's coming from him.

"I have no comprehension of what you're going on about," I reply, slipping my key into the lock and opening the door.

"I'm having fun, Alana."

"You're being an asshole, Blaine," I snap back, throwing my keys on the table and watching him continue to drag Cole through to my office. What's he going in there for? I follow and gape as he drops him, quite unceremoniously, in a pile in the corner. "You just said you wanted to fuck Bree. Come on, that's not okay."

"But you wanting to fuck this is?" He glances at Cole, his brow raised again, which makes me consider the implication. "Did I tell you that you couldn't?" That's not the point. I don't think it is. He just caught me in an off moment. I would never have asked otherwise. And it's all his damn fault anyway. He left me alone without him, made me do things I wouldn't normally do. Now he's telling me I can do anything I want? He's the most possessive man I've ever met and yet we're discussing other partners?

"I'm completely lost," I mutter, my head hanging as I walk away towards the kitchen, hoping that tea might help alleviate my confusion. Jesus. What a night.

"Alana, look at me," he says, as the office door closes. I don't. I'm busy making tea, perhaps trying to avoid a conversation I just don't know what to do with. I shake my head and carry on with teabags and sugar, not knowing what I'm doing as thoughts of killing filter in. "This is what I am, little dove. It's how my mind works." I turn slowly, pretty sure he just admitted he wants to fuck anything that moves if he chooses to and I should allow that openly, join in with him even. "All the filth is coming for you if you want it." I hover, just staring at him as he begins to undo his shirt and walks towards me, his tongue flicking his lips as he drags the shirt over his shoulders and loosens his belt. "No hiding anymore, no refraining to tell you something in case it's seen as sickening. Every sordid little escapism. Every touch. Everything I have, just for you. No care for your possible repulsion, or demise. " *My demise*. The word sticks in my throat as I try to get it out. Death. It instantly sends me backwards, not that I've got anywhere to go. The countertop stops me before I get a chance for any momentum at all. "It's all yours, Alana. I'm not fighting it anymore. I'm done fighting you." He moves in another step, his hot breath filtering over my cheek. "I need you to love all parts of me, if that's what you still want."

My hand goes up to stop his advance. I'm not sure why. Instinctual perhaps, or even fear mingling into the lust I know I have. It's not denial. I'm not denying a damn thing. I'm what he's turned me into and reasonably happy with that, but death? That's my life he's talking about. The hours of Cole explaining his life before all this come back to me, the confusion on his face bringing with it a sense of a younger version, one I need to feel.

"Tell me something nice." He looks quizzical. Good. He could do with not being such a smart arse all the damn time. I need more than this darkness from him. If he loves me, he can damn well show me in other ways rather than saying it. I need that from him right now. I might need this version too, but I have to see the love coming with it. I need dates that mean something to him. Reasons for me actually seeing this as normal. More of those dances he offered. "Something nice, Blaine. A memory, or something that gives me another reason. Something other than just fucking."

He smirks and backs away, his body moving towards the chair until he lets himself sit in it and stare back at me.

"Coffee, one sugar. Black."

"What?"

"You still don't know what I like to drink, do you? Or what makes me happy. That's a start for you."

"No, that's not what I mean."

"Yes, it is," he says, his brow arching as he rolls his shoulders and makes himself comfortable.

"No, I meant…"

"And the sound of starlings calling to each other at night, going home to roost." Oh right.

I gape, completely agog at the thought of birds influencing him in any way. I smile at the thought, though, as he shifts about, his leg crossing over the other and exasperation coming over his features. "Don't stare. I'm being amenable. Enjoy it. Make the fucking coffee." Okay. I turn and keep listening, wondering what else he'll give me. "The smell of autumn rain when it lands on baked earth. It's unpretentious. Grounding. I like that." It's so basic, but it widens my smile nonetheless, making me feel connected to him in a way I've never done before. "At least take those vile fucking clothes off if I have to do this. My shirt looks better on you." Does it? I grin to myself and stir the drinks, then turn back to him to take them over and place them on the table in front of us. "Do it there while I keep talking. Entertain me through this." Okay. At this moment I think I'd do just about anything. His hand comes up to his lips as I take the t-shirt off and let my hands linger on my belt.

"The sound of clattering makes me edgy. There's no silence in it. Like your heels when we met. They drove me nuts. Still do on occasion." Oh, something he doesn't like.

"They're expensive. They should clatter as loudly as they like," I reply, my fingers beginning to ratchet my belt open. He raises a brow and keeps watching, barely acknowledging my words.

"The taste of you first thing in the morning, the moans you make when I come inside you." One button flicks on my jeans, the thought of killing apparently disappearing with just a few words of his memories or privacies. "The look of my sea in the middle of a storm."

Another goes at the mere mention of that sea I long to walk beside. With him. Storm or not. "The way you smile when you look up at me, as if nothing else matters but what leaves my lips. That's soothing to me. Gratifying. It makes me feel alive." He smiles slightly, his finger rubbing his mouth as he watches me undo the last button and then raises his coffee. "And night coming down in the sky. It makes me calmer than the day does, relaxes me." I smile at that as I watch him sip at it, only now realising the connection of how he behaves in the day versus night. He's so much more open at night, more willing to hold onto me. Dance. I begin sliding the jeans down, enjoying the words and feeling bolder with every one that comes from him. "You're like a memory I've never had, little dove. An acceptance I need to complete me." I stall, my fingers hovering around my ankles. That was quite possibly the nicest thing anyone has ever said to me. I could almost cry. "You're like Christmas morning used to be when I was young, full of possibilities and questions finally answered." Oh god, that's beautiful. Fucking jeans. I feel like jumping on him immediately and drowning him with kisses.

I tug at them, willing them anywhere but on me. "Is that love enough for you?" Yes.

"Nope. Keep going." I turn around, my smile growing wider as I reach round to unhook my bra. Sexy is needed now. Sexy and seductive. We're going to do something different to prove this thing between us. He's going to show me with gentle touches and whispered words. I want that from him now. And he needs to do it at least once, just to show himself that he can. "More please, Mr Jacobs."

Charlotte E Hart
THE END

I think I'm starting to grind to music that isn't here, but it's inside me regardless. Some sonnet relays itself around the quietness of his voice, bringing with it a lulling sense of calm, of happiness.

"The feel of your cunt when I try to get my hand in it." I swing my head sharply, frowning at his lack of refinement in such a beautiful interlude. He raises his coffee cup and winks, then tips it to his filthy fucking mouth. "The look of you when you sleep. It makes me want to watch you all night rather than wake you." Better. It's enough for me to start my strip again, my hand hovering the bra out to my side as I turn around. Teasing him. Although, that's plainly ridiculous. "Bend over and tell me you wanted to fuck my brother." I gasp, unsure how to answer that. "Say it. Be honest with me." My mouth fumbles around the words, hardly able to say them out loud, but he's right. I did.

"I did want him," I whisper, the words barely audible.

"Say the word fuck, Alana. Mean what you tell me." I gulp down the embarrassment, slight tears creeping into my eyes at the thought.

"I wanted to fuck him." I go to stand up, my mind broken of his meanderings into dreams and loveliness.

"Stay down," he snarls, his voice full of that dominance I'm used to as I hear him get up. I blow out a breath and gently lower, my eyes closing ready for the slap that's going to land at any minute. "Why?"

"I was aroused." It comes out as quietly as the first words. And I'm becoming more so now with the thought of what he might do any minute because of them, much as I might want that softer version I was hoping for to carry on.

THE END

"Would you fuck him now if I asked you to?" I frown into the floor as I see his shoes come around in front of me. That's too much, isn't it? That's - I'm not sure what that is. "Too much? Alright, would you fuck Delaney if I asked?" Honest. Honesty. He's giving me his version, isn't he? I need to do the same. I do. I can't. I stare at the floor, waiting for him to change the question maybe. He doesn't. He wants an answer to this one.

"Yes." It squeaks out of me, hardly able to understand why it's allowing itself the freedom from my thoughts. I probably would though, if he asked and he was watching. "If you watched." He chuckles and wanders off until I hear him sit.

There's a few minutes silence after that. Me just touching the floor and waiting, for what I don't know. More of his words maybe, ones that make sense and keep us close. That's all I want. A new sense of closeness. One just for me. I want more of that beauty he just offered me, more of those memories. More thoughts of Christmas mornings and completion. It makes me close my eyes and try to calm the expectation that's wracking my bones. I'm neither ready for nor wanting this to fall apart, regardless of those killing hands. And, for now, I'm all his again, waiting for whatever he thinks will make this all fit together. Right and wrong have, at some point, become distorted and insignificant. I'm naked and bent over in front of a man who killed the last version of me, admitted it to me. And all I want is more of him and his words. I want them pumping through my veins, guiding me, winding their way into my heart and showing me the path forward. I want those fucking lips caressing my skin and making me remember the feel of him, the taste of him. I don't care what happened to the last one of me. I don't. In this moment I couldn't give two shits about the whys or the whens. I just want him and his way of being, entrenching itself further and never daring to leave. "You think you should be punished or pleasured for that statement?"

Either or. I don't care about that. As long as he delivers it I'm happy. It's his decision to make. He can do with me exactly what he wants. Tomorrow we'll discuss rationality. Tonight, I'm his.

Chapter 17

ALANA

There isn't any answer to give as I hover here. Not one that's relevant, anyway. Pleasure, punishment. It all ends up with an orgasm, or no orgasm at all. Sometimes fulfilling, other times not quite so, but either way he's taken the decision from me, making my life seem easier somehow. He's done it with nothing but that tone coming back at me, surrounding me with dominance and governance.

It was complicated a few minutes ago, perhaps lovely given the words that flowed from him, but me pushing him seemed to make the air less easy. Now it's quiet again. I can feel it as I stare at the floor, waiting, calling me back to no thought at all and ridding the confusion that was present. I suppose I'm coming to accept that now. That's what he offers once I stop questioning and just be. It's simpler that way. He gives me that freedom by taking away my ability to make decisions, ones I don't want to, or am incapable of, making. It's like that just now. Me telling him I'd fuck Delaney if he asked. It's so much easier if I just let it roll out of my mouth and stop wondering if I should or not, less taxing maybe.

THE END

"Are you starting to understand now?" Yes. I nod at the floor, losing myself in his voice. I am. Perhaps I should just let him take over completely. I could be free of everything then, never caring for meetings or deadlines again. He could do all that. Deal with it. Let me be free to write and dream, lose myself in it all again and do as much as I want whenever I wanted to do it. Dreams and waves. The freedom to not care about responsibility or repercussions.

His feet move into my eye-line, his shoes showing me that solid, dependable walk of his as he moves around me and makes me feel small, protected by the circle he's creating even. Is that what submission is? It should seem weak, did feel weak at first, like I needed to prove myself above it, but it doesn't feel that way at the moment. Certainly not after his offering of the things he loves, the things that make him happy. "This is why we began the way we did." I'm not sure I understand that, not really, but I'm still resigned to staying here whether I understand it or not. "So you'd stop fighting me, learn to trust me." Trust. It seems such a ludicrous notion given what I now know about him, dangerous even. "I needed you to behave and trust me, Alana." I smile at the way my name leaves his lips, the sound of it like some whisper across my skin, calming any hesitation that used to live inside me. It's gone now, rightly or wrongly. It's all gone. "Learn to trust yourself."

I blow out the last breath of fear I have and listen to him as he moves off, the rustle of his trousers making me aware he's getting undressed. It makes me long for him inside me, hope for it. It feels like months since he's touched me. Not that it is, but the separation between us made me fidgety, nervous, like the air had disappeared and I couldn't find it without him.

"What can I do to you?"

"Anything."

Anything at all. Nothing feels as good as when he's on me, in me. He's the storm I never knew I wanted, a force I couldn't be without now. He surrounds me with something other than the average, giving me a sense of passion and warmth rivalled by nothing else.

"What should I do to you?"

His hand touches my back, the roughened feel of it sliding across my skin gracefully, somehow making whatever depraved act might follow seem plausible. Honourable.

"I love you, Blaine. Do what you want."

His hand comes over my shoulder and slips around my neck, a gentle tug pulling my frame upright to meet him until I can feel his chest against me.

"I want to take you home, keep you there." My eyes widen as I stare at the counter tops in front of me. Keep me there? "I want to wake up each day and know that I can have every inch of you any time I want." I smile, the thought as appealing to me as he's making it sound for him. "I want you to bathe in my sea and wash the bruises away each day, let me put new ones on you the next."

I suck in a breath, letting the intensity of that sentence resonate somewhere, see if it scares me from the moment. It doesn't, and his frame moving around the side of me triples the heart that was already beating tenfold at the thought. He arrives in my eye-line, his fingers still cupping my neck, barely applying any pressure.

"Blaine, I …"

He shakes his head at me, his hand coming up and fingering a line along my jaw. He meanders it around, gently drawing lines along my skin, almost testing his resolves against the pressure he wants to apply.

"You're so beautiful, you always have been." I smile at him, staring into eyes that seem as reverent as he's aiming for. It's enough for me to slide my arms around his neck, draw us closer so I can feel him against me again. "The pool, the church. The look of tears when you come, the feel of you in my hands. That's true beauty. It makes me happy." I lean into his hand as he caresses my cheek, closing my eyes to the feeling and letting it fill me with hope that we can do this. This can become normal for me. *"You* make me happy."

My legs are lifted without me realising, and I'm carried to the countertops. It makes me giggle slightly, amused that he wouldn't chose a bedroom for romance. It's sweet in some ways, a show of *him* in the middle of this quiet moment. The sound of crashing behind me makes me jump and fling my eyes open again, only to find him smirking and continue to swipe everything off the surface around me. "Don't push me," he growls, a quick bite into my hip bone as he leans over and clears the decks further. "You've no fucking idea how close I am to letting go at your cunt." Oh, I think I do. I think I know exactly who this man is in this guise. I can feel him inside now, like a caged lion, barely tamed but willing to try for a love he's never known.

"Tell me you love me," I say, softly, my fingers picking up his face to bring him back in front of me. "Please. I need that from you."

"I love you."

It's said with little passion involved, but it is said, and that's all I need. I know it won't come often, just like I know this sense of softness won't come often either. It'll only come when he thinks I need it, when we need for it.

He slides his hand around my back and tugs me forward into him, bringing my crotch directly to the cock waiting for me. Perfect height. Perfect distance. Perfect thoughts and perfect words. And the feel of him splitting me open has me gasping, ready to grab hold and pull him inside. Something feels desperate immediately, not the quiet gentleness of seconds ago. I pant out, waiting for more to come, but nothing does. He just hovers and breathes into my neck, his shoulders flexing under my hands, a tension in them more profound than I've ever felt. Nothing is relaxed here. Nothing. Not even me now I can feel this strain in him. It's wrong, uncomfortable.

"Please Blaine," comes from me, my nails barely restraining the thought of biting into him and forcing him forward.

"Don't fucking move," he snarls, his lips shaking against my neck as his hands leave my skin.

I hover in response to that, unsure what to do for the best as my cheek rests on his, waiting. It's all so still. Nothing but the sound of our breath and the feel of him shaking beneath my cheek. I open my eyes and stare at the ceiling, letting his body rest between my legs as my insides clench around him. This isn't us, is it? I can't feel him here. I can feel something he thinks I need, something that I probably do need, but those words were all I really needed. Those words and me truly realising he meant them. Accepting his way of showing it as normal, for us. I smile at my thoughts and let my fingers move back to his skin, dragging along it gently.

"Tell me what you want to do to me, Blaine." I'm hungry for the answer as I lean back and brace my arms behind me. He looks up to me as I do, a frown on his face. He's so beautiful like this, so torrid. He's a mixture of sin and devilment, just waiting to deliver the thing he's harbouring inside. It's all to do with love, passion. "Tell me. Show me. No more hiding." He licks his lips and flicks his gaze across me, an instant sense of relaxation developing in his frame because of whatever thought just crossed his mind. "Let it go, Blaine. I'm yours. You don't have to do this."

Something happens in the seconds after that statement. Something shifts, bringing the slight sneer I'm used to with it. He becomes the man I know, full of animosity and charge, his hand instantly grabbing at my shoulder and turning us towards the wall. He climbs up onto the surface, never once letting his cock leave my body as he holds me to him. It's a brutal grip, the softness evaporating without any other offer than the one I made. And when my back hits the wall, more objects crashing over the floor as I'm pushed through them, I grunt at the impact. It fills me with a real smile, all confusion and hesitation dispersed as he becomes what I know him to be.

He hovers for a second, his hand bracing the wall behind me as he shunts me up it and takes my weight on his knees.

He snarls, a wry smile suddenly creeping over his features as he pushes on my shoulder to increase his depth inside me. My head tips back at the feeling, my eyes rolling from the pressure I craved before. Fuck, it feels good. Real. Heavy and regressive, just as I know him to be, just as I want him to be. Screw love. Screw all of that for now. This is what I want from him. Real. Truth. And my body gives into it so easily, as I sense the low growl my stomach delvers, needing him deeper, needing his come inside me again for completion. This is who he is, who we are.

I grasp out, my fingers latching into holds on him I know so well, the explicit nature of it more attuned than love making could ever be. This is our love. It's proved as he starts moving, the sensations filling me with more than that quietness ever could. Ruthless shoves, my back scraping on something sharp, his hands giving nothing but pain as he begins fucking into me. It causes groans and gasps to release from me, my mind lingering in the bliss that's coming as all that pain begins to numb down and settle.

My face is snatched, my hair yanked on my scalp, levering me away from him and then back in so he can chew into my neck. Feral. Angry. Stunning. And I want more. My body's acclimatised to this now. He's made it that way inclined. It's becoming needy for the next sensation to dwell in, some new donation of pain I've not had before.

"More," I pant out, my fingers tightening into his skin as he starts to tear me apart. His hands bite into me at the offer, a pain coming from them that makes me howl out and feel tears spring into my eyes. It shocks my eyes open, perhaps needing to see his face to cope with the dense touch. He's smiling as I find a way through my haze to see him, a look of unadulterated sin hovering around the power he's delivering. Still, he's not finished and I know it. I know it because of the way a frown comes across his face as my pained tears start falling.

I'm shoved again, his cock leaving me as I'm pushed off the counter to land on the floor beneath him with a thud. I scurry to all fours, happy to be down here but readying myself for whatever's about to happen.

"You're pushing me," he mutters, his feet lowering to the floor.

"You needed pushing," I pant out, my body heaving from the tumble I just had. He smirks, his fingers wrapping around his cock as he looks down at me and nods.

"Come swallow this for me," he says, calmly. I flick my eyes to the office door as he waits for compliance, suddenly remembering Cole in there. I'd like to say I gave a damn, like to say I was bothered that he might walk in, but I'm not. "Crawl for it like a good little slut." I look back at him again, smiling at my own decadent thoughts and beginning my crawl. I'm too lost in this version of the man I love again to care about anything. Hardly concerned if Cole joined in with the fun. He was right, wasn't he? I probably would fuck his brother if he asked. I'd do anything really, especially when this guise is in control of my thoughts, winding me up with them.

He groans quietly as I sink it in as far as I can, which makes liquid slide down my thighs and causes shudders to race my bones. I adore that from him. Adore its tone, the way it makes me feel relevant, sexy. I need that from him as much as I need the words of love. It's all here as I keep sliding it down, swallowing at the same time to inch it in further. He leans over me and starts to turn, his hand taking my weight to tip me backwards, increasing the angle so I can get more in.

Fuck, it's deep. I can't breathe as he hovers his thumb over my throat, feeling his cock pushing in, moving back and forth. All the way out, take a breath, and then all the way in again until I'm full. I look up at him as he continues, watching the way he keeps staring at nothing but my mouth. He shoves in at one point, causing a gag to come and tears to flow, that makes him smile. I'd laugh if I could. My monster in love. My beautiful sadistic man.

He slaps at me out of nowhere, harder than I've felt before in this position. It shocks me into a reaction as I choke, my teeth barely avoiding clamping closed.

"You fucking bite me and you won't like the result," he growls, as he increases the pressure around my throat and keeps pushing in and out. It speeds up too, the feel of it becoming one fluid movement as I contain my teeth and let him use me. In, out, his hand continuing to tighten, increasing his own friction along with it. I feel like I'm going to pass out at one point, my chance to breathe being restricted on a few occasions. "Put your fingers inside yourself," he says, quietly. "Fuck yourself for me."

Full from both ends. The thought makes the sudden rush of orgasm come quickly, reminding me of illicit teenage visions and dirty top shelf magazines. I can hardly breathe through it as it floods me with pleasure, my mouth still full of pounding cock as it does. It's a rush. Pure and simple. It bleeds through me as I look up at him and whimper around his continued drives inwards. I'm fucking myself with my own stained fingers and relishing its effect on me, my body quaking and shuddering with its effect on my skin. I am a whore, for him anyway. And I don't care. He's in control of me. He can do anything with that thought. Love me, destroy my skin and remind me who I belong to. I don't care about anything anymore. Just this sensation of being held and considered, looked after, used.

His come starts travelling along his cock. I'm greedy for it. Needy. I squirm, trying to reach further inside myself, bring my own orgasm quicker, but his hand knocks mine away completely just as his come surges into my throat. It's pouring into me, little care to comfort as he keeps shoving me into the floor and near choking me. It's a punishment. I know that. I'm being punished for even thinking about Cole. Orgasm denial. I'd smile at the thought if I could breathe, but he's right to deny me my pleasure. He is. That's what I've signed up for with him. I know it all too well.

He draws himself out of me at some point, leaving me gasping for air and racked with an ache only he provides. He's just sprawled across me, not caring if he's heavy or not. I'm just a toy now, something for him to paw around with for a while and enjoy. Deny pleasure to if he chooses. It's exactly what I want to be. I'm happy here languishing beneath his weight. It's like the calm after the storm. Relaxing. My body's primed and waiting for more of him. My arms are unable to move as they lie limply at my sides. I'm just thriving somehow in this sense of degradation, empowered by it. Perhaps empowered by him alone. Nothing else matters. Not calls. Not emails. Not timelines or responsibilities. It's just him on me and the comfort that brings me.

The silence.

"I love you," I mumble, my eyes still closed as he begins ferreting about in me and I listen to the sounds that makes.

He grunts in response. No offering of love in return. No whispered words of endearment. No soft caressing and gentle hands. There's just the feel of him beginning to move on me, his cock becoming hard again against my breastbone as he rubs it back and forth. It just goes on like that. Me accepting whatever he does, him taking whatever he wants, fingers delving into anything he chooses. But there's a quietness here. A calm.

"You want a drink?" he asks, almost bored with the thought. I don't even know why he asked. He doesn't care. I shake my head against the floor, actually quite thirsty but not daring the thought of him moving. Bliss lives here. Quiet comfort, as quiet as Blaine ever creates, anyway. He chuckles and lets his fingers gauge deeper into me. "Yes, you do." I smile a little, enjoying the way he knows everything about me, a slight shiver riding though me because of that fact. "Stay." I snort, amused at his dog like commands, and not entirely sure if my legs would work if I tried to move regardless.

He returns a minute or so later, a glass of water in one hand, the other reaching for me. I gaze at his naked body as he settles himself and lays down. He's so open with it, always has been actually.

"For someone who's been mauled about, you're smiling a lot, Alana," he says.

"Barely mauled. I expected worse," I reply, shrugging my shoulders. He snorts, and then looks at my lips. That's it other than a continued gaze at them, the occasional brush of his fingers across cheek to reaffirm this love we have. "And I like this place we're in. It's nice. Honest."

THE END

It's just quiet again after that, short of the traffic beginning to wake Manhattan up outside. It's as peaceful and calm as I've ever been with him, both of us naked and lying on the floor of my apartment, me barely caring if we ever move again, as I slip a hand under my head to rest. This is all I need from him, from me even. There's a harmony here with him, a concord that no one else could understand. It's not normal or average, and it's far from ordinary, but it's ours, and it's something I won't be without again regardless of what his past holds in his mind for me. I don't care. Nothing is breaking this apart. No judgement. No repercussions or consequences. I need this. This is my future. It's my way out of where I was, out of everyone else's dreams. It's how I write my own destiny.

"Can you tell me about her, now?" I ask, softly, needing to know more about it so that I can sweep the distance away that still keeps a small barrier in place. I don't want it there. If we're going forward, I need transparency so I can understand him fully.

His teeth draw over his bottom lip, his fingers beginning to leave my face again. I clamp mine down on top of them, refusing to allow that hiding again. It all comes out now. Everything. And then we go forward, or backwards, or wherever the hell he feels like taking me. His home included.

Chapter 18

BLAINE

It's a conversation I'm still thinking about as I watch her eyes close, that brattish little huff of hers making me think she's about to give up trying to open me further. It's enough for me to sneer at her lack of resolve, annoyed with her inability to challenge more than she is doing. This languid state makes her less fiery than I'd like her to be. Beautiful undoubtedly, and touching parts of me never found before, but fundamentally it's inadequate for our journey from here. Love alone will not see her through this, no matter its inescapable effect on hearts. The submission is endearing, but the bite is what she needs to keep coming at me with. She needs to mingle those two effectively. Push when required, know me well enough to tell my magician to go fuck himself.

"Why won't you tell me about her?" she snaps.

I smirk at her, willing the hand that slips to the floor to lift again, slap at me and make me tell her. Not that she can until I'm ready. I'm still not. Not here in her insipid little apartment which harbours nothing but boredom and restriction for me, anyway. The only thing of relevance here is the fact that she let me fuck with her like a madman rather than insist on something neither of us want. It was a cleansing experience, filing me with a loyalty to her, one that needs protection or admiration in some way. A fucking collaring probably.

Cole enters my mind as I keep lying here, wondering what she's about to say next. I should get him out of this place, perhaps beat him senseless for daring to find her. And if one of his fingers touched, or went inside, what belongs to me I'll kill him without hesitation.

I roll away at the thought, barely restraining the need to beat her for admitting to wanting him, but thankful for her honesty in the matter. It's good to hear from her in some ways, refreshing. It means there is sanctioning behind her hope, affirmation that she is what I need her to be.

However, she needs to see Eloise rather than be told. Nothing else will do. No conversations of how the woman I killed made me feel. No cherished softening of the facts. Little doves need to see so that they can find a route through that if they choose too. I will not manipulate her thoughts to make that an easier decision for her. She will kneel down and feel the woman who meant little to me, acknowledge that sensation and declare herself in or out of the type of future I can offer.

"What are you doing?" she asks, as I pull my trousers back on and search for my shirt.

I'm not sure. I should make her get dressed and take her straight to the graveyard, show her and then let her leave if she wants, but this fucking heart keeps interfering with that thought process.

"I'm leaving," I snarl, annoyed with my own confusion.

"Why?"

"Because I have to."

"Why?"

I spin on her as I find my shirt and start yanking it onto my skin, all the time fighting the need to go back down to the floor and ravage her again. It's enough to make me turn away and snarl at myself, this time searching for shoes.

"I need to get Cole out of here." I don't. He could rot here for all I care, along with this vile little abode. I just can't bring myself, no matter the importance, to take her to that graveyard yet. The possibility of her refusing me after that is too much for me to comprehend, especially after telling her I love her.

"No you don't. You need to sit the hell down and talk to me." The bite of her tone makes me stop moving, amused at the brattish reaction to my lie. "You're not doing this with me anymore, Blaine. I know you now." That part of the statement is probably becoming truer than she knows. "Turn around." I feel the smile creep further up my lips, amusing me further as I start moving to wake Cole up. "It's time, Blaine. Honest, right? Fuck Cole." That deserves months of fucking edging. I open the door and am elated to find vomit all over her carpet, the reek of it filling the compact space. It's as disgusting as the words of inadequacy she's probably written in here, short of the ones I've been forcing into her. "Honestly, you can't give me … Oh my God," she spits, her little hands pushing me out of the way. She just stands there and looks at him too, her face a picture of disgust. It's provoking, making my cock twitch again. "My office." I'm not sure if she's bothered about Cole's well-being or not as she steps around him, checking the surfaces and her open laptop. "It's all ruined."

THE END

"Good. It's insipid, anyway. You can redecorate." Not that I care if she leaves it infested. I'd rather she came home with me and never returned here again. She spins on me with such venom I half step away for fear of slapping her straight down into Cole's vomit, then chuckle at that thought.

"It's my fucking space, Blaine," she snaps. "Mine." I snarl at her tone, pulling in a long breath to counter the impending reaction that wants to come for such an attitude.

"No it's not," I reply, my eyes scanning and still finding nothing of her but three purple books on the shelf. "Show me yourself in here." She hovers, her face screwing up in thought. "Pick up one thing that means anything to your future or what you want from it." She narrows her gaze of me, then looks around the room, all the time covering her mouth because of the stench. Good, perhaps it will help her see that here means nothing. Her mind is all she needs, that and the freedom to optimise it without restriction or limitations. She needs me and my home, not this fucking place. "It's a box that barely resembles you in any fashion." A fucking characterless one at that. "It was before me, and is even more so now."

"Screw you," she mumbles, irritably, as she picks up her laptop and phone. I smile at that, letting her have her moment's mouthy tantrum. It's pleasing to me, her wrath coming from something she's passionate about.

"You did nothing in here but lose yourself in what everyone else wants," I reply, my feet backing away until I turn and begin putting my shoes on. It's a sad, dingy little room, lacking anything of interest or inspiration. I sit and begin tying my laces, wondering what I should do with her next rather than acknowledge the fact we should go to that fucking graveyard. I should damn well force this is what I should do. It's what my monster screams for. Make her mine without her fucking consent in the matter. "You lost yourself here, Alana. Nothing more than that. It's all a shell of hollow engagement and pitiable fantasies, as vile as the vomit on its surface."

Something comes flying past my head the instant the last of the sentence leaves my lips. It makes me rear up and glare back at her, all sense of calm washing away at the same speed as the object came. She stands there, fury and angst pouring from her, a hell cat being formed because of it.

"You're an up yourself fucking arsehole, Blaine Jacobs," she spits, her feet stomping towards me.

"That I am, little dove," I reply, walking towards the door. "One that you will get down on your knees for should I ask, so be careful with your damn tone."

She stares. No movement. No recourse to my statement. No argument. She just glares at me, eyes like my sea harbouring focused intent. She's thinking, plotting something. It's in her stance now. No fear. No backing down. Purple stripes highlighting her ire.

She's nothing like the woman I saw in here the first time. She's grown from there, strengthened and primed for me now. Ready to take me on in the right moment, should she need to. Force me to admit myself, pushing us forward as she does.

Minutes pass, both of us glaring at each other, push and damn pull finding no damn balance at all, and then she walks in front of the main door, attempting to block me from leaving.

Charlotte E Hart
THE END

"If you leave this apartment without me and avoid this topic once more, you'll never walk back in it. I want to know about Eloise." Her tone makes me check the storm inside, push it away and narrow my gaze of her. She's soft with it, calmed all of a sudden from the venomous insult she was going to distribute. "No touching me. No touching this." She slides her hands, one of them heading towards her cunt. "No clamps or pain, Blaine. No ropes or cuffs. Nothing. Do you understand me?" There's another seductive roll of her tongue across her mouth, a tease that could bring me to my knees if I overthought the issue. "It'll be done. You'll have lost me and our future. I'll never walk that beach with you. Never let you on me. Never kneel. Never kiss you." She doesn't move as she stares back, nor flinch as I step towards her ready to move the pretentious little madam out of my way, or fuck her for being too tempting for words. "I'm finding you, Blaine. I am and you know it." Bitch. Loathsome little fuck toy. "Let me." I growl, more annoyed with myself than her. "I would rather suffer without you than have something half fucking whole." Half whole.

Blood pools in my mouth as I glare back at her and chew at my cheek, the pain rendered inconsequential because of her demand on me.

Not one living creature has fucked with me the way she is doing now. Never have I been tested further than by myself until her. And I still don't understand how she does it. She's inside me even now, her fluids mixing with mine somehow, forcing information about me she has no right to have until I'm ready to give it to her.

"Fuck you." It grates out of me, muttered under my breath for reasons I can't comprehend.

THE END

She moves into me, her fucking body mesmerising me as she glides the distance between us. It makes me want to rip her to shreds for daring to intrude.

"You made me this way, Blaine," she says, her detestable little mouth smiling at me as she stops. I couldn't adore her more for it. "You pulled all this out of me from somewhere, turned me into a changed me. Made me raw and new." I did, but it was always there, just waiting for me to help her find it. Fucks like her aren't made, they're just enhanced when the right mind finds them to play with. "At least do me the curtesy of explaining why you did if not to let me help you."

My fingers twitch in my pockets, as my eyes slight further at her petulant little smile. Madam needs beating, and then fucking until she can't breathe. Clever little bitch. I tap my own thigh, allowing some calm to come back, all the time pushing barriers down to monsters and magicians.

"Get dressed," I scowl out, not knowing what the fuck I'm doing nor caring for the eventuality of it any longer. It will either be or will not be. She wants it all, she can go lay on that odious fucking slab and feel the potential aftermath of such insane manoeuvrings around my mind.

Fucking broken pots with little shards that fit into crevices. Seas with no meaning unless she's drowning in them. Homes with no warmth unless she's residing in them. It's all a fucking lonesomeness of empty and insincere suddenly. Something I was comfortable with before her, safe within, if not bored by. But now, watching as she walks away, a smile still attached to her edible little mouth as she goes to get clothing, I'm not. It's as irksome as the sight of her ass tempting me with no thought whatsoever. She'll fucking tempt me with that forever, won't she?

I snarl at her and walk to Cole again, glaring at his stupidity as I drag him out of the vomit he's laid in. Fucking delinquent. And what was he doing with her in the first place? Trying to gain information I should think. Dig into me, just like she is doing. He shouldn't. He should leave us the way we are, at least he holds an element of respect for me that way.

"You're still there, aren't you?" she calls.

I grunt in response, not able to form coherent sentences for her yet as I wander to the bathroom and watch her get in the shower. She's too far inside for me to know the correct thing to say. Too deep for my magician to manoeuvre around anymore, and too entrenched for my monster to stay away from. I snatch a wet washcloth and go back to Cole, wondering why that not so quiet threat of hers was enough to tip me over the edge. Perhaps that's all I need from her, the continued intimidation that she'll leave if I don't cooperate.

The thought galls me more as I wipe at my near comatose brother's mouth, listening to her hum a triumphant tune, and then lift him to take him to the bedroom. He can stay here while we do this, sleep it off and then explain to me why the hell he was ever within ten feet of my woman.

"Sweet," she says, as she walks out behind me and finds me covering him with her duvet. "Not so arsehole like." Bitch. I might even fuck her on that slab for the remark, make sure she understands what's coming for her should she choose to stay afterwards. "He okay?"

Still I grunt at her, choosing no words at all rather than the confused diatribe that might slip from me should she push any further. I can still smell her from the last time we were here, still sense the feel of her in my hand when I had her against this wall, amusing myself with something I had no comprehension of at the time. Love. It's misbalancing. It causes an unclear route, one lined with break points and delineations I don't care to ponder much more.

"This isn't talking Blaine."

"You've riled me enough for talk to be irrelevant to conversation," I snap, turning to face her and finding perfection in the guise of fluid limbs and soft skin. That riles me too, the look of her in a floral dress and heels exactly what I wanted to see her in. How does she do that, know what I need from her? Maybe I taught her that without realising I was doing. "Have you eaten?"

"What?"

"Breakfast?"

"Erm. No, not other than your .." She points at my cock. "You know."

She sniggers and turns for her coat, somehow not bothered at all by my grunting and aggravated stance. She either can't see it, or simply doesn't care for the ramifications of it any longer. It's something that should worry me. It doesn't. It actually causes a smile to come from deep inside, forging itself through my frustration until it's smirking at her as she wanders away.

THE END

Perhaps this is what love is for me, a constant riddle of not knowing and second guessing, rather than the constancy of always understanding everything before the rest of the world does.

"You're ass looks good in that."

"Why, thank you," she replies, picking up her keys and swinging her coat over her shoulders to leave. Leave. Yes. We should leave and get on with this, not deviate from the destination at hand. It's the one thing we both need. The completion of facts. The show of the last final shove. Backwards, only to go forwards. If she'll have me.

Fuck, I hate her.

~

"You're still not speaking, Blaine."

She's right. I'm not. I haven't spoken since we left, other than to order some food at this restaurant and be polite. I'm avoiding conversation. I'm unable to make any of it sound rational. Other than the one thing we need to talk about, which I'm not ready to talk about let alone show her. I'm not interested in anything else but fucking her again. It's why I deviated from my own agenda and let her walk me to this place a few blocks away. Maybe I thought the subject could still be avoided if I ate something, but every time I look at her, or watch her become nervous because of my silence, it makes me furious with my own denial. Something is crumbling inside, tearing me up and forcing me to acknowledge this love of ours, give it its rightful belief inside a bitter heart.

THE END

"You know, I had a rabbit when I was little." What? I look up from my eggs, wondering where that's come from. "Smitten. That was its name." I smirk a little and push the plate away, more interested in her talking than any element of this food. "I got bored with it, didn't look after it properly. It died eventually. I was young. Careless, I suppose." My brow rises, waiting for wherever this is going. She sits back and folds her arms, a slight wince coming as she shifts her ass around. "I don't know if it died because of me, or whether it just died anyway. Perhaps I just wasn't grown up enough to look after something so precious. Didn't understand the point of it all, you know?" She shifts her body around again and leans in, her elbows resting on the table. "But I do know that things die when you don't love them properly, Blaine." I smile a little more, watching her plot through her conversation of inspiration and hope as I gaze into my sea. "But if you do, love them properly I mean, they should thrive, don't you think?" I pick up my drink and take a sip, not prepared to enter the discussion until she gets it all out and finds the bit I need her to say. "Because if someone offered that amount of commitment, let themselves be looked after without any agenda other than hope," she fiddles with a knife, tipping it about. "They'd have to be pretty sure that person would look after them, wouldn't they?" Yes, they would. "Or they'd need to know that that person would try their hardest, show themselves openly and be honest." Yes. A sane person would. "Because without that confirmation of trust, it would be ludicrous to put yourself in those type of hands, wouldn't it?" I nod at that, knowing full well what she means. "Stupid really." My smile broadens. "Do you think I should trust you further than this, with the little you give me?" I don't answer that. I have nothing to answer it with. How would I know? It would be a lie to tell her she should and yet I will never know unless she does. I pull in a breath and gaze at the way her eyes sparkle in the morning sun, reminding me of those damn stars in the sky at home. "Is it just a leap of faith, Blaine? A hope that I won't die?"

"Yes."

"That's all you've got to give me?"

"Yes. That and something to show you."

"Why don't you just talk to me instead, tell me how you felt, what happened? Why?" she shifts forward, her mouth waiting for discussions I can't give her. "Just talk, Blaine. Help me make decisions about you. I'm getting lost here and I don't know how to find my way through you without something being given in return." I sigh and shake my head, not knowing how to make this point clearer as I feel my own frustration rising again.

"I didn't feel, Alana." I mutter, contented with that fact after all these year analysing it. "I have not felt until you. Her skin was nothing but pliability and amusement. As yours is on occasion." She frowns at me and leans away. Good, she should know the truth along with the facts. "She was my beginning, my creation in some ways. Feelings had nothing to do with anything, other than the want to cause pain."

"But you must have felt something?" I shake my head at her, knowing she's not going to understand this, but also knowing it has to come out for her to even try.

"I'll say this once and hope you understand because there is no other explanation for people like me, Alana." I stand and throw some money on the table, holding my hand out to her so we can get on with what I've been avoiding for too long. She looks at it, and then at me. "Come on, let's see if you're as strong as you think you are now."

She slides out and follows me as I turn, her fingers linking into mine as we make our way out the doors and into the autumn air again. It makes me turn and help her with her coat, the temperature already cold enough for November's energy.

"Where are we going?" I smile at her, a slight sadness in the pitch of it given the content she's about to see. But needs must, and if she's to choose this route willingly, if she's asking for all of me, then she will see the truth this time.

"I shouldn't be out on these streets, little dove," I say, wrapping her arm over mine and meandering my way along the avenue. It's pretty here. This end of Manhattan always is, full of beauty and charm, not like my dirty end. It's the reason she has her home here, some part of it resonating with who she used to be. I smile at that, remembering her as she I saw her in that restaurant the first time. Dirty little smirks into phones, her fingers twirling purple stripes around her fingers. "I should probably be in a psych ward somewhere, having clinicians look over me to test my reasoning and thoughts processes." She snorts in derision, as her heels clatter the ground beside me. "I am an abnormality of human nature, Alana, unfeeling to its normal characteristics. Probably borderline schizophrenic." The heels stop, her arm halting me with them. "If I was diagnosing me I would have locked myself away years ago, thrown the key and abandoned all hope." Her hand pulls away a little. I grab it back, not letting her away from the truth she wanted and turning her to face me so she understands the concept. She frowns as I run a finger along her jaw. "I have hidden in shadows most of my life, waiting for something to pull enough of me through to understand how I should be, little dove. I think you might be it."

She stands there, her feet stumbling from the moment. Truth lies here. Monsters and magicians, professors. I chuckle slightly, amused at her look of disbelief.

"Are you saying you're insane?" she asks. I smile again and move us on, laughing and letting the reality hit the air, finally comfortable because of it. "But. You're a professor, Blaine, I mean…" She stumbles over her words, trying to find reasoning for argument. There isn't any. Based on clinical conclusions and years spent evaluating my own practical evidence, the only sensible diagnosis is more than likely schizophrenia or some other similar disorder. "I don't understand. Are you saying all sadists are mad?" I chuckle, thinking of every other one I've encountered, remembering their sense of solidity against my own turbulent thoughts.

"No. I'm telling you that the three personalities I have make *me* insane, Alana. Not all of them." She gawps and then narrows her stare of me, flicking her eyes across my body.

"Three?"

"Three."

She walks on with me, thinking as she continues holding my arm and formulating her next question. I smile at her, a sense of relief settling because she hasn't run to the road to get away from me. She should. I still believe she should, or at least one part of me does. Neither of the other two give a fuck, at least one of them already working out the next vile thing they can do to her skin.

"That's unbelievable, you know that, right?" she eventually says, little abhorrence to the statement as she processes the information. "I mean, insane, really?"

"Clinically, yes."

Insane. Quite the word of the hour given her little conversation about trust and dreams of happiness with a sadist. I look sideways at her and carry on, allowing her a quiet moment to take a breath and let the facts sink in as deep as they can. It needs to go in. They're not changing, and for me to give my all, for her to understand that, she needs to accepts this and become comfortable with its meaning. Learn to love it, find balance in it. Just as I do.

Chapter 19

ALANA

I don't know what to say. I didn't twenty minutes ago and I still don't know now as we drive down a narrow track, the rumble of gravel beneath the wheels as ominous as the feeling that's creeping deeper into me. I'm not even sure why I got in the car with him, let alone why I'm still sitting here quiet as a mouse as he carries on forwards.

Sane people would have run. They would have picked up their things and run like the wind, choosing safety rather than the thought of absurdity. Not me, it seems. I've become ever more lost in whatever this is, not caring for nor believing in his explanation of insanity. He's not insane. Three personalities my arse. Different maybe, certainly a continuing enigma of jumbled emotions, but he's not mad. Mad people don't do what he does. They don't have reasoning and judgements. They're lunatics, aren't they? I mean, they don't think like we do. They're chaotic and frenzied, their moods changing as quick as the wind. They lash out, unable to make rational statements or decisions, let alone fit into society like the rest of us do. They're not normal, not like Blaine and I are. We're just a little different, that's all. Into it, as Cole would say. We enjoy this thing we're into. That doesn't make us insane, though, does it? Because if he's saying he is, then that must mean I am too because I'm still here with him now, still in this car regardless of his confession. I still love him. Still feel like I need him. Still want to reach over and touch him, have him touch me. Maybe that does make me insane. I don't know. It's all a bloody mess again.

"We're here," he says, his head nodding at a pair of dark gates that loom in the distance. I squint, trying to see the sign before we actually get to it. I don't know where here is. He didn't tell me where we were going, nor did I ask. I just followed, not caring for the destination. Rabbit hole or not.

Turlington Cemetery eventually comes into view, bold, loose script depicting the demise of so many.

"A cemetery?" I say, astounded at whatever that means. "Why?"

"So you can choose."

"Choose what?"

He doesn't say anything else to aid me, he just carries on, his face a mask of silence and harsh features. I gaze out at the unending rows of graves rather than continue questioning, and let my mind wander the pretty shingle path winding around the circumference of the parkland. It's vast. Tall trees and planting border the area, smaller snaking paths intermingling the rows, finding their way to loved ones long since passed on. It's lovely, if one could say that about such a place. Calm and tranquil. I end up smiling at it for some reason, perhaps feeling the sense of harmony lingering around as I watch a couple drifting the edge on their way to the gates.

He stops the car and waits there for a second or two, his fingers gripping the wheel as I look over at him and wonder what this is all about.

"Are your mum and dad here?" I ask, quietly, unsure if it's the right thing to say or not. He shakes his head and looks at his lap, his fingers finally relaxing on the wheel until they fall gently and land in the place he's looking at. I stare at them there, sensing his nerves as I watch them turn over each other. It's so different from him. A wavering of the absolute conviction he normally portrays in what he's doing or saying. He seems like he's tearing himself in two about something, as unsure about what he's doing as I am. "Who then, Blaine? What are we doing here?"

"Eloise."

I stare still, my body becoming a wall of defences that I can't process. I want to know. I asked him to tell me, begged him, and now he is doing I don't want to hear it? He chuckles and gazes over at me. I can't see it because I'm staring out the damn window away from him, but I can feel him all over me nonetheless. I can feel the penetration of those black holes, boring in and refusing to let me disregard this. "You need to do this, Alana."

"No, I don't." It spits back, my mind whirring with every reason not to get out of this car. I don't want to. I don't have to do anything. This, him, is my dream, screwed up as that might be. This is my freedom from the world out there. It's my new me, all wrapped up in his hands so I don't have to think anymore or process shit I don't want too. I just want to write my books, love my characters again, and fuck like there's no tomorrow involved, preferably in his house or by his sea. I don't need to see this. There's nothing to see. I know what he did because he told me. The only thing I need is him to talk about it honestly, not have me going to a grave to look at what he did.

He gets out as I'm still trying to get more words to come out, anything to make him see reason and sense. What is any of this going to achieve? Nothing. It will only make me question all this again, question him. And that's the one thing I've learnt not to do. I trust him, with my life if need be. That's who we've become. Who he's made me become.

I refuse to even look at him for a few minutes, choosing the interior of this car rather than the actuality of doing something he tells me. I'll make my own decision on this one. No amount of him doing anything is going to make me get out of this car. No. I'm just not. I'll wait here and then we can go home and discuss the insane bit of the conversation, perhaps try to rationalise that somehow. Jesus.

Backwards. He said backwards. For me. This is what he means by backwards, isn't it? Making me see her. Making me identify this as a reality to deal with. Him with her. Him killing her. Him with me. My eyes lift slightly at the thought as I grip hold of my dress, their gaze hardly focused on anything other than a green haze coming at me. It's a sea of green, nothing but decisions and thoughts colliding with indecision and hesitancy. I'm a mess of every emotion I've got, each one of them mingling with another adjective to condemn reasoning or self-judgement. I can't do this. Any of it. I might as well have millions of notifications coming at me again, bleeping and flashing their chaotic ramble at me, confusing me again. If he'd order me it would be better than this. It would. I could do it then, I think. I could pull the door handle and heave one leg after another, be guided, but not on my own. I can't do it on my own. I don't want to.

I snatch a glance at the keys, their metal glinting at me, then slide my eyes round to look at the one thing I should look nowhere near. He's there still, his fucking arm holding the gate open, his back facing me as he waits for me to follow. His fingers tap the gate in his hand, his body turning slightly as if he's going to look back at me. He doesn't, it's barely a half turn of his head. It's enough, though. It's enough for every instinct to sink to the pit of my stomach and abandon all hope of winning this fucking argument I'm having with myself. Leave? What fool am I? He's waiting for me to help him, isn't he? Offering what I said I wanted from him to be able to move forward. The truth, all of it. This is my choice. My decision to make. That's what he said. It's the one thing he can't make me do, even if that's what he needs to do to push me through. What future would it be if he forced this last thing? What truth would there be in that, what honesty? This is about me acknowledging our future, not running from it.

My own sigh leaves me at the same time as I pull the bloody door handle, barely any thought to the inclination. It's best if I don't think, noiseless. And apart from the soft crunch of the gravel beneath my feet and the slamming of the door, I don't hear anything other than that as I aim for him. Who knows what this is, or why it is, but it's here inside me constantly now telling me to keep following. Perhaps I'm nothing but a lap dog now, happy to endure anything as long as he keeps giving me that quiet I'm after. And maybe, to others, that would mean I'm nothing more than a toy for him, something to be cajoled and influenced, but that's not what this is. That simply can't be all it is. Not anymore. It's deeper than that, always has been.

I duck under his arm, a slight look back to see his face as I keep walking. There's nothing to indicate happiness or pleasure that I've followed, more a sense of foreboding as he nods his head onwards. I hover as the path separates, waiting to be told where next.

"Right," he says, his body four steps behind me.

I turn and continue on again, each footfall laced with the dread I'm trying to overcome. I'm not sure what it's for, or what I hope to do with the emotion. It's not like I don't know where I'm going to, or what's going to be at the end of it. She's dead. I know that. He killed her. He killed her doing exactly what he does to me. And no amount of that fact has stopped me getting out and coming with him to see this. It seems crazy even to me as I watch my blue high heels crunching each next step, occasionally lifting my head to take in the scenery.

"We don't need to do this …"

"Yes, Alana, you do," he clips, a strident tone snapping back at me before I've got a chance to finish my sentence. "You will look, kneel, and then ask me for what you want again."

I nod at his words, almost expecting them for some reason and wondering if I will do what he's just asked me to do or not. I don't know. I mean, who would? It makes me look up into the sky as another man comes into view, barely aware of him as I keep wandering on. "Left." I swerve to the left, not even looking at the ground beneath my feet as I keep staring upwards. It's all so appealing up there. Perfect skies and perfect clarity, none of it clouded by thoughts or uncertainty. It's seamless, too. Not a join or junction in sight. It's just a continuous horizon, full of nothing but beauty and wonder. It's all my dreams and adventures, ones full of the man behind me and his lips, hands. "Left again."

I don't know how much longer I keep walking, nor care. He just directs me as I keep looking up and smiling at what that sky holds for us. It's so beautiful and clear. Nothing in the way for us, nothing to interfere or veil my judgement of who I am and what I want. He needs me now as much as I need him. It's just this one final hurdle, isn't it? Just this one last thing to see and understand and then we're free. I'm free.

"Stop."

I do, and I do it the second he says it. No stumbling, no tripping over my feet. I'm balanced and quiet again, somehow lost in this meander he took me on, not caring for the eventuality of our destination at all. I know where I am as I watch a small bird dance the sky in front of me, her wings busy flapping madly. I smile at her, wondering if she's going home like I am, willing her there quicker so she can get to those she loves, look after them. It makes me sigh and think of his sea, his bed, the way his arms wrap around me on occasion, the dancing. My head on his chest after our sessions, and the way he cares for me in those moments. Love.

"Blaine, I don't need this." I don't. It doesn't matter to me. I wish it did. I wish I could make a judgement on him and feel the need to tell the world of what he has done, but I can't. I'm selfish about him, barely able to fathom the thought of life without him, let alone the thought of turning him in for something he does with nothing but base need and instinct.

"I do, Alana." I try to turn, wanting to tell him it doesn't matter, that we can leave now and never discuss it again, but he instantly holds me and forces my position still. "You look, find your own conclusions, and then kneel and ask me again if you want to."

I'm still staring up, perhaps trying to ignore what's beneath me for fear it might change my mind. Kneel. He means it this time, doesn't he? For us to go on from here, for us to become more than we are I've got to give everything unreservedly. There will be no games, no teaching, and no entertainment for entertainment's sake anymore. It's emersion he wants from me. Submersion. My obedience. My thoughts. My life should he want it.

A leap of faith hangs in my mind as I slowly bring my eyes downcast, an angel in prayer coming into view on another tombstone. What a leap. And now he's not even touching me anymore, not giving me that confidence in his hold to cling onto. I'm alone in this decision, he's making it so.

"Do you care?" I ask, still gazing at the angel's wings as they stretch out over the grave they protect. It's not something I've thought about before now, only my reaction to the information he gave me.

"About what?"

"Her death." Because if he doesn't, if he doesn't feel remorse of some kind, then what's to stop him doing it again. I shiver at the thought, my arms wrapping me up to keep my heart sheltered from the image of bloodshed at his hands.

"That's not the right question." My eyes glance down at the grave, finally finding the courage as I turn into him. Not the right question? What is then, because this is the only one I need answering. I need to know he gives a damn about what he did to a woman, need to know that he's learnt from his mistake. If he hasn't, how do I know it's safe to go onwards?

"It's the right question for me." He smiles a little, but it's sadder than usual. No charm about it, no sense of amusement at me, frustration even. He's just flat. A depressed line of nothing but what he is beneath the man I first met. "Do you, Blaine? Care?"

"I care about you."

The statement doesn't really surprise me as I gaze at him, his eyes transfixed on mine, no concern to the woman who lies underground because of what he did to her.

"You killed her."

"Yes."

"And now you want me to do the same as she did for you?"

"No. I want you to give me the chance to love you, little dove." He reaches for me, one hand lifting to my face. I don't move or reject the touch that's coming, nor am I scared of it in any way regardless of the reason we're standing here. I want it to land on me, am desperate for it, and have been since that first time in his bedroom. "I want to order myself for you. I want your hope, Alana." I smile at that, watching the way his fingers hover midway between us, waiting for them to find me because he's a part of me whether I like it or not. He's infused in my skin, laced in the way my heart beat forces the blood around my veins. He stops before he reaches me, though, choosing to return the hand and pocket it instead as he backs a step away. "I want your trust. I never cared for hers, nor did I give her the consideration or emotion I'm giving to you."

"But why don't you care about her death? You must have some sense of remorse."

"Do you?"

"What?" He snorts at me, his body backing away again as if he's irritated at my confusion.

"Do you care about her death, Alana?"

"I didn't know her. Why would I? I mean, it's not me we're talking about here." I fumble the words, not sure what answer to give. I glance back at the grave, uncomfortable with my own sense of dispassion for her demise. "I didn't know her, Blaine. It's not …"

"And I did?" Of course he did.

"You were intimate with her, Blaine. She was with you," I snap, confused as to why this has anything to do with me, and irritated with his choreography around the question. He was with her, not me. My care for her death isn't needing discussion. He just needs to answer the question.

He stares for the longest time, a tension forming around his jaw showing his disapproval of my tone. Fuck him. I might still love him, and I did follow him here, but he'll give me more than this for us to carry on. Truth.

I stare back, willing his hand to reach over and soften on me, regardless of my tone, or for him to make me take this and get rid of my questions altogether. I need this from him, I do. We do. It's honest and open and everything I have to get for me to be able to accept this in some way.

"She was with a part of me for a time, Alana. *I* was never with her." He looks at the floor for a second then draws his eyes up me, slowly, taking the longest breath before he exhales it. "Not like I am with you." He tips his head to the side, inspecting the look on my face like he has done a thousand times, watching me get frustrated with his lacking vocabulary, as I tighten my grip on myself. "You want to hear that I'm saddened by her demise, chastising myself for it." I don't know. I just want the damn truth. "You want contrition and penitence so that you can find a sense of happiness in this pitiful vision, don't you?"

"No, I just want the truth. I want your feelings, Blaine."

He frowns for a second, the wrinkle in his brow telling me I'm not going to like what spills out next. That time is over for me now, there's little he could tell me that I can't hear anymore. I'm here at this woman's grave, waiting for the truth, whatever it might be.

He grabs me out of nowhere, the fierce hold of his fingers sweeping me towards the grave before I've got a chance to think about what's happening. I'm shoved so quickly my knees buckle to the ground under his strength, skin grating the floor as I go.

"I strapped her until she bled, then fucked her until she wept, little dove," he says, stepping forward into me, his fingers moving from my neck to my face to force my lips to the marble. The words cause a rush of panic to rise, my throat catching with the choke on tears already forming. "Look at her, feel her death in my hands." He slaps at me, spurring more tears to come as I gaze at the blurred grave in front of me. "And when she couldn't scream anymore," he says, as he tips my head to the side to look back to him, a sneer etched onto his handsome face. "I carried on without thought to consequence." He stands taller with that explanation of their relationship, not seeming to care for the animal it makes him seem to be. "She was my beginning, Alana," he snarls out, flicking me away and letting go of my skin. "My monster's fucking progression." His eyes leave me as he walks passed my cowering form to gaze at her headstone. "She helped me find the other parts of me. Nothing more than a toy to break apart. Keep looking at her, learn."

I stare at the grey beneath me as he mutters more words I can't hear, for some reason trying to see a face I don't know, hear her screams. Some part of me admires him for his brazen attitude to her death, sickening as that might be to my own stomach. It's the same part of me that loves him, I suppose. The same part that kneels here on top of her. That he can be here at her graveside and be honest about the lack of sentiment involved is, while horrifying, authentic to me. No stories, no manipulation, no pretence of prince charming or knights of the realm. This is real here. With him everything is so very real. It's tactile in any given moment he chooses. A mixture of thriller and love story perhaps, both mingling to become something of a freak show bound by my words, his actions, and my obedience to those fateful engagements. A sadist's private thoughts and whims. A masochist's evolution beneath him.

My nails scratch the marble beneath me, finally acknowledging a term I can apply to my situation. I'm a masochist, for him, anyway. Perhaps that's why this position I'm in seems less unconventional than it should be. Hovering on her seems respectful, an acknowledgment of my own future. Death, presumably, is the final call for someone who gives their all to men like Blaine. Perhaps the ultimate sacrifice for love.

THE END

"There's nothing more to tell, Alana." I nod, my mind coming back to the present as I hear his voice strengthen. "I'm both sad and regretful for what happened to Eloise, irrespective of whether it should have or not, but I'm not apologetic for her end. I'm thankful to her for it." I nod. I don't think I really expected anything else to come from him. This is who he wants to be, isn't it? Who he hides, who he keeps away from society so that he can be deemed normal by everyone else. "It is as it happened, and as she wanted it to be, regardless of how." I look up at that, my mouth open, astonished by the last of it and gazing at him for more explanation.

"Are you suggesting she wanted to die?" I ask, my body coming upright. I didn't know that. That makes it completely different. Or maybe it doesn't. I don't know.

He smiles at me over his shoulder, a warm one. It's full of love and memories of the way we danced, the grip of his fingers still entrenched. And I can feel him burrowing his way further inside me again as he turns back to her, more reverence being offered at the slab. It's all such a juxtaposition. Everything is with him. Gentleness over the grave that he put here. Soft words spoken with vile meaning, somehow laced with a respect only he could produce.

"This is your decision to make, Alana. I can't do it for you." He can't do it for me. "I won't make it seem easier to bear." No, I don't suppose he will. "You're free to make your own choice."

Free? Nothing is my free choice anymore. Being with him has changed my perception of what was. It's made me need him rather than the other sense of normality that lingers out there in the everyday world.

THE END

I flick my eyes over her grave, barely giving it any thought other than how it effects the man who is still stands over me. He snarls at himself, moving towards the headstone to rearrange flowers I hadn't noticed. "You always have been. It's why I've made you ask for me."

I smile slightly at those last words, remembering the times he's made me ask. It's been constant the entire time. The need for agreement, the offering, the withheld touches until I nod or present myself accordingly. For a man who has founded a gravestone because of his actions, his self-restraint has been exquisite. And he's done that for me, hasn't he? Trained himself. Suspended himself. Limited his thoughts, put them under quarantine maybe until such time as I accept it all.

"Did you bring those flowers?" I'm not sure why I care, but I do. Some sentiment of romance maybe. Some lingering hope that dates will still reside when I let myself plummet without care to the exploit he chooses. Slut, whore. Alana. Little Dove and Brat. Each one of me ready to offer myself without prudent choice or rebellion as to why or why nots. Just his. To do with as he sees fit, just as long as he gives me that ocean once in a while. That and the feel of his arms around me on occasion, his heartbeat against my back.

"Yes."

"You've never brought me flowers."

It's an absentminded drawl of words, as I stare into chocolate eyes, his frame filling my vision. He's never brought me flowers or presents. Never given me gifts, chocolates, niceties. Never even really said the words most lovers long to hear constantly, announcing their affirmation of worth to each other. One date in all this time. One night of romance, his kind of softening, and even that hindered by the realisation of this place beneath my knees now.

He picks the bunch of roses up and throws them to the floor in front of me, a raise of his brow showing his disdain for my thoughts of romanticism. So I look up, searching the sky for my bird and wonder if she made it home, or whether the cold froze her mid-flight. Perhaps that's what happens when you brave the wind on your own, no hand to help pull you through it. Or perhaps you fly harder until you get to the place you want most, strengthening yourself against whatever tries to stop your descent to the nest that waits. Either way, I won't be kneeling on this grave any longer for anything. If I ask for it all, if I give him that, it'll be somewhere other than the cold slab of the last woman he chose to destroy.

Chapter 20

ALANA

I smile as we walk into a bar I don't know, the effortless rhythm of his footfalls behind me giving me a sense of calm to travel within. He still surrounds me, regardless of the fact that I'm in front of him, somehow casting his shadow out around me so I don't have to fear what's coming. You think I'd be pissed about all this, confused, certainly after nothing but silence from him as we drove away from that graveyard, but I'm not. I'm neither trying to rationalise this anymore nor trying to pick my internal opinions apart. We've just walked all afternoon after the drive back to town, pottered really, all the time with him reaching for my hand and linking his fingers tightly.

We've gone wherever my feet have taken me and he's followed, letting me guide the routes and consider my responses to this morning's events. Insanity and death. Something I never thought I'd be dealing with in real life. Books maybe, but not here in the world I reside in. But then this is my book, isn't it? My story. One written by Alana Williams on an old typewriter, as the man I love shoved the tale through me for the world to read. Although I don't know if the world should anymore. They're our chapters to travel through now. My beginning to our end.

Charlotte E Hart
THE END

He sits me down, ensuring I'm comfortable, still no words coming from him as I look at his face and wonder what our first words will be going forward from this. There's only a smile coming back at me, one that's filled with the more relaxed version I've seen on occasion, before he nods and turns to walk away. I watch him go, his body weaving through the patrons, until he disappears into the fray and leaves me sitting here alone. I don't know why. I'm not concerned either. He'll be back. He'll never leave me alone now, not unless I ask him too. He wants me in his life, in his home. Needs me. Loves me enough to tell me everything he has done.

I turn to the bar and fold a napkin, my fingers needing something to do now he's not holding them. I haven't even asked anymore questions, nor have I tried to probe him more for conversation about either insanity or murder. I don't believe the first, not truly. And the second means little to the here and now. He's told me the truth, let me understand the two elements of him that kept us distanced. That's all that matters to me. He's let me all the way in, and in doing that, he's shown me how much I'm loved. What else should I need than that? Commitment? More words, explanations of in-depth psychological discussions? Why? It makes no difference to me. Nothing will change this internal instinct that keeps me needing to be beside him, under him.

Whatever he was before me is less relevant than what he might become with me. His words proved that. They told me I am worth more than Eloise. That I'm more than she ever was. And time has moved on, anyway. It's fixed us together, the bond between us becoming more trustworthy as it has. We're in tune now I know it all, a mix of two people slowly flattering one another either in spite of, or because of, the reasons why. We have become a new wave, one that still waits for the crash perhaps, but we're both unable to deny the strength of the current regardless. I certainly am. And I'm tired of fighting what I either am or have become because of him. What happened with Cole was all me. What happened with Bree was all me. He might have been the instigator of those types of thoughts, fed them to me, but it's me that acted on those instincts, and me that let them come. If he is insane, it's an insanity I adore. An insanity I'm now a part of, for better or worse.

"Have you decided?" he asks, his hand suddenly on the back of my neck. I chuckle and look back at him, my neck craning round and upwards, desperate to see that smile of his. It's not there anymore, though. He narrows his stare of me instead, a slight hesitation in his lips before he speaks. "Drink?" He doesn't mean a drink. He's doesn't care at all what I want to drink. He wants an answer as to whether I'm going home with him or not. Whether I'm asking for a life with him.

It makes me gaze over his face, looking for any reason not to. Searching, in fact, for the slightest hint of fear still lingering inside myself. There's nothing there, just as there's not the slightest withdrawal of that offer from him.

"I'm hoping you know the answer to that, Blaine," I eventually reply, my legs swinging round to him as he sits on a stool next to me. "I'm tired of thinking about it in all honesty." My hands fiddle with a napkin on the glass topped surface, nervously trying to find something else to say because of his lacking smile. "It is what it is, don't you think? I'm not running scared because of you. So it's got to mean I'm agreeing."

His brow raises as he removes his jacket and begins rolling up his sleeves, still no sign of a smile from him. I don't know what else to say. I don't even know what right minded individual would consider any of this reasonable, let alone be asking for more of it. Perhaps it's just unique to him and me, others like us maybe. I don't know. I just know there isn't anything else without him now, dead women or not. There is only his sea, my words, and the vast expanse of a life without him to consider. I can't do that. I won't, not now I know my life with him.

"That's not good enough for me, Alana," he says, turning to the bartender and pointing at something on the menu, holding two fingers up at the same time.

I snort, amused at his hostile tone. Not good enough? What the hell else does he want? As it is, and irrespective of feelings, I'm all in simply because I can't be out. Perhaps I haven't got the balls or intuition to find myself without him leading me, and perhaps I just don't want to try. Either way I don't care. I just want his hands on me, leading me. Showing me a life I didn't know before him and giving me a sense of freedom because of it.

"Well, it'll have to be, Blaine." That's all I've got for now.

I turn away, my body swivelling before I've given him a chance to respond, and watch the bartender doing whatever he's doing. It is what it is. Possibly not right or normal, but it is here inside me now and I've nothing to fight it with anymore. The tranquillity that rushes through me as I stare forward is borderline insane. All in. All in his hands and not caring for whatever that might hold. The thought makes me smile as the bartender tinkers with varying concoctions of alcohol, mixing them as he does and clinking glass. I'm apparently giving my life and thoughts to another human to deal with, barely caring for the consequence of that. Who would have thought it of the Alana I was a few months ago? I wouldn't. I'm not even sure where it's come from or how it's happened, but this man beside me knows, and he knows what's best for me because of it. He might not know my dreams or aspirations, might not even know what I want from life, but he knows how I work, and knows how I need to work because of those facts. He's inside my brain quicker than I am.

Two dark green short glasses are brought back to us, one of them slid towards him before mine's offered. It immediately makes me glance around the space we're in, searching for other people so I can discern where the hell I am.

"Drink, and then get on all fours," Blaine says, his tone steady and sombre. I stare around, glancing at couples to see if we've entered a rabbit hole I wasn't aware of. It doesn't seem it. Couples are dressed immaculately, high heels and elegant clothes, the cut of their cloth enough for me to assume designer and expensive. Everyone's sitting normally, talking like regular people rather than arses in the air and sounds of spanks and screams. I twist slowly to look back at him, another flick of my eyes over his shoulder towards the back of the long room. "You said you were asking, why are you questioning me, little dove?" He asks. I'm not that I'm aware of, only checking out what's become so fascinating about the view. Its dark down there, and the occasional flash of a light draws my attention to it, as he smirks and sips his drink in my eye-line. "The time for questions is gone. You said you were ready for me. All of me." I slide from the stool, transfixed on the quickening strobe that seems to be pulsing up the room towards us, Blaine's back blocking it. "It's time to prove it now." He stands slowly, his head inclining towards the floor, his original quiet order still intent on being obeyed. It makes me look at him and then the floor, a slow smile spreading at whatever he's got planned this time. At least we're together, I suppose. I'm not being thrown into something with no knowledge, like the theatre.

"Just you?" I ask, the thought of others touching me troubling. I'm not sure why given my penchant for fucking friends in store cupboards, but it's unnerving regardless.

He doesn't answer, nothing other than that stare of his that means he's getting pissed at my hesitation. I guess I won't know what's happening until it happens, and I don't care really. I don't. I trust him. And more than anything, I trust me now. I trust this feeling inside me that hasn't baulked one inch from his order. I feel my knees lowering, my fingers reaching for the carpet without removing my eyes from him. Irrespective of the woman he killed, this is us now. My wants. My needs. He'll give them to me and I'll take whatever he delivers, love helping us both contend with what the other conveys.

He smiles as I hover here, my hands relaxed as I get my knees ready to crawl the distance he asks for. It's down there, whatever it is. I know it is, I can see it in the pulsing light that keeps coming at me, tempting me into something I haven't felt before.

"Are you sure, Alana?" he asks, as the back of my dress is slowly zipped open. It makes me gasp a little, but the warmth of his hand on my skin soon replaces the exposed sensation. I nod in reply as he comes to crouch in front of me, his fingers lifting my chin to face him. "I need to know this is real." I smile at that, listening to the slight quiver in his tone as he gazes intently. I just keep looking at him, focusing in on the eyes I know so well. There aren't any words necessary now. There's no point in them. We don't need them anymore. He knows this look, knows my commitment to him. He asks, I do. That's all there is to this. No questions. No concerns. Just blind trust and the feel of him near. It's in the air somehow when he's close, like he's the other half of me, the dominant half. He leads and I follow, guiding me forwards and stripping me of tensions.

"Sir in here, yes?" I nod at that too as he rises back up, a dirty smile beginning to wrap around his lips, as he begins to walk away. It's the same look I get post fucking, one that fills me with assurance as his fingers tap his legs to tell me to trail him.

My knees hardly feel the floor as I watch him move in front of me and follow, the flash of the strobe continuing to pull me down along with him. It's like a tunnel, the light getting smaller and smaller the closer we get, speeding up and leading me to fuck knows where. It's just one crawl after the other, the shine of his shoes and the tempo of his steps keeping me engrossed. And I ache already, my thighs clenching with every movement, the flex of my back making my arse undulate along this high end fuck tunnel. It's coming in there, isn't it? Pain, exhaustion, the feel of hands and whips. The sting of a belt, the broken gasps for air. The orgasms crashing. It's all coming for me and I couldn't be more turned on by the thought if I tried, my legs pushing me into it, into him. I'm mesmerised by it. Caught in this magical web of sin and self-discovery, barely able to think of anything but fucking and sweat, the tearing of fabric, the grip of manly hands and their delinquent bite into me.

I lick my lips, watching his trousers as they come to a standstill, his hand levering a card into a slot by a door. I could make myself come right here, sink my fingers in and warm myself up for him, make my skin more flexible for whatever he's going to do.

"You dare and I'll cage you for a week," he says, his hand slapping out at my cheek gently. The shiver that rides me is almost enough to make me come without any help from fingers at all. So much so that I lick out at his finger in the hope of drawing it into my mouth. He chuckles at me, allowing me a seconds worth of power over him before he pulls it away and turns to glance back at me. "Last chance to back away, little dove? I won't let you go after this." I smile at him and lick my lips again, not needing any chances. Chances are for those who don't know what they're doing. I do.

The heat that hits me as the door slides open is like entering the tropics. I hover, trying to get my bearings as I stare into the gloom. There's nothing to focus on. It's a blur of bodies, all of them writhing and moaning, the stench of sweat drifting back to me before I've got chance to draw breath.

"Move," he snaps, a slap coming at my cheek again to make me focus on him. "You stay right at my feet. Don't make me show them." I nod quickly, snatching in a breath and trying to ignore everything that's around me. It doesn't work, no matter how I try to zero in on him as we begin moving. Every move of my arms is bewildering, my hands hovering with each reach forward. It's a riot of fucking, whips and chains whistling through the air, screams and howls echoing back to me. Men and women everywhere, subs strapped into positions with tears rolling down their faces as they bellow out. I snatch a look back at the door, nervously looking for an exit. It's not there anymore, the steel frame shuttered closed behind me.

"Blaine?" It slips out before I've thought about it, and the slap that rings across my cheek sends me crashing to the floor, sticky carpet grating on my skin as I land.

"This is the last time I ask nicely," he growls, his shoes nudging my face. I blow out a breath, sensing some comfort in the feel of his frame beside me. Oh god, it's one of the most screwed up sensations I've ever felt, as I pull my body back up again. It's like I need that force, need it to realign me, rearrange the sense of love into a usable fashion. "I love you. Hold onto that and follow me." His words make me pull in my exhaled breath, letting it fill me with strength and courage for what's coming, adjusting whatever fucked up part of me needs bringing through my hesitation.

I crick my neck and look up to find him smiling slightly, his eyes crinkled under his frown. He nods once, another small lift of his lips to clarify those words, then turns and taps his thigh as he walks. *Hold onto that and follow me.* I asked, and this is the result. It's all of him he's offering. This is his world I'm in now, a part of him I have to accept as part of me. It's enough for me to do exactly as he asks, my body crawling the sticky floor with little care to what I'm crawling on. It's not relevant, where's he's leading me is. And I can only hear the noises now as I focus on his legs, the screams dimming to muffled sobs and groans for some reason.

His legs stop suddenly, his voice talking quietly to someone above me. I don't look, I just keep looking at the legs that own me, rather than the new pair in my eye-line, and then follow as he moves off a few moments later.

"Up," he eventually says. So few words now, more simple commands. It's easier like that, and makes me stand up without any thought to why. He gazes at me and then points at a wall, a chain hanging from a high hook a couple of feet in front of it. I walk straight to it, unconcerned by the rusty manacles dangling from the end. Nothing matters, only his pleasure and my sense of happiness. I'll find it there under him, I always do. Pain is only relevant for the first few minutes, and then it disperses, bringing the calm I crave along with his idea of adoration.

I glance around a little as I raise my hands, waiting for him to put me in the cuffs. People are watching, a few of them taking a seat to view the show of this famous sadist of mine. Fine, let them have their fun. It doesn't bother me anymore. Nothing does other than ensuring he keeps smiling at me, his hands finding their peace on me. It's what one does for the love of a good man. They give their all, waiting for it to be returned as and when it's deserved. And I'll get it later. I know I will. This right here is my last show of compliance, my obedience to him. I smile at the thought, imagining his beach and the sea that waits for me to go home to it. No other person here gets that. And no other woman gets to wake up in his arms. Only me. He's more mine than I am his in some ways. Who else gives him this but me, telling him they love him as they do? No one.

THE END

I roll my shoulders, letting the beat of the muted music sink into my soul as I watch him walk to a bench, another person's hands tightening the cuffs into place. I don't know who it is, nor care. I'm looking at the one thing in my life worth enduring. I love that man, adore him for reasons I still can't comprehend. And that puzzle only increases as he turns back to me and pulls the belt from his trousers, all pleasantries removed from his face. He's stone cold here, a mask for the crowd around us, no doubt.

Four strides and he's by my side, the belt already looped and hooked under my chin so he can latch it onto the chain above me. I twist slightly, trying to ease the pressure he's created, it causes him to tighten it and smile eerily. There he is, my monster smiling back at me, his mind getting ready to disperse whatever atrocity it needs to. And if I look closely enough now I can feel him in those eyes of his, see the change. Perhaps that's the personalities he told me of, one of them, anyway.

He gazes at me for a moment, his fingers slowly pushing my breasts out of my bra, then moving down to sink his fingers straight to where I need them most. It's quick, and there's no depth to the move, which makes me groan out and widen my stance hoping for more. Nothing more happens other than a small tease, one that increases what desire was already pooling there.

"Do you remember the main room in the first club we met in?" he asks, his mouth inches from my lips. I nod, the images coming at me as I think about them. "Do you remember what was happening at the end, to the girl?" I frown a little, remembering the initiation procedure that was developing as I left. "That's what we're here for, little dove."

He backs away a step as I let the realisation sink in, his feet covering the ground slowly. The crowd comes forward, some of them standing by his side as if ranks are being formed. "These are my people."

I glance at the faces around him, seeing no one I know. Tall, short. Men, women. Young, old. All of them wearing the same arched brow as him, one that seems to tell me everything I need to know without any words at all. They're all like him, aren't they? There's nothing soft here. Nothing kind. Fine suits on the men. Tailored apparel on the women, make up still perfected. Only the subs are sparsely clothed, some of their moans still echoing to remind me they're actually here too. For now, and with the ring forming around me, sadists are all I can see. They leer and smirk, some amused, some aroused, all interested in me and what Blaine has brought for them to toy with. Initiation.

"You didn't tell me about this," comes from me, another snatched glance at someone behind me as I fidget a little. Perhaps I'm just nervous that I had no warning about what was to come. Or maybe I'm impatient for this last step to understanding him, to finding him and being obedient to his needs. I'm not sure which, but either way I feel honoured in some way. Like I've achieved something to be brought here. It makes me squirm a little, slightly uncomfortable with my own thoughts as I hear one of the men chuckle.

My toes roll over themselves to ensure safe grounding beneath my feet, as I turn to glare at him dismissing Blaine as I do. Something sharp stings at my stomach immediately. The yelp that leaves me rumbles through my skin, making me pull my belly in and draw my knees up, as I twist my body back to face him. He's smiling, affected by my yelp of horror, no doubt, another belt dangling in his hand.

"Don't ever look away from me." I suck in a breath at his tone, trying to regain my calm as I stare at him, bewildered. "Disappointing me here won't end well for you." I don't doubt it.

Another laugh sounds in the room as I crick myself back into shape, letting my body hang. I don't look this time, rather try to let myself fall into his eyes again and forget the rest of them. That's all I need to do. Focus on him. He looks, though. He drops my eyes quickly and glowers across the room. It's hate-filled, proving his disapproval of whoever's laugh it was.

Much as I might hate to admit it, especially in this context, the sight of that glower on his face calms me. That's his fight for me. His love. It makes me feel precious in ways I can't explain, not even to myself. This is a show of ownership. He's proud of me, proud of us. I wouldn't be here if he didn't think me ready, nor would I be relaxed as I hang here if I didn't trust him enough to show me through this. No safewords. No words at all. Just me and him, regardless of everyone else.

I grip onto the chain above me, stretching myself as I roll my shoulders again and get comfortable. This entire thing makes me feel aroused in some way, sensual now I'm doing nothing but gazing at him.

"Who first?" he says, "Your choice, little dove."

I don't care who's first. I won't be seeing or feeling anyone but him. As long as he keeps looking at me and focusing me, he's all I'm here for. This isn't about anyone else but me and him. Us.

Charlotte E Hart
THE END

"Nothing will fuck me like you do. What does it matter?" He smirks, his head inclining to the man on his right, quiet words being whispered.

I glance at the man as he steps forward, then shake my head and look straight back at Blaine. His frown comes again as I feel a hand grab at my arse, pinching into it immediately. It hurts, enough for me to gasp a little and try to get away from it. It's futile. There's no getting away from anything here. And there's no getting away from the slap and second rough grope that lands because of my rudeness.

"You should have trained it better," the man mutters, his fingers snaking firmly around my waist and hovering above my pussy. Blaine sneers at that, his hands flexing as he backs away half a step. "It's a fine one you've got here," he says, his hot breath coming over my shoulder. "Does it fuck well?" Blaine's face turns almost to stone, rigid lines erupting where the softened edges I know once were.

"Be careful with my property, Lazeros," he says, tight lips containing so much more than just those words. I smile again as the man's fingers works their way into my knickers. He's jealous of what's happening in front of him. Probably aroused - definitely I would assume - but he doesn't like this.

I flick my eyes to his trousers, watching the way his stance gives room for his cock to harden. I know him now, know his movements and thoughts. It makes me widen my legs, giving this man room to play as I gaze back and imagine other hands here. I'm not sure whether I should be enjoying this or not, but I am.

My tongue grazes my dry lips as a moan leaves them, and his fingers start to burrow in. They inch in firmly, no care for their function or purpose. He's just finding his way inside, fucking me with hands made for pain. And they do hurt, too. They grate and gauge, his nails shredding me, warning me of the limits I'll be made to endure by the many. Regardless though, I feel my hips starting to move as I watch Blaine watch me, my pussy clamping on fingers as they begin pumping in and out. It's provocative, arousing. The air, the smell, the sight of Blaine as he tenses and inches a step forward. And I quiver at that, my mind readying me for him rather than this functionary dabble at sin another hand offers.

"Please." I mouth the word at the man I love, my teeth drawing back over my lips as I let my orgasm build. I know I'm not allowed to come, no matter what. It's part of this test I'm in. Part of me proving my worth. And I won't until he tells me to. I can do that for him. I will, no matter the squirming and mewling that's coming from me as I try to back away from the feeling.

He flicks his head at the man, causing him to remove his hand, and then nods at someone on my right. Another hand hits my skin quickly, the sharp sound of heels clinking the floor around me. Still, I stay focused on the one in control of me, of the room it seems. The hands are smaller this time, womanly, they caress and cajole, making my eyes roll a little, before they twist perversely on my nipples. They wrench and tug, their small surface heightening the sensations to sharp stings and bevelled grates. And her teeth bite into my neck at one point, making me gasp and groan as I try to avoid her fingers travelling down my stomach.

It goes on and on. One after another. Just as I get close, another pair of hands comes in to replace the previous. Every hole being prodded and poked, fingers delving and diving, some of them in my mouth, the texture of each one different to the last. I feel used here. Used and hung for entertainment. Blaine pulled up a chair at one point, turning it so he could sit and lean on the back to watch me. He smiles and frowns the entire time, enjoying my torment in one breath, but barely restraining himself from intervening in the next. I can see it all in his eyes. The war being waged. The need to stop these people but enjoy them too. It's confusing to me, making me fight and struggle a little, unsure if he's happy or not. And I'm trying to stop the tears coming. Trying to stop the shame that rifles through me. It's some degree of the old Alana trying to break through this free for all on my body, fight against it, but that near satanic smile that comes back at me, oh god that fuels me again. It forces me to harden myself and wait for him, my thighs clenching regardless of the large fingers trying to prise them apart.

"Let him in," Blaine grates out, his chin resting on his forearms as he keeps watching me. I can't. Any more and I'll come, I know I will. I'm a ball of nervous energy, ready to let the pent up sensations explode. Men, women, the look of his gaze as he watches me strain against this man.

He stands abruptly, the chair he's standing on being cast to the side as sudden aggravation sweeps his features. Fear builds instantly, the kind I haven't really felt since my apartment all that time ago. It's the same face he had then, his hand at my throat when he first showed me himself.

"Blaine?" it falls from my lips as I try to scamper backward, the move instantly blocked by the man behind me. He's so fast to move toward me, his fingers reaching for my skin with vicious intent written all over them.

The hand that's on my skin is knocked out of the way, the man's body behind me falling away as it happens, and then just as quickly I'm spun so I'm looking at the wall, my body pushed into it.

"What did I tell you before you came in here?" My skin crushes into the brick as his hands reach in between my thighs and pull them apart, hoisting me up as he does. "What did I ask you to call me?"

I don't know, nor care. I'm flummoxed, my mind reeling with sensations now that I can feel him on me again. I'm about to come, I can feel it as my nipples rough the wall, my wrists tugging at the metal around them. It's all so bright, colours lighting up behind my closed eyes as I feel him grab in harder, his fingers moving the crotch of my knickers away. I'm desperate, moans and grunts coming from me as his clothed body rubs on my back, his cock digging into my arse. I want him inside me. I do. I don't care that these people are here. I don't care that I'm being a show. All I can feel is him and the way he makes me feel. It's all him and me. It's all I want it to be. And the shunt of my body being shoved, the wall grating painfully against me again, only heightens the next spur for orgasm. It makes me desperate to touch him, have him hold me and guide me. I can't think at all, nothing other than the need to fuck.

Sweat pours from my forehead as my cheek squashes the wall, the continued jostling of my body making me rub against it.

"Please," it's mumbled from me, hardly audible in this room of noise and rumbled sound. I can barely hear it above my own breath, sharp gasps and moans still coming from me along with my chanted pleas.

"Ask me." My head's crushed again, a vicious yank on my legs to push my knees into the surface. "In front of these people, ask for what you want. Let them hear you."

"Please, Blaine." Nothing happens other than more pain, my body pushed and turned, new sensations assaulting my body as he keeps coming at me rather than putting his fingers where I need them. "Please. Please."

I'm so close. So very close. And so fucking exhausted. It's coming from everywhere, to the point where I can barely feel anything nice. Pain, more pain, the next bite in, another hit somewhere on me. Bruising, raw, my frame being shoved and pushed, pulled and then tugged again. There's nothing but aching and hurt, my body bound in it as my wrists slip and shear against the cuffs. And then, just as suddenly as the pain came, it subsides and begins to dissipate.

I open my eyes, letting the room come back into view. There's nothing here, and my body's still being heaved and shoved about, but the pain has gone now. I'm floating, just like I was under that water. I can feel him on me, feel the tension and density of him there still, but it's all muted and gentle suddenly.

I sigh out at the feeling, letting him do whatever he wants because the ache just keeps building, beautifully. It's sturdier now somehow, deeper. It builds from the bottom of me, a sense of gravity and surety coming from each continued batter of my skin.

"Sir." It drawls from my lips, finally understanding the merit of that word in this moment.

THE END

I don't know where this space is I'm in, but I'm lost in it, not caring for the next blow or demonstration of his worth. I'm just here, with him, that's all I know. Barely present and yet fully immersed. I'm desperate for his lips and yet not caring if I get them or not. This here is all us. It's where I've longed to be.

Chapter 21

BLAINE

There she is. My beautiful little fuck toy.

I hit out at her, watching as her body holds steady and takes the brunt of the impact. It fires me up, my hands hardening with each next tug on her skin. Beautiful. She shines here, just like my fucking stars at home. The tears have gone, the wailing and screams disappeared. All that's left is skin and flesh, her mind drifted to some other place where she'll no longer feel my wrath.

The thought preoccupies my magician as he thinks and twists the images, wondering if he should let her abandon the pain, but my monster cares little for the amusement. His hands grab at her and brutally yank skin, little care to their effect on her safety. I grip at my jeans, ready to fuck into her till she bleeds and comes back to me, the pain too much for her to stay away from.

I snarl at one of the crowd who dares step into my space, wondering if I should make them all leave, but they helped get her here, didn't they? Helped her find that last little push she needed. And she's so appealing as she dangles, her wrists already bloodied by the cuffs she hangs from. Blackened streaks on her face, reddened imprints littering her skin.

THE END

"The cage, Blaine," one of the fuckers behind me says.

I growl at the thought, aggravated with sharing her. I've never brought a woman here, never found one I wanted to cement anything with enough. Time and time again I've done this with others, helped prepare them for a life together. And this was my own fucking idea, too. Bring her here, let her feel what it means to be owned and chained before I take her home, so she can breathe her way through it all and understand completely. Now I can't find the want to let these others on her. I can't allow it. Or won't.

I let go of her, carefully allowing her body to leave my hands and swing as I turn to scan the room. They're all here still, each one ready to take their turn with what belongs to me. Initiation. I searched to find these people, be included in them at my whims. This is their life, though. Not mine. Nothing matters but this and their little club of iniquity. I rest on the borders of it, half in, half out, using it only when I see fit to try and find my equilibrium with these creatures I've created in myself. Now it's annoying to me, the thought of collarings and life enrolment almost a restriction I don't care to entertain.

"This is your time, Blaine." I glare at Delaney's voice as he comes through the crowd, his shoulders pushing a route through to me. "Accept it." Why is he here? I back towards my little dove, protecting her from his and everyone else's advance. He's not in this club. He's merely a prelude to this, a path out of the real world. He's how I found them, but he doesn't involve himself in any of this. "Do what you need to do, Blaine. Finish this." My skin crawls at the thought, my own fingers rubbing together as I consider permanent fixtures in my life, fucking magicians laughing at my hesitation. "Take her. She loves you. Prove she's right to give you that."

I snarl at his forthright tone, and watch him weave his way further towards us, the occasional heckle from someone angering me further. "You brought her here, didn't you?" I back closer to her, watching him drift around the edge of the floor, skirting all the others. He's not touching her. No one is anymore. She's mine. Just for me and my sins to delve into.

She whimpers as I feel her skin on my back, causing me to turn and look at her. Her head's hanging, the look of her flourished skin making me smile regardless of my cock's still aching condition and these intruders being present.

"Stop where you are," I snap, shoulders squarely aimed at him as he keeps moving.

"Why? What are you afraid of, Blaine?"

I'm not afraid. I'm envious of what all this fucking sharing means. I can feel it in my bones as everything collides inside me. Love, honour, commitment to just one and one alone. It's private to me. Something to be kept behind closed doors and coveted. The stench of death hangs in her arms for me, not them. It waits for me to take it should I choose to. She'll rest in my hands daily, not theirs, waiting for me alone to play with her and offer security to. This fucking depravity around us pisses me off. Sharing? Fuck that. It's enough that I've watched them on her already, touching what isn't theirs to damn well touch.

I glare at him as he closes the gap, slowly. A leap of faith, she said. It's a leap we'll take together, nothing to stop us in our adventures. We'll take it and bed ourselves in, fucking till blood runs dry and screams go silent.

"This is done," snarls out of me, at all of them. "She's mine."

I turn and reach for her cuffs, one arm wrapped around her without thought as I undo them. She's going home, where she can rest, and then we'll see how much of a fucking leap she wants to take.

"No it's not. You don't get to walk out of here without their agreement," Delaney replies, inching in closer to me. I steal a glance passed him, continuing to scowl at anything that dares move in my direction. Fucking purists, all of them concerned with welfare and decency. Not one of them knows how it feels in those final few seconds, and all of them want to. I can see it now in their eyes as they watch me, wishing they felt what I feel. "Take the other option if you have to, Blaine, but she's not leaving here with you alone. You should know how this works for men like you."

"Fuck you, Delaney."

He snatches at my hands out of nowhere, knocking them away from the cuffs and me away from her. It jolts me in front of all these others, enough so that the three pairs of hands that grab me get purchase on my arms before I can fight them off.

"Coward," he snaps, anger reflecting back at me. He lifts her, as I fight their hold, and turns to walk away. "You're right, you don't fucking deserve her."

My feet halt their struggle, unable to move as my three try to reconcile the words and watch him carry her towards the cleansing room. Don't deserve her. He's right. We don't. Never have done regardless of my feelings. We taint and taunt, amusing ourselves with toys to endure us. We ravage, no care to the skin that takes the beating. A frown comes at the thoughts, internal battles of love and lust raging with each other, tearing me apart at the images and thoughts occupying space in our mind. Monsters and magicians fucking with me again, winding me up and not letting me find any sense in all this.

"Why are you so baffled by this?" Lazeros asks, wandering over and interfering with my view of Alana's limp body moving away. "You knew this would come once you found someone. You need it. Your type always do." I've got nothing to answer him with other than frustration and fists that would rage hell if I could get free. Fucking purists and restrictive laws. All they do is slow the process, kerb it's advance with their rules and traditions. I struggle against the hands holding me back, my monster rampant to get to her, my magician spinning furiously to find a way out. "You know you need the guidance and control, Blaine. It's what you found us for, what you've helped us teach to others."

I scowl at him, still too lost in my internal battles to deal with conversation. Discussion screams of reflection and consideration, attributes I achieve because of Eloise, not because of nature's intent. And now, with her, I don't want to consider any longer. I want to live and breathe again, let nature take its course without limitation.

"You can't hide from us, Blaine. We won't let you. The professor must be taught."

I arch a brow at him, waiting for more wisdom to spout forth as I stare at the door Delaney's gone into. He doesn't give any. He does nothing but wait for my acknowledgement that he's correct. He's not getting it. Nothing is keeping me from breathing again. She's my toy.

THE END

My release. Fucking instruction be damned. I know what we need, and it lies in her hands. There is nothing else in my mind than getting to her and making that happen, without him or these fuckers still holding me fast.

"Tell them to let me go, Lazeros," I mutter, trying to snag my arms away and still looking at where my little dove has gone. He doesn't, which only riles me further and sends any hope I had of containing my fury spiralling.

Fucking reprobates, all of them. My weight snatches and pulls until I gain leverage on one of them, hand wildly slamming out to break the others hold too. We spin in tandem, the world blurring by as I focus in on threat, my monster thanking me for the chance and reaching to break anything it can. It's over before it begins, two of them on the floor by my feet and the first clutching his face for fear of it falling off his damned head.

I brush the arms of my shirt down, growling at one of them as it attempts to stand, and then looking to Lazeros to prove my point. I'm in control of this. Not him. Not them. And not anyone else who dares try to influence my stars. They're mine to find. Mine to wander through and revel in, with her beside me for each further step forward.

Eventfully he sighs, as I start towards the room, then blocks me of my path towards her.

"You should trust us, Blaine. You want that below your feet, don't you?" he asks. I glance down at the composure his sub offers, regardless of the volatility that just happened beside her. Brown hair, glassy eyes, her skin as reddened as I've seen my little doves on occasion. "You won't get it without us. You'll lose her without the control you need. Or kill her."

The slow creep of my eyes back to his tells tales I'm not sure if he knows or not, but the tilt of his head tells me he knows something about what I am. Time watching me, maybe. In tune with his own sadism is more likely the cause. He's one of the only others that's taken that second option available, and the only one who would dare have this conversation with me.

"You might not want the rules, Blaine, but you do want her. She needs them from you, no matter how much you crave the lack of them."

He walks off, barely any other acknowledgement to our exchange than that, and a gruff expression that tells me if I don't conform my interlude in their world will be finished. I stare at the sub again, taking in her form and considering the implication of full control. It would minimise my destructive tendencies, make me accountable, her safe because of it potentially.

I could have that with Alana if I asked her for it. She'd give that if I pushed enough. She's followed me here. Shown she's willing, eager even for completion, regardless of my complications to her health. The thought of her walking away from the grave comes into mind, her ass swinging as she wandered calmly, not bothered by the bones she crossed on the way. And she crawled in here, not for me, but for her. She felt that need and embraced it, just as she did when I looked at these cuffs that still dangle in my eye-line.

"I love you." The words murmur from me. I should have said them as she stood on that grave, should have offered them as she kissed the slab. I could have fucked her there, too, made new memories to think of the next time I visited.

"Sir?" I look down and find the sub wide eyed, her lips parted, questioning.

"Not you." *Her*.

I drift my eyes over to the door again, trying to work out what changed in me as the others approached her. Jealousy perhaps. Possessiveness. Protection. Confusion. Or all of the above, cut with my own sins to trounce feelings and hopes. Leave them behind us so I could forget the decency I've aimed for with her. Lazeros is right. Without them to keep her safe, she has little hope of survival beneath me. My mind spun of its own accord, as it wants to do, ready to do it's bidding with little respect to rules and obligations of trust. She frees me in that way, sets us open to possibilities and endless nights of passion.

"Go back to Lazeros, tell him he's right," I mutter at the sub, still intent on that door Alana hovers behind, waiting for me to come for her. "Apologize for me, and tell him I'll take that second option." If I haven't just ruined any chance I had of getting it.

It seems to take hours for me to cross the space between us, effort labouring my steps as I stare into the activities around. Fucking rules. All this time spent teaching them, and yet now I baulk against their constraint, regardless of their necessity. But I'll do it for her. I'll do it for my stars and the horizon she'll bring eventually, if I can make her give it all.

I push on the door only to find it's locked.

"Delaney?" I shout, finally pushing the door. There's no answer. "Open the door." Nothing still. Nothing but the rumble of the club around me which is back in full swing, my interlude seemingly forgotten about. "Delaney?" Still nothing. I stare at the handle, wondering if I can break in.

"Why?" his voice echoes back through the wood, barely audible. I'm not answering that. I don't have a fucking thing to prove to him.

The sudden sight of the door opening and his sanctimonious expression standing there infuriates me, making me step in to him to get to her. He holds up one finger and steps forward into me before I've got any further.

"Think about what you're about to say. She's battered, raw, and confused." He snarls at me, a look of disgust etched into his features. It backs me off, never having seen such a sense of aversion from him before. "And from what I can see, you've offered her nothing but fucking confusion all this time." Frustration forms in the pit of my stomach, veiled by him and his opinion of me. Fucking idiot. He has no right to an opinion of me. "Hesitance gets neither of you anywhere. You go all in, or you don't fucking go at all."

I stare, unable to make a response worthy of air time, and the growl that leaves my throat could well be heard by the entire club. To hear this from him is tantamount to being ridiculed by a teacher for misdemeanours.

"Why are you even here?" eventually snaps out of me. This place is nothing to do with him.

"I knew you'd come sooner or later," he replies, smiling at my quietened tone. "I'm connected to upstairs." He flicks his head upwards, presumably to God. "I've got powers." Dick.

Charlotte E Hart
THE END

My eyes snake the room as my hands find a place on my forehead to soothe the sound of her screams echoing there, monsters calling me to decimate without this restriction I'm considering. Nothing but other couples carry on around the space reminding me of their rules. Fucking, howling. Dark corners, even darker thoughts. Love's heated gaze, levelled at eyes below and above. They resonate so well, the taste of her blood joining the party to highlight the shiver that rides me. All my voices merging into one, enjoying her, needing her.

It's so uncomplicated for them all, a sense of right or wrong drawn from safewords and fragrant displays of affection. Flowers, no doubt. The romantic mingling with the sinful. I snort manically, wondering if the flowers really mean so much when they come from hands like mine. I don't care for them, nor do they offer any resemblance to the beauty of her skin in my fingers, fingers that still long to touch her even now.

"Move, Delaney." I'm not looking at him, I'm watching another man whip his toy, her back arched as the strike lands, her face a picture of hell mixed with heaven's call. "Move before I make you move." My tongue strokes my bottom lip as I stare at the landing surface, hearing the yelp and willing the guy on harder, faster. That could have been Alana there now, her flesh enhanced by more stripes, her groans coming for others to listen to.

"Why?"

"Because she's not your concern," I snarl, my body spinning slowly to look at him, dismissing the other show. "She's mine." All mine. My responsibility. My obligation. My heart. My love. My sense of all this around me now. "Stop protecting what isn't yours to defend."

He nods as I turn, but it's barely laced with agreement. More offered out of deferential respect for position and honour. It forces another snarl of aggravated impatience, my respect for his own position coming forth because of his ability to gain leverage on my emotions. I'd fucking kill him otherwise for blocking me.

"The man who crawled the floor for broken pottery is who she needs, Blaine," he says, taking two steps away from the door he shields. I snatch a glance at the slight opening again, looking for her to no avail. "It's who you need, too."

"Just move."

He stares for a while, not moving a damn inch as he watches me watching him, apparently still in a mind to protect what isn't his. He'll get two more fucking minutes before this turns into something that leaves all rationale behind. The guy might have a handle on his emotions, might even be superior in some ways, but this is becoming tedious to me. Which, while fascinating in my magicians mind, isn't helping Alana understand her worth to me.

Eventually, rather than argue further in silence, he moves. A small sidestep, one that has Tabitha coming out of the depths of darkness to stand at his side. She leans in, his arm naturally draping around her waist as she watches me intently and waits. Love, it seems, comes in many forms, honest or not. Whatever they have, though, is nothing compared to the need that poisons my blood as I stand here hoping for absolution in new arms.

Charlotte E Hart
THE END

My hand is on the door before I've realised I've gotten to it, the cool metal heavy against my palm as I push gently and give one last glance at the man who saved my sanity from ruination. She's the first thing I see, a blanket around her bare shoulders, her purple tipped hair hanging over her face to hide its beauty from me. She doesn't move, nor look at me. She just stares at the floor, her leg hanging to from the sofa she perches on.

There's a few moments of silence, the only sound I'm interested in coming softly from her mouth, and then she sighs as her finger twitches the blanket around her.

"I don't even know why you want me," she mutters, still sheltering her face behind tendrils laden with sweat. "I'm utterly lost here." I stare, transfixed by her form looking so small and fragile in this room. "Why, Blaine?"

Her words sound betrayed and desolate, as if she feels pointless in this idea of love. She's far from pointless. She's everything I need, warped with necessities I shouldn't want.

I sigh and take a step towards her, wanting nothing more than to show her how much care *I* do have for her, but she flinches, her body moving away from me into the sofa. It's a fear, or reaction, I despise instantly. It settles deep inside me, tearing a line through my magician's amusement.

"You shouldn't be scared of me, Alana. Not now." She scoffs a little, hushed noises coming from behind the mask of blonde masses, but the sound of the tears isn't lost from me. They scream over the quiet sense of composure she's trying to achieve, making me long for her in my arms again. I stand firm, giving her some space to acclimatise to me again, hoping that offers her the respect she deserves. "It's me that should be scared of you." She sniffs a little, her hand gingerly coming to her face behind her hair, her body still unmoving. "I *am* scared of you." Her leg pulls up, tightening her into a ball, no other reaction than that. "Do you understand why?" She bounces her head, a slight nod. It's not enough confirmation for me, not enough for me to know she understands the entirety of this thing she's entering. "No you don't."

"Is it fucking surprising I know nothing about your feelings?" she snaps, hair bobbing with the ferocity of her tone. There's my brat.

I supress the smile that wants to come as I finally see those blue eyes glare at me, choosing to remind her of temper tantrums at another time. For now, she has carte blanche to be how she chooses to be, ask anything of me. Now I'll answer. Now, and because of her coming here and offering everything she has left to give, she can have it all.

I move towards the door and close it quietly to drown out the exterior noise, flicking the lock as it clicks to. I don't want anything to interfere with this conversation. No other thoughts to digest. No other person to determine our needs from each other. This the one thing I have to offer her now. The only way being with me will ever work for us. Lazeros is right. It's her only hope.

She blanches again as I walk back and sit, her legs still curled up beneath her as if protecting her heart. I'm not surprised as I cross my legs, lean back, and keep watching, opening up my body to her. It's hers if she wants it. Fuck it. There's nowhere to hide anymore, nothing to keep from her. If she accepts what she already knows, and then accepts the terms of what we're going to need, then we move forward. Otherwise coffee and weekly chats it is, all the time intermitted with me scanning her road, watching her building, protecting the fucking ground she walks on and wishing I was a better man than I am. Or a simpler one.

"Ask what you need to," I murmur, reaching for a glass of water on the table beside me. "Ask anything, I'll talk and tell you."

She narrows her stare, a slight sneer creeping up her lip. That doesn't surprise me either given how hard she's become to take me, even if it is that softness of hers I crave.

"Why do you want me?" The fucking question falls from her lips again, not one part of her eyes removing themselves from mine. I gaze back at them, part entranced with their hold on a soul I never thought could be breeched. She's flawless, especially given this state she's in. The bruises, the marks, the smell of her cunt lingering in the air, the taste of her in my mouth even though she hasn't been in it tonight.

I sip some water, remembering that image of her beneath my sea, then the fear associated with her drowning before we'd even got a chance to start this corruption. Corruption, that's what this is. I chuckle, my eyes flicking to those inked up fingers, the memory of them dragging on my skin almost enough for me to call this talking off so I can fuck the breath from her.

"I don't want you, Alana." Her eyes widen, her mouth parting as a puff of air comes from them. Horror etches in next as I caress my own mouth, waiting to see which version of her erupts first. Nothing else moves as she stares back, just the tremble of her lips and the matching quiver in her hair. Tenacity it is, then. Those damned eyes of hers, asking all the questions of my heart. It moves me in ways I've never imagined, just as she always manages to now I've let her in. Soft fingers on me, that fucking smile of hers, the giggles, the sense of her on my fucking chest as we sleep.

"What?" she says, eventually, her words failing other than that. I smile at her, wishing she was closer so I could run my finger over those blackened streaks running from her eyes, lick them away and hold them inside me rather than have her bear them any longer. That's all this needs to be for completion. A lock and key, a collar buckled and worn with pride so she can breathe eternally in my care offering her skin as my reward.

"I don't want you, Alana. We need you. All three of us." She clasps her legs tighter, the sneer developing again as she tries to deny the truth again. "But I can't contain them when I'm with you. I'm terrified of that." She stares still, a slight narrowing of her eyes as her chin raises. "And you should be too."

Chapter 22

ALANA

The room is warm, the dull throb of music outside coming between our continued gaze, but other than that there's nothing but brown eyes that look glazed as they stare back.

Terrified? I'm not terrified, not of him. I've seen the worst that can happen, stood over her grave. That's not us. It never will be.

"I need your life, little dove. All of it, without questions or deliberation."

The enormity of that statement makes me swallow and struggle to hold his eyes, but I do. There's no backing down. That's not what those eyes need from me. They need tenacity and strength as they bore back, no sense of wrong or care for my argument should I try. It's that way or no way at all. I don't know why I know that, but I do. That's his offer. Full control of me or nothing at all.

"What does that mean exactly?" The question doesn't come out shakily anymore, I'm through that now. Now I'm intrigued and interested, perhaps buoyed up by the sense that he needs me. Need is a feeling, a heartbeat, something you can't be without. It's so much more than wanting anything. But I still want to know why. I *need* to. I want to understand viscerally, to have that power within us so I can feel my way through whatever this will be, trust him further than I already have. And he just smiles again as I ponder his face, some inclination of amusement at my confusion lingering around lips that should be kissing mine.

"You know what it means. You've been learning all about what it means since the floor of the church. You know exactly what it means."

I keep staring, trying to let all the knowledge I have bind together, searching for ways to make this a possibility. It's not just a relationship anymore, is it? Not just him and me together as and when we choose, enjoying sensation and yet living our lives at the same time. This is near slavery in reality. To be kept and used, moulded.

"That's a lot to ask for."

"I told you, I'm an asshole. A selfish one, at that."

"And there isn't anything you've got to offer a girl that's a little more charming?" He raises a brow and stands, causing me to follow his frame as he steps forward. "Something to make this seem nicer somehow? Because I love you, Blaine, I do, but you're asking for my life here."

"No, I'm asking you to trust me with it. All of it. It's the only way I can keep control of me."

I pull the blanket closer as he paces the ground, my eyes still following him to stay ready for whatever he's going to do next. We're both mad to be discussing this, really. Mad as hatters and not caring for the magnitude of killing fingers and lacking care.

"I don't even really know what it is that you want, Blaine. Total subservience? A life beneath you? Whatever you want whenever you want it?" He pockets those hands of his, a smile broadening as my questions pour out of me.

The thought of those attributes is more appealing than my brain will allow comprehension of. Nothing to worry about, nothing to discuss or argue over. No concerns other than his directions and wants. Just pure, simple immersion into this, no thought of anything but that and my writing.

"All of the above. It's the only way to help me contain them," he says, calmly.

I turn away from him, gripping my knees to my chest and wondering what lunatic allows this as a part of their existence, let alone asks for it from men like Blaine. Contain them? He means the three voices he talks of, doesn't he? The insanity.

It makes me wonder which one of him stood out there and watched me be poked and prodded, asked me to do it for them. Irrespective of whichever one of him it was, I still feel alive here with him. Loved, adored even. I felt it out there, and I feel it now as he gazes at me, asking for something so few would be able to give.

"The staining's wearing off," he says, breaking me of my mused thoughts. I turn to look at him as he moves onto the other end of my sofa and sits. "How's the story going?"

What the hell's that got to do with anything?

I glance back at my fingers, noting the dulled ink that lingers there and thinking back to my last typing session on the typewriter. I don't know how much I wrote that day, perhaps a few thousand. It changed the way I wrote on my laptop, though. I don't care any longer for word-count, nor do I care if it meets credible criteria. I just write, letting the words flow until they're finished without care to the chapter's length. My heroine's in love, regardless of her situation. The hero's proving himself to a degree. Villain and plot twists missing because this story isn't how a publisher wants it. It doesn't conform, nor does it follow protocol. This is my story. His story. Our words.

"It's almost finished," I eventually reply, still turning my fingers over. "Not long until the end." He chuckles and reaches his hand forward slowly, the sight of it making me yearn for it to land on my skin and remind me why I'm here again. And it does, without my moving to reach him. He's just there, his fingers mingling with mine and filling me with the same emotions they always do. The end. What a couple of words to write for this journey. I watch his larger hand link with mine, watch it sit there with such ease and calm. No tremble in it, no sense of trepidation or fear. He's so definite in himself, unlike me, still, regardless of his concern. "How should I finish it?"

"That's not my decision to make, it's yours, but my way is the only way forward for us. You know you have to ask me for it." The thought should make me frown. It would certainly make other women frown, but not me, it appears.

"Why did Priest pull me away from you?" He stares, one finger running over mine to keep us coupled again. "What was that? I felt alone without you." I look away, struggling to get the words out under his gaze. "*You* make me secure here, Blaine. Not Priest or any of the others," I whisper, remembering him always feeling so close to me. "Mad or not, when you're with me, I feel safe." There's a clipped sigh that leaves him. It hangs in the air around us, making the heart he's damn near holding almost stop. "I can't do it if you leave me alone, Blaine. I can't. I won't."

"Alana, there are rules and obligations here," he says. I quirk my head, hoping for something to make sense, as I stare into his eyes. "They're ones I don't want, but they're ones we do need. They were reminding me of that out there. Showing me something not all of me wants to acknowledge." Still I stare, hoping for more clarification, until he sweeps me into him and kisses my forehead, soft lips warming everything I've been missing in here before he arrived. "I don't have enough control of you, Alana, not enough control to keep the voices at bay. That's why I'm asking for everything. I'd rather you alive and breathing if I can achieve it. Safe."

I nod into his lips, barely managing to stay as shocked as I should be by the last of that statement. It's the insanity, isn't it? The three of him creeping into us and changing our dynamic, or making it the way it should be. I don't know, but I also don't know if I can give that life. I might want him, might want and need a life that I'm desperate for in some ways, but whatever happened out there with those people just showed me it's far from any reality I know of.

"Blaine, it isn't as simple as that. None of this is. This isn't a life I know." I look at the door, wondering about what that sort of life means and trying to find a rationale in it for us as he keeps me firm against him. There isn't any that I can see. Just me and him in his house is one thing, this other life he needs? Well, it's quite another, no matter how tempting it might be. "I've got deadlines, things to achieve." Although, at this point, and because of the hold he's still increasing around me, I can't remember any of them. "My life, you know? Publishers, meetings. I can't just beck and call to you whenever you feel like it. All this is-" stimulating, fulfilling, overwhelming, and so beautiful I could cry? "Wonderful, but it's not life, is it? I can't just do this all the time and become your-" What? "Thing."

He backs away and smirks, chuckling at my description of myself as he settles himself and then yanks me back to sit astride him.

"Yes you can. You leave the world to me and say thank you, like a good little brat should. You'll make a damn good thing for me."

I gaze in reply, smiling slightly at the thought. I wish I could leave it all to him. Wish it were as simple as the way he makes it seem, but there will always be things that need doing, meetings that need attending. There will always be noise, won't there? There will always be a time when I have to go back, start answering it all again. And the notifications will keep coming, no matter how he shelters me from them for a while.

I sigh as he sits there, letting the strength of his eyes surround me and make me feel warm again. It's over, isn't it? My dream, his beach, the thought of wandering them eternally and popping in and out of the real world when I need to? It's done. I can't give him everything the way he needs it.

It just won't work.

"We should stop this," I mutter, quietly. We should. My logical brain knows that, no matter how my mind screams for the kind of release he promises. He frowns instantly, fingers tightening on my thigh in protest, but it can't be a getaway forever. I can't be hidden away in corners for him to play with, an order of subservience in place. It's just been a holiday into the unknown. A beautiful one, and one that

I'll never forget, but it's not a life I can endure forever, certainly not with the kind of sentiment he's talking of. I'm independent. My life has had to be. "You were right at the beginning. Our lives just don't work that way. I have obligations, commitments and …" He pushes his cock into me, pressing my hips down onto him so my core slicks against his trousers. Fuck. All coherent thought goes out the bloody window, lost from just a touch and more of that commanding force. It's enough to make me close my eyes and forget any reasons why I shouldn't be here.

"You have obligations to me." He muses the words, his fingers wandering around my naked back, testing all the muscles he knows so well. "Remember them." I do. I remember them with acute clarity. He doesn't need to touch me for that. He just needs to fucking exist and I can feel every hold he has over me. "Let me love you, Alana, don't push this away." The statement forces my eyes open, my hands hovering on his shoulders as I feel his lips graze my throat. Such honesty from him, such emotion, and it's so quiet. "I need you now." The words are as hushed as the first ones, perhaps barely spoken for fear they might not be received well. I just watch the way his head keeps moving, his lips meandering the same spots, his eyes tucked away beneath my chin as he traces them across my skin. "I love you."

I feel the cracking of my heart long before the tear that trickles along my cheek. It takes my breath away, making me smile and imagine a life of words like that from him. They fill the void that's been hovering around us, giving true depth to our meaning of love. My arms draw him closer, enjoying the way he curls into me and holds himself together with me, rather than for me. This moment is it, the thing I've searched for from him. And we're here like a pin, balancing on a moment in the hope that I'll give him everything he needs without care to my future. "Walk my beach with me, little dove. Stop thinking about why you shouldn't. Trust me to make this work for us."

"But you want everything." His head comes up to gaze at me, his thumb wiping the tear away that began to fall, then swiping it into his mouth as he nods.

"I do, without questioning."

I struggle away from his hold, feet tripping over themselves until I scramble from his lap and stand to face him. It's just not fucking possible, is it? No matter how much I want it to be. What's he going to do, walk me to meetings and tell me how to react? They're my books. It's my life. My publisher and my contracts. I can't be a slave to someone else's wants and desires. It's not real life.

"I have a life, Blaine. I have responsibilities."

"That you hate."

"I don't hate it, I-" he arches that brow of his and leans back onto the seat, waiting for whatever words I can't get out. "Struggle with it."

"You fucking hate it. What you want is to write and dream. It's exactly what you should be doing. So you write, Alana, and I'll manage whoever Fuckwit the 3rd is. All you have to do is agree." My mouth gapes as I stare back, wondering how the hell he thinks he's going to do that.

Although, I suppose he has done a damn good job of it while I've been on my sabbatical. Still, he can't do it constantly, can he? And deal with Barringer? Jesus, that will just end up with fights and years of litigation, both of them butting heads and using powers they think they have over my mind and body. No, it's ridiculous. Love is one thing. This world is another. The two can't be mingled together in some contract of sorts, him managing the entirety of my life as it does.

"Your life is here now, little dove. With me." He stands suddenly, the speed making me swing round to see him waving his hand around the space, anger suddenly etching his brow. "Your emotions and thoughts about yourself should be here, in our world."

My mouth moves around snarls and snaps wanting to come from it, irritation lacing every fucking breath, regardless of whether he's right or not. My phone and life outside of this are very real. The endless damn deadlines are real, irrespective of whether I want them to be or not. Nothing will make them go away. This is all just a dream, fantasy even, no matter how the love I feel still continues to thunder in my chest.

We just stare at each other. Him impassive but near explosive, me trying as hard as I can to contain the sense of sadness that wants to pour out, until he walks passed me and catches me off guard, grabbing my wrist and yanking me towards the door.

"Your needs are here, Alana Williams," he snarls, unlocking the door and shoving me out into the roaring sound of the club again, naked. "This is why you are lost. You crave the quiet this gives you. It's what you are." I freeze at his words, not knowing which way to look because of them. "It's the same quiet I crave. We are the same breed, searching for our counterparts." I snap my eyes to him, infuriated with his superiority in the midst of my dishevelment. "You came to me asking for my help, little dove. Here it is. This is your world now. Stop fighting and just yield to it. Trust me with everything."

I flinch around, backing myself to the wall and snatch glances at everything going on in the vicinity. Cries and howls, moans, a low drift of smoke glazing the ground as I stare into the gloom and try to make out shapes and sounds. And the smell, it's electrifying, no matter how repugnant it might seem to my nostrils. It's nothing like that first club I met him in. Here is decadence and true debauchery, the display of cunts and cock on show more seductive than it ever seemed at first.

Sweat drips from skin, men and women wander casually dragging their significant others around, and the moans and groans seem guttural, as if bellowed through need rather than the high pitch tones and wails of before.

"This is the real world of sadists and their toys, Alana. No wretched dominants brawling for a chance to fuck the innocent. This is how honour comes into the fold. Out here is where you are worshipped for giving yourself over to pain." My hands cover me as I back along the wall further, trying to get away from the visions, perhaps avoiding the very thing he's been guiding me towards all this time. That's what it's all been, hasn't it? First the pain. Then the mind probing. Then the kneeling and begging, somehow making me want more of it with every next encounter. The trust, the conversations, the little snippets into his mind. It's all been a road to here, one I followed willingly, barely understanding its meaning until now. "You won, little dove."

"Won what?"

"Your war against my heart. For what it's worth, it's yours." His heart. I shake my head from gazing at him and look around the room again, carefully putting one foot in front of the other towards the place I was hanging in earlier. I can't give it all. It'll never work like that. He can't protect me from everything. He just can't. It's not possible. "We can't run from it anymore, Alana. You want fucking proof? Here, let me show you what you're worth to me."

He hauls me up and starts walking off through the throng of people. I snatch and grab at him, trying to push him away maybe, I don't fucking know. It's all a mess inside my mind again, coherent thought lost in the middle of this noise and smell. It's overwhelming me, making me feel scared or panicked. It's not like at his house. It's always so silent there, noiseless. And I can't even see his eyes as we go to help me, his pace speeding with every footfall. It's just a blur of bodies in the darkened murk, some still hollering and yelling, pained and agonised groans coming from corners I can't see.

"You have to put me down," leaves my lips, as I watch a woman stripped and pushed to the floor. I flinch as she screams and writhes on the floor, her body already being pulled at by the others around her. "Blaine, stop, I can't do this for you."

It's a futile plea, one I know won't get me anywhere but further into whatever he's thinking of. I don't even know why I'm protesting, really. I followed him here, bowed and willed us further into this, pushed him, even after he'd shown me her grave. And I love him so much, I do, regardless of knowing I need to leave. It just won't work between us his way.

His fingers are like a vice grip on my skin as he carries on, his arms constricting harder with every breath he takes. And people move, I see them do it, their eyes seeming deferential to him as he forges us through doorways and out into another open space. He's admired here, loved for exactly what he is, just like he was at the stage-show. Women bow and curtsey, all the time smiling at my continued struggle in his arms. The men nod their approval and wave their hand on, some of them beginning to follow behind us as I sneak a look over his shoulder.

It all makes me stop my struggle a little and look at the side of his face, following the contour of his jaw until I reach his lips. They're as tight as his hold is, a near grimace attached to them as he frowns and scowls at others in his way. It's the same look I saw when he stood by her grave, the same one I watched develop when he first told me about her.

"You're scared," I mumble, noticing the emotion on his otherwise elusive features. It softens whatever determination to leave I have, bringing a charm to the situation around us as I bounce in his arms. He really is. And it's not fear of them, or of himself, its fear of me saying The End of us. There's the slightest twitch to his lips, something that no one else would even notice as he stops somewhere. I don't know where, I'm too busy trying to see his eyes, my body hitching around to get in front of him. "You're scared of me leaving you alone again, aren't you?"

He puts me down slowly, the rough fabric of his clothes rubbing against my exposed skin as my feet lower. And then he just watches me, nothing other than that and that slight raise of his mouth as he lets me go.

"Please trust me," he whispers, his chin tipping at something over my shoulder. I don't look. I can't. Looking will mean letting go of those eyes and that's something I don't want to do, not yet. This look

THE END

he's got now, this might keep us safe. Forge a path somehow. It will keep us together as long as I can make him hold onto it. So I stare back, trying to fall back into that sense of freedom he gives me, if only for one last time as I run my finger down his cheek. He's right, at the moment I don't know what I want, or how I do what he's asked for, but I'm not leaving him until this proof of his is done. One way or another, we'll finish this. We'll finish our story.

Chapter 23

ALANA

Maybe I'm eclipsed by something other worldly, or maybe it's just the smell of these people around that begin to encroach on our space, encircling us again. I don't know. I still feel like I know as little about this world now as I did when this started, but what I do know, what I trust, is him. All this around me seems to pale into insignificance now I'm focused again. Noise dilutes, the thrum of chattering and music becomes less intrusive as I sink deeper into his eyes. That's all we need. Just us. None of this matters. None of the real world outside these doors or the inescapable truth of what is about to happen. It's coming for me no matter how I run or try to avoid it. He's showing me that again as he strides us forward.

Perhaps this proof will show me something. Guide me. It's a part of me I can't put a decision too. Right and wrong. Up and down. Stay, go. Leave him or give him what he wants. I can't find the answer. I'm torn in two, losing the will to choose either path by myself any longer. So, for now, no arguing, no debating, no thought other than eyes and need. It's our rabbit hole, our little world that love lingers in. It might be screwed up, might even be something others would deem completely inappropriate, but it is inside me now, he's right. I can't run anymore.

I'm lost in him again, ready for whatever he wants with no real inclination to challenge or disobey. It's as natural to me as the old Alana who asked questions of him once was. My fight has gone, seemingly evaporated because of the hold he forced around me to get me here, the one that's still firm regardless of the five feet separation he's now put between us.

I smile at the memory as I continue gazing into his eyes, listing the endless moments we've had when he's given me nothing other than sensation to answer my pushing. A slap, a shove, a nudge, perhaps all of them guiding towards this very space we're in. Complete trust. Carefree abandon, accepted because of what will eventually be. He's given me nothing to be afraid of, nothing I can't tolerate. And now he's giving me the love I asked for, too. His heart. He's offering himself here as much as he's asking me to give myself over. It's all real this time as I stand in the middle of this floor, naked, and surround by his peers. We're one here. Combined, and stronger because of it.

My life in his hands.

I scan the suitors near us, not knowing exactly what's coming as they smile in return. There's no leering this time, though, no sense of perverted anger or frustration coming from them. In fact, they all seem composed and reflective, as if admiring something, me presumably, or the man in front of me. It makes me turn on the spot, ensuring I see each and every one of them, remember their faces and smiles. Perhaps this is a family in some ways, his family. A community unlike the one he first showed me. There's certainly no leather and outfits on show, nothing to shock the innocent. These people are dressed normally, suits and dresses, with normal behaviour to match, it appears. Not counting the current situation I'm obviously in.

Eventually I end up back at him, my whole body buzzing from the air around us and the anticipation of what happens next. Fucking happens, I do know that. I saw it the second time I met him, watched that girl have them all paw at her and pounce on her as if she were fresh meat to be devoured. It felt like it was going to happen when I was in chains earlier, before he left me hanging. Fingers probing and pushing in, making me wet and encouraging the lust to come. They needn't have bothered, just Blaine is enough. Just his eyes and I'm wet again. I can feel it ready to pour from me at any form of instruction now. It's debilitating in some ways, making me desperate to be touched, but in others it's soothing, quietening.

It only takes a small smile on his face and a glance at the floor and I'm bending my knees, ready to drop for whatever he chooses. Pain, harmony, either or. It's the same thing to me. The same sense of freedom in minutes under devils hands. Under water. On land. Heaven or hell, anything in between. He's my devil. My heart. His beats inside me now, alongside my own to help the continuation of both. End this or not, I am comfortable here as my skin brushes the wooden floor, almost relaxed because of it. He looks as handsome as always, pride beginning to wash across his stoical features as he keeps gazing. And there's so much love that passes between us in this gaze, so much adoration in our silent conversation. It's a true bond. A heartbeat. One I now realise is inescapable, regardless of the muddled future I see.

"Pretty thing."

THE END

I hear Priest's voice and wonder if he'll be the first, as I watch Blaine harden a touch. At least I know him, at least I've already felt his lips on me, felt his appetite. Letting him fuck me won't be hard, not as long as I can see Blaine all the time. I'll imagine it's him, let his thoughts keep me together as I'm rutted at, welcomed in. That's what all this is, isn't it? A welcoming ceremony.

Funny how that seems so calming compared to the first time I saw it. It's warming me now, my insides telling me I've found something here that other people wouldn't ever understand. And why should they? Why would they even try? Sadists such as these aren't meant for the outer world around them. They're meant for communities that harbour them, keeping them safe from interrogation and blame.

I smirk at the thought, readying myself as I hear footsteps cross the floor behind me. They're Priests, I know them. I don't remember how I know them, but I do. I can hear their balance. It's unlike Blaine's, lighter somehow. I smile wider and close my eyes, acknowledging how much I have actually learnt from these people without even knowing I have. All my senses work as one now. Listening, waiting, smell, touch, taste. Different sounds and nuances, helping me anticipate next moves and feelings that will come. I can even feel the tiny hairs covering my skin standing on end, heightening themselves to feel sensation quicker, learn faster.

I'm aware of myself first. He taught me that. He's taught me that without me even knowing he has done. I know me now. I understand me. Inside. My needs. My thoughts. And if I listen carefully, if I let go of all this around me, just listening to it on a top level, I can even hear my own blood pulsing through my veins, sending me inward.

The footsteps carry on around me, circling and warning me of things to come. A click clack of rhythm, one after another, and then more pairs join in, echoing the sound further on the boards. My hearing is on pins as they keep coming, trying to gage each and every footfall around me, waiting for something to land on skin and wondering what will come first. Lash, spank, whip. Kisses, fingers, caresses and cajoling. Fuck it. None of it matters because all I can see as I stare into my own black mind space is chocolate eyes and a devil's grin, one that's widening with every further second that passes by. Pride, lust, love. The sense of closeness in his arms as he folds me into him at night, the feel of his lips as he trails them along me, constantly tempting me with no thought at all. Other than his, anyway.

A kiss lands on my forehead, soft and hovered. It's followed by a finger on my shoulder and then the lips have gone. I frown at the gentle caress, perhaps waiting for something else to come, something harsher, but nothing does. And then another pair do the same, different ones this time, cold and less soft, but it's still brief nonetheless. No punitive pain. Nothing for me to brace for. It carries on like that, one after another. A kiss and then a touch, barley allowing me to feel any pressure, just enough to know someone was there. More lips, more touches. All of them filled with a sense of reverence or compassion. Some lingered, some brief and fleeting. A few leaving lipstick prints against me, only for the next one to wipe the stain away.

It's harmonising after a while, leaving me full of such calm I almost forget where I am. It's dreamy, like a deliberate enchantment being placed on me to soften the blows that will come. And then finally the one I'm waiting for comes, it lands on my lips instead of my forehead. I heard his footsteps long before he got to me, heard them all the time clipping the ground around me as the rest took their turns. I could feel his impatience in each step, his hesitance on occasion, faltering a step and then moving again. I heard him over every other set of shoes here. Not because he's the loudest, but because he's the one that resonates in my mind. The fall of those feet is like the beat of my heart, teasing me with how I should be reacting to everything in life.

I smile into him as he picks up my chin and the kiss deepens, letting every slight hesitance disperse and disappear. It causes a groan to emanate from him, his mouth devouring what little care I had left away from me. And then I feel the brush of his trousers against my knees, the bone in them rubbing against my own. It makes me frown again, wondering what he's doing down here with me like this. Only once did he sit with me, it was in the beginning to tell me about my reflection. My lips soften against his, trying to form thought, getting lost in my own memories of that time. It seems so long ago. And it worked, all these things he's taught me, they have made me feel like he is a reflection of me. It's not dirty or sordid like I once thought it would be, it's a soul's reach for something it knew nothing of, a stretch for continuation in someone else's form. A heart's leap into safety perhaps, regardless of the danger involved.

"I won't let them at you," he murmurs, as his lips break from mine. I slowly open my eyes, and find his shining brightly at me, a smile coming back that leaves me breathless for more of his lips. "You've done your part for now, little dove. Nothing will ever hurt you again but me." I have? I turn slightly, looking at all the others who seem to be lining up or pacing about edgily now, rather than the composure they portrayed earlier. I don't understand what he means. "It's my turn now. For you, I'll take my turn." That didn't help explain. I still don't know what he's talking about. I snap my head back to him, tilting it and trying to find the right question to ask. None of this makes sense. This is about them on me, isn't it? Proving myself. That's what I came in here for originally. It's why I followed him. Why he carried me to this spot. It's the way it happens. "Go and sit over there," he says, nodding his head away from the floor and over to the chairs behind me. "It's my turn to show you how I feel. You deserve that from me. It's the proof you need."

"But I thought …" He snarls, it's so quick it makes me flinch a little as he nods his head again and scowls at me. "You'll make me change my mind if you carry on." Oh. I snatch a look at the others and see one of the men picking up a whip, Priest hovering behind him and smirking at me. "Go, Alana. Sit. Learn. Let me give you this."

So I do, gingerly raising myself up until I'm standing above him and looking down. It's seems odd as I back away slowly, quick glances between him and the hoard waiting for my departure from the floor. He looks so alone there, his large frame kneeling in the centre of the room, veins already breaking out on his arms to prime muscles, no doubt. And he watches me so intently as I go, his body moving to take the shirt from his shoulders and then letting it fall beside him.

Sudden realisation dawns as I feel the floor change to carpet under my feet, they're going to beat him, aren't they? They're going to torment and bruise him, just as he does me. And he's going to make me watch it, show me something that is for us alone. Why? I don't want that. I didn't ask for this. This isn't the way it should be.

My head flicks through the crowd, looking for Priest so he can explain in some way. He's nowhere to be seen, no matter how hard I look through the bodies beginning to form a queue. I look back at Blaine instead, ready to tell him to get up. This is stupidity. He doesn't have to do this in any way, or for any reason as far as I'm concerned.

"You don't have to do …" My hands fly to my mouth as I see a man step in to him and throw the whip, the crack of it making me jump. And then I yelp out as I back into something, my eyes fixed on Blaine as I watch him grunt and lean forward to take the brunt of it. Jesus. "Stop." The word springs from my mouth without thought, my fingers reaching forward as I push away from whatever I crashed into. But hands grab my arms, holding me firm.

"Another," he grates out, as he raises himself back up. I gape at him as he pants a little and then smiles, his shoulder rolling as he steadies himself. "Stand still, little dove."

"No, I don't want this …" He chuckles. It's a menacing sound, not like his normal one. This time it's filled with underlying rage and frustration, pain probably. He's not showing it, though. He's collected, calm. His breath easing in and out, stabilising himself again.

"He honours you, Alana. Let him." Honour?

I snark at Tabitha's voice, her fingers now digging into arms, all the time still gazing at the man I love and wondering what the fuck this is all for. I would have done this for him. I'd do just about anything for him. The last thing I want to see is this happening.

"Why?" He smiles again, but doesn't give any response to me. He just waits for the next one to come, more long breaths being pulled in to help him get ready for them.

"Because he won't share you. He chose option two, Alana. This is his reward, to remind him what he'll get if he hurts you."

"I don't understand." Another lash lands on him, enough force behind it that he doubles forward, one hand bracing his fall. It brings tears to my eyes as I watch him push back for more, no sound coming from his lips. "But he doesn't have too. Blaine, please." I look up at the next man coming in behind him, trying to wriggle free of Tabitha's grasp on me. She tightens immediately, kicking my fucking legs away just as she did before until I'm back on my knees again. "No, please."

"Listen carefully and watch this while I explain," she says, snagging my arms tighter behind my back and kneeling behind me. "This is your highest accolade, Alana. Remember it well. Only one other person in this room has ever offered what he's giving you. We share here. We do it to ensure safety. If he keeps you with no one else to offer guidance, how do you know if it's acceptable?" Oh. My brows raise as I soften my fight against her, my skin bristling as I watch a woman coil a whip ready to cause damage. "Sadists like him like to hide and play, abuse. This is our way of keeping you healthy." Right. "His way of keeping you alive." Yes, alive is good. "You'll get lost in him, lose your mind, probably. He's so very good at that. I've seen it."

I cringe as the tall red headed woman walks in front of him, her fingers scraping the side of his face as her high heeled foot taps the floor.

"Hand," she says, calmly. He places it in front of her, palm up. She tuts at him and kicks it away, a look of disdain levying her features. "You're right handed, Blaine." He smirks and lifts the other one, offering it instead, and within seconds she's strapped it with a piece of leather. She does it over and over again, making me almost feel the welts that must be coming because of the force of them. Still he does nothing other than stare through her, watching me watch him. No flinch, no movement of his jaw to show concern. He just takes it. No fear. No remorse.

"See what he does for you, Alana. He'll remember that pain, use it to look after you. He'll remember what you give him each day you stay and take more from him. He'll love you for it, rather than misuse you because of it, never letting anyone else hurt you again."

A puff of air leaves me at that, my whole frame relaxing the fight it's still trying for to get to Blaine and help. It's his offering of contrition for his acts on my skin, isn't it? His show of love, a reminder of his own force on me. Perhaps it's his way of remembering Eloise and what he can do if he's not contained. I don't know, but the thought brings more tears to my eyes, filling me with a sense of admiration for his offer. I know how those hands feel on my skin, how that whip feels behind him, the one that's being lined up again as we keep looking at each other.

"Do you understand?" Her hand lands on my shoulder, gently trying to tug me backwards into the dark confines of the side of the room. I nod, but snatch my shoulder away from her to crawl forward a little further. I'm might not stop whatever this is, but I'm damned if

THE END

I'm leaving him while it happens. He'll see me and me alone as this continues. I owe him that.

"I stay here, where he can see me," I snap out at her.

He'll see me all the way through it, remember it. He'll fucking hold the pain that's coming inside him, knowing what it feels like, and then maybe we'll find a safety in his mind because of it. If that's what this is supposed to be about then I need him to see me, need him to understand that we're in this together, at least for now. We'll feel this as one unit, right to the fucking end so we can find comfort in it. And, just for once, I'll tend his wounds. Take him home after this, make him bathe in his sea. We'll walk then, talk. Perhaps make plans for the future he talks of somehow. Life can go to hell on its own. He's right. And this show of his love proves it beyond doubt.

"Never letting anyone hurt you again."

Tabitha's words stick in my mind as I watch the woman walk away, her heels forming a rhythm I cling onto because of his lacking sound, until another pair of feet change the dynamic. More force, more power in this set. Heavy steps and an even heavier hand, knocking Blaine from his upright position faster than any other has done. Both his hands drop this time, the pain in his right evident as he clambers back up to take another lash. And eventually his smile begins to fade as another lands. His face flattens, the pain starting to encroach on his carefree attitude, rendering him detached and glazed. I can feel the shiver riding me, not because of my care for him, rather because I can feel where he's going. It's the same place I go to when he's on me. Dark, warm, a place of strength and elevation above the present. I can only hope it's as nice there for him as it is for me. Mystical and strange, the everyday abandoned for those extraordinary sensations he delivers.

I could come thinking about it. I could use my own hands to do it for him, show him how much I appreciate the gesture. I shake my head at myself as I see him finally get into position again, just to have the man slap him so hard it sends him back to the floor again. He's not fighting at all. No grab for the hand that hurts him. No retaliation. He just keeps taking it. Blow after blow. Humiliation after humiliation. This pack of power and guidance doing their worst to him to aid my safety. And while part of me is desperate to stop it all, protect him from it, I understand what Tabitha means and why this is so important. He's asked for my life, this is his community's way of ensuring he protects it.

Eventually it all seems to shadow into one. Feet moving onto the floor and continuing, one after another. Blaine's body coming to rest on his hands and knees, occasionally being shoved to the floor by a boot, another blow levied at his spine to prove their point further. On and on it goes, the room nothing but a pin point of precision for me as I watch him take it all, his breath panted out, hardly releasing any other sound than that. Sweat drips down his brow, travelling along lines I love so much, showing a face I've never seen before. It's exhaustion. Fatigue. He's being pushed to his final limits, no give to the thought that he can't endure their deliverance onto him. No care either. He's big as far as they're all concerned. A surface that needs to feel this energy on it until it has no other option but to show its decimation.

I tilt my head at it all, wondering why I'm not as bothered as I should be. This is as insane as anything could ever be, but it doesn't feel that way. It feels necessary. Praiseworthy even. Principled and worthy of true admiration in spite of its degradation.

"He's so passionate about you, Alana," Tabitha says in my ear. "Priest would never do this for me. It's such a show of love to receive this from us." She gets up from behind me and moves into my eye-line, her tall silhouette holding a hand down to me. "Much easier to let us all fuck with you, don't you think?" Yes, I suppose it would be. Not for Blaine, though. I know that now. Others on me confuses him, makes him obscure within his own actions. "Come. It's nearly finished. He'll need you to help him." I dodge my eyes around her, watching the last of a man's beating being delivered to Blaine's skin. His body is sprawled on the floor, barely any movement left in him as I listen to the first groan of agony leave his lips. "There's only one left now." I scan the line for who is left, finding no one that hasn't already taken their turn on his skin.

"Who?"

"You, of course."

My eyes widen, their pupils dilating at the thought. I'm not doing that to the man I love. No way. There isn't one part of me that wants to further his pain. I want to drag him to a warm space, somewhere he can recover in and relax, not be a part of causing more agony.

"I'm not doing that," I snap, getting myself to my feet and heading onto the floor to get him off of it. This is done now. His proof has been shown. I get it. I do. He'll look after me, never letting anyone else hurt me. "He needs me to help him, not hurt him further. You're fucking insane if you think I'm doing that." She smirks as I stand here, my feet slowly backing me towards him. Something hard stops me, a body coming into contact with my back. I spin, finding Priest there, his ever present smile firmly in place too.

"It's not done until you finish him, pretty thing. This is all for you. I didn't think he would, but he has." All for me. I back away from him, snatching glances across the darkened room between Blaine's exhausted form and Priest's smile between us. "He's done this for you. You've caught him." I frown at that, unsure if I'm happy about the thought or not. A Blaine caught seems a Blaine clipped of flight, trapped somehow, contained. "He knew in the beginning. Did you?" I shake my head, still peering at Blaine as he pulls himself along the floor, his frame hoisting up onto all fours. A tear comes as I watch him move, a sense of love rushing through me now it's over. All for me. It's enough that I move to Priest's side, him turning at the same time so we both stand and watch Blaine push back onto his knees.

"You haven't had your turn on him," I murmur, wondering why not as I keep looking at Blaine's heaving form. "You're like him. Why haven't you done this too?"

"I'm here as a friend, nothing else. I'm too close to be effective on his skin. The others are better suited to scarring him." Oh. I flick a look at him again, searching him for more answers than that. Love maybe. Honour. A sense of compassion lingering. There's none that I can see, only a continued gaze of his friend as he tries to rebalance himself. I look back, wondering what comes next. What to do. How to finish this now that there's no one left but me. "You can do anything with him now. Beat him to remind him again. Kiss him to remind him. Hell, you could fuck him if you want, we'd all enjoy that one." I snap my eyes to him, furious with his amusement given Blaine's pain. He chuckles at me, his hand suddenly pointing at the door we came through. "Or you could just take him home. Give it all some meaning. Give him the life he needs now he's found you." The life he needs. I blow out a breath, trying to remember what I need, other than the man who's just shown me another extraordinary act of care. "Love him, Alana. Make this worthwhile. He suffered without you for long enough. Push those pieces back together for him. Make him whole."

I gaze back at Blaine to find him looking straight at me, his body a surface of colours, their glow as incandescent as rainbows on a summer day. He pants through them, his lips trembling around each breath as though he can hear the indecision in my mind. *Little Dove.* I can hear it in my heart. It's repeating. It's longing clinging onto the flesh as if he's speaking the words directly at it, bypassing whatever my brain might be thinking about.

"You think I can?"

"He does, that's all that should matter to you. What have you got to lose?"

My life, that's what I've got to lose.

I walk away towards Blaine, no care to the skin that shows for the rest of this room to see. It feels okay here to be naked, like this is a home of sorts. Perhaps it is in some ways. It certainly is for Blaine. A place for inclusion, for happiness and freedom. I'm not sure that it's a place for us, though. Not yet at least. More trust needs to come for that. Not mine. I trust him already, but he doesn't trust himself, does he? Never has as far as I can tell, not really. That's what this has been about. It's why I've had to ask, I suppose giving him confidence as I

THE END

do. This reminder here, the one they've been levelling at him, is just another push at him, forcing him in the right direction.

I kneel in front of him, wondering what needs to be said after this. Perhaps nothing needs saying at all. Perhaps it's all been said already, the littered bruises on him now displaying more respect than other people ever could.

He doesn't move other than the continued breathing. He just waits, presumably offering me a chance to do my worst to his skin too, should I choose too. It makes me smile as I gaze across his body, trying to cement those bruises and grazes into my memory, find them a place in my heart so I can hold them there and feel his love for me. Who does this for someone they love? These people do. This man here does, it seems. The one I love without reservation or demand. He still crawls through me, showing me so many new options in life, giving me new perspective and hope. Maybe this can work his way. I won't know unless I try, will I?

Besides, the story isn't finished yet. We haven't walked our beach, felt the sand between our toes and giggled stupidly about irrelevances. I need to find that with him. I do. He does.

Chapter 24

BLAINE

The dark clouds loom over my sea. They remind me of the shadows in that room, their endless roll as constant as the pain that was inflicted on my bones. I stare into them, watching the way they keep coming, warning me of the potential should I choose not to look after those in my care. Fucking obligations have caught me. Love has.

I snatch in a wheezed breath, watching the moon's hover, its dissidence high in the sky lighting the waves below. It keeps me from seeing my stars, infuriating me with its glare across them. I want my fucking stars back, the ones that show my path to her. I've sat here for hours looking for them, barely moving in case I miss their show, but it's just moon and clouds, has been since she left, nothing more to tell me she's coming back at all.

She did. She came back and supported me, drove me here. Looked after me for a few days and tended to my wounds, all the time giving me hardly any conversation to engage in. She made coffee, cooked food, applied creams and ointments, ones I normally used on her, and then she left. She left me as I slept, leaving a note saying she had to do something. I don't know what, but it's been three days now.

THE END

No calls. No texts. No fucking anything to tell me she's coming home, coming back.

She took my car and she fucking left me. Ran like a thief in the night, taking my fucking heart with her. Perhaps she's not. I wouldn't blame her, not now she knows everything. Who'd want a monster like me? Who'd be prepared to endure a lifetime of three minds, all of them working against each other, trying to kill my own sense of judgement on how best to handle skin? She may have watched my offer of love. She may even have seen the determination in my eyes as I presented the only sense of loyalty I have to give, took the brunt of them for her, but that doesn't mean she will bow down and give me her everything.

Why should it? I'm asking everything of her. I'm asking for all she has, all she's worked for, without her questioning anything I ever do. It's a life that raised subs hardly accept, let alone relatively untrained ones like Alana. And I'd take it again. I would. I'd have these bones mutilated every month to know she'll be here when I wake each day, not the once yearly they enforce on my kind of breed. I'd do that to make sure no one ever touches her again but me, that no one ever hurts her again but me. I'd take that for her. Endure it.

I sigh and gaze upwards again. This is my penitence for Eloise. I know that now. It's my atonement. My punishment. I can feel it seeping further in with every next hour she's not next to me. It's the loss I should have felt for the death I produced. The grief I should have absorbed myself in as they lowered her corpse into the ground. It cuts my souls like a knife, raking agonised tears and sobs from my monster, the lacking stars only highlighting his once again deficient life. And it infuriates my magician, his mind still traversing circles in here, trying to find a way to pull her back to us. But this is as it should be, as we deserve. We're nothing but monsters after all, ones who deserve little care to our emotions now they've been breached.

We should be left here to rot in our own cesspool of nightmares, alone. Our life, my life, or the lack of it now she's left, is as it needs to be. Destroyed and shattered, woken and abandoned, a seascape of endlessly crashing tears, wracked with hopeless dreams and insidious reasoning. I am nothing again. *We* are nothing. We are hollow without her support. Empty. We are alone once more, nothing but our night and sea for security. Her hopes gone. Ours, obliterated.

I sit here for a while longer before giving up on my damned stars and moving from the deck back into the house. They're not coming out tonight. Why should they for the likes of me? It's still nothing but clouds and rolling waves, their flow as impassive as my heart feels again. I can feel it giving in, giving up. Its thunder in my chest is becoming quieter, just as I'm forcing it to do. I'm closing it down, some small part of me smiling at the thought of her safety and willing her a future that she deserves without me attached to her. She'll fly out there now, absorbing energy differently, renewing herself in imaginative ways, grasping life by its fucking horns and throwing her dreams into the open again.

I made that come, found it in her again. If nothing else, my professor helped her with that. He did well. He set her free from her confines and showed her how to fuck with courage again, be more than she had become. He did as a good man should do, showing her the life I should have given to Eloise. He pushed her into the world again and showed her a path to manage herself with. I'm pleased with that.

Charlotte E Hart
THE END

It makes me look around my bedroom and then watch the bedsheet's soft bristle in the breeze. I'm contented somehow. It gives me comfort, warming the part of me that's so often not allowed its pleasures. She's free, irrespective of whether I am or not. She's out there again, writing her stories, filling the world with dreams and aspirations, hopefully doing it a little better than she was before.

I glance at the typewriter, its position in my bedroom a conundrum to me. She's moved it here at some point over the last few days, and then left it rather than take it with her. She should have. She should have taken it with her and used it when she traps herself again, used the retention it produces. The manuscript's still there, too. The stack of sheets lined up neatly beside it. I haven't looked at it, nor do I care too. She's probably left it there as a nod to her. A reminder. She shouldn't have bothered. The story isn't relevant to me, only that she wrote it because of me, because of us. It's presumably a love story that should be perused by those who have hope for more, those who long and thirst for something above their average. I no longer have that hope. She's taken the only hope I ever had with her, leaving me with nothing but memories to cling to and the smell of her lingering around my home.

I pull in a breath at the thought, drawing in the last of her scent and gazing at the bed, wishing she was still in it. She's not, though. She's gone. A fucking typewriter doesn't remind me of her. *She* reminds me of her. She is inside of us. Every breath pulled. Every thought made. Every crash of my sea and every night that goes by, she will be inside of us, of me. Her skin, the way she moves, her smile and her frown, even the sounds of her tears. They all live inside us for

Charlotte E Hart
THE END

every moment we are awake, and the image of her haunts our every next unconscious thought, too. She has become our reason for drawing in air. We're somehow unable to stand the thought of not breathing another in case she steps through our door, offering her hope again. We are lost without her and empty of desire. Alone, just the three of us.

I move over to the damn thing, needing to touch her again in some way, and finger the keys. They clunk and clatter, irritating my eardrums with their noise. And she comes reeling back to me again, her ass on the seat, her naked body driving the next chapter down, barely a care to what's around her. I snort, remembering the time I had to beat her to make her eat, forcing food down her throat like a child because she had more words to write and dared argue with me. I adored that fucking arguing. Relished the next one that came.

It makes me smile and look at the top of the pile of sheets, hoping to see her handwriting on it, another note or a letter, anything to bring her back to me again. There's no handwriting, though, only the bold print of the keys, large letters covering the page. The End, it says. The End. I shake my head at her, knowing that she means us. The end of us. The end of something she passed through like a tempest, engulfing me in its path and trying to give me a love I don't deserve.

The smile on my face forces me to turn the page, letting it fall to the floor as I stare at the next set of words.

Ask and you shall receive.
A portrait of love.
Our story,

Charlotte E Hart
THE END

B. A. Jacobs.

Fucking bitch.

I chuckle, letting the sentiment find a home inside me it shouldn't damn well need. It brings fluid to my eyes, the tears produced by the static holding my damn finger on the words there. Our story? Our fucking story should be still going on, still evolving so I can learn more about her and find solace in her arms dowsed with care, let her guide me with her hopes and dreams. I could kill her for leaving me so raw. Beat her ass and make her finish this, take it to its conclusive end rather than leave it open and wanting still. She's left a hole here that will never be filled, be mended either. It's open and weeping, its blood seeping from corners it knew nothing of before her.

That hole makes me run a finger over the name, somehow seeing my professor in its official form. Enjoying its counter across my monster and magician, amused by it even given her hardly ever seeing him. Perhaps she does know me better than I think. Perhaps she always has, regardless of her ability to entertain my other two, love them. Delaney said that. He said the ones that mattered could see inside, no matter how you tried to keep them out. I'm glad of that thought. Inspired by it in some ways. Perhaps she always knew how much I loved her, regardless of me not telling her enough. Maybe that's the only thing that kept her coming back, keeping us together even though she should have run for her life.

I turn the next page, a new intrigue searching for something in her words, and then lift the stack of papers to move back out onto the deck again. It's more comfort I'm after, probably. The sense of companionship I've now lost. If I can't see my stars then maybe I can damn well find them in these papers instead. I'll read and drink black coffee, hoping for a closure to find me as I stabilise to one again, helping me cage my monster somehow. It's all I've got left to do now, that and close the beating of this heart down permanently, something I'm finding harder than I thought. And the barriers just loosen again with the next words read.

Pre Face

She was nothing to me. A barren landscape to play on.
Until she wasn't.
Our story starts here. It isn't pretty and it isn't your average tale of love, but it is a love story, one she forced me to admit to needing. One I proved.
I'm no hero. I'm a monster, but now I'm a monster with a heart.
Life is not without cause or hope. She taught me that.
Our story starts right here, at the end.

Fucking hope.

It allows a smirk to creep up my sullen mouth, my ear trained on any damned sound that might interrupt it other than my sea, and turn the next page. Maybe she is coming back. Until then I'll read and study her words, find her in them, feel her there as well as in my heart. I'll read and study what it is that I taught her, what it is that she taught me, and maybe, by the end of it, I'll have found my containment again, forced this anarchic heart closed.

She'd hate me for that. She'd call me a coward and a liar, but I do it for her. I do it to protect the world she helped me see again, and I do it because it belongs to her alone. We must be contained unless it's for her, kept restricted. We must become quiet again and controlled.

So I sit, bedding myself into this chair and letting the sound of the swell lull me into stories of love and adoration, my smile increasing with each page turned. Such passion. Such a sense of revelry from hands stained with ink and a body battered to its finest disposition. Quite beautiful really. Elegant. Sophisticated.

"Quiet feet," her voice says. My eyes snap over my shoulder, the sudden appearance of her in the open doors near annihilating any form of reserve I was managing. "Finally snuck up on you, hey?" She stands there, a small smile on her face, dressed in a floral skirt that should be ripped from her skin. "You didn't hear me?" I shake my head slightly, my eyes narrowing at why I didn't, as I look over her face and skim outlines I've missed. "What are you reading there?" she asks, her smile becoming more of the contradictory smirk I'm used to from her. "Good is it? It better be." She fingers her hair, the curls in the purple twisting around. "Romance needs to be. And you wrote it, after all. They're your words." She giggles and turns as she says that, her ass calling me to beat it for leaving me. "Drink?" she calls. No, I don't want a drink. I want to rack the bitch for making me think I'd lost her. I want screams and howls and bellows of pain to ring out across her skin for weeks. I might even drag her down to my sea and fuck her in it, holding her head under the damn water as I do. "Blaine?" The sound of my name rings through these walls like a beacon of hope, one that has commitment attached to every damned letter. "You might not need one, but I do. Champagne preferably."

The statement forces me from my dazed seat, causing the heart that was receding to open up fully waiting for acceptance of it.

"There's some in the cellar," I reply, looking into the room for her. She's not there, she's gone again. I frown, wondering if she wasn't here at all and I imagined it. Nothing is beyond the realms of probability in this fucked up brain of mine. I chuckle at myself, amused that I'm even making her up now, ready to join her with the other three of me, then groan at the thought. How quaint of me. Fucking love stories. I turn back out to the deck again, snatching at the papers that have blown about in the wind, desperate to right their numbering again so I can carry on reading.

"My life is bloody heavy. I hope you know that," she shouts, the echo of her along the hall coming back at me. "Honestly, you want it, it's yours. Come and carry it for me." I swivel again, my hands creasing papers as I walk back to the sound of her, feet quickening at the thought. And the sound of clattering echoes too, the familiar tone of her heels resonating in my home as if they've always been here. "This stuff is heavy, too. Come and be manly." Manly? I turn the first corner down towards the entrance door, my bare feet padding me along, wondering what she needs manly for and still not entirely sure if any of this is real or not. "Because honestly, if I have to deal with you forever, I need the gentlemanly bit on occasion." My eyes widen, the words making me halt in my tracks before I get to her. Forever? "And I need the truth all the time, Blaine. You know that, right? All the time, do you hear me? Where are you? Who the fuck are you is probably more appropriate."

My toes curl against the marble, my mind grating against itself, as I smile at the last of her mumbled words. Magicians smirking, monsters powering limbs and pulsing inside my veins. Indecision outmanoeuvring resolution, confusing the process and endangering any boundary I was introducing again. And then she's there in my eye-line, her eyes shining as brightly as my fucking stars always do, skin as ripe as it always is. She hovers in the hall, her face a mask of questions as she opens her mouth and looks behind her a little.

"Blaine?" I raise a brow at her, waiting for whatever the fuck's about to leave her lips. Hate. Vitriol. Love. Sarcasm. Contempt. All things I adore. Slutty meanderings, waking this cantankerous mind up again, readying it for her. An apology even. That might be useful to her well-being. She just hovers some more, perhaps questioning herself given my scowl at her.

"Where have you been?" I ask, barely able to stop myself from grabbing her to test she's real.

"I had things to do. I left a note." A fucking note. I snarl at the memory of it, just holding the need to push her into the den and fuck any form of breath she has left out of her.

"You left me." It's a fucking statement. One I want to ram down her throat somehow. She grabs her hands and twists them about in her grip, the look of fear beginning to encroach on her features. Good, she should be fucking scared.

THE END

"I couldn't just stop my life for you on a whim, Blaine. I had to do …" her eyes scan the floor nervously, her feet inching back a step or two as I begin moving towards her, "things."

"What things?"

"Important things. Meetings. Business things." She looks up again, apparently galvanising herself for an argument. There's my little brat. I smile at her, the smell of her coming at me the closer I get, the taste of her embedding itself further. She should galvanise herself. Get ready for me because at the moment this fucking monster is fit to tear her to pieces for daring to walk away. "They're things we need to talk about, Blaine."

"Are they." It's not a question. I couldn't give a fuck about talking. I'm not intending to talk for at least two days. She's got some making up to me to do, that includes me using anything I haven't used on her before. "A fucking note. You thought that would be acceptable?"

She backs off a step again, her own eyes narrowing at me as she takes another and then turns down into the kitchen, a huff coming from her lips.

"Champagne," she snaps, her ass continuing down the steps. "You get that first. Nothing else happens until we talk." Fuck that. I'm at her back before she's got a chance to move another step towards the glassware. She swings round so quickly it shocks me, her hand slamming out and connecting with my cheek. It brings a wry smile to my face after I've taken the sting of it, making me chuckle and decrease the space again. "Back off," she spits. "I'm asking you. Take. A. Fucking. Step. Away." I do, eventually. One step away. Two steps away. The movement has become alien for me with her, uncomfortable. It causes another chuckle as I remember all those backwards steps in the beginning, all the wasted time. "See? Backwards isn't that hard after all, is it?" Bitch. "Where's the champagne?"

"Cellar."

"Go and get it then. Chop, chop. We're on a date." Are we.

The sarcasm swims through me as I wander off, part annoyed with her fucking superiority and part in awe of it. I'm even fucking hurrying for the bottle, the walls blurring by as I round corners and take stairs downwards. I don't know which I pick out of the store, not caring for the taste of it. I just want her. I want on her, in her. I want her taste and her smile, her nails egging me on again. Fuck Champagne. Fuck talking.

By the time I get back she's got a document on the table, a fountain pen laid out next to it, and two flutes waiting for the champagne in my hand. I stare at it, wondering what fuck paperwork has got to do with anything.

"Sign it without reading it," she says, her body sliding around the side of the table, long legs on display as she sits and crosses them.

"Why?"

"Because I'm asking you too. I only have to ask, Blaine. That's the way this works, isn't it? That's what you told me. I want my proof that that's still true."

"You've had your proof. These damn scars substantiate that."

THE END

She smiles and picks up the document, her ass shuffling across the table until she's able to lean back and put the fucking thing between her legs.

"Not good enough. You want my life, I've brought it to you, but I want that compensated should you fuck it up. Sign the document, Blaine."

Ah, money. Clever brat. I smile at her and move forward, picking up the pen and flipping the bottom of the papers to find the signatory lines. I don't give a damn enough to bother reading it, anyway. It's all hers whatever happens. It was hers the moment she infiltrated this heart. Hers the minute I came inside her cunt. My life, for what it's worth, has been hers for longer than she knows.

"And the others," she says, as I push the first set away. I look back up at her, my hand scrawling with little care to what I'm signing anymore. She smiles down at me, enough charm in the stretch of her lips to make it all seem complete. Life, money, homes. It all means nothing without her with me anyway. It's nothing but a vacuous cavern deprived of life, bland of meaning.

"Enough?" I ask, aiming for the gentlemanly she quoted.

"No. Pop it."

"What?"

"The champagne, Blaine."

I step away and grip the fucking thing, willing it to stay steady in my hands as I peel the top off and push the cork. Fucking champagne. I've got plans for this bottle once we've done drinking it, plans she'll hate me for. The glasses fill, the bubbles making her giggle for reasons unknown, and then she picks one up and turns the documents towards herself. "Five minutes," she says, her fingers laying the documents out one by one, as I back away.

What the hell I'm waiting for, I don't know. Some repose of decency, I assume. Some attempt at this date we're apparently on. I smirk and sip my own drink, barely tasting it over the smell of her perfume in my space again, but I wait nonetheless. I wait because she's asked me too, and I wait because the longer I do, watching as she holds her phone up and take pictures of each document, the more pain she's asking for. She makes exasperation an appealing impression.

Perhaps she always has.

"We're becoming impatient, Alana." We are, all of us. Fucking irritated actually. She frowns in reply and flaps a hand at me, her fingers still going ten to the damn dozen on her phone. Fucking phone. The damn thing's going in the trash the moment this is done.

"There, all done. It's with my lawyers."

"Is it my turn now?"

She lifts her eyes and sips at her drink, her mouth opening to say something more. I've knocked the stuff out of her hand before she gets a chance, my own glass going flying with the act. And she sighs the instant her skin sinks into my grip, causing me to relay the exact same emotion to the sensation. She flows into me instantly. The feel of her, the smell. The taste of us exploding as my mouth finds hers.

"You left me," murmurs from me, my tongue already tracing the lines of her lips, cock engorging itself for a reminder of why that won't be fucking happening again. I snatch her into me, arms wrapping around her, biting in to force the connection again and makes us physical. She's here, in my arms again. She's real and alive, a part of me wanting to kill her for daring to come back.

My hands hitch her skirt up, enough chaos in the move to have her gasping as I shove her back onto the table top. I couldn't give a damn about that either. She'll feel this on her skin for weeks, hate me for days because of it. "You fucking left me alone."

She gasps again as I imprint everything I've got through my teeth, the side of her body taking the brunt of my weight as I force her down onto the surface and level her face at mine. But she smiles at me as I snarl at her, her fingers moving to the side of my jaw and stroking along it, filling me with those fucking hopes and dreams again.

"No," she says, her legs widening to allow me closer, lips leaning in to brush mine. "I just had to let go of my life for you, Blaine. It takes time. It takes me being in front of people. You wouldn't have let me leave." She gazes at me, both hands coming up to my face and running the contours of it, a fanciful expression settling in as she keeps everything loose and soft. Stupid girl. Beautiful, talented, wayward and difficult girl. "I've given it all to you. All the control." She tilts her gaze of me, the smile widening as she looks at my chest. "All the power." Her hand drops down, skimming the edges and making me shudder in reply. "It's all yours now. What are you going to do with it?" I've got several ideas, none of which she's going to enjoy. The damned cage for a start. Her face suddenly changes, a thought jumping to mind. One I'm not going to like much by the looks of it. "I do have a few requests of my own, though." Does she? She's not getting them, no matter how I answer her. "Cole." I groan at the thought, pushing her

THE END

legs wider and burrowing in, hoping to fuck the word out of her mouth. "He needs his big brother, you know?" Fuck that. "He misses you."

Cole is the last fucking thing on my mind, as should it be for her.

I hitch her ass to me, picking it up and walking off with her towards the den, not giving a damn for any other conversation she might think relevant. Nothing is more relevant than me fucking into her again, than me feeling her heat around me so I can let the voices come and enjoy their noise rather than contain them.

"And I think you should consider teaching again. Properly, not just the fucking bit. You're clearly quite good enough at that already." My brow raises at the thought, more interested in it than I'd like to admit. "I think it'll help you. You know, in the long run." Maybe it would with her beside me to level these monsters of mine, give them something to play with. Who fucking knows? I grab tighter and smile as I keep turning the halls. "This isn't talking," she mutters, her lips starting to nibble against my neck, her legs tightening around me and reminding me of how much she takes of my insanity.

"Fuck talking." And fuck the den too.

I head straight for the bedroom, then through it to the open doors leading to our sea. *Our* sea. It calls to me, as it will to her for as long as I can keep her here. It will pull both of us under, not giving a damn for our lives as it does, but that's my curse now, my promise. Nothing will ever hurt her but me. No sea will drown her. No company will force her. Not one damn thing on this planet will ever wound her apart from me. She's my burden to bear. My promise to keep. My toy to honour.

"It's beautiful here," she says, her arms loosening around my neck so she can take her top off. She wrenches it and tugs, throwing it into the wind as she does, purple stripes flicking around my face. "I still want my dates, though." I snort, my cock rubbing against her as we keep going. She can have all the fucking dates she wants. Every fucking day if that's what makes this happen.

"With who?"

"Any of you."

My feet pick up speed, the need to get to the water becoming a necessity I didn't know before her. It begs me to come now, but not for death, for life. It begs me to put her in so I can drown with her and listen to her moans, lose us in there so we can live. We'll fuck in there until we're done, and then we'll fuck again and watch the sunrise come, finding warmth in the sun for once.

She kisses me softly again, her hands wrapping around and caressing the back of my neck.

"Tell me you love me."

"No."

"Why."

"You've been a brat." She giggles and holds tighter, the sound of her ebbing into me at the same speed as my heart beats for the one she's got against me. "Brats don't deserve love." She snorts and wiggles against me, lowering herself slightly to arch against my jeans.

"This brat deserves everything you've got, Blaine. She's giving you her life."

That she is.

THE END

My feet slip into the cool water, and I lower her immediately, enjoying the yelp that comes from her as she hits the temperature.

"Fuck, that's cold."

There's nothing but cold and dark, just the way I fucking like it, the water swelling around us as the moon dances above. It's as we are, a dark and dangerous endeavour, still warning of things to come and trials to be endured. But the stars are coming out as she turns in my hold, her body clambering onto me as I wade deeper and let the current take her weight. They're coming and lighting up our sky again, giving me my path back to her. I still don't deserve it, but I'm taking it. We'll cling onto her until there's nothing left to cling onto.

"You'll remember your vow, won't you?"

I don't answer, I just push deeper again, my hand reaching for her neck to tilt her over onto her back. She floats there, her body undulating within our waves, hair cascading out behind her as I twist myself between her legs and wrench at her skirt. And the house just lingers there in the background, the deck lit up as I stare passed her towards it. A home. *Our* home. Beaches and fucking dreams. Promises of insanity, smoothed with some fucking emotion called love. But I do know it now. Because of her we feel it in our souls, somehow making it a part of the confused three, linking it there to defend the adored and cherished. Preserve it.

"You give me your hope and I'll protect it, little dove."

She sighs at that, her arms spaying out at her sides. I hear it even over these waves coming, the tone of it rooting into my heart like a morning chorus of starlings. It makes me pull her to my mouth, feasting on salty waves and the equally salty tang. She groans and bucks in my hold, her legs scrambling for purchase around my neck, hands still outstretched as I devour the sense of missing I've felt without her. I'm licking my own wounds. Reaffirming my love for her and gauging out our future. Life is here. It's in this sea I've known so long. Our life. It will ravage holes and roughen itself, finding it's equilibrium as time passes for us. She will bear me and I will love her for it, shielding her from reality's grasp until we're ready for the real world again. She'll pull me back to that. I know she will, but for now we'll stay here and endure ourselves. Her weathering me. Me allowing her to guide me back together piece by piece, or rip me further apart. Find my three and give them credence. Perhaps that's the truth of it all. Perhaps we need to evolve further before we merge, becoming a new man as we do. Who the fuck knows. I don't.

    Either way, she'll be the one that finds me eventually. She'll be the one that settles me into coherency, tolerating my three and opening their paths. I'm bound to protect whatever she chooses now, ready to lay my life down should she see that as the only route forward for sadists like me. I'm taking my chance whatever the consequence, because I'm nothing without her to guide us onwards. My life is owned by her.

THE END

Charlotte E Hart
THE END

Acknowledgments

The journey of these two books has been a revelation to me, showing me a world outside my first 6 books. It's been soul quenching to dive into new characters and enjoy their torment, hopefully producing another new life for you to read your way through. Stories are now my world, giving me a chance to channel thoughts and images into yours. As always, my only intention is to provoke thought and help you see something you've not seen before. If I've done that, I've succeeded in my goal.

I'd like to send out love and thanks to:

My PA - Leanne Cook, without whom I wouldn't survive this booky world. She's the calm in my storm. Mostly.

My beta Readers – Jodie Scott and Katie Matthews. You helped no end. Even if you did make me swear and spit. Yes, Slavey, you also helped with the swearing and will continue to do so, I'm sure.

My Editor – Heather at Heathers Red Pen Editing.
As usual, love you. Thanks for everything. You're still a star.

My other half – Who is my world and gives me this chance. You don't know how much you mean to me or my words. I love you.

Bloggers – You're stunning. All of you. To offer the support you do for no other reason than the love of books, well, I've no words for how awesome that makes you.

Charlotte E Hart
THE END

And, of course, all of my readers.

You all amaze me with your kind words and encouragement. There will always be a story in me ready to come out, but it's you lovely readers that help me believe the words are worth reading.
I can only hope that I continue to provoke thought with every novel and encourage your minds to search horizons new.

Charlotte E Hart
THE END

Also Available by the Author

****

The White Trilogy
Nominated for best BDSM Series of the Year

Seeing White (Book 1)

"OMG. Amazing writer, amazing books. Deliciously dark and …"

****

Alexander White, the wealthy business man with looks to die for. Just like the other colours you'd think…….but no.
He came from a very different place and made some of his money a very different way.
And he keeps it well hidden because the truth would destroy everything he has. All that he's worked for would be gone in an instant if they ever found out what he's capable of, or what he really did and who he did it for. So he keeps people far away with metaphorical games and walls to deceive and confuse.
He doesn't do relationships, he doesn't do emotions and he certainly doesn't do love.
He does money. Making it, manipulating it and spending it whist he plays with women who know what they're signing up for.
Three people shaped who he is today. One damaged him beyond repair, another taught him to control the rage, and a decent one helps him to consider his options more appropriately.
But be under no illusions ladies, Mr White has not been a nice man, and he will probably never be a decent man, but as long as he keeps up his image, and nothing gets through his barriers, no one will ever see the truth.

Life's good for Elizabeth Scott, successful business, happy kitchen and a great sister who deals with all the expensive people so she doesn't have to. She just cooks, bakes and smiles her way through each day……well most of the time, anyway, that is when her great sister isn't

Charlotte E Hart
THE END

pushing her to, "get out there a bit more," or "sort her shit out." Then the biggest contract of their lives comes up..... And the ever useless London tube, with her sister in it, catastrophically breaks down. Unfortunately, that means only one thing. She'll have to deal with some of that wealth herself, and that means the devastating Mr Alexander White in all his glory.
Life suddenly couldn't get worse, regardless of his unfairly gorgeous backside.
She has no idea what the hell she's doing.
******

This book is followed by:

Feeling White (Book 2)
Absorbing White (Book 3)

Charlotte E Hart
THE END

The VDB Trilogy

(Best read after The White Trilogy)

The VDB Trilogy begins a week after the end of The White Trilogy and is told from new POV's. It is, in some ways, a continuation.

****

The Parlour (Book 1)

Above all else Pascal Van Der Braak is a gentleman. Devastatingly debonair and seductively charming. Always styled and perfected.
He is also a cad, scoundrel, rouge and kink empire founder.
Tutored in the highest of society, having been born of royalty only to deny it, he found his solace in a world where rules need not apply.
Where he chooses to ensure rules and duty do not apply.
Some call him Sir, others call him master, and no one would dare risk his wrath unless they required the punishment he favourably delivers.
Except one, who has just strapped a collar around his throat, one he asked for. So, now he needs to appropriate his businesses correctly for peace to ensue. He needs to find the correct path forward for everyone concerned, so he can relax, enjoy, and finally hand over the responsibility to someone else.
Simple.
But where comfort and a safety of sorts once dwelled, there is now uncertainty, and a feeling of longing he no longer understands. A need unfulfilled. And as problems arise, and allies scheme, he finds himself searching for answers in the most unlikely of places.

Lilah

It's the same every day. I'd found it odd at first, but I'm used to it now. I was so tired and weak when I got here that it was helpful really. That small woman comes in to help me wash and get dressed. I don't know where the clothes come from, but they're nice enough, and at least they're clean and dry. Not like the rags I arrived in. They were taken from me the moment I took them off to get into the shower, the first shower I'd had in god knows how long. Nearly a year I'd been running

Charlotte E Hart
THE END

the streets, a year without a real bed or a home of any sort. There isn't a long and awful story to tell about an abusive family member, or a broken home. I suppose I just slipped through the cracks and got lost at some point. I lost my job first, and then I couldn't afford the bills on my apartment, so the landlord threw me out. I don't blame him, he did the right thing by himself. And then it was just a long and never-ending road to nothingness.
So now I'm here, wherever here is.
And I don't know why.

****

This book is followed by:

Eden's Gate (VDB 2)

Serenity's Key (VDB 3)

Charlotte E Hart
THE END

The Spiral

******

Maddy has only one decision left to make after the final bruise—leave him.

And she's doing it. She's finally free.

Her own home. Own life. Own decisions.

There's no-one to answer to anymore.

But when her job as an antiques moderator leads her to the mysterious Blandenhyme estate and the intriguing Mr. Caldwell, that freedom begins to turn into an unconventional love lost in shadows and fog.

And as chilling voices whisper words to cloud her judgement, and dangerous liasons bring terror and dread to the fore, she finds herself struggling to survive Blandemhyne's sinister misgivings regardless of its beauty.

They say the dead never sleep, that they stalk this earth until retribution is served.

That time has come.

Standalone. Dark Romance. Spiralling. Thriller.

*****

Charlotte E Hart
THE END

Innocent Eyes
Cane Novel 1
(Hart De Lune)

****

"If he's gross, I'm bailing."
That's what I said to my supposed best friend when she asked me to take her place. A blind date, she said. What harm could it do? He was charming. Beautiful. God's finest creation. He wined me and dined me. Made me do things I'd never before dreamt of in the bedroom. It was perfect. Dangerous. Arousing.
But Jenny didn't tell me the full story. She didn't tell me about the debt she owed. And now Quinn Cane wants his money's worth, and he's going to make me pay whatever way he can.

"A debt needs to be paid."
The woman who came to meet me didn't owe me money. I could tell by her innocent eyes. Still, the debt will be paid either way.
She was something to play with and use as I saw fit, but something about Emily Brooks made me want to keep her. So she became my dirty girl. Pure. Innocent. Mine.
Then she whispered my damned name and invaded my world, changing its reasoning.
She wasn't meant to break the rules. But she rolled my dice and won.

Shame. Forgiveness. Dark. Erotic. Romance. Mafia.

This book is intended for mature audiences. 18+ only.

Charlotte E Hart
THE END

Printed in Great Britain
by Amazon